MASTER of EARTH and WATER

The First Chronicle of Fionn mac Cumhal

"PAXSON AND MARTINE-BARNES HAVE PUT
NEW FLESH ON THE LITERARY BONES OF THE
ENDURINGLY POPULAR IRISH OUTLAW/POET"
Orlando Sentinel

"UNUSUALLY GOOD CELTIC FANTASY...
The story sings...
The book comes to life wonderfully"
Kirkus Reviews

"AN HEROIC, HIGHLY SATISFYING
COMING-OF-AGE SAGA...
Artfully blends the mythic and mundane"
Publishers Weekly

"SUPERIOR SCHOLARSHIP
AND STORYTELLING...
Diana Paxson and Adrienne Martine-Barnes
have joined the ranks of the creators of the good stuff."
Chicago Sun-Times

"SPLENDIDLY PACED, ACTION-FILLED,
GORGEOUSLY WRITTEN...
Magical exploits...A vividly imagined world...
MASTER OF EARTH AND WATER whets
the appetite for the rest of the trilogy."
Booklist

AvoNova/Morrow Hardcovers by
**Diana L. Paxson &
Adrienne Martine-Barnes**

THE SHIELD BETWEEN THE WORLDS

MASTER *of* EARTH *and* WATER

DIANA L. PAXSON
& ADRIENNE MARTINE-BARNES

AVON BOOKS • NEW YORK

MASTER OF EARTH AND WATER is an original publication of Avon Books. This work is a novel. Any similarity to actual persons or events is purely coincidental.

AVON BOOKS
A division of
The Hearst Corporation
1350 Avenue of the Americas
New York, New York 10019

First AvoNova Printing: June 1994
First Morrow/AvoNova Hardcover Printing: May 1993

AVONOVA TRADEMARK REG. U.S. PAT. OFF. AND IN OTHER COUNTRIES, MARCA REGISTRADA, HECHO EN U.S.A.

Printed in the U.S.A.

RA 10 9 8 7 6 5 4 3 2 1

For Our Demnes,
Ian, Geoffrey, Robin, and Simon

People and Places

CHARACTERS

[Note: the following pronunciations are my attempt to transliterate the words as pronounced in a way that will be vaguely comprehensible to the modern reader. Dh = "th" as in the; qh = a gutteral "ch" or "gh" sound. A dash indicates a syllable separation, an apostrophe indicates a hesitation. "Mac", meaning "son of", has been left in the modern form (the medieval spelling would have been "magg") out of deference to the sensibilities of the reader. Gaelic is an inflected language, and names may change their spelling in different grammatical positions.]

Our thanks to Alexei Kondratiev for correcting spelling and word forms, and to Paul Edwin Zimmer for advice on pronunciation. Any mistakes are the result of artistic decisions or pure ignorance, and are our own.

Fionn mac Cumhal [FYONN MAK KOOWEL] called Demne [DEM-NEH] as a child (or Demne Mael, or Demne the Gilla)

Cumhal mac Trenmor [KOOWEL MAK TRENMOR] of the Ui Tairrseg [OO-EE TARSHEG]—Fionn's father

Muirne Fair Neck (Muirne nic Tadhg) [MURRN'YUH NEEK TA'KH]—Fionn's mother

Tadg mac Nuada [TA'KH MAK NOOADAT]—a druid, Fionn's grandfather

Donait [DUNATCH]—a woman of the Sidhe

Brigid [BREE-ID]—goddess of healing, smithcraft, and poetry

Fiacail mac Conchinn [FYAKIL MAK KON'HINN]—a *fennid*

Demne's fosterers:
Bodbmall [BODHVULL]—a wise woman and wife to Fiacail the Liath Luachra [LIAH LOOKHRA]("Speedy-legs")—a warrior woman

Boys from the Rath at the edge of Mag Life:
Gort mac Dubthach [GORT MAK DOOV-HUK]
Bran mac Conall [BRON MAK KONIL]
Cormac mac Conail [KORMAK MAK CONIL]

People at Tailtiu:
Conn [KONN] of the Hundred Battles—high king of Eriu,
Cormac mac Airt [KORMAK MAC ARTCH]—his grandson

Boys in the House of Youths:
Aonghus mac Conail [EWN'GUS]—Bran's older brother, a *fili* apprenticed to Fionnéices
Lugna mac Ronain [LOOGNUH MAK RONIN]
Diarmait mac Fergusa [JERMATCH MAK FERGUSA]
Oscar mac Mebh [OSKAR MAK MEV]
Dael mac Conain (of Clan Morna) [DAYL MAK KONEEN]

Women in the household:
Blathnat Nic Aedh [BLA'NAT NEEK AYDHUH]
Moriath [MORIAH]
Samhair [SAWERE]

Clan Morna (sons of Daire the Red):
Conain the Swearer [KONAN]

Goll [GOL] (One-Eye) (formerly called Aedh mac Daire) [AYDH MAK DERRY]

Airt Og of the Hard Strokes [ART OHG]

Garra [GARA]

Uirgriu mac Luigech Cuirr [UR'GROO MAK LOOGESH COOIR]—lord of the Luagni, who was one of Cumhal's rivals for the post of *rigfennid*, the king of Benntriage at Dun Coba near Sliab Luachra

Gléor Redhand, king of Lamraige [GLEE-OR]

Lochan [LOCK-UN]—a smith

Cruithne [KROO-INYE]—his daughter

Eochaidh [YO-KAI]—a fisher who courts Cruithne

The Grey Man of Luachar [LOOAKAR]—formerly one of Cumhal's men, transformed into the Otherworldly boar of Siiab Muicce

Béo [BEE-O], the Red-Mouthed woman—mother of the Grey Man

Aife [EEFUH]—second wife of Manannan who was transformed by her rival into a crane and whose spirit remained when her skin was made into the magical *corrbolg*, the treasure bag of Cumha

Crimall's fian:

Crimall mac Trenmor [KRIMUL]—leader of Cumhai's old *fian* and Fionn's uncle

Dithramhach mac Cumhal [DI'RA'WACH]—Cumhal's assumed son by a bondwoman

Reidhe mac Daei [RAY'YUH]—a survivor from Cumhal's old *fian*

Coll mac Diarmaita [KUL MAK JERMUTA]

Aghmar mac Domnaill [UQHMAR MAK DOWNIL]

Glanna [GLENA]—hearth keeper for Crimall's *fian*

Grimthann [GREEMHAN]—the dogboy

Duibhne [DWEE'NHYE]—the cupbearer

Fionnéices [FYON-AY-KISH]—(Fionn the poet), formerly Aonghus' master and once *fili* to Cumhal

People (and deities) in the Background:

Aonghus Og [EWNGUS OHG]—god of love, son of the Dagda and Boann and owner of the Brugh na Boinne

Boann [BOW'UNN]—cow goddess, the river Boyne

the Dagda [DOIGDA]—"the Good God" of might and plenty

Goibhniu [GOVN'YU]—the smith's god

Luchet the Fair [LUKETCH]—one of Cumhal's warriors who took out Goll's eye at the battle of Cnucha and was killed by him

Lugh Samildanach [LOOQH SAMILDUNAWK]—multi-skilled champion of the Tuatha dé Dannan

Ogma [AH'MAH]—inventor of the Ogham magical script

Conchobar [KON'OVUR]—1st century king of the Ulaid

Cuchulain [KOO'HOOLIN]—the champion of the Ulaid in the time of King Conchobar

Ferdiad [FERDIA]—his friend and opponent

Medbh [MEV]—Queen of Connachta who fought Conchobar

the Morrigan [MORIGUN]—raven goddess of battle

Tailtiu [TALTCHU]—foster-mother of Lugh, after whom the Tailtiu fair at the Feast of Lughnasa was named

PEOPLES

Sons of Mil [MILL]—Milesians, Gaelic speaking rulers of Eriu

Tuatha dé Danann [TUA'HA JAY DANAWN]—the **Sidhe** [SHEE'UH], euhemerized as the race preceding the Milesians, or deified as the Celtic gods

Galeóin [GALYOWN]—(Gauls) Fir Bolg [FEER BOLUG] and Fir Domnann [DOWNAN] (Dumnonii)—Brythonic-speaking subject peoples

Ui Morna [OOEE MORNUH]—a clan of the Fir Bolg located around Loch Derg in southern Connaught

Ui Tairrsigh [OOEE TARSHI]—a clan of the Fir Bolg located in the land of the Ui Failghi [OOEE FALYI] (West Offaiy, County Kildare)

Ui Uirgriu [OOEE OORGRU] and Luagni [LOOANYI]— Tuath Luaighne, in Midhe

Fir Bili [FEER BILI]—a tribe located near the pass of Kilbride, Mydhe

PLACES

Midhe [MEEYUH]—Meath

Laigin [LAYIN]—Leinster

Mumu [MOOMOO]—Munster

Connachta [KONAQHTA]—Connaught

Ulaid [ULADJ]—Ulster

Alba [ALAPA]—Scotland

Sliab Bladhma [SCHLEEUV BLADHMA] (Sea-monster mountain)—Slieve Bloom mountains

Mag Life [MAG LEEFEH]—the plain of the Liffey

the Curragh [KURRAQH]—plain surrounding Kildare

Fidh Gaible [FEE GAV'LA]—forest between the Curragh and the Bog of Allen the Gaible—River Figuile

Loch Lurgan [LOQH LOORGAN]—where the Liath Luachra dwells

Almu [ALMOO]—Tadhg's dun on the hill of Allen near Kildare

Tailtiu [TALTCHOO]—in the valley of the Boyne along the Blackwater between Navan and Kells

Temair Brega [TCHEMER BREGA]—the hill of Tara

the Boann [BOW-UNN]—River Boyne

Sliab Luachra [SHLEEUV LOOAKRA]—Caha Mountains in Cork

Lamraige [LAMRAYUH]—Limerick, near Loch Gair

Benntraige [BENTRAYUH]—Bantry

the Siuir [SHU'UR]—River Suir

Lochan's forge—on the Dingle peninsula

Sinnan [SHEENUN]—River Shannon

Loch Dergdeire [LOQH JERUGDERRY]—Loch Derg

Bri Ele [BREE AYLUH]—a fairy mound near Cloghan

An Uaimh [UN OOIV]—Navan, Meath

Brugh na Boinne [BROOQH NUH BOYNYUH]—the palace on the Boyne, Newgrange

Linn Féic [LING FAYK]—a pool at the edge of the River Boyne below Newgrange

TERMS

Ard Ri [ARD REE]—high king

bendrui [BUN-DROOEE]—woman-druid

caman [COME-ON]—hurley stick

corrbolg [KORBOLUG]—crane bag

drui [DROOEE]—druid

fennid [FENITCH]—member of a fian

fian [FEEAN] or *fianna*—national guard

fidchel [FISCHELL]—a board game, something like chess

fili [FILLEE]—poet

filidecht [FILJECHT]—the poets, poetry

gilla [GILLYEH]—lad, young man in service or training

grianan [GREEANUN]—"sun house," building where the women work or relax

mael [MAYL]—crop-headed

ollamh [OLLAV]—highest rank of poet

rigfennid [REEGFENNITCH]—chief of a fian

Imbolc [IMBULK]—Feast of Brigid, beginning of February

Beltane [BAL-TEEN]—May Day

Lughnasa [LOONASAH]—Feast of Lugh, beginning of August

Samhain [SOW-IN]—Hallowe'en

Foreword

Of the three great legendary cycles of Irish literature, the tales of the outlaw/poet Fionn MacCumhal have had perhaps the most enduring popularity among the people of Ireland. The stories of Cuchulain and the Ulster heroes were written down in an early form, and the memories of the various peoples who settled Ireland were preserved in the *Book of Invasions*. But like Robin Hood in England, Fionn has always belonged to the people of his land.

The rulers whom Fionn serves or battles in the tales belong to the third century C.E. in Ireland, the dawn of the age of the high kings. The *Annals* date the reign of Cormac mac Airt from 218 to 256 C.E. Certainly someone at this time united Ireland sufficiently so that the Irish could begin raiding Britain, much to the Romans' dismay. Why not Cormac, with the assistance of Fionn? Eoin MacNeill and others believe that the stories of the *fianna* are based on the relationship between the Gaelic lords of the land and the subject races, descended from these earlier immigrations into Ireland.

The original locus of the Fionn stories seems to
have been northern Leinster, the country around
Kildare. They remained popular, especially in the
south and west, which the high kings controlled by
drafting their warriors to form independent fighting
forces to give them the balance of power among the
Gaelic clans. These warrior bands, halfway between
a corps of mercenaries and a national guard, were
the *fians* of Ireland, the greatest of them being that
of Cumhal mac Trenmor, the father of Fionn. Perhaps
the fact that Fionn, though a great hero, was not
actually a member of the ruling class, contributed
to his popularity when Ireland was conquered once
more.

The stories of Fionn were not written down until
the ninth century, and by that time the tales were
already part of a rich oral tradition that continued to
flourish throughout the Middle Ages. Gaelic settlers
carried the stories to Scotland, where they were
eventually retold, in a form appropriate to eighteenth
century sensibilities, by James MacPherson as the
Poems of Ossian. One cannot help but wonder if some
Irish immigrant to America told Fionn's story to Mark
Twain and inspired both the name and character of
Huckleberry Finn. In the twentieth century, James
Joyce worked his own bizarre magic on the tale in
Finnegan's Wake. But literary treatments have always
been less important in the history of the legend than
the popular tradition, which speaks of Fionn as if his
adventures happened yesterday.

Fionn's amazing survival should not be so sur-
prising. As Nagy's excellent book, *The Wisdom of
the Outlaw*, points out, Fionn is above all a liminal
character. Like Huckleberry Finn, he operates on the
fringes of society. His is basically the way of the
shaman, and he moves freely between the worlds
of the outlaw and society, between the natural and

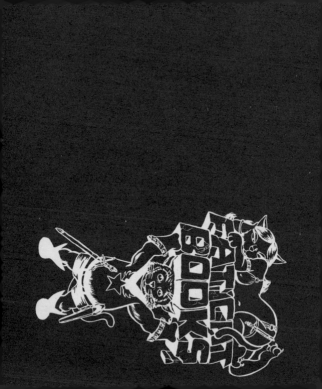

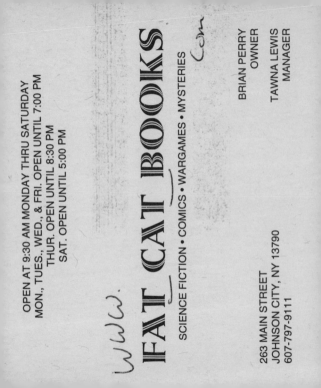

FAT CAT BOOKS

SCIENCE FICTION • COMICS • WARGAMES • MYSTERIES

OPEN AT 9:30 AM MONDAY THRU SATURDAY
MON., TUES., WED., & FRI. OPEN UNTIL 7:00 PM
THUR. OPEN UNTIL 8:30 PM
SAT. OPEN UNTIL 5:00 PM

BRIAN PERRY
OWNER

TAWNA LEWIS
MANAGER

263 MAIN STREET
JOHNSON CITY, NY 13790
607-797-9111

the supernatural, animal and human, action and intuition, male and female.

The adventures of such a hero transcend any single retelling. Even the three volumes of our own attempt to tell Fionn's story cannot cover the whole, but we have done our best to select the episodes that would create a coherent narrative. The Boyhood Deeds of a hero were one of the traditional classes of Irish tales. *Master of Earth and Water* presents the Boyhood Deeds of Fionn.

As a final justification for tackling a story to which we were led by the encouragement of our editor, Chris Miller of Avon Books, and by love of the lore of Ireland and a good story, we offer the following observation by Eoin MacNeill:

> *The legend of the Fiana, as it spread from race to race ... was constantly undergoing reformations. ... It remained always modern, not only in its language, but in the sense of being entirely the property of each succeeding generation of story-tellers and ballad-makers.*
>   *Duanaire Finn* xlii

In this tradition, we present our version of the story to you now.

We consulted many books in the writing of this tale. Among the most important were:

Duanaire Finn: The Book of the Lays of Fionn translated by Eoin MacNeill. London: Irish Texts Society, 1908.

Máire MacNeill, *The Festival of Lughnasa*. Dublin: University College of Dublin, 1982.

Vivian Mercier, *The Irish Comic Tradition*. Oxford: Clarendon Press, 1962.

Joseph Falaky Nagy, *The Wisdom of the Outlaw*, University of California Press, 1985.

Alwynn and Brinley Rees, *Celtic Heritage.* Thames and Hudson, 1961.

Robert D. Scott, *The Thumb of Knowledge.* New York: Institute of French Studies, Inc. 1930.

Prologue

◆❧

FIACAIL LED THE WAY THROUGH THE FOREST. OLD though he was, a lifetime in the *fianna* had taught him to step with a maddening deliberation that crushed no leaf and broke no branch to tell their pursuers which way they had gone. Bodbmall shifted the warm burden of the infant she carried from one arm to the other and trod carefully after him. Mist clung and curled among the upper branches of the oak trees, deadening the air.

At every movement she could feel the weariness of the long hours beside the bedside of the laboring woman. For a moment she thought with longing of the great hollow oak which had sheltered the birth, then hard-learned lessons allowed her to banish the awareness of her fatigue, as she banished her grief for Muirne. It had been the girl's own decision to stay behind with her new daughter, to live or die when her father found her, so that the old druidess might give her twin-born son a chance to live. At least the binding Bodbmall had laid on the baby still held, though she could feel him struggling against it.

They came to a clearing, and Fiacail turned. A nod from the druidess was sufficient signal—they were

1

companions of long-standing, familiar with one another's ways, and needed no words. The Liath Luachra was close behind her, weapons ready. But the small sounds of the forest were all that could be heard around them. Then they paused to skirt a thicket, and in the far distance heard the shouts of men.

The old warrior woman made a face. "Oafs," she muttered.

A quelling glance from the druidess silenced her. Tadhg's men might be no mightier than any other warriors, but the strength of the lord of Almu lay not in men but in magic. Bodbmall stilled, letting her own subtle senses quest outward. There was a stirring—she flinched and strengthened her wardings as the mist stirred to the beat of silent, broad-barred wings; round yellow eyes gleamed and were gone. Tadhg had learned the owl shape when they were children together. Now he was the greatest druid in Eriu, and he was using all his powers to hunt down his own daughter.

The Liath Luachra glared at Bodbmall, then nodded at Fiacail's back impatiently and lifted her grizzled brows. Bodbmall shifted the child to her other hip and gave a shrug. They were all getting older, but she and Liath could still run like deer if there was need. Still, despite stiffening joints, it was Fiacail's woodcraft and her own magic that must save them if Tadhg should get on their trail.

She glanced at the man's bent back with the exasperation of old affection. Though they lived apart as often as they did together, he was her husband. But the warrior woman had been Bodbmall's companion for almost as long. She could never quite choose between them, her two loves. The silent infant she carried was not the first she had borne into the wilderness to foster with Fiacail's warrior band. Years before she had carried this babe's father, Cumhal, on

a similar journey. It had been easier then. Her bones
had ached less. He had grown to a fine, fair man and
the greatest of warriors, lord of the *fianna* that served
the high king, but no match for a druid enraged by the
theft of his daughter. And now Cumhal was dead, and
the druid was trying to destroy Cumhal's child.

There was a faint ringing in her ears, and she slowed,
sending her awareness outward. That sound always
presaged some imminent crisis, and she was too wise
in the ways of knowledge to ignore it. Tadhg had found
Muirne, she thought then, and was searching for those
who had helped her.

She nudged Fiacail, pointed, and they set off again.
The sensation was maddening, shifting from side to
side, from ear to ear like a mayfly winging through
her skull, but each change led her in a surer direction.
Mist still shrouded the trees around them, but the
oaks were giving way to ash and black poplar as the
land sloped downward. A watery yellow light now
set their shadows moving darkly across the brighter patches between the trees. Their general direction
was west, towards the hills. There were many hidden
places within them; surely one would provide refuge.
Bodbmall's arms ached with fatigue, as if the child
were growing heavier.

A swift river rushed across their path, swollen with
recent rains. There was no obvious ford, so they followed its banks. The roar and rush of water seemed
to rouse the child, though he made no sound. But he
pushed free of the folds of the cloak and turned his
head towards the noise. A smile crossed the tiny face,
and he looked up at Bodbmall with an expression of
delight so great that her heart was lightened. She saw
a flash of white upon the upper gum. The ridge of a
tooth gleamed in the pink mouth.

Even in her weariness, Bodbmall felt the quick-
ening of excitement. The boy was a *drui* born! Finally,

she would have someone to instruct in the ways of wisdom. *A tooth, a tooth*, her heart sang. *A child such as I have always longed for*, her mind replied. Contentment lent new ease to her limbs, and she hugged her precious burden to her.

They came to a fairly smooth stretch of water where the stream had scoured out a deep pool. Above it, the river narrowed, and several large boulders offered a crossing. The space between the rocks was not beyond a bit of nimble jumping. Bodbmall kilted her skirts up into her belt and knotted the corners of her cloak together behind before she nodded her readiness. They started across, Fiacail still leading. The child coiled a small fist into the cloth of her gown, pinching the flesh beneath it.

The rocks were slick and wet, and patches of moss made the footing treacherous. Bodbmall watched Fiacail carefully, then copied his movements. But despite her care, the weight of the babe unbalanced her and her foot slid on wet lichen. She flailed helplessly, felt the babe flung away as she went down. She glimpsed the small form splashing into the pool below the rocks, grabbed, and the blanket came away in her hand.

The Liath Luachra plunged into the water, came up for air, and, swift as an otter, dove again. The seconds seemed like eternities as the warrior woman surfaced again and disappeared. Bodbmall felt her heart go still. Were the gods toying with her, giving her a child and then tearing it away? She pulled herself upright, ignoring her soaked gown and a bleeding scrape on one hand, and stared bleakly as the head of her companion moved further downstream. It was hopeless. It had been too long.

Then mist above the river shifted and sunlight dappled the water. The Liath Luachra emerged in a spatter of golden drops, thrusting the naked child above her, then rolled onto her back and set him upon her flat chest. Kicking mightily, she swam towards the shore, cursing.

Bodbmall scrambled up from her knees and in her haste nearly missed the next rock. If the child had been dead, Liath would not have made a sound. Fiacail jumped back to steady her, there as he always seemed to be when she needed him. A strong hand beneath her elbow got her back to the bank. He brushed tears she had not known she'd shed from her wrinkled cheeks and led her to where the Liath Luachra had come ashore.

The warrior woman plopped the wriggling child down on a pile of leaves and sank to the ground, bowing her grey head between her knees and gasping for air. She pounded her head to clear the water from her ears and glared at the child with red-rimmed eyes.

"Brat! He was playing with the fishes! I have a mind to toss him back!"

Bodbmall knelt beside the boy, ignoring her companion's fury with the ease of habit. Complaint and water were the Liath Luachra's elements. The child kicked his sturdy legs and gave a little crowing cry. In his arms he gripped a plump salmon, still twitching as it gasped its life away. The baby's eyes, blue as the water when the sun broke through, danced with delight.

Fiacail stared down at them. "Well," he said in his deliberate way, "I see he got us dinner."

Chapter 1

DEMNE SLIPPED BETWEEN THE SHADOWED FIR TREES, listening intently. He tightened his grip on the bone-tipped spear and ignored an itch beneath the deerskin wrap that was his only clothing. His throat tickled at the dry-dust smell, but he did not cough, nor did his bare feet stir the dry needles that covered the forest floor as he passed. Someday he would have a pair of shoes, like the Liath Luachra, his warrior foster mother, and a fine-woven cloak of colors, such as his other fosterer, Bodbmall, wrapped about herself, but not until he finished growing. He wondered when that would be. He was almost nine and already eye to eye with Bodbmall.

He heard scratching ahead of him and saw a red squirrel scrabbling beneath the root of a tree. Demne laid his spear carefully down and crept forward. Then he snatched, and his fingers closed on the bushy tail. For a moment he had it, but the luxuriance of the brush had been deceptive. The squirrel exploded into action and the tail slipped through Demne's fingers, leaving him with a handful of russet hairs. In another moment the beast had scurried up the rough trunk, leapt for a low branch, where it swung precariously, then launched itself safely to an upper bough, where it turned, chittering furiously and dancing from foot to foot for all the world like Bodbmall in a rage. Demne brushed the hairs from his hand and began to laugh.

If he had no squirrel for the pot, at least he had found its hoard. Still laughing, he squatted at the base of the tree, opened his game bag, and began to scoop out the kernels the squirrel had cached there.

Suddenly Demne paused with his hand in midair, listening. The branches of the fir trees were holding their own conversation with the wind, but the sound he had heard was like the rare laughter of the Liath Luachra, only higher pitched, sharper. Demne pivoted slowly, all thought of food for the moment forgotten. His neck hairs prickled, and he pushed a length of pale, tangled hair off his brow. Somebody was laughing at *him!*

Several days before he had heard the same tittering sound. It had been followed by a patter of footsteps as though another person were running away from him. But whoever, or whatever, it ran as if the wind had feet. If only he could be *sure.* This was not the first time he thought he had heard or seen something that neither of his foster mothers seemed to know was there.

The sense of being spied on—and laughed at—persisted. Demne narrowed his blue eyes and hunched his wide shoulders, staring. But no one was there. Still he kept hoping. Sometimes he got so tired of the Liath Luachra and old Bodbmall and their bickering and the way they pulled him one way and another. If only there were someone else with whom he could play!

Bodbmall was a wisewoman, a *bendrui*, who wanted him to learn the secrets of the trees, the course of the summer stars, and the wisdom of the waters. The Liath Luachra demanded that he master spear and sword and bow. No one asked him what *he* wanted. This made Demne think of the man who had twice visited them. They called him Fiacail, and he was a warrior. Fiacail had stayed for some time, and Demne gave a rare smile as he thought of the older man. He was tired of the women, weary of hearing the same things over and over again. Fiacail had shown him new things. He wished he had someone to hunt with as he had done with the man. But not a sneak who laughed at him and hid.

A low squeal snapped his thoughts back to the present. A second later he heard the rooting grunt of a pig from somewhere ahead of him. Demne's mouth watered. He remembered pig. The last time Fiacail had come, he had killed one, and the women had cooked it. They had praised Fiacail, and the boy had been pierced with longing to have them give *him* such words. The taste of pig and the sound of approval were a single sweetness in his memory.

Demne knew how to snare squirrels; he was a mighty hunter of hares. He could bring down a bird with a sling stone and catch fish with his hands, and he had helped the Liath Luachra to run down the fleet-footed fallow deer, but until today he had never caught more than a glimpse of the prey he most desired. He closed his pouch, edged backwards to recover his spear, and, heart drumming, passed silently from the shade of the firs into the dappled space beneath the oak trees beyond.

Demne crept closer, grasping his spear, and the rooting stopped. The boy froze in place. There was a snuffling noise, a high squeal, then more rooting. The forest seemed to still around him, the slight breeze dying against his sweating skin. He felt as if the wood were holding its breath too.

In the stillness, the whisper of breath in his throat was a storm wind, the thud of his heart like thunder.

With an effort, Demne silenced his body. Then he squeezed shut his bright eyes and tried to do a thing Bodbmall had been pestering him about for days. He tried to hear the air. . . .

It was like slipping between two trees that stood side by side without touching either. With a quiver as if he had passed some invisible barrier, Demne slid into a place where he could hear the deep silence at the heart of the world, and the sound of his heart and laboring lungs faded away.

Abruptly he plunged among the oak trees. A young pig gave a startled grunt and exploded out of the glade with astonishing swiftness for something so ungainly, its stripes blending into the light-dark dapple of the forest floor. It dashed into a thicket, and Demne dove after it, laughing, heedless of rocks or branches. He smashed a toe against a hidden stump and did not feel it at all.

Squealing discordantly, the beast darted across the floor of the forest, leading him away from the sparser vegetation of the hilltops where he usually hunted and deeper into the wood. Demne felt the ground dip, and he hesitated. He had never been this far from the rude huts that were his home. One thing the women had agreed was that he must *not* go down into the thick of the woods. Then his yearning for the sweetness of pig overcame him. Demne grinned in anticipation and loped after his prey.

A glade opened before him. The pig scooted across it on blurring legs, leaping for the shelter of the trees beyond. Demne gave a bound and a shout as he hurled his spear into the animal's side. It struck; the pig shrieked, then scrambled into the underbrush with the spear still dangling from its flank, banging against rock and tree. A trail of splattered blood showed where it had gone.

The boy chased after it, howling. His foot slipped on

a gout of sticky blood and he staggered. The toe he had smashed in his heedless running had skin torn away at the nail, and the blood of the pig smeared into the cut in his flesh. Where the two bloods touched, Demne felt a strange tingling. But as he plunged forward he barely noticed, until he tripped over a branch and went down on his hands and knees.

Demne could hear the pig squealing from somewhere ahead of him, but at that moment he was incapable of following. Where his hands and knees touched the earth, it held him. He saw the forest in a hazy way; only the things close to him were clear. At the same time, he smelled things he had never known before.

Who would have believed the earth held so many scents, so many sounds? He could almost hear the bark growing on the trees. Demne wagged his head from side to side, feeling as though his neck had somehow shortened, and sniffed and listened.

The boy made a sound not unlike the squeal of the pig and dragged one scraped hand up off the leaf-strewn forest floor. The tumult of smell and sound diminished, and now he was able to heave himself upright again and follow his prey. Broken ferns and blood-speckled leaves told where the pig had gone by. A little winded, Demne rested his hands upon his bloody knees. No wonder Bodbmall and the warrior woman had made such a fuss over Fiacail. This was a lot harder than catching a hare or even killing a hind.

Demne trotted along, savoring the praise to come and the taste of boiled pig in his mouth, admiring the animal's endurance even as he pursued it. A deer would have collapsed already. Why, a pig must be the most powerful animal of all! So busy was he with this idea that he barely gave attention to the grunts of his prey.

The little pig staggered just ahead of him. It collapsed, then pushed itself up again. Demne rushed forward to finish the kill, then flipped awkwardly aside as sharp milk tusks raked the air where his belly had been. The animal's dimming eyes glared at him as its head sank once more. Demne stared back curiously. No hare or hind had ever given him such a look as it died. What he saw in the pig's eyes was anger. He knew the expression well, for his foster mothers were frequently angry with each other or with him.

Then the pig gave a shudder and was still. Demne bent down cautiously and yanked the spear out of its side. He stroked a hesitant forefinger across the rough-bristled hide. It was different from anything he had ever touched before. It was not just the roughness—he sensed something about the animal. . . . Perhaps when he was grown he would know the words.

Burst branches rattled like sudden thunder, and an immense black sow smashed through the shadowed bracken beneath the trees. The boy glimpsed red-rimmed eyes and sharp teeth, gasped, and grabbed for his prize as he took to his heels. He could feel the hot, moist breath of the sow on his legs. He risked a glance over his shoulder, caught his forehead against a branch, and reeled back.

The sow gave a grunt of fury and swept her snout towards his belly, hooking the edge of his garment. The sinew holding the skins together snapped. Demne dropped the pig, grabbed leather as it fell, and flung it at the sow's terrible eyes.

She tossed her head and the skin went flying; Demne thrust his spear into the unprotected throat with all the strength his young body could muster. The point stuck in the thick-muscled neck, not deeply, but it hurt her—he heard a squeal of rage. He snatched up his kill and ran, while the angry sow roared and tore at leather and bracken as she strove to shake loose the spear.

Branches whipped his naked flesh, and the dead pig was a heavy burden, but Demne hardly noticed as he plunged deeper into the forest, splashing through gurgling streams and scattering showers of golden pollen from flower-laden trees. Then he began to ascend again.

Arms, legs, and lungs aching, Demne raced until the trees were a blur. He wondered if he would ever stop. He had left the great black sow far behind, but still he ran as though something pursued him. Perhaps he would run to the end of the world. That thought finally slowed him. He had never even been to the edge of the forest.

The trees took shape around him. He was naked, torn, and bruised. His head throbbed and his arms felt afire with the pain of muscles stressed beyond their power. His mouth was dry and tasted as if he had licked the outside of Bodbmall's cauldron. And none of it mattered. He looked at the little pig that was stiffening in his arms and grinned triumphantly.

By the time Demne reached the huddle of small huts, he was aching all over. His head pounded where he had struck it against a branch, and his leg muscles jumped and quivered with strain. His unclad skin itched with dried sweat and blood—his own and the pig's—and the toe he had smashed against a rock was throbbing afresh with every step. He could not recall ever having felt so weary.

But despite the discomfort he was happy, and he knew that something inside him had changed. It was more than the simple pride of slaying a pig as if he were a grown man. Beneath the thud of his headache, he could hear a wordless soft sound that was almost like a song. Music he knew, for the two women often sang as they worked; but this was different. It was not the clear, high voice Bodbmall used to chant her druidic teachings or to accompany herself while she ground the grain or tanned a hide. Nor was it like the deep-voiced melody of the Liath Luachra, intoning battles and famous deeds of heroes. The sound was unlike anything he knew, except perhaps the tone he had once heard when Bodbmall's knife had struck the bowl of the glass goblet she kept for special rituals like the Eve of Samhain, when the gateway between the worlds stood wide.

Demne never understood quite how she knew the day, for all days were alike for him. He knew the seasons, the passages of the moon from dark to full to dark again; and still it was a mystery, like so much else. *He* was a mystery, and it puzzled him and made a hot, hard feeling in his chest. Where had he come from, why was he here, and what was going to become of him? Beasts had mothers and fathers, and the birds in the trees as well, so how could he have none? Why did he live hidden away from other folk? He knew there were other people, for he was forbidden to venture beyond the forest lest he encounter them.

More telling were those times when Bodbmall would suddenly gather up the herbs and simples she used for healing and hurry down the mountainside. How had she known someone needed her, and where had she gone? After a time he had learned not to ask, for the Liath Luachra just shook her head and set him some new task.

The song in his ears carried him past pain and brought him by swift paths of memory back to the three round huts in the clearing. Their thatching of brush and reeds bound to a framework of woven hazels seemed to have sprouted from the hollow on the side of the mountain. The sighing of the oaks that shaded them mingled with the laughter of the nearby stream.

At the sound of his footfall, the Liath Luachra started up from the rock on which she had been sitting, oiling her sword. Her eyes widened at the sight of his naked body and the rigid carcass in his arms. Then they narrowed, sharp and critical, and she took a stiff step towards him. Her long plaited hair was the grey of twilight, and her skin was seamed and puckered with weather and age.

"Where is your spear?"

"In the throat of the mother pig, unless she tore it out of her. I did not stay to see." Demne fought to keep his voice as steady as hers, but his shoulders slumped as he lowered the pig to the ground. Fiacail had not lost his spear. . . .

Was that why she had not praised him?

He felt ashamed and dull-witted now. It had taken a long time to make that spear, to harden the hind's shoulder blade, to sharpen its edges and shape it to its deadly purpose. Days had been spent smoothing the shaft, making certain the thongs that held the point in place were strong and secure. He had been impatient, and the Liath Luachra had scolded him, while Bodbmall had complained that the making of it took him away from his studies with her. But that had been a long time ago. Something in him rose up to protest the injustice.

"Being that close for that long was enough—the shaft of that spear was too short for me," Demne said defensively.

The warrior woman looked at him with eyes as grey as her hair, up and down, as if she had never seen him before. "It is so. You have grown since we crafted it. I had not noticed."

That was it, he thought, only a testing. Now she would praise the way he had used that spear.

She crouched down in a series of movements, like a crane, and examined the carcass. "Your aim was poor. It was not a clean kill."

"No." A sudden appalled guilt closed his throat once more. Why had he ever gone after something they were always telling him he was not old enough to kill? He remembered how the piglet had squealed. It had been hurting, and it was his fault. The Liath Luachra had taught him better than that. Once more he had failed her, no better at hunting than he was at the lessons Bodbmall beat into him. He wondered if he would ever do anything well.

"Still, it was a hard thing, and I can see you did not falter."

Demne's heart leaped. She *did* understand! The Liath Luachra stood up, painfully, for he could hear the creak of her bones, and Demne wanted to reach out a hand to aid her. He did not, for he knew she was still quite capable of boxing his ears, even though he was nearly as tall as she.

Bodbmall came out of the storage hut at the sound of their voices, a willow basket in her hands. Demne's heart began to beat, slow and heavy, in his breast. Now the Liath Luachra would tell her what he had done, and they would be pleased with him.

The wisewoman swept the scene with her bright eyes and bustled across the space between them, wisps of white hair springing back from her broad brow. "What's this, lad? Where is your wrap? You cannot be running about that way. And you are all cut! What have you done to yourself? Is it every moment that I must be keeping my eye upon you?"

Demne felt his skin go hot and words burst out of him. "The sow tore it away with her snout, and then I threw it over her face. We have not had pig since Fiacail last came. I thought it would be a good change from hare."

"Thought! Thought!" Demne jerked at each word, as if she were beating flesh already bruised. "You heedless child! If you had been thinking you would not be naked and bruised now! Go wash yourself. Do you think clothing grows on trees? Threw it in a sow's face, indeed! 'Tis lucky you are that you found her alone, without her daughters around her." Her shrill voice rose, and a huddle of crows took flight from a nearby tree, cawing. Demne shuddered. One sow had been bad enough—the thought of a whole clan of them coming after him was enough to haunt his dreams.

"Come, Bodbmall. There is no need to be so harsh with the lad." The Liath Luachra's deep voice was calm.

"You! You encourage him to foolhardiness. He is not to be a warrior. It is your tales that are filling his head with this nonsense. How can I teach him the paths of the wise while you—"

"He is almost a man!" The Liath Luachra snorted with bitter laughter. "You cannot be keeping him swaddled in your cloak forever. You could not even manage it the day he was born, when he escaped your clutches and went to play amongst the fishes!"

For a moment Demne's pain receded. This was a tale he had never heard! For all he knew, he might have popped out of a rock or fallen from a tree. But he remembered an odd question Fiacail had asked on his last visit there—"Have you caught any more salmon, boy?" And then Bodbmall had glared and ordered the boy to go get more firewood, even though there was plenty at hand.

"Fool, be still!" Bodbmall cried.

"You cannot keep him a child forever, old woman! I know how you are."

"How can you say it? You go distracting him with your stupid tales of old heroes when he has so much still to learn! He was born with the tooth of wisdom—he's not meant for the warrior way."

Demne glanced at the body of the piglet. Had killing it been the deed of a warrior, and was that why she was angry? But they needed food!

The Liath Luachra shook her head and her braids flew. "Do you forget that I have seen you foster afore? I remember how it was with his—with the others. Conn and Cumhal. You would have kept them children forever."

"This is different."

"It is the same. You still want a babe for your barren womb."

Bodbmall rounded on the boy. "Go clean yourself. I shall be surprised if you do not take a fever from one of those cuts. Go! Now!"

Shivering a little at the overtones in their words, Demne moved reluctantly away. He strained to catch the rest of their argument.

"Have you finally lost what wits you ever had to be speaking of Conn?" Bodbmall lowered her voice to a near hiss, and Demne could not catch the Liath Luachra's reply, though he saw her grey skin flush. He was accustomed to their endless bickering, and their scoldings as well, but this seemed different. He had bungled the hunting, but at least he had tried. Why was it so wrong for him to do something on his own?

When the low laughter of the stream rose above the sound of the women's voices the ache in Demne's throat began to ease. It was all more puzzles. Who was Conn and the other man whose name he could not recall? It made his head blaze to try to remember the name.

The ache of emotion was giving way to confusion. Then he waded into the chill water, and gasped as the cut on his toe opened again. His feet were hard from running unshod, but it felt as if several of Bodbmall's needles had been thrust beneath his skin.

Since there was nobody to hear him, he let himself moan softly, then caught the rapid patter of feet above the gurgle of the stream. He looked suspiciously at both banks, but there was nothing. Then he glimpsed, just for a moment, a sparkling flash like the flicker of a leaf tossed by the wind. He blinked, then the stinging in his flesh reclaimed his attention. He dipped his torn hands into the stream and cupped water against his bruised and sweaty face.

The smell of the water overwhelmed his senses. Never had he noticed that water had a scent, except when it was still and thick with scum. He lowered his long body down into the cold liquid, ignoring the sting as it touched his cuts, and put his whole face into the stream. The scent seemed to go through his skin, his entire flesh, until it was in his very bones. He drew a breath and came up, coughing and choking. But the smell lingered, sweet and clean, better than air. The water caressed his legs like a touch he had always longed for but never known.

After a time the chill drove Demne reluctantly ashore, looking back at the stream with a hunger he could not identify. The strange ringing in his ears was stronger now, almost a discernable melody. He strained to capture it as his damp body dried in the light breeze. But like the name he could not recall, it was just beyond his grasp.

He looked up at the path back to the huts and tried to summon the strength to follow it. The ache of betrayal was back, but distant, on the other side of the wonder of the stream. Still, he felt as though he had chased not one small piglet but ten boars.

By the time he returned, the two women had skinned the animal and gutted it, and the fire was alight beneath Bodbmall's great bronze cauldron. He watched the Liath Luachra tie the pointy hooves of the pig to a long wooden pole. They were still arguing, but about domestic matters, not about him. Demne was both relieved and disappointed. He had hoped to learn more.

"What were you doing, then? Drinking the stream dry? Get your old tunic and start hauling water, child. It will take most of the night to boil this beast. Then I will see to your hurts. You do not look as badly injured as I thought you were. Most of the blood must have been the pig's."

Bodbmall's orders were a familiar irritation, but Demne decided this was not a good time to protest. His old garb no longer covered his back, for his shoulders seemed to have widened since the winter. The deerskin was tattered and stained, and he put it on reluctantly. The sinews over the shoulders strained and pulled, and his arm sockets protested; still, it was his own fault. Somehow he should have kept the new garment away from the flashing jaws of the sow. *And* recovered his spear. If only he could imagine how.

He seized a leather bucket and scurried back to the stream. But now that he had remembered her, the terrible red eyes of the sow seemed to glare from behind every tree, her hot breath to touch him with every shift in the breeze.

The clean smell of the water eased the ache in his chest. It was fear, and he knew it. The light hair along his arms bristled at the thought, for he knew that no matter what they faced, warriors were never afraid. At least, neither Cuchulain nor any of the heroes in the tales the Liath Luachra told him would have run away.

For a moment he paused with the bucket in his hand. Perhaps he was not really brave enough to be a warrior. That left the wisdom in which Bodbmall so endlessly instructed him, that wearied him far more than the pig had weighted his tired arms.

He dumped the water into the great pot, then hastened back to the stream. Now was not the time to stand around thinking. It would take a great many trips to fill the cauldron. He hauled water mindlessly, except when he could not help pausing to savor the smell of it, to listen to the faint, elusive ring of melody that seemed more intense here beside the gurgling stream. His hands hurt and his feet ached and his head pounded, but he did not even consider complaining.

Finally, when Bodbmall was content with the level of the liquid in the cauldron, Demne and the warrior woman lifted the pole and lowered the piglet inside. The water lapped near the edges of the container, but did not overrun it. Exhausted, the boy flopped down on a rock while the *bendrui* dropped packets of herbs into the warming water. Then she made a bag of porridge and dropped it inside as well. The water would cook everything at once for them. As the sun sank towards the distant horizon, steam began to rise.

"Here, now," she began in her sharp way, "let us see what you have done to yourself, lad." She brushed aside his thick, pale hair with a touch more tender than her words and inspected the bruise on his temple. "What did you do, fight with an oak tree?"

"I ran into a branch," he muttered sullenly.

"That will teach you to look where you are going. Now, these are just scratches," she went on, looking at his arms and legs. "But that toe—how did you do that, now?"

"A rock." He wanted to cry out, to throw himself into her arms, but he did not dare. The old ache was making speech painful. Even now, with the savor of the beast he had brought her scenting the air, she had not praised him. Even now, when she could see his wounds, she did not pull him to her soft breast, as she had done when he was a little boy. . . . He loved the smell of her, warm and herb-smoked, her skin and garments drenched with the odors of her rituals. Demne ached for something more than this brisk examination. Why must she treat him like a stupid animal?

"You have torn the nail. You will be fortunate if it does not rot. I will get the ointment." She grunted as she stood up and scuffled away to the hut where she did her rituals and kept her store of vile-tasting and terrible-smelling medicines. Demne hoped he would not get a fever, because Bodbmall's cures were almost worse than illness.

While he waited, he thought about the footfalls and the laughter he had heard in the forest and beside the stream. He wondered if he should tell Bodbmall about them, or about the faint music that still rang in his ears. He opened his mouth, but the ache in his throat was still there. *Bodbmall had not praised him.* This was a magic thing, but he was not going to tell her. It was the only thing he had that was his own! The decision made him hot, for he had never hidden anything from the two women before. He felt very strange, as if he were not Demne at all. But he was not yet a man like Fiacail. Who was he? What was he?

The old woman came back with a loaded wooden tray. Demne studied the array of little pots warily. There were the oils that she made every year from the fruit of the oak and the berries of the yew, from the stiff foliage of the rosemary or from flaxseed. Some of it the Liath Luachra used to keep her weapons from rusting and her leathers supple. The oil of the lavender plant, he knew, eased headache when rubbed into the brow. Both women combed the oil of the rosemary into their hair after washing, and into his, when they could get him to sit still. He hated the stink of it. He knew better than to ask which one she was going to use now. Bodbmall only told him what she wanted him to know.

Besides the oil, there was a pot of evil-smelling ointment, a small bone needle, and strips of linen. She poured some oil into a tiny-handled pot and held it over the fire for a brief time. Then she took a bit of cloth, dipped it into the oil, and rubbed it over the injured toe.

Demne held back a scream while she cleaned the wound with several applications of hot oil. Then she examined it closely, the needle in one wrinkled hand ready to remove any inground dirt or splinters of stone. He held his breath until she set it aside. The relief was enormous, even while his toe throbbed and sweat beaded his forehead. She took a large dollop of ointment and rubbed it over the toe. It burned for a moment, and then a wonderful coolness penetrated the injury. At last she wrapped a strip of linen around the toe.

"Next time, look where you are going."

Demne looked at the grey head still bent over his foot, and his hands clenched into fists. His skull pounded as if it might burst at any moment. Only the curious, ringing music seemed to keep it in one piece. He focused on the chiming melody. Bodbmall looked up at his face, alert and sharp-eyed, and he forced his features to stillness lest she should see.

"I will," he muttered. Then he stood up and limped across to the sleeping hut, ignoring his aching head and growling belly.

Demne huddled on his reed mat, facing the wall and pretending to be asleep when they called to him that the piglet was done. Grief rose in his throat—for what, he was unsure—and closed it. They were eating his kill, but it seemed almost that it was his flesh they were consuming. He was the one who had been chased, and had bled, and in the face of their silence, something within him had died. Only one hot tear escaped before he stifled all feeling and retreated into a mute emptiness where nothing could reach him but the soft lilt of the music within.

Chapter 2

❧

DEMNE NEVER DID EAT ANY OF THE PIG HE HAD KILLED, nor did he hunt pig again. His toe gradually healed, and from the piglet's striped hide, Bodbmall made a bag to carry her herbs in. He even came to realize, with his waking mind, that she and the Liath Luachra had been so cold because they had been afraid for him. But at night sometimes he still dreamed of the moment when he had brought home his prize. In his dream, the two women would be giving him the praise they had denied him, and then the pig would begin to change into something terrible. When he had such dreams he woke sobbing, sometimes so loudly that Bodbmall had to give him a sleep draft, scolding him for being a silly child.

But the daylight hours were a delight. He watched the spring pass in a kind of wonder, for the forest seemed a new place to him after his encounter with the piglet and the sow. Whenever he could escape from the camp he would sit and listen to the subtle sighings of the wind, the secrets the trees whispered to one another in the darkness, and the soothing murmur of the stream.

On a morning shortly after Beltane he was finishing

his porridge, wondering how soon he would be able to slip away, when he saw the Liath Luachra coming towards him with a branch of blackthorn in her hand. He eyed the thorn-studded branch warily. They had not played this game since last summer, but he still had scars.

"I will give you a head start," she said, grinning so that all her strong white teeth were displayed.

"I would rather you were giving me a thorn branch of my own," he muttered as he got to his feet, and her grin widened.

As he followed the warrior woman up the slope to the cluster of hazels they usually used for this exercise Demne reflected that at least it was better than burying the garbage or carrying water, and by the time his teacher had put him through the exercises to limber up, he was almost beginning to look forward to the game. Since last summer his legs had grown longer. Maybe she would not catch him this time.

"Remember now what I have told you about beginning," she said softly. "Let your awareness sink down through your center into the soil, then draw up the energy to fly!"

The path their feet had beaten out the year before still showed faintly as a ring of greener grass around the hazels. Demne remembered how he had felt the earth after he killed the piglet and nodded, wishing he could do this four-legged. The pig had certainly gone fast! As the Liath Luachra disappeared ahead of him Demne took a deep breath and settled himself to run.

He felt a sharp sting across his calves as he sprang forward and knew he had not been quick enough off the mark, but between one breath and the next he hit his stride. The Liath Luachra got him once more, and then he pulled away. Exultation filled him. He was going to beat her at last!

Around the hazel copse they ran and then twice around again. Demne glimpsed the grey-green flicker of a cloak ahead of him. He *was* faster! He was gaining; in a moment he would have her! The breath sobbed in his chest as he stretched himself to full speed. He saw the Liath Luachra clearly, then she leaped between two young oak trees and disappeared.

Demne stopped short, panting. "That's not fair!"

"War is not fair," said a disembodied voice from the opposite direction. "Do you think your enemies will always play by the rules?"

What enemies? Demne wondered rebelliously. *Nobody knows I'm alive except Bodbmall and you!*

"Follow me through the woods, lad, and take your revenge!"

A thorn flicked his shoulder and he whirled. The Liath Luachra grinned at him, then seemed to fade backward, dropping the thorn branch at his feet. Gritting his teeth, he snatched it up, then plunged after her through the trees.

Once more she had become invisible. After a few moments Demne forced himself to stand still. As the pounding of his heart eased he began to hear the subtle sounds of the forest: the whisper of leaf on leaf and the creaking of branches stirred by the wind, the faint scrabbling as a mouse scurried through a patch of last year's grass. Where was there a greater silence, an emptiness in the web of life where a human could be?

Setting his feet carefully he moved forward, and presently was rewarded by the sight of a grey shadow that slipped through the trees ahead of him. For a moment he paused, admiring the movement that seemed to be part of the shifting shade cast by the trees. She was heading back towards the huts. Gripping the thorn branch more tightly, Demne followed. They were almost within sight of the hearth fire when once more the Liath Luachra disappeared. Demne stopped in his tracks, scowling. This near the huts all he heard was the birds and other creatures that were used to living close to humanity. He stretched on tiptoe, peering around him, but saw only shadows.

Had she doubled around behind him? Angrily, Demne stomped forward, switching his branch against the clumps of fern that lined the path. He was tired of this game. He was almost out of the trees, and Bodbmall was looking up from the cauldron, when the branch was wrenched suddenly from his hand. The sharp thorns scored his shins as the Liath Luachra seemed to rise from the ground at his feet, laughing.

"I think that this time I have won the game," she said, grimacing as she followed him into the clearing. "And you must pay the forfeit."

"How did you do that?" he asked, too amazed to be angry.

"Child, you must learn to look for the unexpected!" The warrior woman pointed back at the woodland. "I moved only when something else was making a sound, something that you would know belonged here. And when I stopped, well, you were searching for someone tall and you never thought to look down."

"I understand," he said, rubbing away the thin line of blood that was welling from one of his scratches. "Can we try again?"

The Liath Luachra stared at him and snorted. "You have too much energy for an old woman. Run the training course through the wood and bring me some cresses from below the waterfall, and mind you don't miss any of the leaps or bends."

Demne nodded. A good run would release his frustration at not being able to catch his teacher, and he would not be tempted to cheat, for despite her show of exhaustion, she was perfectly capable of lying in wait for him along the path and assigning some worse task if he missed a single obstacle.

When he was done, he found the old warrior woman basking on a rock in the sun. His breath was a little uneven, and he was covered with a fine sheen of sweat, but Demne felt wonderful. He plopped down beside her, listening to the bird song, and she gave him a big-toothed grin.

Encouraged by the Liath Luachra's good mood, Demne decided to ask her something that had puzzled him. "Old one, what is the *fianna*?"

Her eyes narrowed and she looked at him. "Where did you hear that?" she snapped. "Have you been listening at walls?"

"I could not help it! You and Bodbmall were screaming so loud they could have heard you on the moon!" He felt guilty that he had heard something he was not intended to, even if there had been no way to avoid it. "Three nights ago. You said I should go be with them, and Bodbmall said no. What is the *fianna*?"

The warrior woman sucked her teeth for a time, and Demne knew this was a signal she was thinking deeply. At last she spoke. "The *fianna* are those warriors who serve to defend great Eriu from its foes, mighty men, fearless and stalwart. They live upon the land from Beltane to Samhain, and they reside with the king at Temair from Samhain to Beltane." A frown crossed her brow. "The *rigfennid* is their chief, and second only to the king in dignity and honor. It is his task to lead the *fianna* in war, to see to the ordering of the men and the defense of the land."

"Oh. That doesn't sound like something to keep secret from me. Tell me, was that man, Fiacail mac Conchinn, one of them?" She was holding something back, something he needed to know! His heart pounded even as he pretended disinterest.

What foes? Demne knew that Eriu was an island, that water surrounded the land on all sides, and he could not imagine where foes might come from, nor how they would arrive. Were there enemies within Eriu already? His mind raced even as he forced his face to reveal nothing.

"He is. Why do you mention him?"

Demne giggled. "He is the only other person I have ever seen, save you and Bodbmall. Why haven't you told me about this before?"

"I should not be speaking of it now! Bodbmall would have the skin off me in a second if she knew, and off you as well." The Liath Luachra gave a deep, feeling sigh. "Your father was of the *fian*, and Bodbmall fears you will wish to follow in his path, instead of in that of the wise, and perish as warriors often do. Say nothing to her of this, or we will both be in the cauldron."

"How does one become a member of the—"

She shook her head, making the braids writhe. "I cannot tell you more, Demne. It would give you ideas. Now, help me back to the fireside. Our morning's work has wearied me."

Sullenly, he aided her to her feet, and let her lean across his broad shoulders as they returned to the huts. *Ideas!* He wanted to scream his fury at the secrets that surrounded him until the very trees split. Demne swallowed his rage and comforted himself with the knowledge that at least the Liath Luachra had told him something worth knowing. A band of warriors, defending the land. He liked that a great deal.

Bodbmall met them, and began scolding both of them immediately. "You old fool! Do you not know better than to sit on a cold rock after running. You will be stiff in the morning, and it will be your own fault. Here, now, lie down and let me massage you. You, Demne, get some water and set it to boil. I must make some cress tea to keep the muscle cramps away."

As he hastened away, Demne saw the Liath Luachra grinning at him over Bodbmall's shoulder. He grinned back, and felt a lightness in his heart, for no reason.

As THE SEASON ADVANCED, DEMNE FOLLOWED HIS TWO guardians ever farther afield. Bodbmall needed to restock her store of herbs, and the Liath Luachra took advantage of the opportunity to teach Demne how to move through different kinds of country. But all their ranging was in the wilderness. Demne knew that there were other people in the world, for he saw smoke rising from the conical thatched roofs of dwellings tucked into folds of the forest. Sometimes he would glimpse a single figure watching over a herd of dust-colored sheep, assisted by eager dogs, or people on horseback chivying bands of bawling cows to a new pasturage. But these sightings were all from a distance; a man was no sooner glimpsed than the three wanderers melted back into the forest again.

After Midsummer they made an expedition to the wetlands east of the wood. The bogs were a place of deceptive beauty, whose delicate grasses and shining golden asphodels waved above unstable muck that could suck a man down. Here the herons stalked through the mists like grey ghosts. Dragonflies glittered in the sunlight, and moths fluttered through the dusk with the eyes of predators painted on their wings. Under the Liath Luachra's careful tutelage he learned his way between the islands that dotted this verdant sea until he could traverse the marsh almost as quickly as the forest.

Where there were pools of open water, Demne learned to drift beneath the surface as silent as a log in the stream. These waters sang to him of slow transformations beneath the sun. But despite their soothing, he learned to come up beneath a fat teal or a mallard, grabbing its paddling legs and bearing it to shore to be killed by a swift twist of the Liath Luachra's strong hands. But it was just as much fun to tickle a bird's belly and watch it explode from the water, squawking with outrage.

One afternoon he miscalculated and came up beneath a patch of pondweed. For a moment he flailed wildly, sure that some beast of the marshes was smothering him, then he realized what it was and pulled the weed away from his eyes so that he could see. As the dark waters around him stilled, he glimpsed a form streaming with water and maned like an aughisky with weed. Or perhaps he was not the water-horse, but something stranger, a fierce and shining serpent all fringed and spiky about the head and jaws like the one that tried to eat Ferdiad when he went to court the daughter of Queen Medbh.

He cast a quick glance shoreward, wondering if his guardians had seen. But the Liath Luachra lay stretched beneath a tree, her knotted hands clasped upon her breast and her mouth a little open so that her long horse teeth showed clearly as she snored. The heat of the afternoon had overcome Bodbmall as well. The old woman sat with her back against a willow, the mortar full of half-crushed herbs forgotten in her lap and the pestle rolling from her hand.

Very carefully, Demne began to make his way towards the bank. It was hard to move quietly through the water, but the Liath Luachra had taught him how to ease along with never a drip or a splash. With painstaking care, Demne reached to the bank and clawed out a handful of black, sticky mud. He smeared it along his arms and across his belly, a slow grin stretching his face. Then he inserted himself into the clump of reeds just below their camp. The two women were still asleep. Shivering with excitement, Demne picked up a stone with his toes, lifted his foot so that he could grab it, and threw.

The pebble hit the trunk of the willow tree and rebounded towards the Liath Luachra. As it hit the ground, Demne erupted out of the reeds.

"*Aooragh! Aoorawr! Awroogh!*" he cried, waving his dripping arms.

Bodbmall sat bolt upright, the mortar rolling unheeded from her lap, but the Liath Luachra had already blurred into motion; metal flashed in the air as her dagger left her hand. Demne started to duck, knowing already that he would not be in time. In slowed motion he seemed to see the knife arrowing towards him and Bodbmall's fingers flickering in a sign of warding. Then time stopped as the *bendrui* sang out a *Word.* . . .

The dagger shattered in midair. Demne hit the earth hard as the pieces sang past his head and buried themselves in the reeds. He gulped in breath and expelled it again in a grunt of laughter, gasped, choked, and crowed once more, beating his fists against the ground.

His cry changed to a yelp of pain as strong fingers closed on his ear and hauled him upright.

"Don't you ever"—a callused hand smacked hard against his backside—"do that again!"

"I'm . . . a monster!" he protested, trying to squirm away.

"You're a wretched evil imp! And you were almost a dead one!" With one arm the Liath Luachra clamped him against her belly while the other hand expressed her feelings more directly. "Haven't I taught you . . . never to sneak up on a warrior . . . that way?"

"But you looked so funny!" The last word tailed off into a grunt as a particularly effective smack stung his rear.

He remembered her face in the single moment before she reacted, eyes bulging and mouth agape like a netted fish. And Bodbmall's astonished glare had been funny too. Laughter was squeezed from his lungs in a series of whimpers he hoped she would take for pain as he danced beneath the steady blows. He could hear the air wheezing in the old warrior's lungs as well when at last she released him.

Demne's rear end was burning as if he had sat in the fire. He eyed the cool water longingly, but he knew better than to move. His head bowed beneath the torrent of abuse that streamed over him; as one of his guardians paused to draw breath the refrain would be taken up by the other one.

"After all our care for you!" screeched Bodbmall. "You cannot allow two old women a moment's rest? What return is this for the nights I have stayed wakeful nursing you?"

"Disobedient, thoughtless brat! Are you just stupid, or were all my words no more to you than wind?"

Now that Demne thought about it, he did seem to remember the Liath Luachra lecturing him about the safe way to wake a trained warrior. *Well enough if you can slay a man sleeping, but a man just waking will attack without waiting to distinguish friend from foe, like a beast disturbed in its lair.* And he knew that was true, too, for once he had poked a stout stick down a badger's holt and brought it back bitten clean through.

Eventually all three of them were exhausted, and Demne was brusquely ordered to wash himself off in the pool.

"Good reflexes—" he heard the Liath Luachra say to Bodbmall as he eased gratefully into the cool water. "You've lost none of your power!"

"Nor you," said the *bendrui*. "I had barely the time to say the Word!"

"*Hunh!*" grunted her companion. "I'll be paying for it tomorrow! This old carcass is no longer up to such alarms."

She was a true prophet. The next morning the Liath Luachra could barely move. Something seemed to have gone wrong in her back, and despite all of Bodbmall's potions and manipulations, it was three days before she could walk, and then only by leaning heavily on her spear. In the meantime, Demne was kept close to camp and given all the most disagreeable jobs that Bodbmall could think of for him to do. When the *bendrui* had gone off to gather some more herbs Demne gathered his courage and knelt beside the pallet where the old warrior woman lay.

"I'm sorry," he said. "It's my fault that you're hurting this way."

"Ah, Demne, the enemy I am fighting now no one can defeat in the end." From her stringy throat came a cracked, barking sound that he finally realized was laughter. "It is not your fault that I am growing old. You meant no harm, surely, but you acted foolishly!"

He swallowed. "I only wanted to make you laugh."

"You did not think," she said, growing stern once more. "And that is a thing that you cannot afford. There are dangers in this world you do not dream of, child."

He sighed. He had grown up in the shadow of mysterious dangers that were never explained. How would he ever learn to protect himself if he always ran away? He was sorry that the Liath Luachra was hurting, but he still could not believe it was so wrong a thing to want to play.

THE SUMMER WAS TURNING TOWARDS ITS GOLDEN ENDing when they started back to the forest of Gaible once more. The Liath Luachra could only go slowly, but they made a virtue of the leisurely pace, stopping often to dig for roots or gather berries or herbs. Fall was a good time in the forest, when the nuts ripened on the trees and the seed heads on the grasses. The animals grew fat then, getting ready for winter, and their coats were thick and warm. Demne had always liked autumn because then they were too busy to spend time on lessons. But the *bendrui* had a way of testing him when he least expected it.

"Tell me what are the chieftain trees, Demne," said Bodbmall as they went along. It was probably the oakwood through which they were passing that had prompted the question, Demne thought as he gazed around him. The day was drawing to an end, and amber light slanted past the green leaves.

"The oak," he answered promptly, "and the hazel and holly that grow with it—" He pointed to the smaller trees that had planted themselves where the oaks let some sun through. "And . . ." he frowned, thinking, "the apple, the ash, the yew, and the fir." For a moment he had a vision of them as chieftains in council, marshaling their hosts for war. What would it be like, he wondered, to watch a battle of the trees?

"And the peasant trees?" The next question came before he was ready.

"Is the alder one of them? And the hawthorn?" Demne asked.

"And the willow, birch, elm, aspen, and rowan trees," she answered him. "You must remember them and their uses."

He nodded, but he did not entirely believe her. He had heard the song these trees sang in the silence of the wood, and it was no less noble than the music of the trees of the first rank. The hawthorn and the birch tree, the rowan and willow especially were holy, used often by Bodbmall in her charms.

Swiftly she led him through the lists of shrub and herb trees, and Demne filed the information away in his memory, hoping he would remember it when she

asked again. She did not hit as hard as the Liath
Luachra, but she was better at catching him unpre-
pared.

The warrior had halted, staring at a long meadow
that lay beyond the fringe of trees. The color in the
sky had deepened, and the grass and the red deer who
were feeding on it were all edged in flame.

"Yum, venison! Can we hunt one?" Demne stopped
as he glimpsed the grief in the old woman's eyes.

"I cannot run," she said harshly, and looked away.
A hot red guilt flared through him, and suddenly he
could not stand still.

"I will run for you! I will give you meat to make
you well," he exclaimed, shaking his spear with the
head of flint that he had chipped himself.

"Demne!" cried Bodbmall, and the horned head of
the stag came up, its ears swiveling. But the boy had
already plunged into the undergrowth, and he knew
that neither of the two women could follow him. This
time he would do it right, and then they would praise
him.

The wind was blowing towards him, and after a
moment the deer returned to their grazing. Demne
stilled, remembering his lessons. They might not be
able to smell him, but there was nothing wrong with
their ears. The stag was strong and dangerous, and one
of the does had two half-grown fawns nearby. But the
other doe was barren, and one hind leg dragged just
a little when she moved. An injured hip, he thought,
frowning. If he did not take her, when winter came
she would surely fall to the wolves.

Now he was at the edge of the meadow. The deer
moved slowly away from him, and he slipped from
behind a birch tree onto the grass. The stag's head
came up, and he froze. *I am a birch tree . . .* thought
Demne, rooting his toes into the grass. *I am nothing
to fear.* Moving only when the deer moved or had

their heads down grazing, he eased towards them, the spear held ready at his side. All awareness narrowed to the shrinking circle that enclosed himself and the deer.

And then the wind changed.

The stag threw up its head, snorting as Demne's scent reached him. For a moment the fawns hesitated, ears flapping, then they bounced into motion after the does. With one bound the stag soared into the lead, and Demne launched himself after them as if the Liath Luachra's thorn branch were stinging his heels.

Wind blew back the tangled locks from his brow as he ran, but the deer, even the lame doe, were bouncing away across the grass. Demne's legs pounded the earth and his heartbeat shook his breast with the effort he was making, but they were drawing away from him. Then at his ear he heard a ripple of laughter.

Demne gulped in air and blurred forward. He passed one of the fawns, and the barren doe's stride faltered.

I am your death, old one, thought the boy. *Wait for me.* He shifted his balance, still running, so that his arm would swing free.

And then he could see the stretch and bunch of muscle beneath the ragged brown hide. The doe's head was low, her flanks heaving; he focused on the bare spot behind her elbow, and all the hours of practice that the Liath Luachra had put him through became the single moment in which he cast the spear.

Sharp stone bit through tough hide with all the momentum of Demne's running behind it. The doe stumbled, eyes rolling in surprise that changed to desperation as she began to understand. She tried to leap away from the pain, but the spear had struck too deep for her to dislodge it. And in that moment,

Demne reached her, caught up the spear shaft as it banged along the ground, and with all the strength in his wiry body, bore her down.

For a moment she heaved beneath the spear, and Demne danced to avoid the thrashing hooves that could split his belly as easily as his spear had pierced her side. Then some last resistance gave way and all the strength went out of her.

The piglet Demne had killed had looked at him with hatred before it died. But in the eyes of the doe he saw only grief. *I cannot run . . .* said her dulling gaze. *I will never run any more. . . .* And then there was nothing.

The boy fell to his knees in the grass beside the creature he had slain, his vision blurring with tears. Its look reminded him of the gaze of the old warrior woman, for no reason he could discern. And it had been so fine, so beautiful. Why must he slay such beasts, to eat and live? He heard the crunch of footsteps and rubbed his eyes dry, smearing dirt across his cheeks to disguise any tear marks. When his fosterers arrived, he had already begun the task of removing his spear, as if nothing had occurred, though his heart pounded as if he were still running.

"Fool!" said the Liath Luachra, "to start a stalk without scouting your surroundings. You do not know what else might have been hunting those deer. You still act without thinking! It will be your downfall one day." At her words, despite himself, Demne began to sob once more. Why did they praise one another, but never him?

"Are you hurt?" the *bendrui* said sharply, "Where did she strike you? You see the penalty that disobedience brings!"

Still sobbing, he shook his head and flinched away. He did not care whether or not they praised him;

he would not, *could* not, look at the Liath Luachra
now.

"Well, now that you have done it, you had better
finish the job," the warrior woman said more kindly.
"There is at least some use in this game."

Still sniffling, Demne nodded and drew his knife
to gut the slain deer. Later, as he staggered after the
two women through the gathering dusk with the deer
on his shoulders, Demne was able to be glad that the
Liath Luachra would have a good meal, but he knew
that he would not be able to eat this prey either.

SUMMER RIPENED INTO AUTUMN, AND DEMNE WAS KEPT
busy with all the tasks that the Liath Luachra could no
longer do. After days spent ranging the forests, Demne
usually slept dreamlessly, but on a night when the sky
was clamorous with the cries of migrating waterfowl,
it seemed to him that he heard the *bendrui* talking to
a stranger. No doubt it was a woman from the lands
beyond the forest where he was not allowed to go,
thought the boy, but there was something different
about this one. He stirred sleepily, calling Bodbmall's
name.

The flicker of firelight that filled his doorway was
blocked as the *bendrui* looked in.

"Be still, child, and rest. All is well. . . ." Her voice
trailed off in a murmur of nonsense like one of her
spells. He knew the tone and the rhythm; it brought
him sleep when he was wakeful. Vaguely he wondered why she felt the need to use it now. He knew
better than to try to see or hear when folk needed a
wisewoman badly enough to seek her out in these
hills. But it seemed to him that there was an edge
to Bodbmall's voice that was different from the other
times, and though his eyes closed, there was a part
of him that continued to be aware of the murmur of
voices by the fire.

"Healthy?" came the Liath Luachra's deep tones. "Oh, indeed, he grows healthy as a young salmon on its way to the sea. And he courses the forest like a wild thing. That potential, surely, is being fulfilled. You may think it a rough life, but you know it is no worse than he could expect in the *fian*."

"He is as big as a child three years older," said Bodbmall, as if she disapproved, "and bright enough, though he runs from his lessons when he can."

The stranger laughed, and the sound was like the laughter that had mocked Demne in the forest, but warmer, more golden. Demne drifted a little closer to consciousness. Were they talking about him? It hardly seemed likely, but nonetheless it was strange. The stranger woman spoke then, too low and sweet for him to catch the words.

"Ah, my heart, you must not," said Bodbmall. "What if he should wake and see you? Where would all our care be then?"

"In Brigid's name, Bodbmall, have some pity," the Liath Luachra said roughly. "Go chant some more of your spells over him if you have to, but the lass has come a long way. You must let her see!"

Forewarned, Demne burrowed into his blankets so that only the side of his face was visible. Through his closed eyelids he sensed the glimmer of the oil lamp in the doorway and controlled his breathing, though his heart was pounding so furiously that he was sure Bodbmall must be able to hear.

"Come then, if you must," he heard her whisper. "He sleeps as only the young and healthy can."

He sensed that the lamp was being lifted, but most of its light was blocked as someone came in. It was not Bodbmall. The *bendrui* moved with deliberation, and the folds of her woolen gowns were permanently scented by her herbs. And the Liath Luachra's leather garments had a rank scent, intensified lately by the sour smell of illness, and she moved as if she were always in pain. But the person who had entered came into the hut and knelt beside his pallet in a single smooth movement and a rustle of finely woven cloth, and the smell of her was like a stand of apples in the spring.

Demne's breath caught, and he forced it to steadiness. No fawn left alone by its mother could have been more still than he. He was not in bodily danger, but something in the women's voices had told him that to open his eyes would bring him pain such as he had never known.

He could hear the woman settling beside him, the quick, indrawn breath as the lamplight fell full upon his face. Her nearness was like a flame, and the need to see her grew in him. He heard her uneven breathing, and then a whisper of melody.

"In the dark forest the young fawn is sleeping,
Sleep now, sleep safely, oh child of my heart.
In the green pasture the cow her calf is keeping,
Sleep safely till the morning—"

Her voice was like honey made sweeter by the warmth of the sun, with the huskiness of suppressed pain. Carefully Demne sighed and stretched his arm across his face as if to shield his eyes from the light. But beneath that shelter he was peering through his thick lashes.

"In the top of the oak tree the eaglet is nesting,
Sleep now, sleep safely, oh child of my heart.
Deep in its den the red fox cub is resting,
Sleep safely till the morning—"

He glimpsed folds of rich violet-colored wool and the glint of gold, but Bodbmall was holding the lamp behind the stranger, and all he could see of her face was backlit russet-red hair.

> "In a pool in the forest the salmon parr is dreaming,
> Sleep now, sleep safely, oh child of my heart.
> In the depths of the sea the secret sun is gleaming,
> Sleep safely till the morning—"

Suddenly afraid, he shut his eyes tight, and at that moment she leaned forward and lifted the tangled locks from his broad forehead.

"Come away now, my heartling. It is enough for him, and for you," said Bodbmall from the door.

For one dizzying moment, Demne felt soft lips brush his brow. Then, with the same supple movement as before, the woman was rising. He heard the whisper of her garments, and the apple-blossom scent of them swirled through the air. And he heard her soft weeping.

Then the light was gone, and with it the presence of the lady. Demne opened his eyes, but the fire outside had sunk low, and if the women were still there, they had gone beyond his hearing. He wanted to get up and go after them, but he was afraid; and presently, though he had meant to listen for Bodbmall to return, the darkness turned into dreaming.

In his dream, Demne ran across grass of an impossible green towards a lady whose hair was a radiant auburn that brightened to a blazing gold. There was a broad river between them. He plunged into it, and suddenly he was a salmon. For a time then Demne floated in dimensionless clarity that led at last into dreamless depths of peace.

When he woke in the morning, Bodbmall and the

Liath Luachra were already bickering, and there was never a glance between them nor a print left on the ground to show that anyone else had been there at all. Demne carefully eyed the earth, when his fosterers were busy elsewhere, but at last decided he had only dreamed that he had smelled apples and felt a kiss upon his brow.

Chapter 3

❦

THAT WINTER WAS A HARD ONE. THE SNOW STAYED late, and the Liath Luachra coughed a good deal. But spring came finally in all its wonder, and Demne welcomed his new role as hunter for them all. At Midsummer, he would have lived ten winters, but he knew that already he was doing the work of a grown man, and this heartened him when the bickering of the women became too great. He was less enthusiastic about his lessons with Bodbmall.

The *bendrui* was teaching Demne the history of the tribes who had come to Eriu from Gaul—the Galeóin, who surpassed the others in valor, the Fir Domnann, who built the great earthworks, and the Fir Bolg, who carried the earth in bags. But it did him no good to learn the names of the streams at which each ship had come ashore, for he had never seen the sea. Nor did he care that once his people had ruled all the land of Eriu, since he himself was not allowed to leave the shelter of Fidh Gaible's trees.

What the trees themselves had to say to him seemed more vital than Bodbmall's recitation of chieftains long in their graves or the lessons of the old warrior woman. These had become only verbal instructions, since age had stiffened the Liath Luachra's hand so that she could no longer close it around the hilt of a sword.

Demne used his sling to bring down waterfowl. He hunted hare until he was heartily sick of the taste, no matter how the *bendrui* flavored it with her herbs, and stalked the deer. He dug roots to spare the *bendrui's* back, and often carried the Liath Luachra from her bed to a place beside the fire, until the rays of the sun warmed her old bones and allowed her to move about a little.

His height had increased another couple of fingers, so that he looked down at both women when they were standing, and his chest and shoulders had expanded as well. He had a new kilt of deerskin and a cape pieced together from the hides of hares. There was already a gap between the bottom of his laced goatskin vest and the belt that held his kilt, but he hardly noticed. He wandered among the trees half lost in dreams of a land where the music that teased at his awareness could be clearly heard.

On a day when sunlight dappled the forest floor with green and gold and the warm wind sported with the maturing leaves, Demne's wanderings brought him far to the eastward of his usual range. Somewhere above, a lark was trilling in its ecstatic ascent of the skies. Ahead, the foliage was thinning. Demne ran forward, hoping to catch a glimpse of the bird.

But what he saw when he came out from among the tree trunks was a line of rocks piled into a low barrier. With a speed that had become instinct, he faded backward into the woods; for fences meant plowed fields, and the one thing his constantly bickering guardians agreed on was that he must never leave the forest. Once or twice he had dared ask why, but Bodbmall just pursed up her mouth and answered, "Because I tell you so."

From below came the sound of voices. Silent as if he were stalking, Demne eased from shadow to shadow until he reached the last outpost of the trees. Beyond the wall lay a broad sweep of pasture. On the hillside beyond it, a cluster of round dwellings roofed with tall cones of thatch was surrounded by a palisade of stout logs. Cattle skulls gleamed white from the gateposts, and pale wisps of wood smoke drifted towards the sky.

On the other side of the fence, several short people were tossing a ball. Demne looked more closely, then touched his own hairless chin. They were like him; they were boys. But these boys shouted and ran and grinned. When one fell, the others laughed and called him clumsy. But Demne knew the sound of scolding too well to think them angered, and in a moment the boy who had fallen got up and laughed too.

He liked the sound. Like the music the trees made, it filled Demne with a wordless longing to understand. These boys who looked so much like him seemed to be having such fun. . . . Without thinking, he left the shelter of the forest and moved into the open slope that lay between the wood and the wall.

One of the boys saw him and hallooed a warning. The others turned, and in seconds, they were clambering over the fence and racing towards him.

"Who are you," one demanded, "and where do you come from?"

"Are you a bogle?"

"He looks like he came out of the earth."

"Why is he dressed all in skins? He hardly looks human."

"A wildman, then, all covered in fur!"

They surrounded him, chattering about him as if he could not hear. There were six of them, all in bright short-sleeved tunics of woven stuff, embroidered with yarn. Demne shifted his hard, bare feet and looked at the calfskin shoes that were bound to their feet with thongs. They were, he guessed, his age or a few seasons older, but only the one who had asked him his name was as tall.

"Who are you?" the boy asked again. He had coppery hair and carried himself with the same assurance as the Liath Luachra. The other boys grouped behind him a little, wary but curious.

"I am Demne," he answered slowly, his glance as busy on their gear and clothing as theirs were on his. He was not used to the idea that anyone but Bodbmall could wear cloth, although the Liath had a cloak of rough grey wool. The old warrior woman and Fiacail had both worn leather garments; somehow he had thought that fabric was only for females.

"What kind of name is that? I am Bran mac Conail. Who is your father?"

Demne considered this question for a moment. "I do not have one."

"What about your mother?" said one.

"I do not have a mother either," Demne replied.

"He must be simple," a boy said.

"Everyone has a father," another added.

"Not *everyone*," came a mean snicker. "There is that Leide, whose mother grinds our grain. He has no father." All the boys seemed to find this extremely amusing, for they chuckled and elbowed one another in the sides.

"Well, a mother, anyhow . . ."

Demne frowned. He did not like their laughter anymore. Their faces distorted before his eyes, until he saw the narrow features of a stoat on one, and the cruel beak of a rook on another. A hot, red feeling rose in his chest. They were just stupid boys. It was not his fault he had no father. It was Bodbmall's. She would tell him the courses of the stars, but she denied him the knowledge of his parentage.

"Then we will call you the Lad of the Skins," Bran said peaceably, ignoring his companions. "Where do you come from?"

Demne studied him suspiciously, seeking to understand why the boy asked. He was becoming more and more certain that he should not have let his curiosity get him into this. If he was not careful it could turn into as great a disaster as the pig or his attempt to play monster had been. Bodbmall had always been quite clear that he must not leave the forest or go near any of the several small raths that crouched at its skirts. Still, Bran's face was open and friendly and interested.

"The forest," he said at last.

"No one lives there," jeered a boy, the one whose face seemed like a stoat's.

"Not so. My mother says the midwife lives up in the wood somewhere. Maybe she is his mother."

"Is that true?" Bran asked.

"I am alone." Demne answered, not sure what they meant. He had revealed too much already, and would get a proper birching if he told his foster mothers what he had done.

As he spoke the words, Demne felt suddenly as if a wall had come down between him and the others, and on his side, it was cold. It was true—he *was* alone. He wanted to be at ease, like this Bran, and to have companions. But he was locked within himself except when he listened to the trees and the wind. They were poor companions, but they did not jeer at him. He took a step backwards, towards the safety of the trees.

"Look! The big oaf is frightened!" Stoat-face grinned wickedly.

"What a coward!"

The red heat swelled in Demne's chest once more. He was not afraid! None of these boys had ever faced an angry sow. They could not spear a pig or run down a hind. They could not move through the woods as silently as he did, not in those clumsy shoes. White-knuckled, he gripped the haft of his new spear.

The boys crowded towards him. One kicked, and another swung a balled fist at his hard belly. Demne shot out his free hand, grabbed Stoat-face by the hair, and yanked. The boy's head jerked back, and the others scattered as swiftly as they had charged. Only Bran stood his ground a few feet away. Demne tossed his captive to the ground, and Stoat-face hit the earth with a grunt.

"Why do you call me names?" His shout sent several ravens in startled flight from the nearest oak tree.

Stoat-face got up, his face red and his tunic smeared with mud and stuck all over with straw. "You big bully. Why don't you grab someone your own size?"

Demne looked down at the smaller boy. "Why don't *you?*"

Bran and the others roared with laughter. "He has you there, Gort," one said. "Your mother is going to be mad at the mess you have made of your clothes."

"He shoved me in a mucky spot!"

"Gort mac Dubthach, you *are* a mucky spot." This provoked fresh laughter, and several of the boys capered around crying "Mucky spot, mucky spot," confusing Demne entirely. One moment they were ready to kick him, the next they were making rude remarks about their own companion. Gort the Stoat, he decided, was not well liked by his playmates. What a puzzle it was.

"Why not play ball with us?" Bran asked.

"I have never played that." Demne could not think of anything, at that moment, that he had played. Everything he knew was work. Everything was hard, and very serious. Except when Fiacail visited, the two old women rarely laughed. Sometimes the animals

he watched did things that were funny, but these
boys, with their gibes and laughter, seemed stranger
than any beast of the wood.

"Come along. It is very easy."

"What are the rules?" Demne asked.

"Rules?" Bran cocked his head to one side for a
moment. "We just throw the ball back and forth. I
do not think we have any rules."

"Oh." Demne found this astonishing.

Everything he knew had rules. There were rules
about how to make a spear or tan a hide or gather
herbs. The paths of the wise—the druid way—had
more rules than he could count, for each thing must
be done at the correct time and in the proper manner,
so that the balances of the world were maintained.
One did not take more than was needful, or even rob
the trees of their limbs carelessly. One never took all
the honey from a hive or removed all the eggs from
a nest. Did the boys know these things? Somehow he
doubted it. Uneasy, he followed Bran back over the
low wall and into the grassy field.

One boy scooped up the ball and darted away, then
spun and hurled it at another. From the look on the
face of the second boy, he had not expected it, and
Demne suspected that part of the game was to surprise the receiver with a hard-flung ball. He leaned
his spear against the wall and followed Bran out into
the field.

He heard, just for a moment, the ghost patter of
unshod feet nearby, and glanced towards the sound.
At that moment, the ball arched towards him, and he
almost missed it. The leather stung his hard palms
as the boys fanned out around him in a pattern he
could almost understand. Then he flung the ball at
Bran. The smack of leather against the other boy's
hands was audible, and his eyes widened a little at
the force with which it had come. But he was already

in motion and casting the ball at another boy.

Suddenly Demne realized that the game did indeed have rules, but apparently the boys were not conscious of what they were. That surprised him, but now that he understood what was going on he darted swiftly among them, catching the ball and hurling it at the least ready of his companions. From their expressions, he realized his throw must be harder than they were used to. He tried to do it more lightly, but his strength still outmatched theirs.

The stoat-faced Gort, especially, seemed unable to field his throws, for twice he dropped the ball and shook the red hands at the ends of his thin wrists as if they were hurting him. The second time it happened, he charged Demne, forgetting the game completely, and ran his curly brown head into Demne's flat belly. Demne overbalanced and started to laugh, as he had seen the other boys do.

Then Gort began to pummel him with small fists. The laughter died on his lips, and the game stopped. Gort, astride Demne's stomach with his little face twisted with rage, was no more trouble than a mayfly, for his blows were too weak to really do any harm. The other boys ran towards them as Demne grabbed Gort beneath his flailing arms and flung him lightly aside. The boy landed several paces away, the wind knocked out of him.

Demne got to his bare feet as Gort began to howl. He looked at Bran for some signal, and the big boy grinned and shrugged. He grinned back, feeling the muscles of his face strain at this unaccustomed exercise, and a small, wonderful warmth stole into his chest. He liked Bran.

"Oh, stop blubbering, Gort. You are such a baby!" a medium-sized boy said then. "Come on. Let us get on with the game."

Demne realized it was past midday and that he had

gotten nothing for the supper pot, so he shook his head. "I have to leave, but it was fun to play with you. I am sorry I threw so hard."

"Come again another day," Bran told him.

"I might do that," Demne said quietly. He picked up his spear, leaped over the wall, and dashed across the field and into the shelter of the trees. He did not see how surprise changed the boys' faces, nor did he hear them wonder how he could run so fast. Neither did he hear them arguing about whether to tell their parents about the strange boy with whom they had played.

IT WAS CLOSE TO EVENING BEFORE HE RETURNED TO THE three huts with a dead hare and a brace of ducks banging against his shoulder. The Liath Luachra was lying near the fire, shivering slightly, although it was still warm and pleasant. Her big hands lay useless in her lap, and her large, square teeth seemed too big for her puckered mouth. The stiffness which had plagued her last fall had increased as the seasons had passed, until Demne thought she was turning to stone. All her strength had drained away without warning, and it was all she could manage to walk from her sleeping pallet to the fire without assistance now. Her temper had worsened as her vigor diminished, and she no longer sang.

Bodbmall was preparing one of the vile-tasting mixtures she gave the old warrior woman when these shivering fits came on. She gave the boy a quick, piercing glance as he crouched down and began to clean his kill.

"You were gone a long while," Bodbmall said, grinding dried herbs with a pestle.

"Was I?" Demne answered with as much surprise as he could muster, keeping his face lowered to hide the tinge of red he knew colored his pale skin. "I got lost."

"Lost?"

"In thought," he lied quickly. "Because of the voices of the trees . . ." That was not entirely untrue. Today he was conscious of the trees as he had never been before.

Bodbmall gave a pleased sigh. "Which trees did you hear?" She nodded triumphantly at the Liath Luachra. "You see, woman. He is on the druid's way. My teaching falls upon fertile ground. Now"— her attention returned to Demne—"tell me what you heard."

"Much good tree talk will do him when—" the Liath Luachra sputtered, then fell silent under the *bendrui*'s glare.

Her interruption gave the boy a chance to remember other days when he had listened to the forest murmurs in silent awe. He frowned. "It is hard. I do not have the right words." He slit the skinned hare's belly and gutted it. "The oak says that its roots reach to the heart of the world. I did not know the world had a heart."

Bodbmall gave a short bark of laughter, and Demne remembered how the boys had laughed when they thought he was being naive. He wondered if one could say things like that on purpose. Being laughed at was better than being scolded, anyway.

"Of course it has a heart, silly boy. Is it not alive? That is a good beginning, to hear the oak, for it is full of strength and wisdom."

Demne nodded, but in truth he found the oak somewhat proud and full of itself, and rather dull. He preferred to listen to the hazel, but something compelled him to keep this a secret. What the hazel whispered was precious, and he lacked the words to express its beauty. Were there words for the yearning that made him tremble if he thought of it too long? How could he ever sing the hazel's song, which seemed to him infinitely sweeter and wiser than the ponderous booming of the proud oak trees.

Bodbmall was looking at him, waiting.

"The alder sings of water, but not the water of the lake and river, so I do not understand it."

"That is the sea it sings of, boy."

"The sea?"

Bodbmall sighed, scooped the herb mixture into a cup, and added some warm water from a small pot. She stirred it thoughtfully, then handed the cup to the Liath Luachra. The warrior woman took the smooth wooden bowl in her twisted hands and lifted it to her puckered mouth. Her teeth gleamed hugely above the rim of the bowl. She choked down the contents and made a horrible noise. For a moment it seemed she might be about to spew it out again. She snorted and glared at the other woman.

"Why do you make it taste so foul?" she complained, settling back again. The shivering in her limbs ceased, and her muscles slackened as the potion took effect. Her swollen, twisted hands rested limply on her chest and her breathing slowed.

Demne watched and then returned to cleaning the hare. He was afraid, for he knew the old woman was nearing the end of her time. He hated the thought, because he could not imagine Bodbmall without her companion. Time, which before had been a vague and meaningless notion, had become real to him, and with it he had begun to have some sense of the future, of time as it had not yet occurred. And this frightened him. No longer did he exist from day to day, from season to season, obedient and unquestioning.

Bodbmall frequently had to snap her strong fingers under his nose to bring him back to her lessons. But the secret he wished most to learn remained hidden. Who was he? Who were his father and mother?

Sometimes he almost thought he knew, and then the knowledge would recede into the world of dream once more.

His encounter with the boys had opened this wound afresh, and he wished he could speak of it. Demne had been feeling uneasy about keeping his own counsel since his brush with the sow. But revealing as little as possible to his foster mothers had become a habit now. He had not told them about his heightened senses, of how the water whispered to him, and how the stones murmured beneath his bare feet as he ran.

He let the old wisewoman assume that it was her instruction that had taught him to hear the voices of the trees. And of the ghostly patter of running feet and soft laughter that swept by him now and again, he said nothing at all. These were his secrets, the only possessions he had.

Finished with the hare, Demne began to pluck the birds, taking some heated water from the cauldron to soften their feathers. "Tell me about the sea," he said then.

"What? Oh . . ." Her voice held such an unaccustomed note of tenderness that Demne looked up. Bodbmall was gazing at the sleeping face of the Liath Luachra, and the sorrow in her eyes made him look away again.

"Never mind . . . I was just thinking of how she was before she was so grey. . . . The sea," she went on more briskly, "is the mother of waters. It is all around us, all around Eriu, ever moving, restless and changing. You will see it one day. It tastes of salt, and fishes swim in it, as do other creatures."

"Salt?" Demne knew about that, for he had tasted the white crystals at the salt springs to which the deer and other beasts went, and gathered it by throwing the water on coals as Bodbmall instructed him. But there were no fish in those springs. He was not sure he believed in the sea.

This thought disturbed him. Never before had he really questioned any of Bodbmall's words. But if she knew who his parents were, why did she refuse to tell him? Were they monsters? Or beasts? He remembered how his body had seemed to change when the blood of the pig had mingled with his own, his neck shortening, his snout swinging low. While it lasted, it had felt very real.

Remembering, the red heat of the sow seemed to run along his flesh and through his blood. He could not trust the old woman. She had not praised him for killing the pig or running down a deer, and she would not tell him who he was! Then the sensation passed, and he went back to plucking feathers from the flesh of the duck again, unaware of the trouble in the wisewoman's watching gaze.

FOR SEVERAL DAYS, DEMNE STAYED WITHIN THE FA-miliar fastness of the forest and ignored the persistent memory of the ball game. But the companionship and the easy laughter of the youngsters haunted him. He knew he should tell Bodbmall about his adventure. Instead, he forced himself to listen intently to her teachings, although the lessons chafed his patience. He was not a woman—what use could this knowl-edge be to him?

He assumed that all the wise ones were women, for Bodbmall never spoke of any other practitioner of her art by name. In fact old Fiacail the warrior was the only man he had ever seen up close. Sometimes he thought the old druidess was trying to change him into a younger version of herself. But when Bodbmall talked about the trees he listened, fascinated especial-ly by her words on the nature of the hazel, the tree of poetic wisdom. The fact that not all of her ideas agreed with his own knowledge, he kept secret. It pleased him to hold his thoughts from her. Though she did not know it, they were playing a kind of game.

But even though the slow decay of the Liath Luachra distracted her, Bodbmall was not unaware that her fosterling was beginning to have thoughts of his own. That was quite natural. She had reared his father and other boys, and knew. Demne's small secrets did not worry her, but the fact that she could no longer probe his mind with her art was disturbing. It was as if he had retreated behind a shield, and she had never encountered self-protection so seamless in a student so young. She sensed his mistrust of her as well, but she was too weary and worried to try to allay it. It was like a spring storm, she told herself. It would pass.

"THE YEW—DEMNE, TELL ME AGAIN WHAT ITS USES ARE."

Demne jerked back to awareness, trying to remember what Bodbmall's question had been.

"The wood is good for making bows, and chips cut from the branches can be inscribed with sacred signs and used for casting oracles . . . and those who sit beneath a yew tree on a hot day may have visions," he finished hurriedly.

Through the open door of the hut the whole bright world was beckoning. The wind was warm and sweet with the smell of gorse blossom and the murmur of bees, and he sensed a change in the air, as if something were about to occur. It made his hair prickle and brought a tingle to his skin. It made him long for the sound of laughter and piping, boyish voices, the slap of the leather ball against his large hands.

"Very well," said Bodbmall. "Now tell me what the birch tree is for."

"You bruise an oil from the twigs to keep wounds from going bad and to rub the Liath Luachra's mus-

cles when they are sore. You boil the leaves to make
a soothing tea. And you cut the branches to switch
me with!" he finished without thinking, then stared
at her, appalled.

The wisewoman's face stiffened, then suddenly she
began to laugh.

"I should give you a birching now for your inatten-
tion!" she exclaimed. "But I see that I'll get nothing
but silliness from you today. Be off with you then—
even I can see that it is a fair day!"

Without even taking up his spear, Demne sought
the forest, and almost without noticing, drifted down
the slope towards the plain of Mag Life and the rath
where Bran mac Conail and his playmates lived. He
could hear their shouts long before he came to the
edge of the forest. He paused, still shadowed by the
trees, and peered between the leaves.

The meadow beyond the low wall was filled with
boys, but not the ones he had met before. These carried curved sticks and were hitting a small ball back
and forth across the field. They were older than the
youngsters he had seen before, bigger, with deeper
voices. Finally, he saw Bran mac Conail among them,
his coppery hair tied behind his head and his pale
face flushed with excitement.

Heartened by the sight of his friend, Demne ventured forward. With more assurance than he really
felt, he crossed the open slope, climbed the wall,
and leaned against it to watch the game. For several minutes the boys, intent on their game, did not
notice him. He observed them carefully, figuring out
the pattern they were following now.

Then Bran saw him and gave a yell and a wave
of greeting. Demne waved back, grinning delightedly. Then a hurtling ball drew his friend back into
the game. Demne stayed where he was, enjoying the
warmth of the sun and the action on the field. This

game seemed to have more pattern than the one the boys had played before. After some time, one boy shouted a halt, and the game ceased.

Bran, his face flushed with exertion and pleasure, ran across the field to Demne. "You came back! I was starting to believe I had dreamed you—and Gort wishes he had! He got a proper tanning from his mother for coming in so dirty. I am glad you are here," Bran added cheerfully. Demne decided he was glad to be there as well.

"What are you playing?" he asked.

"Hurley. This is the first time they have let me play." The pride in Bran's voice was unmistakable, and Demne guessed it was some sort of honor to play the game.

"Who is this?" It was a young man, the one who had called a halt. His features were very like Bran's, although his hair was a darker red, and he lacked Bran's warmth and friendliness.

"This is Demne. Demne, this is my older brother, Cormac mac Conail. Why don't we let him play? He is big enough."

"Demne who?" Cormac's blue eyes narrowed suspiciously.

Bran scratched his head. "Just Demne. The Lad of the Skins. He came some days ago and played ball with us. He is very strong, Cormac. You should see him throw. And he runs like a hind."

"I care not if he runs like the grey of Macha. We need no nameless brats on our team. What were you thinking of, Bran? You have less sense than a mouse. Be off with you, slave."

Demne did not understand the last word, but he knew it was an insult. The other young men had gathered around to see what was happening. They were looking at him the way Bodbmall might look at a louse she found in the bedding.

He hated them then, and he hated Bodbmall for denying him his parentage. Why were the boys were so hostile, and why did his heart hurt so? He felt the red mist begin to swell in his chest and fought to control it. He had only wanted some laughter to fill the emptiness. What had he done wrong?

As he began to rise, Cormac shoved him in the chest.

The red mist caught fire, and Demne smashed a balled fist into the unprotected throat before him. There was a slight rasping sound, a feel of soft bone snapping, and the other boy gave a gasp and fell backwards.

There was a moment of stunned silence. Demne stared down at his assailant, waiting for him to attack again, but Cormac's blank blue eyes remained fixed on the open sky, and even when two ravens flew overhead they did not move.

"The outlander has killed Cormac. Let's get him!"

Demne looked up and saw a mass of contorted faces, pumping legs and waving fists, bared teeth from behind which hoarse voices snarled his name.

He responded without thinking, using the skills that the Liath Luachra had been drumming into him for as long as he could recall. Demne's fists flew, and his bare feet struck out furiously. A half dozen of them managed to knock him to the ground and piled on top of him, kicking and screaming, but Demne fought back, tearing a swinging arm from its socket and gouging out an eye before he rolled free.

He sprang to his feet, scooping up a stone no larger than a robin's egg and hurling it straight into the brow of the closest foe. Time slowed as he watched bone crack and the rock smash into the soft stuff within the skull. Then he was aiming a sharp kick at someone's knee. There was a howl of anguish and the boy fell to the ground. Yet another one charged in, swinging one of the playing sticks. Demne ducked, came up beneath his foe, and heard ribs snap as his hard shoulder hit the boy's chest. There was a terrible wet sound and the other dropped the stick, blood foaming on his lips as he fell.

The remaining boys took to their heels, screaming. Demne stood swaying in the midst of those who could run no more. His skin garments were in shreds, his face bleeding from a dozen gouges. One of his eyes was swollen almost shut, and blood smeared both his arms.

Panting, Demne looked at what remained of his attackers. Five were still, and one was crawling away with his leg bent at an ugly angle, moaning with every move. The boy whose chest he had broken gave a final gurgle. Another youth staggered to his feet, clutching his arm, and tottered towards the rath. Shouts came from within.

As he turned away, Demne's eye fell on the face of the one whose skull the thrown rock had broken. It was Bran. In his fury he had not known him. . . . He stopped short, feeling as if something had broken inside.

Demne knelt beside his dead friend. He touched the other boy's smooth cheek with trembling fingers, and tears washed through the blood on his own. "*You do not think . . .*" the voice of the Liath Luachra echoed in his memory. "*It will be your downfall one day.*"

"I did not mean to harm you, Bran mac Conail. You were kind to me and I returned your kindness with this! The women were right—I am a beast, a monster! How could I have not known you, oh my friend."

Then he heard the patter of bare feet; small, bare feet, racing towards him. An invisible hand touched his torn shoulder, cool and tiny, and a breeze cooled his face.

Run!

Demne heard the command, and was on his feet without thinking. He leaped the low wall, and fled for the shelter of the forest. By the time Conail mac Conair found the bodies of his two sons upon the churned earth, Demne was gone. He did not see Conail gather the men of the rath and lead them towards the wood, vowing vengeance.

Chapter 4

"WHERE IS BODBMALL!"
Demne was gasping by the time he reached home. The Liath Luachra had been resting in the sun. Painfully, she pulled herself upright, staring at his bitten flesh and torn garments and the blood on his hands.

"Gone. . . . She took her herb basket and left shortly after you did. But no beast made those wounds, Demne! What have you done?"

"Acted without thinking!" he said bitterly. "Oh, old one, I didn't mean to do harm! But I went to the edge of the forest, and there were boys playing there. They called me a slave and pushed me, and . . . I went mad, I think."

"Dead?" she asked.

"Not all of them—" he said, shivering. "The others ran back to the rath, and there was shouting. Surely someone will follow! We must get away, for they will find us here."

The warrior woman thought for a moment, tapping her huge white teeth. "Douse the fire so the smoke will not betray us. Then get your spear and go. Keep to the ridge, as I have taught you."

"I will not leave you here to face the anger of those

men," he said stubbornly. "I have done enough evil today!"

"I am old. It does not matter. Get you gone!"

"Not without you!"

"Demne, I can barely walk from the hut to the fire." She gave a long sigh. "Once I could have run with you, but not anymore."

"Then I will carry you!"

"Foolish boy. It will only slow your flight."

"Today I killed the only friend I have ever made. Even if you slowed me to a *seislide's* pace, I could not bear to leave you." The little snail that crept between the grasses was the slowest thing he knew.

The wrinkled, pale old face flushed. "You are a good boy, Demne."

He shook his head, swallowing the sickness that still rose in his throat when he thought of that field. "Good? I killed the one boy who was kind to me when the other boys called me names! I did not know him in the fight, old one! I threw a stone the way you taught me, and it broke his brow."

"That was the battle heat, Demne. Men lose their wits when it takes them. I have seen it many times before."

"I will never do it again!"

"Perhaps you will not have a choice . . ." she said slowly. "You have the gifts of the warrior, whatever Bodbmall may say. Put a young horse on the Plain of the Curragh, and he will run. Put a warrior in the battle, and he will fight. But when the battle lust comes on a man he is no longer even a warrior—he is a creature that only knows how to kill."

"I do not want to be a monster!" Demne cried. "Teach me how to stop it, old one—There must be a way!"

The old woman shook her head sadly. "I never learned. Oh, Demne," she went on, "why did you

venture towards the raths? Have not Bodbmall and
I told you not to go out of the forest, and to keep
away from other folk?" She plucked up her cloak and
reached for her own spear.

"You have been telling me to stay in the wood for
as long as I can recall," he said bitterly, "but you
never told me *why*. I wished to see other people,
to know how they lived, and I forgot. I longed to
talk to someone my own age." He paused. "I was
lonely. . . ."

"I understand." She nodded. "I suppose there was
no preventing it. I warned Bodbmall that we could
not confine you here forever, but she never listens
to any counsel but her own. She was always headstrong, even when she was a girl, and now she is old
and even more stubborn than me!"

The Liath Luachra picked up a small stick. Clumsily her crippled hands fumbled her knife from her belt,
and she made a number of nicks along the edge of
the wood. She bent down and placed the stick in the
shadow of the rock beside the fire, where it appeared
to be merely a bit of dropped kindling. "Well, this
will tell her to beware. Thus do we learn the folly of
our own obstinacy."

Demne knelt and got the Liath Luachra onto his
back, then picked up his own spear. She managed
to clasp her arms around his neck, and he got his
arms beneath her skinny legs. She seemed to weigh
no more than the piglet he had carried into the camp
the spring before.

From the woods came a shout, much closer than
he wanted it to be. Tightening his grip on the spear,
he trotted out of the circle of huts and towards the
stream. With the old woman on his back he could
not look behind him. As he lengthened his stride he
wondered whether he would ever again have even so
much of a home as this had been. Surely he would

never again see this one—the men of the rath would destroy it when they found him gone.

The smell of the water drew Demne, and he stepped into the stream. As he splashed upstream, the chill clear waters frothed around his calves, washing away fatigue and lending energy. When he came to a small rapids he paused. He could hear the shouts of his pursuers faint from below. They were arguing about which direction to go, and he let himself smile for a moment. Clearly the men of the rath had no woodcraft, to be thus proclaiming their presence to their prey. How did they ever catch any game?

There were rocks here on the shore that would show no sign of his passing. On the far bank of the stream he drew reluctant limbs from the water's cool embrace, and began to run. Where he passed, damp footmarks steamed for a moment in the sunshine, then disappeared.

Demne felt his feet fly, and the air brushed his face; he was barely aware of the old woman clinging to his back or the rocks in his path. He heard snatches of tree song and the rasp of ravens and the enraged shouts of the men of the rath, and they were all one. His battered spirit forgot everything but flight. His strong, young legs pounded the earth, and he felt that he could run to the end of the world.

Demne lost all sense of time or place or even purpose as he ran. He fell into a trance of movement for its own sake, and forgot the men who pursued him and the old woman clinging to his back. He outran memory of Bodbmall and her teachings, of the piglet, of the broken face of Bran mac Conail, dead upon the trampled soil. His body seemed to thin until it was like a part of the wind, moving swiftly through the trees and setting their leaves to rustling. He had never known or imagined such power.

It was not until the sow rose out of the earth and

hurled herself into his path that Demne came back to himself. She grunted, pawed the earth with her sharp, small hooves, and charged. Furious to be earthbound, he jerked away from the slashing jaws and glimpsed in the beast's throat an old but festering wound.

The sow turned with astonishing speed and came after him, and once more Demne ran. Bracken whipped at his bare limbs. He could sense the hot breath not far behind him, and knew it was not the first time. She knew the scent of the human who had killed her piglet, and she would pursue him until one of them died. The woman who had borne Bran mac Conail and his brother must hate him the same way.

He wished he could give the piglet back to the sow, and Bran and Cormac back to their mother as well. He would have traded anything he had to see Bran's friendly grin and easy shrug once again. But it was done, and to escape those who sought vengeance for the boys he must fight this older enemy.

Demne spun around, wrenching the Liath Luachra's arms from his neck so that she fell, and grabbed the spear from her hand. A weapon in each fist, he crouched to face the furious sow as she tore through the bracken. She was even bigger than he remembered, her tiny red eyes glowing with lust to rend and slay.

The sow hesitated as the sharp points jabbed at her, heavy head swinging on the muscled neck, indecisive and wary. The wicked teeth flashed golden in the afternoon sun.

The boy drew a long, slow breath of sweet, bracken-heavy air into lungs that burned with strain. His limbs felt leaden and his flesh frail before a power that seemed fashioned from earth's bones. He gripped the spears firmly in each hand, yearning for a shield against the sow's terrible gaze.

The Liath Luachra's shorter spear was in his right hand, its balance awkward and unfamiliar. He loosened his grasp, shifting his hand a little to find the right grip. The sow's mouth gaped as she snarled, and Demne flung the spear into that hot maw with all his power. The shaft snapped as the strong jaws closed.

Demne gripped his own spear in both hands and ran towards the sow. She snorted and blood welled from her snout, and then she charged. Demne jammed the butt of his spear into the earth and then she was on him, head lowering to gore, and the hard barb of the spear drove through her eye deep into the brain within the bone. The sow roared, and blood spouted from her skull as Demne tore his spear free.

Her tusk slashed his calf as she convulsed, and once more, as her blood mixed with his, his consciousness spun away. He *felt* her battle rage as her life ebbed, and knew that although he had killed, he had not conquered her. He fought for control, but the monstrous magnificence that twitched at his feet would be a part of him forever now.

The sow jerked, quivered, and was still. Demne leaned on his spear, shaken by fine tremors that ran from his head to his heels, his stomach churning. Cautiously, he bent to touch the cooling snout, and ran a finger over the tooth that had wounded him. His own blood reddened its gleaming, yellowed surface. Without knowing why, he took his skinning knife, haggled the tooth out of the jaw, and thrust it into his pouch.

He straightened, willing his pulse to slow, and heard the distant shouts of the men who still pursued him.

Demne turned back to the Liath Luachra. Her blue eyes bulged and her wide teeth gleamed from a fleshless mouth. Her garments hung loosely from her aged body; he could almost see the bones beneath the pale skin.

"Demne." Her low voice was a whisper.

"What is it?"

"Quick. The lake."

"The lake," he repeated stupidly. He could not imagine what she was talking about.

"Carry me to Loch Lurgan." She pointed in the direction of the lowering sun with a bony finger. "Hasten." The cries of the men of the rath were much closer now.

Demne scooped her up in his arms and got her across his shoulder. She weighed almost nothing now. He took a ragged breath, gripped his spear, still dripping with the sow's blood and brains, and summoned the strength to move. Every bone and muscle in his strong young body was screaming protest. He ignored them as he ignored the aching wound in his leg and his weariness.

Setting off at a smart trot, he left the clearing where the body of the sow still lay as the men of the rath came into it. He heard the gabble of wonder as they saw the great carcass, and the undertone of fear, but he paid them no mind. The water was calling to him now.

The scent gave him fresh strength, and Demne went faster. The Liath Luachra's heart throbbed against his shoulder, and the crystal song in his mind grew louder. It swept aside his pain and tiredness, summoning him.

A faint glimmer of gold flickered through the trees. As the sun began to dip behind the mountain, he tore through the alders, crossed the damp soil of the shore, and plunged into the cool, gilded waters. He could feel the liquid soothing the cuts that scored his legs, and he stood utterly still, letting the water suffuse his senses.

The sun had gone beyond the far mountain, but behind the stark silhouettes of the trees the western sky was a clear gold that shaded gradually into a translucent blue the color of a kingfisher's wing. The only thing that moved in all that stillness was a heron, picking its way with angular deliberation among the reeds.

"Child . . ." The Liath Luachra's whisper dragged him back from the ecstasy of the water's song.

"We are in the lake," he answered.

"Cast me into the water."

"What!"

"Do as I say."

"I carried you away to save you, not to drown you," he exclaimed.

"This is my place, Demne. This is my true element. Here. Loose my cloak. I need it no longer."

Demne drove his spear butt into the soft bottom of the lake, then shifted his foster mother from his shoulder so that he could cradle her in his arms like a babe. Her bony fingers tore at the cloth of her cloak, and he helped her peel it away. Now the fabric hung across his outstretched arms like a shed skin. The woman who lay there was nothing but skin and bone. Somehow, in his swift flight, her very flesh seemed to have vanished.

"Oh, I have killed you too!" he choked.

"Demne, you have not failed me! I knew the time was near, but I clung to my old life. You have brought me to the place where I must bide. A quick parting is better. Here in the water, I will live again. I was not born of man and woman, child, but of the waters of this place. Return me to it, quick! I ask for nothing more." Then a soft smile touched her face, hardly covered by the skin now. "I do ask more. Bear my affections to Bodbmall, and tell her where I have gone. Now, kiss me in your sweet way, for I must go swiftly."

She sounded excited, not sad. Demne was dizzy with confusion, but he had obeyed her for too long to argue now. He pressed his lips against the withered cheek. With a skeletal finger, the Liath Luachra stroked his brow, smoothed down the length of his face, and touched his lips closed. Her eyes shone with some emotion he could not name. Then she twisted in his arms and dropped into the waters that lapped about his knees.

The withered body of the Liath Luachra broke through the gilded surface of the lake, breaking the golden sheet for a moment, so that the darkness of the blue beneath was visible. Then it closed over her.

And the world stopped. The air had ceased to move; Demne could not breathe. It was only a moment, but to the boy it seemed forever. The water shone around him like a mirror of gold, and he saw his gilded image within it, waiting—for what? His fists closed in the cloak's soft folds. It was all of her that remained to him. He lifted the material to his face, smelling her scent, ignoring his own tears.

The shout of male voices dragged him unwilling back into the turning world. He looked towards the shore. The men of the rath, now reduced to a dozen weary, sweat-stained warriors whose cloth garments had been torn and dirtied in the chase, trotted to the edge of the lake and stopped, eyeing him across the shallows.

Swiftly Demne knotted the cloak around his waist, yanked his spear from the mud, and began to wade deeper into the water. He ducked as a spear was cast at him from the shore. It fell into the water ahead of him, overshooting him by several lengths. Someone was too eager, and careless as well. He felt a sharp contempt for anyone who did not wait until he was sure of his target, as the Liath Luachra had taught him to do.

Now the water was waist-high. The mud of the lake bed squished through his bare toes; the heady scent of the lake overcame the sweaty odor of his own body as the sweet waters washed him. He heard a splash as men came after him, and promptly dove under the water, kicking his feet strongly and propelling himself forward as he had learned to do in the marsh the summer before. He stroked with his free hand, but kept his grip on the spear. Only when his lungs ached did he break through to the surface again.

Demne blinked the water from his eyes. He had gone a good distance, beyond his depth, but if he moved his legs as if he were running and waved his arms, he found that he could stay upright. The dark shapes of his enemies were wading out into the shallows, peering about in confusion.

He rocked as something stirred in the waters between him and the shore. The depths boomed. Water fountained from the lake bed, cascading from the huge head and shoulders and down the endlessly extending flanks of a long leathery body with a square snout and great gleaming fangs. The snapping jaws opened, bellowing a challenge at the screaming men who were flailing towards shore. Spray scattered sparkling from the finned mane as the great head swung back and forth above the heaving waters.

A spear flew at the beast, and a leathery arm knocked it contemptuously aside. Then a taloned paw closed around one of the warriors, crushing his chest like an egg. He screamed as he died, and the others flung their spears. One bounced off the monster's thick hide. The rest of the men floundered shoreward through water that seemed to be trying to drag them down, but the beast caught another and broke him in two before the remainder of the party reached the edge of the lake.

Demne, treading water, watched in a bewildered horror. Oddly enough, he felt no fear of the monster, or perhaps he no longer cared. The beast thrashed towards the shore, roaring, and the boy turned and began to swim in the opposite direction. He had never

been to this lake nor did he know this part of the
mountains, and despite the blessing of the waters,
he was tired. It was all he could manage to force his
weary legs to kick, to keep his head above the cold
waves, to leave the fading sounds of the turmoil on
the farther shore behind. His mind was empty of all
but the effort to move his arms and legs in a steady
rhythm that propelled him forward.

The cold of the water crept into his flesh and seeped
through his bones. Each stroke of his aching arms and
kick of his weary legs was a greater effort. Finally his
body could no longer serve him. Demne felt himself
begin to sink. It seemed proper that he should drift
down into the chill, still darkness, to leave at last the
world of air and light. He struggled a little, but he had
lost the heart for it. Too much had happened today.

He seemed to sink forever, but the ending he
yearned for still eluded him. His lungs ached for
air, but he drew no water into his chest. Demne felt
as if he were dangling between two states of being,
like a spider on its thread.

Something brushed his leg, and he felt the water
swirl around him. Then a leathery claw grasped him,
and he was thrust up through the water into the fast-
fading light. Demne gasped for breath as the great eyes
of the monster regarded him solemnly, and his own
widened in wonder. He knew them! Since the day of
his birth they had watched over him.

Demne could not imagine how the Liath Luachra
had become this fearsome creature who now carried
him tenderly in a taloned paw, but he knew it was
so. *"I was not born of man and woman."* Her odd
words rang in his mind. Bodbmall, in all her wisdom,
could not have explained this wonder. He made a little mewling noise of greeting and spewed up the bitter
contents of his belly.

Demne shook with cold as the beast carried him

across the lake. She set him down on trembling legs waist-deep in the water, and made a fearsome noise that echoed in the twilight. His teeth chattered as he dragged himself the last few lengths to the shore. The torn hide of his vest clung to his skin as he tried to still the spasms that shook him.

The head of the monster was silhouetted against the violet sky, dark and featureless as the trees on the shore. Demne clutched his spear as if it could stop his shivering and drew several long, slow breaths, trying to warm himself as Bodbmall had taught him. A little heat seemed to swell in his chest, though it did not reach his limbs.

The creature waited, watching him. "Thank you, my mother," he cried. "Thank you for my life." The monster gave a low rumble, the great head dipped, and it turned away. It swam towards the middle of the lake, its dark head drawing a ruffle of wave through the water, until it vanished in the twilight and he was utterly alone.

Chapter 5

❧

DEMNE STAGGERED WITH WEARINESS, USING THE BUTT of his spear to help himself along. He was cold and tired and lost. The energy which had carried him and the Liath Luachra was spent. When something scratched in the underbrush ahead his mind told him that it was the fox whose tracks he had just seen, but what could he be sure of when so much had betrayed him? The oaks and birches around him seemed remote; their voices were not friendly like those of the trees at home, and the shadows beneath them stretched monstrous fingers across the path. He was too tired to be afraid, but he shivered when he looked into them.

When he came to a small glade, Demne stopped, unable to go further. He untied the cloak of the Liath Luachra from around his waist and spread it out over some fern. Then, despite the growing chill of evening, he peeled off his damp goat-hide vest and kilt and hung them from the low branch of a young birch tree. With a handful of grass, he rubbed his skin dry. It stung the cuts on his arms, but he barely noticed that now.

Demne wanted a fire, a bowl of Bodbmall's broth

hot from the cauldron; even her thick porridge would have been welcome now. There were enough dead branches scattered on the ground for fuel if he had had the strength to gather them and some way to make a fire. He flapped his arms, but before the motion could warm him he was felled by exhaustion. He slumped against a tree trunk, legs splayed across the soft fern. The night deepened, and his eyes shut, but he did not sleep.

The skirmish with the young men of the rath played itself over and over again against his eyelids. He saw the stone fly from his rough hand into the broad brow of Bran mac Conail, and he saw the blood blossom where it struck. It was like a flower, a terrible bloom bursting through the bone. How could anything so terrible have beauty?

The moon rose above the trees. As the silver light touched his closed eyelids, Demne opened his eyes. The moon seemed to look back, its marred face mostly hidden, so that the thin sickle shone like the curved tooth of a pig. The gash on his calf throbbed as he remembered his encounter with the sow. He could feel the heat in his flesh where the tusk had entered his body, though his body was shivering. He got back on his feet and swung his arms back and forth. His blood seemed to have frozen in his veins.

His head swam, and the birches around the glade whirled dizzily. Demne fell to his hands and knees in the fern. He wanted to lower his head and bury his face in the sweet-smelling plants, to root and grub in the moist earth below. His human hand seemed hideous, his fingers soft, ugly pale things that threw stones and flung spears. He wished they were small, hard hooves that could not grasp anything.

Demne lay in the moonlight, unable to move. The heat in his leg pulsed up his thigh into his groin. It was not unpleasant, but it was alien. Something was

inside him that had never been before, and he was
both drawn to it and afraid. From within came a low
grunting. He swung his head from side to side, seeking the source of the strange sound, but the forest was
utterly still.

With an enormous effort, he lifted his head and
looked at the moon once more. The curves of the moon
were the teeth of the sow, and the darkness between
its horns, her face. He was sure he could see one red
eye in the sky above. Demne bowed his head slowly,
shame heating his body even more than the fever that
gripped him. He had never killed except to eat, until
today. He remembered how he had thrust his spear
into the sow's glaring eye, and a pain filled his chest.
Hot tears slipped unnoticed down his cheeks, as he
grieved for the sow and for the young men who had
died at his hands. He wanted to beg forgiveness, but
his throat brought forth no sound but wretched grunt-
ings. His mouth was dry and no longer seemed fit for
human speech. A tear trickled onto his lips and stung
the raw flesh. He licked the salt of it onto his tongue
and moaned.

The moonlight stroked his burning skin. Demne
shuddered and shrank down against the cool earth.
Ferns brushed his belly and caressed his skin, and
he shivered with pain. He tried to scream, but only
made another ugly grunt. The moonbeams pierced his
fevered flesh with silver needles of light.

Demne crawled a few lengths, trying to escape the
touch of the moon. The scent of crushed fern rose and
filled his senses, and he lifted a green-stained palm to
ward away the terrible light.

But he was too weak, too weary. He sank into the
greenery, defeated. Let the sky sow take her vengeance, then. Demne felt a kind of lightness fill his
flesh as he surrendered. He flopped over on his back,
barely noticing a rock beneath one shoulder, and let

the moonlight stream into his body. He stared into the terrible beauty of the moon, and lifted his aching arms, trying to embrace the red-eyed vision that swam before his stinging eyes.

A dazzling whiteness filled his entire being, a cold flood of knowledge too vast for human words. For an instant there was no secret and no mystery. It was a gift, a great, unrelenting outpouring that swept away his consciousness like a single leaf on a rushing stream. For a moment he knew the lives of all things that trod the earth, from the first small thing floating on the great waters at time's beginning to the pale-haired stranger who had fathered him. He was a single note within a many-voiced song. He could even see the face of time to come: children he would father, men he would slay who were yet unborn. And within it all there was a meaning that he knew he must learn. It was nothing in which Bodbmall could instruct him, nor did it belong to the way of the Liath Luachra. It was something beyond, a hidden spring he had not ever guessed was there. It beckoned him, but he knew that once he tasted that knowledge he would be changed. He struggled to deny the call.

But Demne yearned to sink into that silver flood with an ache that was greater than his need for food or sleep or companionship. His arms strained upward and a sound too formless for a human throat and too poignant for a beast's stiff jaws throbbed in the air. And for a moment, then, his emptiness was filled. . . .

It was a moment beyond knowledge, but the moon had scarcely moved in the sky when his arms fell to his sides, and the fading of the vision drained all his delight away. He ached with emptiness. All that remained was a faded confusion of images. For a long time he lay unable to move, while the moon wheeled across the night sky and down the far slope to dawn.

His head was pillowed by the cool fern, but his flesh burned. He became aware that he was desperately thirsty. Then he heard the little trickle of music which had haunted him since the day he had slain the piglet, deeper and stronger than it had ever been before. In that moment it seemed to him quite comprehensible to be companioned by a melody. As long as he could hear that rippling lilt, he would never be entirely alone.

With a deep grunt, he rolled onto his belly, got his hands and knees under him, and crawled out of the glade. There must be a stream nearby. He sniffed the air, turning his head from side to side. He could smell the fern, the birches, the oaks that stood beyond them. Little rocks, he discovered, had a scent of their own, quite distinct from that of the mosses that grew upon them. He could not see very well in the darkness, but his ears caught the sweep of wings as some night bird passed overhead, and he heard the faint rustle of the leaves in the breeze.

His flesh was still burning. He tried to get to his feet, but the very thought made his head swim. He paused, one hand uplifted, then plunged his fingers deep into the moist earth and felt a rush of security. Better to stay close to the ground . . . it was safer there.

When he found the gurgling freshet, he grunted and plunged his head into the water. An icy mouthful coursed into his throat, but his body was still burning. He pulled his head out and lapped the water. The taste of it awakened a sharp pang of hunger in mouth and belly. He had a fleeting memory of hare, of honey-sweetened porridge, of oatcakes and boiled roots. He closed his teeth around fronds of fern and tasted their bitter greenness. Grunting, he foraged on all fours along the bank of the stream, grubbing some wild carrots and eating them, dirt and all. From time to time he paused, shaking his damp and tousled hair and trying to recall why this seemed odd. He could not. Finally he burrowed into a patch of dockweed and fell into an uneasy doze.

Piping voices roused him. Demne rolled to his hands and knees and peered around him. It was past mid-morning, and the light was golden on the trees. They appeared indistinct, and he blinked his eyes in a vain attempt to clear his sight. Bewildered, he crawled out and sniffed the air, then turned his attention towards the sounds.

Three strange creatures emerged from the shadow of the trees. They walked on two legs and their loose skins were soft blue and green. When they moved their mouths, sounds came out that he knew and did not know. He lifted his snout and scented sweat and wood smoke and wool. They smelled like enemies.

Demne drew his head against his hunched shoulders and pawed the earth. He narrowed his eyes and snorted as heat raced along his veins. They *were* foes! With a shrill grunt, he charged through the underbrush. He heard a shout as he butted his head into one and tried to slash at its legs. His nose grazed cloth and he snapped, but the taste of wool made him gag. A thin branch struck his back with all the might the enemy possessed, and as pain pulsed through him another cry tore through his throat. His foe jerked away. Their eyes met, and it came into his mind that these were too short to be true enemies, that these were boys no older than his former self. Before he had time to consider this prospect, both creatures had taken to their heels, screaming. For a few paces he followed, and then his gorge rose, and all he had eaten spewed out onto the ground.

Gasping and spitting, he crawled back into the wood. When he found water once more he lowered his aching flesh into the stream. Mist surrounded him, and consciousness flickered. His leg hurt most, but heat rippled up through his flesh in pulsing waves, and this time the water could not quench his thirst or cool him. After a time, some instinct drove him away from the water and into the shadow beneath the trees.

The light faded, and cool darkness returned. Sometimes he crawled and at others he slept, a fitful, restless sleep that gave him no peace. Faces glimmered before him; they spoke to him, but he could not understand the words. The golden light returned and disappeared again, but it had no meaning. He knew neither time nor place; he drank when he was thirsty, slept when he could no longer crawl. Gnawing at the bark of trees and clawing up nameless plants he sought to ease his agony. The faces in his dreams drew closer when the world around him was most dim. They shone with their own light, and he liked to look at them. They danced through his awareness like a trill of music. The sounds they made almost made sense to him then. He wanted to stay and listen, but always he fell back into his body again, trying to remember what that meaning had been.

After a time, all of the yammering faces swirled together. As the haze cleared, for a moment he saw a tangle of green that he knew was called *moss*. Waking, he crawled and snuffled, seeking it. His long hair, matted with sweat and soil, clung to his neck and fell into his eyes. When he found the moss he sought, he barely had the strength to scrape it from the tree. In his mind, a voice spoke, a remembered voice he could not name. It told him that this stuff would drive heat from the blood and cool the mind. He paused, grasping at the wisp of memory, then forced the moss between his torn lips. It tasted terrible, but he chewed and swallowed it, and presently his body began to cool.

The mist in his mind dissipated, and Demne found himself crouching between the roots of an enormous oak. It was night, and through the branches he could see the moon riding above. He stared in wordless wonder, for he could dimly remember seeing its slender sickle in the sky, and now it was close to full. He tried to get to his feet, and the world spun dizzily. His muscles screamed when he moved, and his skin seemed to be all one smarting bruise. He took a deep breath and forced himself upright.

A few wobbling steps brought him to a tree. He clung to it, breathing carefully, listening to the steady thumping of his heart. He had only a wispy memory of the days and nights that had just gone by. His sight was no longer fuzzy, but when he looked around he saw nothing to indicate where he was. But to his left, the ground rose slightly. Had he descended the mountains from the lake where he had left the Liath Luachra? He forced his aching limbs to carry him upward.

It took a long time, for he had to rest frequently, but a trail of broken ferns and little patches of earth where the print of his grubby hand could still be seen marked the way he had come down. It was close to dawn when he finally came to a birch glade that looked familiar.

Demne stood at the edge of the clearing for a long time. He could see where he had lain among the ferns, for the outline of his body was etched in white, as if the moon had burned him. The cloak of the Liath Luachra lay where he had spread it to dry, and his tunic hung from a branch. Nothing had disturbed the place since he had crawled out of it, grunting like the pig he had slain. He shivered, but not from cold. The white outline in the fern frightened him, and he skirted it carefully. Then he grabbed the cloak, wrapped it around his shoulders and curled up near the trees. Exhausted sleep claimed him almost before he pillowed his head on one bruised arm.

Awakening ravenous and filthy several hours later, Demne sat up and peered around the glade. The sun was high in the heavens, and on a branch overhead, a mother bird was feeding her nestlings. He scratched his head, puzzled, then walked unsteadily to the stream to wash. The water was cool on his injured flesh, and it stung his cuts as he washed the dirt away. His knees and palms were brown with ground-in earth. A piece of the fatty soap that Bodbmall made each spring would have been useful, but he ducked under the water and rubbed his itching scalp, hoping to remove the worst of the soil. Beneath the rippling stream, he heard the lilt of song, and felt his spirits lift.

When, dripping, he returned to the glade, he used the cloak to dry himself. Then he took down his vest. Demne's wide mouth twisted as he realized it had shrunk as it dried. Or else he had grown larger. Frowning, he clasped the belt around him. Certainly he felt different, though whether bigger was the right word for it he could not tell. Demne looked around the glade for the last time. The fern where he had lain was a blur of sere fronds, the outline of his body fading now. He picked up his spear, tossed the damp cloak over his arm, and set out in search of something to eat.

Feeling a little light-headed, he wandered until he found a bush heavy with bilberries. He ate these greedily until their sweetness began to cloy. As Demne wiped his mouth with the back of his hand, he heard the rapid rush of small, bare feet and a faint giggle nearby. He looked around sharply, but saw no one. It was the same sound he had heard just before he saw the piglet, and when he went to play ball with the boys. It struck him that some danger followed whenever he heard that sound.

"Who is there?" he hissed. There was no answer, not even a giggle, and he shook his head. Then he heard a distant murmur of voices, the deep tones of men and the higher ones of youths. They sounded as if they were hunting for something. Quickly, silently, he moved into the forest away from the sound.

So intent was he upon avoiding the hunters that he nearly ran into the arms of a second group moving through a little clearing. Demne ducked into the underbrush, but it was too late. A shout rang through the air. The men turned towards his hiding place.

A whisper of wind touched his cheek like a small hand. *This way!* Without pausing to reflect, Demne followed it. He heard the rapid fall of small, swift feet, and the ripple of his secret song even above the cries of the men who saw him clearly now. He pushed weak limbs into a run.

A spear flew past him, narrowly missing his arm, and he lengthened his stride. He ran into a thicket of trees and nearly tripped over a huge root. Demne slipped among the trees, and behind him heard the rattle and clatter as the men struggled through. They called and shouted, and he could tell that the first hunting party had joined the second. The trees thinned ahead, and he began to run again, following the faint patter of invisible feet.

In a few minutes, he felt his wind failing. With each breath, a stitch burned in his side. The cut where the sow had gashed him burned like fire on his calf, and his head throbbed. Demne's weakness frightened and angered him. Why were these men chasing him? He had done them no harm.

Then he remembered the skirmish on the playing field and the broken face of his friend Bran. Demne had a vague memory, too, of seeing several boys by a stream. They had not seemed human to him at the time, but they must have told their elders he was there. Perhaps they had said he was a beast. Gasping, he wondered if this might not be true. Then his aching feet plunged into an icy freshet and carried him across to the further bank.

The men broke out of the woods behind him, yelling, and another spear flew past him to bury itself in a tree trunk. Furious, Demne wrenched it out, whirled, and tossed it back. It sped with deadly purpose and pierced the chest of a big man in the middle of the stream. His bearded face looked startled as he died.

That victory lent Demne a little energy, and he dashed into the wood ahead. He raced between the trees while the hunting party paused to deal with the fallen man. Ahead he could hear the footfalls of his invisible guide, and he pursued them in simple desperation. Behind him, he heard the angry voices of his hunters. He dodged low-hanging branches as his unseen companion led him through a small glade and into the stand of rowan beyond it. For a moment he leaned against the smooth bark of a tree, trying to get his breath. He wondered how much further his legs would support him.

A vague memory of one of the wisewoman's lessons glimmered through his clouded mind. Demne threw his arms around the slender trunk of the tree and rested his head against the bark, pleading silently for strength. A warmth kindled in his breast, and his legs stopped trembling. His breath slowed and his heart beat steadily. He whispered his thanks, then pressed his cracked, dry lips against the bark. He saw the bloody imprint of his kiss as he turned to follow his unseen ally once more.

He could hear the men shouting and cursing and knew that they were close behind. He darted between the rowan trees and quietly and with more assurance moved forward. The rowan had refreshed him enough to keep him moving a bit longer, but he knew he could not go on forever. The worn hide of his garment slapped against his bare thighs; sweat poured down his face, stinging his eyes and the many tiny cuts all over his body. Even the leather-hard soles of his feet hurt now.

Demne longed to be back in the circle of huts with Bodbmall and the Liath Luachra. If he had known what it was like to be running for his life, he would not have been so impatient at sitting quietly, learning the lessons he had resented so much. But the old warrior woman was no more, and he had no idea what might have become of the *bendrui*. He hoped the angry men of the rath had not found or harmed her.

He had never meant to cause such trouble. He had only wished for friends, for companions, and for praise. Why did he have to flee?

The trees began to thin, and Demne realized he had been ascending the mountainside for some time. The ground became more rocky, and he burst into the open. Behind him he heard the men shouting from the cover of the trees.

"There he is!"

"Now we have him."

Demne tore across the rocky ground, spiky bracken scratching his calves. And then the earth opened before him. He teetered at the edge of the abyss and threw himself backwards. The hunters behind him howled with glee.

Demne looked from them to the chasm. In its depths fierce rocks tore the rushing stream to shreds of spray that swirled upward in shimmering veils that hid what was on the other side. The waters roared hungrily. In the depths, he glimpsed the white gleam of shattered bones. The sheer sides were slick with moisture, faced with ragged slabs of broken stone where not even a tuft of grass could find a niche in which to grow. No foothold there for man or animal. He lifted his eyes, striving to peer through the veil of spray.

He felt a touch of wind and the mist thinned. Beyond it he glimpsed a smooth expanse of a green more vivid than anything he had ever seen. After a moment he identified the swirl of blue that glimmered upon it as a woman's gown. Then for a moment the mists parted, and she lifted a graceful arm and beckoned to him. Her golden hair hung in two plaits on each side of her face, more fell unbound down her back, and even with his enemies belling like hounds at his very heels, Demne's heart leapt at the beauty of her, the perfection of that simple gesture, for which all else was only a frame.

A spear rattled along the stones next to his foot and shot into the chasm. Demne's fear transformed into a sudden fury. He swung around, lowered his rough head, and charged directly into the men. Another spear whispered above his hair, and he hurled his own weapon into the breast of the man in the lead and saw the eyes of the others widening as their leader went down. Anger gave him strength. Another spear sped towards him, and he caught it in midair. The shaft stung his palm; swiftly he flipped and cast it back again.

Two of the men had fallen, and three were now spearless. They scattered as he ran towards them while the others stood their ground, jabbing at his moving body, scoring the air where he had been. But they still outnumbered him, and now they were beginning to move in.

Come to me!

The words caressed his mind, and abruptly Demne knew he could fight no more. He whirled. The woman was still there, and she was the only thing that mattered in all the world. He drew a deep breath, and faster even than he had charged his attackers, sped across the rocky ground. His hard feet struck the edge of the chasm; with his last strength he propelled himself into the air. The depths beneath him yawned hungrily. He stretched out his arms to the lady, reaching for her beauty.

Then the green ground on the other side rushed up to meet him. The impact knocked his breath from his chest. He rolled over onto his back and lay, half conscious, clutching the sweet grass with his torn hands. His head was pounding. From what seemed an immense distance he could hear the angry voices of the men who had pursued him, and closer, the chirruping giggle that had haunted him. Slowly, the thumping of his heart began to ease.

Painfully he sat up and pushed the matted hair off his brow. The mists had closed in again, completely cutting off the world behind him, but the woman in blue stood serenely a dozen paces away, a grave smile upon her face. She held out a soft hand to him. Demne reached up, then, ashamed of his filth, drew back his hand. He clambered to his feet and wiped his palms on the tattered leather of his garment, watching helplessly as she began to move away. Then, still smiling, she turned and gestured to him to follow her.

Chapter 6

STEPPING CAREFULLY, DEMNE FOLLOWED THE WOMan across the grass. The turf had a close, springy texture like the pelt of some live animal. He felt an almost painful expansion of his senses, as if he had come suddenly out of darkness into the full light of the sun. The life and wonder he had first encountered in the cold water of the stream were flooding him once more, but now they were magnified. Each blade of grass spoke a word in his mind that was both a name and a song, but he did not know how to sing it. The rumbling in his empty belly was a minor hunger compared to this need.

The grass gave way to a path of gleaming white rock that led over the hill. Light was everywhere around him, softer than the golden glow of sunlight, richer than the silver radiance of the moon. It was almost palpable, like honey made into air. He breathed it into his aching lungs and felt the weariness begin to slip away. His head swam with that richness; he was too giddy to still the trembling of his limbs.

The music of his invisible guide chimed in his memory, and he knew that he had not strayed between the worlds by chance. The important thing was that he was here, and not lying somewhere with a spear through his heart, bleeding his life away. A swift rush of gratitude washed away his fear, and he started down the hill.

Before him lay a glimmering land of wood and meadow within which stood a noble hall. Demne gaped, knowing that this must be one of the dwellings of the fairy folk, the Sidhe, whom Bodbmall called the Tuatha de Danann. It was nothing like the round hut in which he had grown up, nothing like anything he had ever heard of or seen. It seemed neither crafted nor grown; or perhaps it was both, for its walls were formed of many trees lined up and joined together, interlacing trunk and twig in an entrancing complexity. The branches intertwined inward to form a slightly peaked roof which shimmered with the greens of many leaves. His skin pebbled with wordless excitement as he began to sense the pattern within its intricacies.

The woman in blue stood waiting in the high doorway of the hall, and it was only then that Demne realized how large the structure must be, for the lintel was well above her proud head, and the peak of the roof was at least three times her generous height above the cross beam. Demne followed her through the door, wondering if he were shivering from reluctance or curiosity.

He passed into a confusion of light and color. He found himself trying to see everything at once and forced himself to stand still. The floor was made of colored stones laid out in lazy spirals that bewildered the eye. The walls were the trunks of the living trees, but most of their bark was hidden by shimmering weavings whose figures seemed to move.

Demne found his gaze drawn back to one hanging in particular. It showed a battle-garbed warrior whose hand gleamed like silver around the hilt of his sword. The face was half-hidden beneath the metal helm, but

the sharp blue eyes seemed to look directly at him. He
saw a gleam of long, pale hair across the shoulders, as
fair as his own.

The woman followed his gaze and nodded, and
Demne found himself smiling back shyly. Surely he
had seen her before, perhaps in some dream. Who was
she? Would she scorn him because he did not know
his father's name?

"Do not be afraid, lad. It is Donait of the Sidhe who
welcomes you," came the words. The voice sounded
like part of the light-filled air, like the lilt of melody that throbbed in his bones. Had she even spoken
aloud?

"I am called Demne." His voice seemed raucous as
a rook's after hers, and he felt his face go red.

"I know." She reached out and brushed the matted locks off his brow. Demne shrank back. The cool
whisper of her fingertips upon his skin sent an odd
sensation tingling through his flesh. The scent of
apple blossom was in the air, stirring memories
that made him afraid, but suddenly he wanted to
fling himself against her softness as he had done
with Bodbmall when he was very small. That need
frightened him more than the hot breath of a hundred
enraged sows.

"What do you want from me?" The words that
escaped his cracked lips were graceless. The conflicting kindness of Bodbmall and the Liath Luachra
had always led to some new demand. This beautiful
lady had to want *something*.

Did she need a servant to carry water and gather
firewood? The fire pit that ran down the center of the
hall blazed brightly, but he could see no logs within
the flames. And where would he gather wood? The
trees that formed the building itself he would not
consider touching, and those without seemed sacred
as well.

"I want you to take a bath," she answered calmly. "Then we will eat."

Demne nodded. Remembering Bodbmall's high voice scolding him to get clean before he ate made this moment marginally less strange. Donait gestured towards the fire pit, and beyond it he saw a great basin of gleaming stone looking as if it had grown out of the floor. Surely it had not been there a moment ago! The sides of the basin were covered with spirals. Above it, curls of mist shimmered in the rich light.

Demne approached the basin warily. He had never had a *hot* bath before. He inserted a grimy finger, but it was really water. Reassured, he removed the torn remnants of the Liath Luachra's cloak from around his waist and smoothed the ruined fabric as well as he could before folding it. *She* had always kept her gear scrupulously neat and clean.

The little clasp gleamed from the top of the pile. It was made in the form of a long-snouted beast grasping its tail in its mouth. He stared at it, and suddenly saw once more the strange, scaled monster that she had become. The dragon had saved his life, but when he remembered the Liath Luachra's strong hands and sardonic words his eyes smarted with more than steam.

He unhooked his belt and pulled the slashed hide tunic over his head. It reeked, even to his nostrils. He was looking for somewhere to hide it when the woman Donait plucked it from his grasp, her eyes warm with amusement. He wanted to smile back at her, but suddenly he was acutely conscious of his bare body. He scrambled over the lip of the basin and slid into the steaming water. For a moment the heat was dizzying, and he bit back a yelp of pain. Then it began to feel wonderful.

Donait handed him a slab of some stuff that smelled of wild roses. Demne looked at it and decided it must be soap, though it was as unlike the strong-smelling substance the *bendrui* made from ash and fat every spring as Donait was unlike . . . him. He lathered it into his skin as if it were part of some ritual that Bodbmall had never revealed to him. He rubbed the slab across the sopping strands of his filthy hair, and scrubbed at his scalp until his fingers ached. He forgot everything but the task of cleansing, and only gradually began to realize that no matter how much dirt and soap he rinsed into it, the water around him remained clear. He ducked his head beneath the water and felt what seemed like a great weight dissolve away.

Renewed and refreshed, he popped his head above the water and wiped his eyes. Donait stood beside the basin, tall and serene, holding a large, rough-textured cloth.

"You bathe well, Demne."

He felt a glow in his broad chest. "Do I? I did not know you could do it poorly."

"You give it your entire attention—and that is the way to do things well. Come out now."

As he reluctantly abandoned the basin, Demne considered what she had just said. Bodbmall had pestered him continuously to heed her teachings, but she had never seemed pleased. The Liath Luachra had insisted on full attention too. Occasional grunts had approved a difficult shot or a swift run. But never had he heard that it was possible to do a simple thing well. He liked the way he felt when Donait told him so.

Donait wrapped the cloth around his body and began to rub him dry. Even through the layer of fabric he could feel each gentle movement of her hands. She was stroking the moisture from his skin, not pummeling him as Bodbmall used to do, smoothing down the long muscles of his arms, the firmness that had filled out his chest during the last weeks, the length of his spine. He twitched beneath her touch, skin pebbling with some sensation that was not cold.

Her hands moved over the tender skin of his sides and along his flanks, and Demne jerked back, suddenly afraid.

"Complete your drying while I get a comb," she told him, handing him the cloth with a faint smile.

Demne rubbed the soft cloth roughly across his skin, drying his thighs and groin. He looked around for his tunic, but it was nowhere to be seen. The woman came towards him, a bronze comb in her hand and a tunic draped over her arm. The garment was the green of new bracken, with threads of moon-silver worked at all the edges in curling spirals. Demne dropped the cloth he was holding in front of himself and pulled the garment over his damp hair. It fell nearly to his ankles in fluid folds that caressed his skin. *Like her touch*, he thought, stroking the stuff with his battered fingers, pleased and uneasy at the same time.

Donait stepped behind him and began to comb the tangles out of his long hair. Demne stood still even when it hurt, acutely aware of the warmth of her tall body behind his. The sleeves of her gown brushed his arms and shoulders with a soft, sliding sound. If he leaned back, he would feel all the firm warmth of her breasts and the softness of her belly. He held himself rigid, forcing his gaze to follow the spiral paths upon the floor.

Finally she stopped, apparently satisfied. "We will eat now."

There was a table, which had not been in the hall when he entered it, and a kind of padded bench beside it, covered with an embroidered linen cloth. Demne wondered what else would appear. The bathing basin was gone, and the floor was bone dry. Of his clothing, only the folded tatters of the cloak remained.

The brooch gleamed in the glowing light. He bent down, freed the pin, and lifted the heavy silver circle away. A small green stone glinted in the face of the creature where an eye should be. For a moment he saw his old teacher's eye wink approvingly. He stroked the curving body with his finger, then pinned it at the neck of the new green garment he wore.

"Did you care for her greatly?" the fairy woman asked quietly.

Startled, Demne looked up. What could this beautiful woman know of the old warrior?

"The Liath Luachra was my teacher. She showed me how to run, how to hunt, how to fight. And she saved my life. If *caring* is the reason my throat hurts and my eyes sting when I remember her, then it's true."

"It is good to value one's teachers as well as their lessons, however hard. Now, come. Let us sit and eat."

Donait led him to the table. There was a single flat plate on it, made of some silvery stuff that gleamed dully, the edge worked cunningly with curving swirls. He seated himself on the edge of the padded bench. Donait shook her head, laughing, and lay down on her side behind him, leaning on one arm. The pressure of her hand drew him down beside her, and Demne remembered that Bodbmall had once told him that chieftains ate this way. Once more he felt the warmth of her body through the cloth of his robe.

A round loaf appeared on the plate, warm and honey-scented, and she broke it in two and handed Demne a portion. He accepted it uncertainly, even though his mouth watered at the smell and sight of it. Used to porridge or boiled game served in rough wooden bowls, it seemed strange to eat from such a thing. He took a bite of bread as a gleaming apple shimmered into existence on the dish, then saw a goblet slowly forming beside the plate.

Demne looked over at Donait. She chewed her bread serenely, so he ate some of his. It was marvelously filling, and the flavor of it was sweet. He could not eat very much of it, which puzzled him. He peeked at Donait once more, worried that he might offend her if he did not eat all that she had given him.

She swallowed what was in her mouth, and took the goblet, sipping daintily. Then she offered it to him, and as he reached out, his fingers brushed hers. He drank a little and realized he had placed his mouth where hers had been. The taste of her lips was still on the rim, and the sweetness of it woke the wordless yearning within him once more. He felt a warmth color his cheeks, and turned his eyes away from her calm smile. There was barely a hand span between their bodies. But if he tried to move away he would fall onto the spiral floor.

He set the goblet down carefully. Suddenly he was hungry again, and he tore off another mouthful of bread. But the loaf's softness reminded him of the softness of the breasts of the woman beside him. . . . He thrust the thought away.

Instead, he concentrated on thoughts of the old *bendrui*. Even if she had found the message that the Liath Luachra had left for her, she would be frantic with anxiety by now. How long had it been since he had slain Bran mac Conail? Why had he not heeded her and kept away from the rath? Donait placed her left hand over his right one, and he realized that he was gripping the table painfully.

"Demne, there is no need to sorrow here."

"I never do anything right," he replied bitterly.

The woman laughed, and the sound lifted his spirits like the first burst of bird song after a storm. She reached out and patted his face tenderly. "You do many things very well. True, you did not obey your foster mother, but you could not remain a child forever. You made an error, but the first error was not yours. The *bendrui* wished you to fulfill her dream as if you had no destiny of your own. 'Tis a common mistake, one that even the gods have made at times."

By now, Demne no longer wondered how Donait knew. Someone who could make tables appear out of the air could probably find out almost anything, including the one thing that he had wondered for so long.

"Do you know who my father is?" he asked.

"I do."

"Tell me about him."

Donait thought for a moment and began to slice the apple with a little silver knife. "He was very brave . . . and very headstrong. Such men make enemies, and he did that very well too. It was to protect you from those enemies that Bodbmall has kept you so long in ignorance."

Demne frowned. "What has that to do with me?"

"Your father's foes would injure you if they knew you lived."

"But *I* have never harmed them. . . ."

"It is the way of mortals to carry their enmities from generation to generation. They owe you the price of his blood, and so they are afraid."

Demne remembered some of the songs the Liath Luachra had chanted and knew it was true. "Tell me his name then—my father's name."

"It is forbidden to me to reveal it. Eat some of the apple." She held a slice out to him.

Demne hunched his shoulders angrily. "You are no better than old Bodbmall, telling me to eat my food and be still! I am sick of secrets." He glared at her.

"Yet you have kept your own. . . ." she said quietly. "You did not tell your foster mothers of your visit to the rath."

But if the old women had given him answers, he might not have been so desperate for a friend. And when the boys asked him the question that started all the trouble, he would have known what to say. It was not the same! Unable to say so, Demne sank his teeth into the slice of apple. For a moment, all his senses focused on the sharp, sweet flavor. Then his tongue began to tremble.

A nameless sound swelled in the back of his throat: words, images, struggled for form within him. He was the tree just before it falls, the cloud just before it releases its rain. But no words came. The Liath Luachra had taught him how to use the strength of his body. Who could teach him to release the splendor that swelled in his throat and beat against the barrier of his breast?

Frustration brought quick tears to his eyes. Then he swallowed, and felt the flood subside. But it did not vanish. He could sense it within him, a new part of his being, and one that would not settle into his bones for a long time. Had the magic been in the apple, or had the apple only now awakened it, as the horn of the hunter startled sleeping swans from the reeds?

He was afraid to eat more—he would burst with another mouthful of eloquence. He put the apple down and fought to remember what they had been saying before.

"Is it forbidden to say who my companion is? I heard the music again as I came across the grass."

"That music is your sister's song."

"A sister!" Demne laughed with joy. He was not alone; he had a family. "Where is she? Who is she?" The questions burst out, his voice rising. He trembled all over.

"She is your twin, Demne, and one day you will see her. She loves you very much, and she watches over you as a faithful dog guards its master. That is all I can tell you now."

"I do not believe you!" Abruptly, Demne's anger returned. "All this is yours—you can make food and drink appear from the empty air! Who can tell you what to do?"

Donait shook her head slowly, the unbound hair along her back rippling like wheat in the breeze. "Someone who is more powerful than you can even imagine. And you are her servant as well, for you have eaten her flesh and taken her into your heart and spirit. You know her, feel her, and even love her. But it will take many years before you begin to understand her."

Demne scowled. "And her name is another secret, I suppose?"

The fairy woman chuckled deep in her throat and hugged him against her, passing her fingers through his silky hair.

"Poor, angry Demne. I know it is difficult being who you are. . . . The name is not a secret. Men call my mistress Brigid. 'Tis as good a name as any other." She stroked his hair until he was weak from the touch of her hand. "She is the fire, Demne."

"The fire?" His voice squeaked like a fox kit's. Her fingers were the flame, laying a halo of heat upon his hair.

"Look!"

Donait touched the nape of his neck, and he found himself forced to gaze into the fire pit that blazed radiance without visible fuel. For a time he saw nothing but the leaping flames, dazzling and dizzying in a thousand rainbow hues, and then a figure emerged from within. For a moment, he thought it was the woman beside him, for this one had the same golden hair. Then he saw that the face was not like Donait's at all, for it was much older.

But how could She be old? Demne felt his mind scrabble like a hind on loose shale as he looked again.

This woman was a girl, a maiden. Bodbmall must once have looked this way, and the Liath Luachra. Now he recognized the vitality he had seen sometimes in their eyes, and the comparison between this beauty and their age disturbed him. The image flickered in the flames, and he felt the power that pulsed from the woman who floated above the fire. This mix of majesty and mystery must be what called the old *bendrui* to his mind.

The hem of her gown fluttered above the flames and seemed to flow into the spirals upon the floor of the hall. They were pathways, though he could not guess where they led. Each path sparkled with a different color. And each of them beckoned him.

Demne felt his heart leap as he looked at a pathway the color of burnished bronze that turned to gold as it went on. It was nearly straight, but he *knew* that it did not lead to content. He looked up into the face of the Goddess and sensed there was something important to be learned from the shape and even the color of the way. Bodbmall had droned on about such matters, and he had been impatient, but now he closed his eyes and tried to bring back the lessons. Why hadn't he paid more attention! He heard the voice of the *bendrui* in his mind. "*Things are not always what they seem, Demne.*"

When he looked back again, the path had grown red, twisted and bristling with spear points. Big men danced between the barbs, their faces contorting with ancient angers. Their hair was like old copper, and their skins were ruddy as well. Someday he would meet them, but he knew already that they were his foes.

Demne turned his gaze to a green spiral that curled away from the Brigid's skirts in another arc. Somehow he recognized it as the path of wisdom upon which Bodbmall had already set his reluctant feet. He had never guessed that it contained so much power. But he saw now that it was perilous. As his eye followed its windings, he saw an imperious figure standing upon a high hill, peering outward. The man on the hill turned and looked towards him, and Demne cringed against Donait's soft breast, knowing him for a foe more formidable than any of the ruddy warriors. Why had Bodbmall wished to set his feet upon that way, and who was this fierce, proud old man who glared at him so?

He looked into the lambent countenance of the Goddess, and found only a calm patience that could wait for years. She seemed neither pleased nor disappointed, and he, who had risked his life for a piglet and a word of praise, felt the old sorrow shake him again. Then, aware of the warmth of Donait's body against his, he drew himself away and studied the final spiral that wound away from the rippling of the Lady's gown.

It was blue, and so convoluted that he could barely distinguish one curve from the next, paling into silver where it disappeared. If the way of wisdom was full of traps and pitfalls, the blue path was beset with madness. Demne shuddered, for he also sensed that all the knowledge he longed for was somehow contained within this blaze of blue. It looked like a river, and indeed there seemed to be a man fishing in it, intent and serious. He felt from the man both kinship and a sense of danger that made the soft hair at the bottom of his scalp bristle.

Brigid was fading back into the glowing fire, and he felt a sharp pang of loss.

Stay! his heart cried. *Tell me*—But already the colored paths had vanished, and now the floor of the hall was only white and grey stone. He felt Donait's hand leave his nape as hot tears welled out of his eyes.

Demne sniffed noisily. He felt very small and very lost, and he wished that he had never let his curiosity draw him down the mountain. If he had never played with the boys, he would not have slain his friend Bran, nor had to carry the Liath Luachra to her monstrous immortality. But he knew now that he would have ventured away from Bodbmall soon, no matter what the consequences.

"What did it all mean?" he cried.

Demne heard Donait's soft sigh. "I think you know what it meant, Demne."

"Why have I so many foes? I do not even know those men."

"Those are the enemies of your father, and they would seek to kill you if they knew you lived. The old man you saw, the *drui*, suspects, but for all his art he does not know." She sounded faintly amused. "Your foster mother has frustrated him since you were born."

"Bodbmall has frustrated me too," he snapped.

"She is a most maddening woman, but she has had your best interests always foremost, Demne. She has loved you since the day of your birth. But she is old, frail, and human."

"The Liath Luachra said that she wished to keep me a child."

"Certainly she was tempted to try. That is her battle, Demne. It has not been easy for her to let you go your own way. Try to understand even though you are angry now."

"If you love someone, you cannot hold them."

"That is wisdom beyond your years—and I hope you will recall it when you love in turn."

"Will I ever do anything correctly?"

"Ah, Demne. You will do many things well, as well as you bathed, but the outcome will not always be happy."

Demne squared his jaw. "If you do something right, then it should be good!"

Donait was silent for a time. "How many colors of green do you see in the roof?" she asked at last.

He looked up and studied the wonderful traceries overhead. "I cannot count that many," he answered.

"Which greens are not good?"

"What?" He mulled her question over. "Each one is right for the tree. All of them are good."

"So, the hazel leaf is right on its tree, but does not belong upon the willow. People are not like trees. They are like whole forests—like my hall—many leaved and hued. And sometimes people put out the correct leaves at the wrong time, and that is not good. But it is not bad either."

"You confuse me even more than Bodbmall."

"You are weary. Come—we will sleep, and you will see more clearly in the morning."

It was as light in the hall as if no time had passed while he bathed and ate and saw. Once, in an expansive moment, Bodbmall had told him that time within the mounds of the fairy folk was different from time in the world. Perhaps night never came here. Demne remembered the cool night and the sickle moon of the forest with a pang, longing suddenly to see the silver light upon the birch trees.

Demne found his eyes itching with weariness, and he half staggered as he stood. The table and its contents faded into the air, but he was too tired for wonder. He simply followed Donait towards the far end of the hall, where stood an enormous wooden structure like nothing he had ever seen. It was flat, like a table, but covered with layers of soft material. One end curved up as high as Donait's head, and the other was lower, but curved as well. He could not decide if the thing had been made or grown, for where it appeared carved there was no mark of any tool.

Donait pulled aside the heavy woven stuff and revealed smooth cloth, as white as the moon. "It is a bed, Demne," she said, smiling at his wonder.

Demne had slept on a woven reed pallet beneath a worn and patched blanket of ancient wool for as long as he could remember. Each spring Bodbmall gathered fresh reeds and made new pallets for each of them. Demne had learned to help her to gather, dry, and weave. The bed before him was beyond his experience, and if he had not been so weary, he would have wanted to examine it more closely. But Donait was waiting.

He pulled off his gown and saw that a bench had appeared on which he could lay it. He climbed into the structure and felt it yield softly to his weight. Demne stretched out and sank into softness. Against his bare skin the silky smoothness of the cloth was almost as intoxicating as the cool water of the stream. He felt his muscles loosen. Then Donait slid into the bed beside him and drew the embroidered covers across them both.

Demne shrank away. He could not remember ever sleeping with another person, although the Liath Luachra and Bodbmall always laid out their pallets side by side and shared their blankets. The nearness of this tall, beautiful woman disturbed him, although he could not say precisely why. She was not threatening like the ruddy men on the red path or the crowd that had pursued him from the rath. He knew there was nothing to fear, but still he kept a forearm's span between them.

He looked up at the leafy roof, following the intricate traceries with aching eyes until the regular rise and fall of breath told him his companion slept. Only then did Demne allow his lids to close and his body to ease entirely into the enveloping softness beneath him. But despite his exhaustion, sleep still eluded him.

The bed was too soft. He could sink into it and drown. The clean scent of the sheets and covers and the sweetness of Donait beside him bothered him too. He longed for the hardness of his pallet, the smell of the warm earth beneath it, the tang of a wood fire, and the familiar scents of Bodbmall and the Liath Luachra. He hoped the *bendrui* was safe. No matter how she frustrated him, he could not bear the idea that the men of the rath might have hurt her.

He tried to visualize what she would have done when she returned to the huts to find them gone. And then it seemed to him that he was there too, but he was a little boy once more. He called to her, and she smiled and held out her arms to him as she used to when he was small. But as she bent down he saw that it was Brigid Herself who was opening Her arms to him. *Are you my mother?* his heart asked. He rolled over. His fair head pillowed itself against soft breasts, and the steady beat of a heart beneath his ear soothed him as the woman drew him closer. His mouth found a nipple and closed around it. Held securely in that soft embrace, Demne suckled like a babe.

He dreamed that the long, strong hands of the Goddess caressed his face, calling him to some surrender he could not understand. Then the hands ceased their touch and held instead an object—a square, flat board, beautifully fashioned, bearing little figures that begged to be touched. Despite a fear that he was doing some forbidden thing, Demne reached out to put a finger on one of the figures. It felt alive against his skin.

What is it?

This is fidchel, *Demne, the game of war. See the king pieces, and the spearmen and the warriors. Each king is in the hands of his foe, and the purpose is to*

*rescue him. It is a simple game that defies ease. You
will play the white pieces first.*

Why?

That you may learn.

It seemed to him that he now sat at a table, and that
Donait sat across from him, not the Goddess. Without
quite knowing why, he moved one of the spearmen
forward. She gave a little nod, and made a move of
her own. He felt his brow furl, and a light sweat
began to dampen it. There were patterns to be seen,
opportunities and chances to be had. He forgot the
lovely creature whose hand moved the dark pieces,
forgot everything but seeking the patterns that would
free his king piece from its captivity.

The pieces moved very quickly after a time, as if
indeed they were alive, and it seemed the board
returned to its original setting more than once, and
each time he had not brought his king to safety. Demne
concentrated deeply, breathing until his lungs ached,
and somehow at last rescued the precious piece that
had become the most important thing in the world to
him. He heard a warm chuckle and felt soft hands
caress his damp cheeks.

Demne glanced up, and it was not Donait who
stroked his skin, but shining Brigid. There was nothing in her eyes but warmth, no hint of danger, but still
he felt threatened. *You have learned well, Demne. I am
pleased.*

He felt caught between the pleasure of praise and
the odd terror that he might drown in the depths of
her blue eyes. *Good. I am weary. Can I rest now?*

A finger traced the line of his cheek, then drew
away. *Rest, child, and sleep. I shall ask no more of you
at present.* He pulled away from her, felt the softness
of the bed beneath his muscles, and made himself into
a tight ball. He thought of Bodbmall now, longing
for her sharp tongue and ready hand. The *bendrui*'s

seamed face swam before him. Demne reached out and clutched at her wrinkled hands, seeking the safety his foster mother had always provided. Then he gave a little sigh and passed into dreamlessness.

WAKING WAS SLOW AND BEWILDERING. DEMNE SAW THE branches overhead, and he thought he was in the forest. He felt the soft cloth over his body, and for a long, slow moment he could not imagine what it was. Then everything came back in a flood of smells and tastes and colors and sounds. He turned over quickly, but he was alone in the bed. He wondered why that should relieve him so.

Demne sat up and looked down the hall. The fire pit glowed, and he remembered how the glorious figure of Brigid had risen out of it. Of the basin he had bathed in and the table he had eaten at there was no trace. The building seemed quite deserted. The only sound was the flutter of the fire and the slight rustle of leaves in the roof above his head. He pushed the covers aside and climbed out of the high bed.

Donait came through the doorway of the hall, humming softly, and he grabbed for his gown. She looked at him. "Did you sleep well?"

"Well enough."

Demne remembered wisps of disturbing dreams, but he said nothing of them. He shifted restlessly from foot to foot, tensing in response to her grace as he had before. Was it because she was still treating him like a child? Donait smiled, and her beauty made him forget his fear.

"Good. Come here and we will eat."

The table reappeared, but with two stools instead of a single couch, and Demne sat across from the fairy woman over a breakfast of ripe berries, soft bread, and foaming milk in carved wood cups. It was simple food, but he found himself replete with mere mouthfuls. The milk was warm and fresh, rich tasting, and the berries brimmed with both sweetness and a tang that lingered on his tongue. He wondered how he would ever again eat the food of men with any pleasure. The board vanished as soon as he was done, and Donait stood up.

"Now it is time to do something about that hair of yours." She seemed somehow gayer than she had the night before.

"My hair!" He stared at her. She had already gotten it clean.

"It is too shaggy. You look more a beast than a man."

Demne recalled crawling around on all fours and shuddered suddenly. "Perhaps I am a beast. Certainly I am not yet a man."

"You are closer than you know to manhood. Still, it is time for your hair to be plaited, and for you to step out of the women's domain."

Donait plucked a comb and a strange implement out of the air, and walked behind him. She pulled the snarls of his restless sleep out of the pale locks, and then began to snip the ends of his long hair. Demne submitted to her ministrations meekly as he recalled the many braids that old Fiacail had worn. He wondered if braids were the mark of a fighting man, for his pursuers from the rath had not worn their hair as the old warrior had. He began to have a warm feeling in his belly. Demne felt different this morning—special, and more—cared for. A hurt, a loss he could not give name to, was eased and healed. He gave a small sigh of content as she completed the task.

"You are very kind to me, and I thank you," he said. Then he remembered what had happened to Bran mac Conail. What if he did something terrible to Donait? He felt her hand rest on his shoulder for a moment, warm and reassuring. His neck itched where a bit of hair had stuck to it, but beneath her touch, calmness seemed to pour into him.

"Now we must garb you appropriately." She sounded pleased. "First a shirt and tunic. Green, I believe, will be best. The green of oak leaves." She chuckled over some secret jest. "And brogues as well. I would prefer to give you blue, but green is more suitable for now."

"Why does the color matter?"

Donait mused beside him, touching her full lip with a long finger. Watching the movement of the tip of her finger across the rosy skin made Demne tingle most peculiarly. "Color reveals a man's calling," she answered slowly. "You will understand soon."

The garments she had named dropped into his lap, one by one, except for the shoes which fell out of the air and onto the spiraled floor without a sound. Demne looked at the pile of fabric, then shook the pieces out. The undertunic was plain linen, bleached to the color of milk, and the wool overgarment was woven in as many shades of green as the leaves of Donait's hall and embroidered in tan at the edges of the sleeves and the hem. There were breeches as well, dyed a deep brown. The garments were like those Fiacail had worn, subtly distinct from those of the men of the rath or the boys with whom he had played.

Demne unpinned the brooch of the Liath Luachra from the long gown he still wore. Then he stood and pulled it off over his head, brushed off the cut hairs that still stuck to his shoulders and neck, and slowly put on the new clothes. He felt as if he were becoming another person, one he did not know. All that remained of his former self was the worn belt with its leather pouch and the pin. He opened the pouch and looked inside. The curved tooth of the sow still lay there. He dropped the pin in beside it and pulled the belt around his waist. Then he moved back and forth, feeling the touch of leather against his callused feet.

"You must leave me now, Demne."

He turned, startled. It made him feel oddly ill to see her serenity marred by distress. On impulse, he pressed a light kiss against her cheek. The apple-blossom scent of her breasts was almost overwhelming, and he had a hazy memory of his fair head pillowed against them. He ached to stay, held close by her soft arms, and he twitched with the need to get away. He whimpered then and let her go.

"Will I ever see you again?"

Donait sighed. "When you have the wisdom, you will return to me for a time. But it will never be as sweet as this first meeting has been."

A single tear glistened on her cheek, and he brushed it away. It burned, so he brought the finger to his mouth. He tasted the salt of her sorrow as he had tasted the sweetness of her mouth upon the goblet the night before. For a moment his whole body burned, and he knew he would never forget the taste of her tears.

FROM THE RIM OF THE HILL DEMNE LOOKED AT Donait's house with its spiraled floor and branching eaves. The entrance was empty, and he struggled with the desire to run back to its peace. But he had to find Bodbmall and tell her what had happened. If he found her alive, he thought he could bear her scolding.

Demne squared his shoulders and strode down the hill. The cloth of the tunic Donait had given him was strange against his skin. He felt lighter, as if during the night his flesh and bones had become more like *hers*. Was it because he had eaten her food and drunk her wine? His callused feet felt trapped in the caressing brogues. Suddenly he wanted to tear away the fine garments and become the rough and familiar person he had been before. When he returned to the world, would it be the same?

He would find out soon, he thought, for the chasm yawned before him. Some great force of water seemed to have rushed through it, ripping away rocks and leaving slick mud behind. He frowned, for during the night he had heard nothing, and gave a quick look behind him. Donait's house had disappeared. He had no choice but to leap the chasm now.

Demne brushed his hand across his eyes as if the distracting thoughts could be flicked away like the gnats that teased him when he stalked ducks in the reeds. He retreated several lengths up the hill, remembering how the Liath Luachra had taught him to clear his awareness of all but the leap before him. Then he heard a trill of laughter behind him.

He whirled, and for one flickering moment glimpsed a slender girl with hair of brilliant red and eyes pale as moonlight. His heart leaped—Donait had spoken truly. This must be the invisible sister who had run with him and laughed at him, so many times before. Now she was challenging him. Demne reached out in a gesture half wave, half embrace, and began to run. He heard the patter of feet beside him and a slender hand pressed into his.

For a moment they raced side by side. Then her fingers slipped from his grasp. Suddenly the abyss was before him and he was jumping, warm sweet-scented air streaming against his skin as the force of his motion carried him over the gulf. For a moment he understood what the bird feels, flying, then the earth came up to meet him and he tumbled head over heels into a tangle of bracken.

When the world stopped spinning, Demne sat up, staring. Had all these ferns been here yesterday? He scanned the ground, but could find no trace of his battle with the men of the rath. Puzzled, he looked back across the chasm, but instead of the gleaming greensward that led to the fairy hall, there was only a rise covered with bracken like the slope where he had landed. And the chasm over which he had leaped was only a crease in the ground.

Demne flushed with a familiar outrage. He had been cheated again! But the embroidered tunic he was wearing had not turned to dry leaves, and Donait's scent still clung to the fine wool. Perhaps he could believe her promises after all. He got to his feet and stilled, staring. The leaves of the beech trees were fading to a pale gold, and ripening nuts hung in heavy clusters from the boughs. Surely it had been high summer the day before. His heart began to beat heavily as he remembered the other things he had heard about the Sidhe. How long had he been gone?

The season might be uncanny, but at least the contours of the land had not changed. Demne took a deep breath and began to run.

He did not pause until he glimpsed the lightning-riven oak tree that shaded their campsite. He had not been gone for centuries, then, but would the huts that were the only home he had ever known still be there? His steps slowed as he made his way down the path.

At last he stepped into the clearing and stood, staring. A fire burned beneath Bodbmall's cauldron and the smell of porridge cooked with onions and apples filled the air. The huts looked ragged, as if no one had repaired them after the winter's storms, but otherwise everything looked as if no time had passed at all.

"Bodbmall!" he called, heart hammering.

The hide that covered the door to the largest hut quivered and the old woman pushed past it, peering around her. She seemed more bent than he recalled, smaller and more frail. A trickle of fresh terror slid

down Demne's spine. Perhaps she could not see him.
He had heard that folk killed suddenly did not know
it. Perhaps his pursuers had slain him and this was
all a ghostly dream.

Then she swung around, blue eyes widening.
Demne's throat closed. Wordless, he could only run
towards her and hold her to his heaving chest as she
muttered his name. The old woman's skin was cool
beneath his palms, her bones fragile as a bird's, but
her grip on his arms was painful. She smelled of herbs
and wood smoke and age. She smelled of home. He
looked down at the top of her silvered head, wondering how she could have shrunk a hand's width in the
time he wandered as a beast and slept in Donait's bed.
The huts seemed smaller too. That was as disturbing
as the old woman's sudden affection.

Abruptly it came to him that he himself must have
gotten larger. That was why his body had felt so
strange.

Then Bodbmall thrust him away, sniffed, and gave
him a resounding box on the ear.

"And where have you been, wretched one, when I
have been mourning you for a year and a day and a
whole moon more?"

Chapter 7

"AGAINST MY WISHES AND MY JUDGMENT, I WILL take you into the world, but you will be sorry. . . ."

Bodbmall's words echoed in his memory as Demne turned to look back the way they had come. Beneath the low-hanging clouds that had drenched them several times already and looked ready to do so again, the slopes of Sliab Bladhma and the forest of Gaible were a dim haze on the horizon. Now they were moving northward through a gentle landscape beside a clear-flowing stream that the *bendrui* had told him was the beginnings of the Boann; and despite the amazing collection of things that she had ordered him to carry, his heart lifted with every breath of damp air. They were going to the Tailten Fair!

Before she would start, Bodbmall had made him put away the fine garments with which Donait had clad him, and given him some ancient clothes of the Liath Luachra to wear. He had not dared to refuse them, knowing how she grieved because the other woman was gone. The clothes smelled of old sweat and age; the tunic was too narrow for his broad shoulders, and the leggings, which did not even reach his ankles, were nearly threadbare between the thighs. She had

113

taken away the beautiful brogues, too, and made him go unshod. But Bodbmall herself was resplendent in a gown of embroidered white linen with a mantle checkered with all the colors to which her rank entitled her. When he had protested, she snapped that she knew best, and he had been afraid to provoke her into changing her decision.

The trail beside the river had become a road, and as they trudged onward, it began to fill with folk headed in the same direction. There were old men with carts drawn by goats and women with bundles almost as big as his own. Young men drove lowing cattle before them, and young women walked in chattering groups, the twirling spindles swinging up and down, up and down from their hands as the woolen yarn spun out from between agile fingers and was caught up again. When folk saw Bodbmall's cloak and staff they signed their respect and cleared the way. Demne stuck close to the *bendrui's* heels, watching the people as avidly as once he had watched the birds in the forest, and said not a word.

The third night out they camped beneath a cluster of oak trees. Bodbmall had gotten chilled in the afternoon rain and she was coughing. Demne did not like the sound. Their companions on the road had settled farther down the hill. As if in mockery of the old woman's wheezing he heard a girl's sweet song.

> "*Cattle herd down from the heights,*
> *Harvest bright corn growing,*
> *Berries bring from bush and vine*
> *Where the kine are lowing.*
> *Tailten Fair, Tailten Fair—*
> *'Tis there my love is going!*"

"What folk will be at the fair?" He asked Bodbmall. "Will I see the high king?"

"Did you expect he would meet you at the gate and welcome you? The *Ard Ri* has better things to do than talk to stubborn boys," the *bendrui* muttered, huddling closer to their little fire.

"And what about you?" he asked, suddenly angry. "Will you keep me an ignorant child even now by refusing to tell me what I want to know?"

"In ignorance you are safe."

Demne stared at her. "Then why did you school me in the ways of wisdom? That is not the way of a wisewoman, but of a fool!"

"I wanted to protect you," she muttered, and her gaze fell before his accusing glare.

Demne sighed. "Protect me or hobble me, old one?"

"I never meant to harm you, Demne," she whispered. "I only wished to spare you your father's fate. You are so much like him it makes my blood go cold. A man to charm the birds out of their nests when he wanted something, he was. Wanting things cost him his life. Eriu does not need your blood to feed her soil. Demne, child, ask me no more!"

Who was my father? his heart screamed, remembering the men who had waited for him upon the crimson path. *What did my father want that killed him?* But even now, he did not dare to ask that. Nor could he ask the next question that came to him: *What do I want in this world?* In the silence, he could hear the song once more.

> *"The noble horses challenge call*
> *To all before the racing;*
> *Bold youths in bands are gathered here,*
> *With spears their targets facing*
> *Tailten Fair, Tailten Fair—*
> *'Tis there we'll be embracing!"*

"You are so stubborn!" muttered the old woman, rocking back and forth on her heels. Demne felt his anger seeping from him like water from a cracked pot.

"No more so than you," he replied, but there was no force in it.

"I know what is best for you!" she said then.

"Do you? Does anyone truly know what is best for another? That would be a wonder—"

"That woman has ruined you!" Bodbmall exclaimed, and laughed as Demne sat upright, staring. "Did you think I did not know where you had been, when I searched for you in spirit and your name had gone out of the world? Do you think I would not recognize the handiwork of the Sidhe in the garments in which you returned to me, and that I would not smell the scent of another woman in those fine clothes?"

"She was kind to me," he muttered resentfully, wishing once more that he had words for the splendor he had experienced. At first, he had assumed that Bodbmall had known all about his adventures in the Otherworld and was simply refusing to discuss them. And then he had thought that perhaps she did not, and determined to keep his secret. Now, all he wanted to do was to preserve the secret of Donait's name. Bodbmall snorted scornfully and then began to cough.

"And what price did you pay for that kindness?" she said when she could speak again. "The Sidhe give no free gifts to the children of men!"

"And do the Wise?" he snapped back, though his thoughts were in turmoil. Donait had not tried to keep him a child, but he was no closer to knowing why she had befriended him now than he had been when he sat in her hall. "Old woman, I honor you for your care of me, but I will not be shaped to your devices. What use did you hope to make of me?"

Bodbmall closed her eyes, then drew dignity like a

mantle around her and caught his gaze with a fierce possessiveness that chilled his blood.

"You were a gift to me!" she hissed. "From the moment I took you into my arms, squalling defiance at the world, I knew you had the Power; you were the one I had prayed for!"

"Old one!" he exclaimed. "I do not belong to you!"

From the distance came a mutter of thunder. A damp wind sent droplets spattering across them as it shook the branches of the trees.

> *"Milk and honey on the height,*
> *Bright season without sorrow,*
> *Fair the harvest; feast we here*
> *Nor future fear shall borrow.*
> *Tailten Fair, Tailten Fair—*
> *'Tis there we'll meet tomorrow!"*

Once more the song drifted up through the darkness. As the wind stirred the coals to life Demne saw that Bodbmall was weeping, and felt the first touch of fear, but even then he could not express the conflicting emotions that struggled in his throat.

ON THE FIFTH DAY, DEMNE SAW A LONG GREEN HILL rising on their right, its steep sides bright with the golden flowers of the broom. The summit was surrounded by an earthen wall crowned by a palisade. Above it rose the smokes of many cook fires, and the conical tips of house roofs whose thatch had been dyed in patterns like the *bendrui*'s mantle.

"It is Temair of Brega, the queen of the fortresses of Eriu," said Bodbmall, taking pity on his wonder, "where the *Ard Ri* dwells."

"Temair? Where the *fianna* abide during the winter?" he said without considering his words. "I thought it must be Tailtiu!"

A gnarled hand smacked his ears. "What do you know of the *fianna*? How dare you—"

She sputtered to a startled halt as Demne grasped her fragile wrist in one strong brown hand and refused to let her strike him again. "The Liath Luachra told me a little of them, because I asked and because she loved me, in her way."

"Loved you! Hah! She never would understand that you belong to the way of wisdom, and that nothing, nothing can be allowed to lead you astray. The *fianna*! A bunch of bloodthirsty fools, puffed up with pride and vainglory! How dare she speak of what I had expressly forbidden?" The last words were spoken sadly, as if they hurt.

Demne hardly noticed, intent on learning more about the warrior band. "She told me that the *fianna* defended Eriu from its foes."

Bodbmall sniffed. "They do, when they are not killing one another for no reason whatever. Put out of your mind any thought of joining their numbers— you are not fit, and I would not permit it. I have lost too much."

"Lost?"

"Do you think you are the first child I have fostered, Demne?" she asked with a shaky laugh. "I have had many, including your father and the high king himself, and I have seen too many of them feed their blood to the Morrigan. The way of the battle goddess is not for you, my child."

Demne frowned fiercely. "I do not think you have the power to choose for me, Bodbmall. But, let us not dispute." He could not bear the thought of her hints that never led to any learning, just more secrets. As much as he longed to know the tale of his father, he could wait. "If this is not Tailtiu, then how does that place differ from this one?"

"Tailtiu is not a fortress. It is the crossroads of Eriu,

the center of sovereignty. Tailte herself, who was the foster mother of Lugh, cleared the Wood of Cuan and made her home on the plain. Lugh was a good son"— she cast him a quick glance—"and when she died, he buried her where she wished to be, and established in her honor the festival and the games."

Demne felt his lips twitch, appreciating the emphasis. Bodbmall seemed calmer now, and he felt pleased that he had played the peacemaker. He also savored the resentment at her reminder of the duties of a good fosterling, and felt safe enough to tease her a little.

"When you die, old one, what competitions shall I hold on your grave? The thorn-bush race or the water-carrier's walk?"

Bodbmall gave a bark of amusement. "You are a pert lad, and you had best keep your tongue between your teeth when we get to the fair or others will make you bite it."

He shrugged, then grabbed wildly as the bundle began to come undone. From behind him came a rattle of wooden wheels and the rapid hoofbeats of a chariot pony. Demne leaped out of the way, cursing, and went down in a clatter of pallets, blankets, pots, bowls, and bundles of herbs. As he dusted himself off and began to strap the bags up again, he heard an odd, repeated rasp and wheeze from the *bendrui*, and realized that Bodbmall was laughing.

THE DIN OF THE TAILTEN FAIR WAS INCREDIBLE.

Demne, still staggering beneath the heavy pack, thought he had never heard so many human voices. They argued, sang, bargained, and gossiped all around him. His head rang with the noise as he picked his way carefully across the sodden turf, wondering once more how they were ever going to use all the things the *bendrui* had insisted they bring. He hunched his shoulders and managed not to grind his teeth in frustration. When he had agreed to wear these rags he had not realized that he would enter Tailtiu looking like a slave.

Tents and bothies of woven branches filled the ground in the loop of the river. The feet of so many had trodden the moist earth into mire. Demne was only grateful that at last the heavens were clearing, for the old woman was still coughing. Torn between his nagging concern for her and the clamor of more voices than he had thought existed, he felt surprisingly weary. Where did they all come from, and how could they bear to be all crammed together this way?

Battered by sound, Demne began to be sorry he had ever left the mountain. Besides the endless chattering of the people, he could hear the yapping of dogs and, beneath that, the endless lowing of vast numbers of cows. That deep music had caught his quick ears even before he heard the sound of the crowd. Until they came out from the trees and he saw the moving brown carpet of the herds he had wondered what terrible beast could make such a sound. As they trudged through the pastures to the central enclosure, the cattle looked back at him with soft, stupid eyes, and he was glad he had not voiced his fear. Then they came to a pen where they were holding a bull, an enormous animal that snorted from reddened nostrils and stamped its hooves. It had curving horns as wicked as the tusks of any boar, and its eyes gleamed with a malevolent cunning. Demne realized then that there was nothing shameful in being afraid.

Bodbmall led him towards a new wall of hazel boughs, interlaced and plastered with mud and dung. At the opening in the wall a man stood, tall and leather-shirted, holding a heavy spear. He thrust the weapon across to bar the old woman's way.

"And where do you think you are going?" the fellow asked.

"We go to the Women's House," Bodbmall snapped, her breath wheezing and her voice reedy with impatience. "And who are you to question me?"

"I am a warrior of the royal *fian*, placed here to keep out persons of low blood or poor character." He was a big, fair fellow with his lime-bleached hair done up in a multitude of braids, and as he drew breath, his chest swelled like a cock's on a dunghill. Demne wanted to smash the smug face, but was curious at this first glimpse of one of the *fianna*. He found he was not impressed. And to speak to Bodbmall in such a bold manner! Even the Liath Luachra had never done that.

"I am Bodbmall the *bendrui*, and I was rich in the ways of wisdom when you were still in swaddling strings. Get out of my path."

The guard flinched, then he gave a quick glance around him to see if anyone else had seen and drew himself up again. "So you say. You, perhaps, may go to the Women's House. But your boy is a little too old for that, don't you think?"

"I shall enjoy informing the *Ard Ri* how his *fennid* behave under the leadership of Goll mac Morna," she hissed dangerously.

The guard laughed in her face. "*Bendrui* you may be, but I disbelieve you have the ear of the king."

"Do you indeed? Then the land is lost indeed when a man no longer listens to the woman by whom he was fostered," she answered.

Demne stared as the guard turned a most interesting shade of grey beneath his ruddy skin.

"So you say," the guard began to bluster once more, "but whose kindred is your slave?"

"I am an old woman. He is arms and legs for me," Bodbmall snarled, then broke into a fit of coughing that threatened to unfoot her. "He is no concern of yours!"

Demne turned red to the roots of his pale, tousled hair, fighting the impulse to toss his burden of goods onto the mucky ground and stalk away. She made him sound like an ox, and she ordered him around as if he were indeed only a beast with no will of its own. But when she staggered he reached out a large hand to steady her, and pity stabbed him as he felt the fragile bones beneath the skin.

The guard lifted his dark brows, shrugged, swung his spear aside, and waved them into the enclosure, gazing about for fresh victims. Demne cast him a glance of loathing as he helped Bodbmall across the larger puddles towards one of the buildings.

Within the enclosure it was, if anything, noisier than outside. Demne felt battered by the ceaseless murmur of voices, yapping dogs, and howling babes. He could hardly distinguish the constant song of earth beneath it, and felt as if one of his senses had disappeared. As he helped his foster mother ease among the many moving bodies, he wondered how the earth could bear the gathering of so many without injury.

Puffing as he strove to keep his load balanced in the throng, he said, "This is a great crowd, surely. How can they stand —"

Bodbmall gave a snort of what might have been amusement. "A crowd? Why, boy, this is nothing." She gestured at the standards fixed in the ground before a round house set on a raised mound. "The high king has not yet arrived, and several of the greater clans are absent as well. This is hardly half of those who will come to the games and the rites of Tailtiu."

Demne tried to imagine this, and found it daunting. Then he was distracted by the sight of a horseman who was reining his beast through the crowd. The horse was a wonder, but the boy's attention was fixed by the man. He knew those sharp features and foxy hair, neatly braided back from sharp, high cheekbones. Demne had seen this man bearing a spear upon the red-hued way that wound from the skirts of the Lady. He was an enemy. Demne stopped short, fingers curving into claws. He could pull the man off his splendid mount, crush him into the mud—

A twisted hand caught his wrist, old fingers dug into his flesh painfully.

"Lower your head," whispered the *bendrui*.

Old habits brought Demne's head down. He stared at the churned-up earth as Bodbmall went on.

"Fool! Do not cause trouble. To glare at the guard was bad enough, but you must not antagonize that man."

He could feel it when the rider passed them without ever having looked their way. "That is my enemy," Demne muttered furiously.

"There are no foes in Tailtiu, child. This is a sacred place where blood may not be shed. Can you not feel its sacredness?"

Demne gave a quick glance at the old woman, but her bleak eyes were empty of humor. This place, sacred? Distracted by this remarkable notion, the boy forgot the rider. All he could feel was the unnatural press of too many folk and too many beasts on one small piece of ground.

Just then a dog dashed out and snapped at Demne's calf. The boy's bare foot lashed out, releasing his frustrations, and caught the animal just beneath the belly. He lofted the startled dog off the earth, and sent it flying without actually injuring it. The beast came down in a sprawl of legs, and several bystanders chuckled. It turned and came back, fawning and lapping with its pink tongue at Demne's dirt-caked feet.

"Did you see that? His foot was a flash. He should excel on the hurley field."

"Very quick, indeed. But servants do not play at hurley. Pity. I have wanted to kick that cursed hound of Cairell's for ages myself."

"But he did not kick it. He merely tossed it. Most skillfully."

"Well, he should have kicked it, then. I never knew a dog that wanted kicking more."

"Not even that old wolfhound of . . ." The speakers moved out of earshot, leaving Demne bewildered. He hastened after Bodbmall, suddenly afraid to lose her. If he had known how strange the world of people was, Demne thought he might have remained in the mountains.

The smell of cooking food made him realize he was very hungry. He caught up with the *bendrui*, shifting his bundle to another position as uncomfortable as the last, and hoped he would soon be free of it. The moving crowd was a fascinating spectacle, but it had none of the glimmering beauty of the tapestries of the fairy woman Donait. The peace of her fair house beckoned to him from the clamor of Tailtiu.

The House of Women was not a single structure, but several round houses ranged in a rough circle, ringing with the shrill voices of many females. The sound reminded him of the arguments between the Liath Luachra and Bodbmall, and he cringed. The guard had been right. He did not belong here.

He followed Bodbmall to the very back of one of the smaller houses, where the noise was not so great. It had the look of a place not often occupied, the white-washed daubing had fallen away from the outside of the wall, and shafts of sunlight flickered through the woven withies and the gaps in the thatching to the leaf-littered floor. The smell of must made him curl his nose. The stones of the fire pit were coated with ash and dust, cold and unwelcoming.

Bodbmall sank to the ground, a huddle of weary

flesh and bone. In the shadows, the only life left in
her was in her eyes. Demne could see how she tried
to disguise her weariness, and felt remorse for having
dragged her away from the safety of the mountains.
She gasped for air as he lowered his bundle to the
littered floor, and all questions fled. He concentrated
all his energy on clearing away layers of moldering
leaves, until he reached the bare earth beneath. When
he had cleared one side of the small chamber, he
opened the pack and removed the *bendrui*'s straw
pallet, spreading it out and smoothing the bedding
as if it were the most important task in the world.

The old woman remained motionless, too exhausted
to criticize, wheezing like a breeze across river reeds.
Her silence disturbed Demne more than any nagging,
and he peered across at her anxiously. When she still
did not stir, he scooped her up, cradling her in his
weary arms as gently as he could. She seemed to
weigh nothing at all. He laid her down on her bed,
and tucked her garments neatly around her shrunk-
en body. He covered her with a blanket and began to
clear out the fire pit.

When he had completed this task, Demne built a
small blaze, using some of the leaves for kindling and
a handful of dried sticks from a little stack outside the
hut. It was anything but chill in the stuffy chamber,
and there was hardly need for a fire, but it made the
place seem more homelike.

Bodbmall was staring at the ceiling, her twisted
hands clutching the edge of the blanket. For a moment,
Demne looked at her, feeling helpless. He felt his own
raging hunger and a throbbing headache and, worse,
an overwhelming feeling of guilt. He had no idea
what he should do for the sick old woman, whom he
might ask for help, or anything else. At last he gently
removed the old woman's shoes and began to massage
the ancient, bent feet with care, remembering how she

had taught him that the rubbing of the feet restored vitality.

After what seemed an age, Bodbmall stirred. Demne's calves were cramped from crouching, and he flexed his toes.

"You are a good boy, Demne," she muttered. He flushed with mild pleasure at this praise, and hushed the voice within that snarled he was a boy no longer. "The years weigh me down. Go to the cook house and bring us back some supper, now. Take the bowls. They will be filled."

Demne covered her feet with the blanket and stood up, brushing his soiled hands on his worn tunic. He took their wooden bowls out of the bundle, placing the small cauldron of riveted bronze that they had used on their journey beside the fire pit. Then he went out and followed his nose until he found where those tantalizing smells were coming from.

Great cauldrons hung over fire pits beneath a shed next to the largest building, and an entire cow was being roasted on a spit turned by two sweating boys. A sharp-faced woman swung a wooden spoon almost as long as her leg, commanding the whole enterprise. She scolded the boys if they slackened their movements even for a moment, chastened the women who stirred the contents of the cauldrons for no reason Demne could perceive, and ordered more wood placed on one fire, but not on the others. He was so amazed by the sight that he forgot his purpose until she rounded upon him with a green-eyed stare that nearly froze his blood and made his tongue cleave to the roof of his mouth.

"Well, what do you want, boy? Don't just stand there like a log—at least a log would be useful!"

"Bodbmall sent me to fetch some supper, mistress," he mumbled, ashamed of his grubby hands and tattered clothes.

"Bodbmall? The old *bendrui*? Why, she hasn't been here for at least five years! Are you her *gilla*, then? Odd. I never knew her to have a lad before. Always took some strapping girl to do her bidding. A fearsome tongue, that one."

"She is old, mistress." Demne wanted to escape those prying green eyes. He did not like her at all.

The woman gave a snort. "Old! I believe she was born old. Here, give me those. Why are you standing there like a moonling, lad? Give the bowls to me!" As she handed them to one of the other women her fingers flickered in the scornful gesture the boys who taunted him had made.

Demne felt the familiar flash of anger, followed by sullen resentment. He stared at the ground and choked it down.

One of the cooks, a rosy-cheeked, plump woman whose eyes seemed full of laughter, shook a finger at the speaker. "Simple he may be, but he certainly can hear you. Must you speak ill of everyone and everything, Blathnat nic Aedha? One day that mouth of yours will get you into deep water."

Demne did not hear the response, for he saw a pack of boys running across the far side of the compound. They were laughing and shouting, tossing a ball, and he remembered the boys of the rath. He wished he could join them in their game, but he could not forget what had happened the last time he had played with boys. He thought of Bran, who had befriended him and who had died at his hand, and his appetite faded. He wished he had never returned from the house of Donait to the world of men.

Then the plump woman handed him back the bowls, each one covered with a thick slab of bread. She patted his cheek softly. "There now. You take this to your mistress, there's a good boy."

"My thanks to you," he said, dragging himself from

the pleasant memory of the fairy woman into the harsh present. "You are most kind."

As he moved away, Demne heard the plump woman speak. "A moonling, Blathnat? I think the lad is just shy. He would be rather good-looking if he were washed up a bit. I wonder who he is? He puts me in mind of someone, but I cannot think just who."

There was a sound of derisive laughter. "A little young and tender to spit you, isn't he, Moriath? He probably reminds you of some old bed warmer—you've had so many, you cannot recall their names. You must be ravenous to think of a moonling boy, and lowborn into the bargain. He's young enough to be your grandson!"

"Young he may be, but not lowborn," Moriath replied sharply. "I'll snatch you bald for saying so. Open your eyes, you sour-mouthed bitch. Anyone can see he's neither slave nor simple." What else she said was lost as Demne hurried away, puzzling over the ways of women.

The bowls were hot in his hands. Demne wondered briefly, as he avoided a curious dog and a tottering babe, if there was anyone in the world that he could comprehend. The actions of the beasts of the forest were logical, and those of the birds of the air. But human words and deeds were supposed to make sense, and they didn't, at least not to him.

When he returned, Bodbmall was sitting up on her pallet, stretching her twisted hands towards the tiny fire.

"Where did you go to get supper—the moon?"

Demne handed her one bowl and pulled spoons out of the pack. "Do they make stew on the moon? That is a mystery you have not taught me." He grinned when the old woman glared at him. "There was a hard-tongued woman called Blathnat who said I was simple, and she took her own time."

The *bendrui* gave him a stern look that softened into a partial grin. "So, they still have her over the fires. She is a good cook, but a bitter woman. Not without reason," she ended cryptically.

Demne knew better than to demand any explanation, and he was too hungry to really care. He dug into his meal happily, dunking the thick bread into the liquid of the stew and chewing the boiled barley and beef. The bread was the sort that Bodbmall had sometimes brought back from her midwifing in the raths, yeasty and flavorful. It made a wonderful change from oatcake.

Bodbmall handed him most of her piece. "These old teeth are not up to chewing that, Demne." She gave a long sigh and spooned some broth into her mouth. "Soon I will be fit for nothing but gruel, like a muling infant."

"Is that what happens to the old, Bodbmall?"

"Sometimes. Few have seen as many years as I have."

"Then I will never get old," he declared, horrified by the idea of his teeth failing him and his flesh becoming weak.

The *bendrui* gave him a thoughtful look. After a time she said, "That is probably truer than you know, Demne."

He squirmed in his place and changed the subject. "I saw boys playing ball. Can I join their games sometime?"

"I cannot prevent you, though I wish I could. I have such a foreboding, child."

"Why?"

She shook her head, and white wisps of hair fluttered across her wrinkled brow. "Even the wise cannot know what the future holds. We pretend we can, but it is not true. I will say no more. If you are finished gobbling your food, go fetch some water in the cauldron. The well is not far." She extended a bony finger towards the rear of the compound. "And be courteous to all who speak to you, no matter what they say. You are in peril here, and you have enemies you do not even guess exist."

He frowned. "I saw one of them—the mounted man—when we arrived. What is his name?"

He swallowed as she stared at him.

"I will not tell you. Not yet, Demne, not now." Bodbmall gave a racking cough and gasped for air.

"When, then?" he asked desperately. "What if you can't tell—"

"If I can help it you will never have to know," she interrupted him. "Now go. Can't you see I need the water? Once I've brewed up a draught of bitter herbs I'll be well."

Chapter 8

※

D EMNE HUNG UP A BLANKET TO PARTITION OFF THE area around Bodbmall's bed, and stuffed rags into the worst of the holes in the walls. He gathered more wood from a communal stockpile, and did his best to make the place warm. The women who were quartered nearby stared at him and whispered behind their hands, but his sullen frown discouraged questions.

Despite the heat of the day, night mists from the nearby river chilled the air, and the old *bendrui* alternately shivered and burned. Demne brewed foul-smelling mixtures in the cauldron, and she drank them down and cast them up almost as quickly. Finally, just before dawn, she fell into a slumber, snoring and snorting. He touched her skin and found it cool but not cold. Reassured that she was past the worst of her illness, he curled up under his worn cloak and fell into an uneasy sleep plagued by dreams in which the multicolored spirals of his vision became a web in which he struggled helplessly.

When he opened his itching eyes, the sun was above the stockade. It took him a moment to realize where he was. Bodbmall was sitting up, her blanket

131

draped across her sagging shoulders. Her skin was an unhealthy grey. Still, her eyes were clear, and her jaw had that determined line that usually meant something unpleasant for him.

"You must go to the House of Youths," she announced.

"What?" He sat up, knuckling his eyes. "I thought—"

"What you thought is of no matter. Sleep brought me vision. You can no longer stay with me here."

"But who will look after you?" He did not add that her sudden offer of freedom made his blood run cold.

"One of the serving girls can take care of me, but you must be with boys your own age." She gritted her teeth. "Do not think I want to let you go."

"I don't want to leave you in the hands of some girl."

"You will do as I tell you. Now, gather your things— and comb your hair! Remember to think before you act, and keep your mouth closed and your ears open."

"Who shall I say I am?"

"Why should you say anything at all? I just told you to be silent!" She coughed and beads of sweat popped up on her skin. "I am in no state to argue with you."

"The boys will tease me if I cannot give more of a name than Demne, and there will be trouble," he said darkly.

The old woman wiped her brow with a shaking hand. "Boys are the cruelest beasts in nature. Indeed, I have not forgotten what happened to you before. But it should be enough to tell them that you are my fosterling. Now, go fill the cauldron for me and build up the fire." She sank back and shut her eyes.

BY THE TIME DEMNE FOUND HIS WAY TO THE HOUSE of Youths, the sun was arching towards its nooning. He felt like two people, one of them sure the *bendrui* could not get along without him while the other exulted in being free of her demands. When he entered the long building where the boys slept, it seemed to him that the place was as confused as he.

Most of the pallets arranged along the walls were unmade, and belongings were scattered everywhere. Boys were lying down or sitting on the benches, talking, mending hunting gear, or playing games of chance. The whole place smelled of sour sweat and unwashed clothes. Demne made his way down the rows of pallets until he found an empty place, and put his things out tidily. The conversations around him were a blur of noise, but Demne clearly was not the only one whose voice sometimes slipped from a deep boom to a high piping in mid-word. That had been happening since he had passed his twelfth year at Midsummer. It still puzzled him that he had lived a whole year in a day and a night with the fairy woman, but he had decided there was no use in thinking about it.

He took a moment to study the youths around him. Some were finely garbed, but others had clothing as shabby as his own, tunics popping at the seams with sudden growth and leggings too short for lengthening legs. Relieved that his garments would not draw unwanted attention, he returned to his task.

Woods-trained senses told Demne that as he worked the others had been gathering around him, but it was not until all was tidy that he stood up and looked around. He returned their stares, hard or curious, with an expression of wide-eyed interest. This second encounter with other boys would be different. At least he was a head taller than all but the eldest of the youths, whose voices were deep and whose chins were shadowed by budding beards. They might think twice about tackling him.

A large red-haired lad whose little eyes reminded Demne uncomfortably of a sow's swaggered across the room.

"Well now." He favored Demne with a rude stare. "And who might you be?"

As a cluster of youths grouped themselves expectantly behind the questioner Demne began to wonder if his own size was going to help much after all. He forced himself to grin sunnily.

"Guess."

The other boys clapped hands over their own mouths to stifle giggles as the red-haired lad's jaw dropped in surprise. His face flushed as ruddy as his hair, then he lunged at Demne, meaty arms swinging like clubs. "*Think, Demne!*" the Liath Luachra's voice whispered in memory. He feinted and bobbed as she had taught him, and then stepped aside so that the fist met air. The other boy's eyes widened, and his gaze flicked to his fist as if he wanted to make sure it was still there. Their audience had grown, and a whisper went through the crowd.

"You tell me who you are, or I'll beat you silly!"

Demne scratched his head, playing for time. He noticed several swollen lips and blackened eyes on the faces around him, and guessed that his would-be opponent was used to pushing the others around. He had seen how wolves in a pack enforced their status; perhaps people were the same. Except that this lout was no wolf, but a dog. The woman, Blathnat, had called him simple the evening before—perhaps it might be safer to be thought a fool until he learned the signals that this boy pack used.

"Silly?" He gave a high-pitched giggle. "But I already am. And besides, you have to catch me first."

Instantly he regretted adding that. Now he understood why the old woman had warned him to keep silent. That remark had been as provoking as a wolf's

waving tail, but there was something about this boy
that demanded it. Although Demne was exasperated
with himself, there was none of the dreadful red rage
that had betrayed him before.

He ducked a wide, wild thrust that would have hurt
if it had connected, grabbed the lad's thick wrist as it
shot past him, and yanked, then let go. The big youth
sprawled onto the floor, cursing.

"That will show the big bully," someone whispered
in the crowd.

Roaring, the youth scrambled to his feet and sprang
at Demne. Sidestepping gracefully, Demne shot out a
foot and tripped his foe. Then he leaned down and
hauled his fuming opponent to his feet, bobbing under
another wild swing. He put a big hand firmly against
the other boy's broad, heaving chest and shoved just
hard enough to put some distance between them, but
not enough to unbalance him again.

"I don't like to fight," Demne said plaintively. "Do
you always pick on strangers this way?"

"He does that. And it is a courtesy in you to treat
him so charitably." A young man just into manhood
himself eased through the crowd. He was tall, willow-
slender, and oddly familiar. His carefully braided hair
was the amber of sunset, and his cheeks were high-
colored below grave grey eyes.

"You will come to a sorry end, Dael mac Conain, if
you do not have a care," the newcomer said, frowning.

"He would not tell me his name," Dael whined.

"And after you were asking so courteously, too,"
the young man replied gravely. "The lad's name is
his own, to give or keep as he wills. Will you stay
brawling in this sty when the high king is here? He
is almost at the gates! We run the first races soon, and
I expect the House of Youths to be in order before
then. Dael mac Conain, was the charge of this abode
misplaced in you?"

There was a thick, sullen silence. The younger boys scattered, folding their blankets and picking up discarded clothing and shoes. Dael turned an unlovely red, and glared at both Demne and his inquisitor. "Go ahead. Give yourself airs, Aonghus. I will get you one day."

Aonghus shrugged. "The men of Clan Morna have been saying that sort of thing for years. But before they can fulfill their threats, their hot blood always carries them away."

Demne kept silent, marveling at the quiet assurance of this young man. Aonghus's clothing was simple and good, but not as lavish as Dael's, and he certainly did not have the physical strength to overcome the boy. But he was obeyed, and the other youths displayed a respect for him that bordered on fear. Demne wondered why.

And Aonghus seemed so very familiar. At last it came to him that he had seen just such eyes in the face of Bran mac Conail, whom he had slain with a stone. Demne blinked back tears. When Aonghus had moved away he turned to the small boy who had the next bed.

"Who is Aonghus? Is he the leader here?" He reached over and helped straighten the blanket of his neighbor.

"Aonghus is apprenticed to Fionnéices," the boy replied, as if this explained everything.

"What power does that give him over a bully like Dael?"

The boy goggled at him. "You are big and strong, but you must be silly indeed. A trained *fili* can raise black boils on your face with a mere word, and Fionnéices is one of the most famous poets in the land."

Demne digested this. Bodbmall had told him of the poets' path, a way of the wise not unlike her own. Did Aonghus hear the ceaseless song of earth which even through the clamor of the House of Youths pulsed up to him from the soil? He longed to ask.

"That will be it, then." He grinned foolishly. "And these races he spoke of—are they fun?"

The boy shook his head in wonder. "Fun? I would not say that. You are the strangest creature, and I wonder if you are as simple as you pretend."

"Sometimes it is safer to be an acorn on an oak than to be a squirrel in the pot." Demne let the grin fade, eyeing the boy with interest.

"Is that why you play the fool, to keep out of the pot?"

Demne grinned again. "You have found me out."

The younger boy gave a sly smile in return. "I think I like you, whoever you are. I am Lugna mac Ronain."

"And I am called Demne. Now, tell me more about the high king and the races and . . . well, everything."

A HUNDRED YOUTHS CROWDED TOGETHER BEYOND THE walls of the enclosure as a dozen horses tore around a roughly circular pathway laid out across the fields. As they rounded the turn and thundered past, Demne saw the red-haired man he had noticed when he entered Tailtiu, whipping his beast mercilessly. He frowned, thinking that Dael mac Conain would look exactly like this man someday.

With a last surge of speed the horses sped between the flower-decked posts that marked the finish, and the riders turned their mounts aside, stroking lathered necks and sopping flanks. He rejoiced silently as he watched the winner of the race receive the praise of the others, and was glad that the red-haired man had finished a poor third. He schooled his face into a mask of amiable stupidity, and waited to see what would happen next.

Several men with rakes went around the course, sweeping away steaming droppings, and an old fellow walked among the boys, grouping them by size for the footrace to come. The sides of the track were walled with watchers, and, at the far end, a standard fluttered in the breeze above a platform where an old man was seated in a great chair. He was like the wreck of a lightning-struck oak, thought Demne, whose mighty limbs retained a memory of its strength and all its pride. This must be Conn the Hundred-Fighter, the *Ard Ri* whom everyone spoke of, but he was too far away for Demne to see whether there was any kindness in his eyes.

Then the monitor was chivying the boys into position. Demne had not realized they would let him join in the racing, but surely even Bodbmall could not wish him to make a fuss about it now. His heart leaped at the thought of winning a place among the boys, and he ignored Dael mac Conain's glare, knowing that in a moment the bully would be too busy running to trouble him.

A tremor ran though the runners, then the oldster's hand flashed down. Dael's leather-shod foot lashed out, catching Demne just below the knee. Dots of pain were dancing in Demne's eyes. He felt a flash of rage as his leg started to give way, and fought to control it as the backs of the boy pack seemed to shrink before his gaze.

Then his flaming cheeks were kissed by the brush of a breeze, and he recognized the touch of his invisible twin. She was gone almost before he thought of her, but his blood quickened. His first steps were a wobble, and people began to laugh, but the pain was forgotten as he sprang forward. His bare feet began to fly, toes springing off the rough track so fast they barely stirred the dust.

The heaving mass of small, square shoulders and pumping limbs grew swiftly larger. The leaders were strung out ahead with the rest of the racers blocking the track behind them. Demne held his position, seeking an opening. The racers were supposed to be all of a size, but the stronger boys elbowed the weaker aside. A boy went down in front of him, and Demne leaped across the fallen racer.

He felt a twinge as he landed on his left foot, but he bit back his pain. He had endured worse while chasing deer in the forest. He sucked in air and surged ahead, speeding towards the next knot of runners. These were older boys, bigger and stronger than the previous group, and much rougher. His anger against Dael mac Conain extended into a general sense of outrage as he saw one boy's swinging arm catch another in the belly. This was not a race, but a brawl!

Boys fell and yelled and punched each other. Demne dodged and jumped, his steady stride faltering as he swerved to avoid a fallen runner or duck beneath a flying fist. At least when he ran through the forest the branches did not try to hit him first. He was distantly aware of shouting, but he could not tell whether the adult voices were raised in protest or were cheering them on. He darted under someone's swing and felt sweat sting his eyes.

Then he was in the open again, and there were only a dozen or so big boys still pounding ahead of him, strung out a stride or two apart. Demne dragged a sleeve across his brow and stumbled on a loose clod.

A breath of breeze lifted his hair, and suddenly Demne found his second wind. He no longer heard the shouting from the sides of the track or the yells of the boys running behind him. Presently even those before him became a blur. Now he thought of nothing but speed, felt only the yielding earth beneath his feet and the wind in his hair. One by one he passed the leaders, but he did not see their faces, nor did he notice the ferocious glare of Dael mac Conain as they ran even for a dozen strides.

He left the Clan Morna boy behind him in a fresh spurt of power. Now only three racers ran before him, their feet kicking up dust and clods. But Demne's new strength was failing him. Suddenly his lungs ached with effort, and his limbs were like fire.

Then Demne heard something, and his skin crawled. Was all this a dream, and he still in the forest after all? His stride faltered as he glanced behind him, but he saw only the blurred shapes of the runners. It came once again, invisible, or perhaps sounding within him—the squeal of an enraged sow.

She was there—behind him—shadow taking the shape that haunted his dreams. Terror sparked strength through leaden limbs; aching lungs gulped dusty air. Demne's stride lengthened, his feet skimmed the soil. He spurted past two more boys, then hung, as if fixed there, a pace behind the front-runner.

He could almost touch him, yet he could not seem to get past. *I outraced the sow,* he thought dimly, *and the men who would have slain me. Can't I run for something? I've no one to carry but myself this time. . . .*

His sister had refreshed him once, and he had been spurred a second time by fear. This time he sought inward, to some part of himself he had never tapped before. For a moment he strained, then something swelled from his aching loins and burst through his breast like fire. His pounding heart narrowed towards its goal and drew the rest of him with it, arms pumping, legs thrusting the earth behind him. The crowd blurred; the leader was a shadow in a stilled world in which only Demne moved.

And then there was nothing before him but the raised platform. From the whirl around him a single face took form—ice-pale eyes ablaze now with excitement, silver hair bound with a circlet of gold. Abruptly the power that had propelled him let go.

Demne staggered and strong hands caught him. The face disappeared as his bearers turned.

As the roaring in Demne's ears eased he became aware that people were shouting, carrying him around a great circle. The cheering battered his senses as he struggled to get upright. He mopped his face with a grimy sleeve, and the world came into focus once more.

Piggy eyes slitted with rage, Dael mac Conain was saying something to one of the men who had judged the race. He jabbed a finger at Demne and his cheeks purpled.

Aonghus walked serenely towards Demne and his cheering supporters. He lifted a smooth hand to the boy, and the men who were carrying him let him down. Impressions rioted in Demne's awareness— warmth for the young *fili*, shame when he remembered how Bran mac Conail, who was so like him, had lain dead on the ground. Something warm trickled down his left leg. Demne looked down and saw blood seeping through the worn fabric of his old teacher's breeches. He had not realized that the kick he received had broken the skin. He blinked back giddiness, but he could not help limping as he followed Aonghus.

They came to the cluster of men around Dael. The redheaded boy's narrow lips twisted, and he pointed a grubby finger at Demne.

"He fouled me on the track. That was no fair win!"

Demne gaped at the injustice, but the men, all grey heads, were dressed in tunics of embroidered linen and cloaks of good wool. They all carried carved sticks, and he guessed they were the judges. Demne was abruptly aware of his own shabby clothing and wild hair. His lamed leg began to hurt and he rested his weight on the other, trying to find the words to deny Dael's outrageous claim. But even if he had fouled Dael mac Conain, could they fault him for it?

It seemed to him that half the racers had been trying to trip up the other half.

Aonghus cleared his throat. "I have not yet completed my studies, but it will one day be my task to create the truth of events by my reporting, and I know what I have seen. This lad no more fouled mac Conain than he crawled around the track on hands and knees. You all saw him running like the wind itself, and if you will look now you will see that he bleeds still from the kick he received from none other than this . . . dog . . . who presumes to accuse him of cheating."

Dael turned even redder than before. "Is he your new favorite then, Aonghus mac Conail? Will you cuddle him in the night? What can you know of footraces and manly things, mooning around, memorizing a bunch of—"

Demne felt his heart go still as he heard the full name of the young *fili* for the first time. The breath paused in his lungs, and hot tears threatened to spill from his eyes. The world was a terrible place, when you could slay a man's kin, and have him come to your defense. He forced air into his chest, and reached for the calm stillness the old *bendrui* had been at such pains to teach him. Until this moment, he had never known what a gift it was.

"Enough," snapped one of the greylings. "One day, lad, that tongue of yours is going to get you killed. You have not the sense of a blaeberry in that thick head of yours. Is it not enough to cry foul when it is untrue? Must you also insult the student of great Fionnéices?"

"Fionnéices! The *fili* are a bunch of woodlice, sucking blood out of hapless beasts," Dael shouted. "They grow fat on the labors of better men."

Another old fellow shook his head. "Indeed the mac Mornas have no love of poets, since they are blamed for the death of Cumhal mac Trenmor when the tales of the *fianna* are sung in Temair. Still, Dael, that is no cause to speak intemperately."

"The tale that we caused Cumhal's death is one of Fionnéices's lies!" Dael, clearly out of his depth, was sweating with unease. "Cumhal was an outlaw and deserved what he got!"

"A *fili* must speak the truth or lose his power," the older man answered.

"A *fili* can twist the truth as a fisher bends wicker into a weir," Dael mac Conain muttered, but his voice was no longer so loud.

"Who, besides myself, observed this lad in the race," Aonghus asked, ignoring him. Two of the judges stepped forward. "Did either of you see him do anything dishonorable?"

The old men looked at each other, then at Demne. One rubbed his wrinkled chin. His lips were sunken across toothless gums. "It was quite otherwise, to my mind. I saw him jump over fallen racers when he could have trod on them as the others were doing. And we can all see that he is bleeding. Not only is he the victor, but he has acquitted himself with great courtesy."

"Your eyes must be as useless as your gums, old man," Dael growled. "You wait until my father hears this. I am the finest runner in all of Eriu."

"You ended a poor fifth, child of Morna," said the other judge. "And when your father hears that you kicked this youth at the start of the race, where all could see, he is more likely to beat you than give you praise. Has not your clan had enough trouble these last years? I saw that blow! I really do not know what the world is coming to. In my day we did not brawl on Tailtiu's holy ground. But the boy needs to get that hurt seen to—"

Dael was still scowling, but to Demne's surprise, the others were nodding and turning away. He was glad he had kept still. Men crowded around him, asking where he came from, how he had learned to run that way, but Demne made himself smile foolishly and mutter disjointed comments until they shook their heads and turned away.

His injured leg was stiffening up, and he knew it needed cleaning and one of the *bendrui*'s poultices of smelly herbs. When the men finally left him alone, he limped back towards the enclosure. Bodbmall could treat him, and perhaps she could explain to him what had been going on. She might even be pleased with his victory.

As he reached the edge of the field, Demne felt an itch between his shoulders. He paused, turning. From his high seat the *Ard Ri* was watching him intently, and even at this distance, the boy thought the gleam he saw in those eyes was one of recognition. He took a quick breath, aware of a sudden impulse to go back to him. But what could one of the great ones of the world want with such as he?

Then lack of sleep and exertion caught up with him. Demne hobbled away from the field and back into the enclosure, towards the House of Women. It would be good to see the *bendrui*'s aged face once more, even if she scolded him.

When he reached the doorway of her place, a rather pretty young woman was sitting in the sunlight beside the entrance. Her long braids were the russet of autumn leaves, and her cheeks blushed like roses. Her lap was full of withies that she was plaiting neatly into a basket, and she was singing softly over the work.

She glanced up from her work and frowned. "Go away, you dirty boy. You do not belong here."

Suddenly the girl no longer looked so pretty. Demne brushed sweat-matted hair back from his brow and scowled back at her. "I want to see Bodbmall."

"She is asleep. You cannot see her now." The patronizing patience in the girl's tone was far worse than Dael's truculence because there was no way he could fight it.

"Just who do you think you are, saying whether Bodbmall will see me?"

"I am the servant of the wisewoman"—the girl looked him up and down—"and you are a grubby beast."

Demne's vision darkened. Bodbmall had replaced him before even one day was gone! He felt his fist rising and fought the urge to strike the insolent girl down.

"What is this racket! Can't I get some rest?" Bodbmall pushed aside Demne's blanket, which still covered the door, and poked her head out like a tortoise. "What are you doing here?"

"I told him you did not want any dirty boys around," whined the girl.

"Do not give yourself airs just because you are my servant, Samhair."

Demne swallowed his anger as he heard this rebuke. "I got hurt in the race, and I thought you could fix it. I won, Bodbmall."

"Did you?" she asked indifferently. "I am hardly surprised, with those long legs of yours. Come in and I will see what I can do. You look like you've been rolling in the dirt. Girl, go fetch me some water."

"Who is she?" Demne demanded, when the young woman left carrying a large pail. "Why can't I take care of you, as I always have? Why did you send me away?"

Bodbmall hawked up a viscous yellow gobbet onto the floor of the chamber and took a labored breath, though it seemed to him that she was breathing easier than she had been the day before. When at last she stopped coughing, she answered. "Because, Demne child, I can give you no more. Look at me—I can barely breathe on my own. I am a cask from which all the mead has run." She shook her head, then gestured him down. "Here, now, let me have a look at that. How did you get a cut like this in a race?"

"A boy called Dael of Clan Morna kicked me just as we started to run. I do not know why. He started being ugly as soon as he saw me."

She sighed noisily. "I let you out of my sight for half a day, and already you are in trouble," she said, as if it was his fault. "Stay away from the sons of Morna, Demne. They are a bad lot, even the best of them."

"It is hard when we share the same sleeping quarters. Couldn't I come back here?" As she peered at his hurt knee, he heard the wheeze of her lungs, and a cold finger of fear moved up his spine. She was so ill, and it was his fault. She never would have gotten chilled if she had not brought him to Tailtiu. And what did a mere girl know about nursing?

As if his thought had created her, Samhair flounced into the chamber, glared at Demne, and poured water into the cauldron. He scowled back at her, but held his tongue. Let her look. It would not harm him.

The old woman sat across the fire with her eyes closed while the water warmed. After a time, she roused and sorted through the bundles of herbs he had carried across the leagues from their home. At last she found the one she wanted, and emptied its contents into the cauldron. A pleasant smell rose in the close air of the chamber. When the liquid was heated to her satisfaction, Bodbmall took a pad of cloth and soaked it. Then she cleansed the cut with the cloth.

It was very painful, but Demne forced himself to practice the exercises of mind and body that the *bendrui* had taught him and he had learned with such reluctance. He breathed deeply until he could hear only the song of the fire. After a while, the pain receded. Bodbmall handed Demne another bundle of herbs.

"Wash that cut with this, if it gets ugly. But I believe it will heal well. Now go, boy, for I am weary, and do not return here unless I send for you."

Demne stared at her white hair and seamed face with a rising sense of desolation. His heart yearned to tell her of the young *fili*, of his certainty that Aonghus was kin to the boy he had slain, but he could not. He hardened his features, determined not to let his feelings show. Donait had sent him away too. He wondered if he would ever find a place where he belonged.

"As you will, Bodbmall." He caught the smug look on the face of the girl and hated her. "I thank you for your ministrations." His heart swelled with the need to say more, but he could not speak in front of that thief who was taking the old woman away from him.

He pushed past the door hanging, empty of all but anguish. Bodbmall had not praised him for winning the race, just as she had not when he killed the pig. A kind word from her would have been such a little thing.

In the dust before him he saw the scurrying track where a mouse had run the night before and the brush of the owl's swooping wing. But the mouse had gotten away.

He let out his breath and forced the emptiness out of him. Then he turned towards the House of Youths.

Chapter 9

THE HOUSE OF YOUTHS WAS NEARLY EMPTY WHEN Demne returned. At one end, three unknown boys and Aonghus were gathered around a flat board with carved figures. After a moment, Demne realized it was *fidchel,* the game he had learned in the house of Donait. For a moment, time froze: for he could not recall learning the game in that single night Bodbmall had told him was a year and more. Then the dream returned to his mind, and he could see the face of the woman across the board from him, and she was both the Goddess and Donait, slim fingers moving pieces that almost lived. He found he was holding his breath in wonder, and let it out slowly, the walls of the place dancing before his eyes.

Curious to see how the game was played in the world of men, he crouched down as comfortably as he could with an injured leg and observed the play. It was instantly obvious to him that the boy was going to lose several important pieces if he did not alter his strategy, but he kept his tongue well behind his teeth.

Aonghus defeated his young opponent swiftly, then made a few soft-voiced suggestions to show the boy how he might have played more skillfully. Demne's admiration for the young *fili* increased. The skill he most longed for was this: the ability to find the right words for all the things he wanted to say. *And Aonghus is kind*, Demne thought then. It had never occurred to him that one could teach by combining small praises for moves well chosen as well as criticisms, without scolding or sarcasm.

"Do you know the game, boy?" Aonghus asked, and before he could remember to pretend ignorance, Demne found himself nodding. He started a little, trying to cover, and scratched his sweat-salted locks.

"I think so—a little," he said, hoping that Donait would forgive him. Sometimes, thinking back, he felt as if he had been with her as long as he had with Bodbmall.

"A woman taught me," he added defensively. Someone snickered behind him, but Aonghus smiled his grave smile.

"Good! They are often the best instructors."

One of the youths protested. "How can that be? *Fidchel* is a game of war, not birthing and bedding!"

"If that is all you believe women know, Diarmait mac Fergusa, then I fear your education has been sorely neglected."

Diarmait shook his head vigorously. "My mother does not play *fidchel*, and my sister just giggles at everything."

"Perhaps, but when a woman does become a warrior, she is more terrible than all but the most fierce of men, and more cunning at it. Have you not heard of Queen Medbh?"

"Surely, but that was long ago. My mother doesn't charge about in a chariot, making trouble."

One of the other boys snickered. "'Tis true she does not ride about in a cart. . . ."

Diarmait turned an ugly color and started to raise his fist. Aonghus lifted a smooth hand.

"Enough." He did not lift his voice, but the single word carried unmistakable authority. Demne stared. Clearly, you did not even have to use many words. It was something in the voice and the manner. He sighed. That air of certainty was yet another thing to long for.

"In any case, *fidchel* is a game not of strength but of strategy and of cunning, in which women often excel. Let us play." Aonghus began placing the defending pieces in the middle of the board.

Demne moved over to take the place of Aonghus's defeated opponent. His injured shin protested, so he half knelt with his good leg tucked beneath him, and the hurt one bent up, his dusty bare foot firmly on the floor. He wished that there had been time to wash or to change his clothes. But the only other garments he had were the things Donait had given him, which Bodbmall had forbidden him to wear. For a moment he wondered why he still obeyed her. But, if he had worn his good clothes in the race they would have been ruined by now. Then he began to place his pieces, and forgot all about Bodbmall, Donait, and his leg.

The carved pieces fit into small holes bored into the playing tablet, the two opponents each having wood of distinct colors. Demne had pale pegs of birch, and Aonghus darker ones of oak, as befitted one who pursued the poet's craft. The board itself was divided by a series of grooves into squares, seven rows of seven each with a hole for the playing pieces.

Demne's kingpiece looked over the pale knobbed heads of his defenders from the center of the board at the pale pieces ready to encircle him from the edges of the board. His gaze flicked up to Aonghus's impassive features and back again. The young *fili* had been

kind, giving him the easier task. He had only to get his
kingpiece safely to one edge of the board before the
attackers could pin him. Unless one was a very stupid player, the advantages were all on the side of the
king. But it would not do to discount Aonghus's intelli-
gence. Demne looked back at the board planning what
moves would change the cross-pattern of his defenders into a sun-wheel that would open a file for him to
escape while protecting against the long, straight,
swoops of his foes.

Demne touched his pieces and pulled back his fingers in surprise. Donait's *fidchel* men had felt alive
in his hand. These were just bits of old, long-dead
wood. Distressed, he looked up at the roof, but no
shining leaves entwined there. But why should he
have expected it to be the same? He shrugged and
made his first move.

Aonghus gave a little grunt, and Demne looked up
at him. "A most interesting opening, boy. She who
instructed you must be an unconventional player
indeed."

Demne gave a long, slow smile, remembering Donait
and the Shining Goddess. He was not certain which
had instructed him. "She is like none other," he
replied.

Aonghus made his opening move, and the other three boys settled down to watch. They clearly
expected the *fili* to be an easy victor, and it was clear
that he was an excellent strategist. Demne frowned
over both his opponent's moves and his own, but he
did not hesitate. He saw the trap being laid, and he
avoided it, breaking Aonghus's pattern before it was
established. The problem of the game was complex,
to rescue his own white kingpiece while preventing
the dark ones from overwhelming him. Spearmen
and warriors fell on both sides, opening up the
board.

The *fili* paused, and it was he who hesitated now. His smooth hand hovered over one piece, then moved another. Demne held in a grin and breached Aonghus's defenses. He heard a soft whistle from one of the boys, and a whispered phrase of comment from another. The young poet rubbed his jaw and looked across at Demne.

"You play a perilous game, boy." He placed a warrior to close up the breach.

Demne swallowed another grin and pushed his shaggy hair off his brow. He was enjoying himself thoroughly. He covered the pieces with his large hand, and when he withdrew it, one of his defenders, appearing from nowhere, pinned the warrior. Aonghus gave a grunt and studied the board.

"Who *is* he?" came a hiss from somewhere behind him.

"Who cares? Just watch the play."

The whispers distracted him for an instant, while Aonghus made his move. It was a good question. Demne only wished he did know who he was and where he belonged in this world of young men. Then he studied the change, drew a breath, and chose a move that would free him again. The *fili* clicked his tongue against his teeth. After a little thought, the poet made a move to close in on the king. Demne countered by shifting it between two white pieces. Now the king was protected on two sides. Two others already stood in position, close by. It was a pattern called the Barb, a spearhead to bring the king to safety, and a bold, challenging move that Aonghus would have to answer with an attack. At the same time, half the poet's oaken warriors were hemmed in, and he must try to release them.

With a grimace, Aonghus captured one of the spearmen in the Barb, and Demne immediately recovered with another move. The *fili* lifted his eyes from the board and looked at Demne. "I would very much like to meet your instructor, boy."

Demne stared at him. If there was anyone with whom he would have wished to share Donait, it would be this man. But he could not even be sure when he would see her again. "If you are fortunate, perhaps you will," he answered finally.

Aonghus made another move, seeking to free his men once more, and Demne countered by turning the Barb into the Tusk, moving his own king piece forward to the third file of the board. None of the *fili*'s men were in place to threaten it for two moves, which would allow Demne to reach an open file and freedom.

"I must concede, I believe," the *fili* said quietly. "I thank you for a most challenging game. I have never seen this style before. It is most bold. . . ." He sighed, then looked up. "Is your leg bothering you?"

It was, but Demne was reluctant to admit it. Dael mac Conain's kick had done a good bit of damage. "Not really. But my breeches are ruined."

One of the watching boys chuckled. "I'd say they were done before you ever ran the race."

Demne stared at the board, but he felt his face reddening. He hated feeling dirty and shabby before these well-garbed boys. It made him remember the hide tunic he had worn when he first encountered the boys of the rath. Worse, it reminded him of the death of his first friend, Bran mac Conail, whose face was so like that of the *fili* sitting across the board.

Aonghus mac Conail, kin to my only friend Bran, whom I slew . . . For a moment Demne thought he was going to be ill.

"Now, let me think," Aonghus said. "I believe I have a pair of outgrown trousers that might fit you. I was going to pass them to my younger brother—" He bit off whatever else he had been going to say, rose, and drew Demne after him away from the others, and out the door.

Is he dead, Aonghus? Demne wanted to ask. *Was he killed by a wild boy out of the woods? Was his name Bran?* But he was all too afraid that he knew the answer.

"You are a lad of hidden talents," said Aonghus as they crossed the courtyard. Demne stared at him.

"Not for words," he said desperately, trying to cover his anguish. "What does a *fili* do?"

Aonghus gave him a sharp look, then spoke softly.

> *"A fish in the stream,*
> *first gleams and is gone.*
> *The word within the mind*
> *To find must be known.*
> *The poet drowned in sleep*
> *In the deep casts his line."*

Demne blinked as a silver salmon swam upward from the glimmering depths of his mind and disappeared into the light of day. Without knowing what the poem meant, he knew that it was true.

"Did you make those words?"

"Is that what you want to do?" Aonghus's high-boned pale face grew faintly pink with pleasure.

The boy ducked his head, for once grateful for the thick hair that fell over his eyes. "How can I tell? Sometimes I feel like a pig caught in a thorn hedge with folk pulling on both sides. One of my foster mothers taught me the way of weapons, and the other the way of the wise. I don't know if I want to be a *fili*, but I do wish to make my words do my will."

Aonghus gave him another odd look. "Well, if you seek a teacher, I suggest you try another master than Poet Fionn."

"Why?"

"He is a master of his craft. But he can be . . .difficult. He has many secrets, and he makes even me uneasy sometimes, when he looks into the dark places in his past."

He sounds like me! Demne thought bitterly. Was this some subtle poet's way of discouraging him, or was Aonghus too good at heart to understand such a man?

"It is hard to imagine a master more difficult than the teachers I have already had," he said quietly.

"Then you will find your teacher in this also, if it is meant to be. . . ." Aonghus had gone suddenly somber. "Here are my quarters," he added abruptly. "I will get the garment. That building there is the bathhouse. You should soak for a time."

Demne waited, feeling like a gadfly that has been slapped down. Had he been too forward, or did some magic of the *filidecht* tell Aonghus that here stood the slayer of young Bran? Did Aonghus himself know why he had drawn away? Demne shifted from foot to foot anxiously, thinking of things that might go wrong, until the poet returned.

The breeches were sewn from a sturdy green cloth that looked hardly worn. Demne thanked Aonghus as well as he could, but he was acutely aware of how awkward and clumsy he must sound. The slender *fili* smiled gently, as if he was used to the stupidities of young boys. He clapped Demne on the shoulder and urged him towards the bathhouse, then vanished into his own quarters. Demne felt as he had when Bodbmall sent him away. He stood for a moment, gazing at the shut door, then made his way to the bathhouse to get clean.

EXCITING AS THE GAMES MIGHT BE, THE FESTIVAL OF Tailten was above all a cattle fair. Demne heard them as he slept and ate and followed the other boys to view the fair's wonders. Their incessant lowing was a music that lay beneath all other sounds. It was not quite like the song of the earth to which he had listened in the forest. This was a harmony of living beings, from the skittishness of the unbred heifers to the calculating patience of the old milk cows, from the stolid content of the oxen to the power and pride of the bulls. But all these notes were blended in a single music by the beasts' shared awareness. It was the voice of the herd that spoke to Demne at the fair.

He realized presently that the same thing was true of the people. Each clan and kindred of the four fifths of Eriu had its own music, and when the high king sat on his platform with his druids behind him and judged the people, all of them blended together into one song. Fragile though the harmony might be, each man of them knew where he belonged.

Weaving in and out of the clans and kindreds, Demne discovered the *fianna* who had stirred his curiosity. By the simple act of keeping quiet, he learned much about these men—and a few women—who stood prepared to defend Eriu from foes at any price. Even they were part of the song of the peoples, though they were bound by rules and customs he could not quite understand. A man might not join them unless securities were given that if he were slain, no vengeance would be demanded by his kin. This was Demne's first encounter with the law of the land, and he eyed it as he would a thorny thicket, suspecting traps.

Most of all he learned that while the *fianna* were respected, and in many ways feared, they were also outcasts in many ways. At first he felt a sense of kinship with the warriors, until he grasped that their leader, the *rigfennid*, was one of the red-haired men who he knew to be his foes. He listened to complaints and resentments for the cost of maintaining the men of the *fian* from many, spoken quietly but nonetheless forcefully. Protectors they might be, but popular they were not. Yet even though the *fennid* were outside the general community, still they belonged to the song of Eriu.

I belong nowhere, Demne told himself, the thought gnawing at his belly. His victory in the race and the calm approval of Aonghus had won him a measure of acceptance in the House of Youths, but that only seemed to intensify his awareness that inside he was not like the others at all.

But Demne took care not to let them know it. He smiled whenever someone spoke to him and encouraged his thick forelock to flop over his eyes. Soon the youngest ones learned that they could tease him without fear despite his size. But the older boys remembered how he had fought Dael of Clan Morna, and treated him with more care.

THE CONTEST IN SPEAR THROWING WAS HELD TWO MORNings after the race. The sun was already hot upon Demne's shoulders and back as he moved with the others across the trampled grass of the race course. His leg was healing well, and at least this time he knew a few of the other boys who were crowding around him. Still, he felt uncomfortable in the press of bodies, and he uneasily eyed the spectators who ranged on all sides. He saw the stuck-up girl who was looking after Bodbmall in the crowd, and wished he could speak to her. Still, if she was there, the *bendrui* must be on the mend, which made him feel a little easier.

Across from them, several rounds of thick wood hung from heavy ropes that were in turn suspended from long poles. The purpose of the arrangement puzzled him. The older men who were supervising the occasion each had a dozen or more spears stuck into the soft ground beside them, their metal barbs a dull grey in the sunlight. Demne waited with the willed patience he had learned as a hunter, ignoring the gabble of the boys around him.

The contest began with the smaller and younger boys. One judge set the targets swinging, and another handed out boy-sized spears. Demne watched young hands grip wooden shafts. He could see the tension in backs and shoulders, and felt his own. He ran a finger across the serpentine brooch of the Liath Luachra, which still pinned his tunic closed. Nervously, he pushed his tangle of pale hair away from his forehead.

He had half expected the same chaos as the footrace, but perhaps the spears enforced their own discipline, for as the judges approached, everyone stilled. Each boy stepped to a mark drawn on the ground, gripped the spear he had been given, aimed, and tossed at the gracefully swinging target. Half missed altogether, and few of the rest hurled with enough power to sink their weapons into the wood. The air rattled as spears bounced off wood and tumbled to the ground.

Almost before Demne knew it, it was the turn of the older boys. Their mark was a fresh line further back than the one drawn for the first group. Demne stepped forward and accepted the weapon offered by the judge. Once more he felt the prickle between his shoulders as if someone were watching him, but he forced himself to ignore it and concentrate on learning the balance of the unfamiliar spear. He shifted his hand up and down the ashen shaft until it felt comfortable, then waited for instructions.

The targets were set swinging, more rapidly than for the younger boys. Demne took a long, slow breath and balanced his spear. All the world narrowed to the moving round of wood against the pale sky.

"Toss," cried a voice, and he threw.

For a moment the air shimmered with weapons like some strange rain. Then one struck the earth short of the swinging targets, and others began to hit the edges of the rounds and skitter to the ground. Only a few flew true. He saw one strike the center of a round and dig deep into the wood. When it ceased to quiver he recognized the bit of green cloth that was his mark trembling at the end of the shaft.

A brown hand clapped his shoulder. "Well thrown, lad. You've a good, steady hand. Now, go over there with the others until the next round."

Demne shuffled across the churned earth and smashed grass and joined a little cluster of youths. Dael mac Conain stood with them, and he glared as Demne joined them. In the two days since the footrace, Demne had tried to avoid the other boy. He had kept silent or played the fool to disarm envy and disguise the gaps in his knowledge. Mac Conain had been relentless in his persecution, not only of Demne, but of any boy smaller than himself, and his only friends seemed to be those who had been beaten into following. They copied his manners, and bullied the littler ones too.

Once all the boys had completed their first spear toss, the targets were taken down, and smaller ones put in their place. Because they weighed less, they swung more rapidly. Those who had not been eliminated in the first rounds were divided into three groups of fifteen or sixteen boys each. Demne watched the first bunch as it was led out to the mark.

Beside each boy, three spears were stuck into the earth. The youths hefted each one, checking the balance, then shoved them back into place. The targets were set swinging, and the signal given. Strong young arms swung spears up and sent them flying, one after another, as rapidly as possible. Several boys hit once or twice, but only two sank all three spears into the rounds. These came back, flushed with triumph, to receive the praises of those waiting. As he followed his group to the marks, Demne felt the old, familiar yearning for such sweet words.

He stilled his thoughts, as the Liath Luachra had taught him, and touched her brooch. Then he tried the balance of each of his three spears, handling them until they felt comfortable. He put two spears back into the ground on his right, the other on his left. One of the men in charge of the contest looked at this and stared hard at Demne, as if trying to penetrate the shaggy locks which shadowed his features.

The boys on either side of him had set their spears in a neat row. Demne wondered if there was a rule that one must arrange things that way, but surely if he were doing wrong someone would have told him so. The Liath Luachra had trained him to cast the spear that way. He could almost sense her presence, and his ears echoed with the memory of her harsh voice as she had forced him to practice until his arms ached and his shoulders burned with pain.

The targets were set swinging, and the signal given. Demne hurled the first spear with his right hand, took a half step back, and reached out with his left hand to the spear on that side. Almost before his first spear had reached the target, the second had followed it. With a simple forward step his right hand grasped the third. The impact of the first spear had altered the motion of the target, and the second affected it again, a wobble so subtle that it was difficult to follow. Demne knew only the weight of the spear in his hand, the shifting balances as his body strained to match the movement of the target. So profound was his concentration, he might have been alone on the field as he hurled the final spear.

The shafts of his weapons stuck out of the target in a neat diagonal line. But Demne scowled and shook his head. They were too far apart! He had intended them to cluster together. The Liath Luachra would have scolded him and slapped his ears, and Demne was deeply grateful she was not there to see the muddle he had made. Once he had completed this ruthless evaluation of his own performance, Demne studied the throws of the other boys. As in the previous round, most had failed to get all three spears into the target. But this did not make him feel any better.

The others were competing with each other, Demne realized then, and he was measuring himself against the standard of the Liath Luachra's training. As he neared the remaining youths who had not yet had their chance, and the two who had succeeded in the first round, a foxy-faced lad in a fine linen tunic grinned at him.

"That was splendid. How did you learn to use both hands?"

Just a few minutes before, Demne had longed for praise. But now he felt no pleasure in the words.

"I practiced," he muttered finally, sullen and hot. What a stupid question. Clearly he had not practiced enough.

The lad laughed and slapped his upper arm. "I could practice till Samhain and never do that well."

Demne felt slightly better. He might not be as good as his teacher had wanted, but apparently he could do things that other people could not. He had only begun to realize that since coming to Tailtiu. But he could not laugh or tease or boast like the other boys. If only he had been reared in a rath instead of spending his childhood with two old women, he would have known how to behave.

It was not enough to throw a spear or know the ways of the wise. If he had known how to move among men, his friend Bran mac Conail would still be alive, and, like as not, in this very field. Demne watched the third round of the contest without really seeing it. He knew that one of the black moods he struggled with so often was destroying what little pleasure he might have had, but the light seemed to have gone out of the day.

Nonetheless, the sun had reached the high point of the heavens. The seven boys standing in the field were all that remained of those who had entered the spear toss that morning. Demne watched as the rounds were removed and replaced with targets no wider than his forearm was long. The judges brought out new spears, slightly longer in the shaft than those used before, and with narrower barbs. The Liath Luachra had possessed such a spear, and he knew it could be thrown a remarkable distance.

Indeed, the judges were marking a new throw line, even further from the targets than before. They shoved five of the long spears into the ground at each place, and gestured the seven forward. Demne stepped up to one, and a hard fist smashed him in the small of his back. Furious, he turned and found Dael scowling and ready for a fight.

"Get away, you fool. This is my spot."

The pain in his kidneys was dizzying for a moment, and Demne wanted to knock the other boy down and kick his face in with his bare feet. He clenched his fists as one of the judges bustled forward. "Here, now. What's all this?"

"He's in my place, the upstart," snarled Dael.

"Mind your manners, boy." Demne had started to retreat before he realized this remark was not directed at him. "The *Ard Ri* is watching. He won't take kindly to you behaving like some lowborn brat. Go over there and use the red spears."

"Lowborn brat! He's the one who started the trouble, and I won't use red. It is not a fortunate color for me."

The judge gave Dael an amused look. "What an odd thing to say, considering the amount of blood Clan Morna has spilled on Eriu's soil. I saw you strike this youth without provocation. We all know what a troublemaker you are, Dael mac Conain, and we won't have any of your nastiness on my field. Do you hear?"

The boy wilted a little beneath the judge's keen gaze. The pain in Demne's back begin to ease, and he glanced towards the high platform. The great chair was once more occupied, and he felt the eyes of the king piercing him.

"I will take the red. All you needed to do was ask." He rubbed his back. "Red is a very fortunate color for me." He bared his teeth in a grin as he remembered the red path that had swirled away from the skirts of the Goddess.

"I don't speak to nameless nobodies!" Dael smirked as if he had said something clever. Demne decided that if no one else got there first he was going to kill that boy one day. His heart pounded as he moved away, and he had to control his breathing to calm himself.

Demne hefted his weapons, testing their balance. One seemed very wrong, and he looked at it more carefully. He was holding it in both hands when one of the men came over. "What is it, boy?"

"Uh, these thongs are broken," he said, wide-eyed.

"What! Nonsense. I personally checked every spear myself. Let me see. . . . These are not broken. They've been cut." He looked at Demne, who stared back stupidly. Then he looked at Dael mac Conain, who was nearly shining with smugness, and shook his head. "The mischief that boy gets up to. Unfortunate color, my eye. He wanted you to use a damaged weapon. It is a good thing you noticed."

"My teacher told me to always study any new weapon," Demne answered.

"And who was that, boy?"

"My teacher was the Liath Luachra."

"That explains a great deal. The way you ran the footrace, for instance. She was the swiftest thing I ever saw. Long ago, of course. She trained you very well. I could only wish—well, never mind. Better a sweet nature than a clever bully. Better for Dael mac Conain, anyhow. Here, lad, I'll get you a good spear."

Demne choked back a hearty laugh as the man hurried away. He felt anything but sweet. Dael must fear him a great deal to have tried such a stupid trick. He wondered why the boy felt he had to cheat to win. Still, it calmed him to realize that the other was afraid. He measured the balance of the four spears while he waited for the fifth to be brought, and glanced towards his adversary. Dael had his shoulders hunched in rage.

Demne considered the placement of his spears, which to the left and which to the right. He was still thinking about this when the judge brought him the fifth spear, with a narrow strip of red cloth tied around the butt end. Demne took the last spear and held one in each hand, feeling not only their balance, but something of the hands that had crafted them. It was the first time he had ever noticed the voice of anything made, and it was a new and remarkable thing.

Then he heard Dael complaining about the delay, and he turned and grinned. Something in his wolfish smile made the other boy go silent in mid-word. Demne positioned his spears to his satisfaction, rubbed his palms across his thighs, and waited. All the tension drained from him as the noonday sun beat down on the crown of his head.

"Have you ever seen a warrior set his spears like a thicket around him?" someone muttered behind him.

"Only one, and that was long ago," came the answer. Demne wondered why that was so remarkable, but the judges had set the targets swaying. Their movement lulled him like the singsong of Bodbmall's chanting. Then the signal to begin sent a rush of power through his veins. His hands flew and his feet danced. The spears sped across the distance with effortless ease. Perhaps he had not awakened after all; perhaps he was dreaming.

Demne reached out and found empty air. All the spears had been thrown. He scratched his head to conceal his surprise, and looked towards the target. It bobbed just a little now, the fluttering red cloths around the shafts at the butt almost touching each other. The heads of the five spears stood no more than a finger's breadth apart in the center of the round. Demne gave a great sigh, and his wide shoulders sagged in relief. This time, even the Liath Luachra would have been pleased! If only she were here to see it. He barely heard the cries and cheers from the boys on the field and the watching crowd.

Demne turned slowly away from the triumphant cluster of spears and looked at the high king. Even at this distance, he sensed approval, knowledge, recognition in that pale gaze. Demne lowered his head in a slight bow. Then he was engulfed by admirers, slapping his back and praising him, and this time he was able to rejoice in the praise.

Dael mac Conain was standing in bewildered isolation, deserted even by his hangers-on. Demne almost felt sorry for him, until he remembered what Dael had tried. But his desire to slay the other boy had faded before the radiant joy of winning the spear toss.

For the first time in his life, Demne found the present delightful. He was having the best time in the world.

Chapter 10

❧

TWO DAYS PASSED IN LENGTHY RITUALS OF CATTLE blessing, trading, and more races, both foot and mounted. The earth of the oval course was almost bare from constant use. Demne spoke little and listened well, beginning at last to understand something of the petty intrigues of the boys in the House of Youths and the more serious involvements of their clans.

To his discomfort, Demne's triumph at the spear throw had gained him a small group of admirers. He had always longed for companions, but when some of the boys from the House of Youths began to follow him about, he was wary of their sudden friendliness. He wished he could ask Bodbmall what it all meant, but the ancient *bendrui* had made it clear that she did not want him. Thus, even his newfound friends could not keep him from feeling lonely. He could beat the other boys in games, but that did not make him like them. Claiming Bodbmall as his foster mother satisfied the more curious, and even bestowed upon him some status, but he still had neither kin nor clan.

THE THIRD MORNING, AS THE CATTLE LOWED AND THE dogs barked, Samhair, the girl who was caring for the

bendrui, came to the House of Youths to find him.
Demne was standing silent in the midst of a pack of
piping boys who were discussing the coming game of
hurley. He had no idea what they meant, and was not
sure he cared. The name rang a distant tone of memory, but it gave him a sense of unease he could not put
his finger on. Even so when Samhair beckoned, he
scowled. Then he noticed that her lips were set in a
grim line and his hostility turned to alarm.

Demne left his companions without a word and followed her across the compound. He was afraid to ask
any questions, and after the constant chatter of the
House of Youths, her silence was restful.

The hut was full of darkness. For a moment Demne
stood blinking, then he realized that the heap of blankets upon the pallet was Bodbmall. She lay without
moving, and what he could see of her seamed face was
empty of color. Blankets were heaped over her, and
her cloak as well, even though the day was already
warm. They trembled slightly as she shivered beneath
them. Her breathing sounded loud and terrible above
the flutter of the little fire.

Demne knelt beside the pallet and looked down
into the weary face. She was dying. Sweat had matted her white hair, and she smelled foul. In the few
days since he had last seen her, the flesh had wasted
from her bones, and the hand that gripped the blanket was like a raven's claw. Was there some curse that
destroyed everyone he loved?

Then Bodbmall stirred, and the thought was forgotten. She rasped for air, her eyelids twitched, and
painfully she dragged them open, staring at him without recognition for what felt like an eternity. At last
her gaze seemed to clear, and a hideous smile twisted
her mouth. But even this movement made the lips
crack and bleed. Demne saw a bowl of water and a
cloth beside the pallet. He wrung out the cloth and

caught the sharp, clean smell of willow bark as he reached down and wiped her face with care.

The labored rattle of her breath sounded like the bubbling of her great cauldron. Demne took her hand gently. Against his fingers it burnt like a brand.

"I never told you what a fine lad you were," she wheezed, "and now I do not have the time."

"Be quiet, dear heart. Save your strength to grow well," he told her. Demne felt that she was the child now and he the parent. It was a terrible sensation, like standing on his head until the blood came into it and then standing up quickly. He struggled to remain calm.

"I shall not recover, Demne. You will have to look for me at Samhain, when the spirits return."

"Please, Bodbmall," he whispered, "do not die."

Do not leave me. You are all that I have. If I had not insisted that we come, you would not have caught a chill. His thoughts were like the piping of birds against the finality he had heard in the voice of the *bendrui.* She had chosen to come here, as she was choosing now to let herself die. He told himself that no arguments of his could have persuaded her to leave the mountains if she had not wished it. But if that was so, she could choose to live. She had to live—he still needed her!

She made a noise that might have been a laugh. He rinsed the cloth and washed her face again. After that the *bendrui* was still for a time, shuddering beneath the blanket as he had quivered when he waited for the race to begin. When she spoke her voice was marginally stronger.

"Everything I could, I have taught you. The gods have played a game with me, to give me one born to wisdom and then turn him away from me. I know you will not follow the ways of the wise, Demne. But use what I have taught you well. Be honorable to all,

even those who would injure or destroy you or take
from you what is yours."

"And what is mine, Bodbmall? Who is my father?
Who is my mother?"

The *bendrui*'s eyes glazed over. "Be a good boy. . . ."

Then her lids fluttered closed and her hand went
limp in his grasp. Only the rasp of her breath told him
she yet lived, so still was she. But after a few minutes
even this reassuring sound faded, and he could no
longer see her chest rise and fall.

Demne staggered to his feet. Grief burned in his
breast, but his aching throat was too tight to let it
free. Or was it rage? Bodbmall could not be dead—
not without giving him the one piece of knowledge
he most needed. It was almost as if she had died rather
than tell him who his father was.

He wanted to scream his anger at the roof of the
hut or the vault of the sky. He wanted to destroy
something. But there was nothing to smash except
Bodbmall's baskets or the girl sitting outside the door.
He was sure she had not cared for his foster mother
as he would have done if he had not been sent away.
Suddenly the tears came. Blindly he plunged through
the door of the hut, blinking as he came out into the
light of day.

Samhair looked up, eyes widening, and read his
news in his face. Something odd came into her
glance then. Was she blaming him for the death of
the *bendrui?* Demne fought down the urge to slap
her. He whirled away from her and for several seconds could do no more than stand shaking like a wet
dog. Southwards lay the mountains from which they
had come. He wanted to run back to them, run without stopping until his heart burst and he fell in his
tracks. He was alone!

Presently the shaking ceased. Demne could feel the
first flame of his grief sinking into embers of despair.

He brushed his eyes with his sleeve and sniffed miserably.

"She just . . . stopped . . ." he said dumbly, looking at the girl.

Samhair nodded. "She was old, and very tired."

Demne's big hands clenched and unclenched at his sides. Fresh tears welled into his eyes.

"She was very pleased that you won the spear toss and the footrace," Samhair said quietly. "But she sounded as if she expected you to win. Even when I told her about that mean trick that Dael mac Conain tried with the spears, she only laughed."

Demne glared at her. Why could Bodbmall not have told him that herself? He wished he had heard that laughter, had shared with her that moment of pleasure. Why had he been robbed of her last few days? He had yearned for the *bendrui*'s praise, but he did not want it from this intruding female who eyed him with such cool calculation in her gaze.

"Now you should go," said the girl. "The game begins in a little while."

"Game!" he sputtered. "Why should I care?"

"Because Bodbmall wished you to enter, no matter what happened to her. She told me several times that you *must* play."

Demne gaped at her, and then, oddly, felt comforted. It was almost as if the old woman were still ordering him around, complaining and crabbing. It did not ease the pain, but suddenly he felt stronger. All the times he had resented her orders were forgotten; he felt a dim relief at having something purposeful to do.

THE HURLEY COMPETITIONS HAD ALREADY BEEN GOING on for some time when Demne arrived. On the field now were two teams of smaller boys from the House of Youths. Each child had a strip of colored cloth tied around his brow to show which side he was on, and carried a wooden stick curved at the lower end. The field was an oblong of well-trampled grass. At each end were poles that supported a crosspiece, painted the same colors as the headbands. The purpose of the game seemed to be to drive the round leather ball either under or above the crosspiece, using the stick but not the feet or hands. Sometimes a boy caught the ball in one hand, then promptly dropped it to earth and hit in the direction of his team's goal, while the other side tried to keep it from getting there.

The curved sticks looked wicked, and several times he saw one barely miss a young head. Above the murmur of the watchers Demne could hear the thud of wood striking flesh alternating with the sharper sound as it hit the ball. He rubbed at his aching eyes and pushed the tangle of pale, curling hair back off his brow. He recognized it now, the name. The boys of the rath had been playing at hurley the day his friend Bran had died. Bodbmall had wanted him to be here. He must not think of her, or his dead friend, but about the game only.

Eventually he began to pick out a pattern in the apparently random movements of the boys and the ball. The game was essentially the same as the one the lads of Mag Life had refused to let him play with them, but more ordered and skillful. It could be perilous. Either by chance or intent, the *caman* sticks seemed to strike flesh almost as often as they did the ball.

Then someone started shouting for the boys from his own age group to form up at the end of the field. Demne was handed a green strip of cloth. He bound it firmly across his forehead, glad of a way to keep his hair out of his eyes. Nearby was another cluster of lads with yellow headbands. With a sigh of relief he saw Dael among them. They seemed to have chosen him as their leader, or perhaps he had seized the role. Their heads were bent together. Once someone glanced towards the greens and laughed, and Demne knew they were planning some mischief. He squared his jaw and narrowed his eyes at them.

He wondered if his own team leader, a big lad called Cormac mac Airt, had seen. Cormac had arrived only the previous day, and Demne found it hard to understand why he should be the leader, for he seemed as arrogant as Dael, whose father was called Conain the Swearer, but he kept still. Everyone in the House of Youths had treated the newcomer with great deference, and Demne tried to copy them.

Now Bodbmall was gone, and the only thing that mattered was to fulfill the last command she had given him. Silently he took his *caman* and hefted it to find the balance.

"Listen," began Cormac. "We have to keep an eye on those yellows, and we have to win. It's my only chance to achieve anything in these games, because I missed getting here until too late. You understand. But the Morna brat will do his best to prevent us winning, and we are the lesser team in size and weight."

"Except for Demne," piped up Diarmait. "He's as big as you are, Cormac."

Cormac continued as if he had not heard. "The judges will not lift a finger to stop any fouls, even with me here. They're too afraid of the mac Mornas and the *fianna*. When I am in the high seat, I am going to change that."

Still in the grip of his grief, Demne found Cormac's words incomprehensible. He knew there was more going on here than a simple hurley game. He just did not grasp what. A knot of frustration hardened in his belly. He did not know the things he needed to know! Still, his few days at Tailtiu had taught him to avoid such intrigues as much as he was able. That was the problem. He had an uneasy sense that these rivalries could be as deadly in a ball game as on a battlefield.

Cormac glanced over his team, and his impatient gaze rested on Demne.

"Try not to trip over your own feet, dummy, and stay out of the way. I swear the luck always falls against me. First my fosterer does not start out until three days after we planned to go, so I must miss the races and the spear toss, and then I am stuck with striplings and mooncalfs. You, Diarmait, keep to my left, and guard me while I hit the goals."

Diarmait nodded, but gave Demne a grin and a shrug when Cormac turned away, as if they shared some jest. Without understanding, Demne found himself smiling in return, but it felt stiff and false. He did not feel like smiling at all.

The two teams trotted out onto the field and faced off. The judge tossed the leather ball into the air, then scrambled back as a dozen curved sticks swung for it. A second later it arched into the air, curving towards a spot well behind the green team's line. Demne could see a boy with a yellow headband racing forward to follow up this first advantage.

He launched himself to intercept, and his stick cracked against that of the other boy just as they reached the ball. But Demne's was in front. The same stroke that knocked his opponent's *caman* aside whacked the ball back down the field towards the green goal. As the rest of the yellows converged on him, Demne saw one of the other greens deflect the still-rolling ball into an agile pass to Cormac.

Then a *caman* hit his foot, and he suppressed a cry. That had been no accident, but he ignored the pain and leaped towards the green goal. Cormac caught the ball on his stick and lofted it above the onrushing yellows in a lovely turning movement like a swan beating its way up from a stream. Two other greens were close behind him; one hooked the ball out of the way of a yellow and hurled it towards Demne.

The leather smacked into his big palm, and he dropped and slammed it towards the goal in a single, continuous motion. He hardly heard the shout of the onlookers as the ball flew beneath the green bar and hit the ground.

A youth from the yellow side put the ball back into play, and there was a mad dash down the field. In seconds, the yellows had gotten the ball down the long run, and hit it above their own goal. There was another huzzah from the crowd as the greens began to play the ball back down the field. This time Cormac hit the ball over the goal and watched with a grin of pleasure as the people cheered.

As the yellows began their return, Demne darted in and stole the ball away from Dael mac Conain. He barely noticed his enemy's glare of outrage as he smashed the ball upwards and watched it arch over the green goal. As he ran, he felt his hair stirred as a *caman* whizzed close by. Dael was chasing him, as if he had forgotten the game.

The greens took swift advantage of this diversion, and for a few seconds the yellows milled about, leaderless. Cormac made another under-post goal, and there was a pause in the play. Dael stopped running after Demne, his face flushed with heat and exertion, and motioned his team to gather around him. Demne trotted over to where Cormac waited, brushing the sweat off his brow, but breathing easily.

Cormac looked at Demne for a long time with measuring eyes. "We are ahead, but those yellows can catch up. There is more to this game than strength. It also takes strategy. So let me make the goals. Just keep the ball on our side, and keep the yellows away from me. Do I make myself clear?"

Demne frowned. He hadn't any idea what Cormac

meant. From what he had seen, any player was allowed to hit a goal, but Cormac seemed to wish to play the game alone. From the expressions on the faces of the rest of the team, he thought they didn't like the leader's orders any better than he did.

Oscar mac Mebh, one of the youths who since the spear toss had been trying to befriend him, came up to Demne.

"That big hound. Is it our fault that if he doesn't do well, he will not be allowed to stay with his grandfather this year? We should all have a chance to score. I am glad you have made some points, Demne, and I'd like to see Cormac try to wallop you. You'd make him eat dust, I'll wager."

"What does his grandfather have to do with the game?"

"I keep forgetting how simple you are. Don't you know that Cormac's father was son to the *Ard Ri?* He has to prove to the old man that he is as good as his father was."

"That is just his excuse," one of the other boys added. "You know how he is, always sure he can do things better than everyone else."

Demne listened to this with slowly dawning understanding. During his days in the House of Youths, he had learned that many of the boys were like himself, reared by others than their fathers and mothers. The difference was that they knew who their parents were. It was also clear that the games were only one of the reasons for the festival. The high king's time was filled with negotiations and judgments. Even watching the play seemed only an excuse to gather his chieftains. Demne remembered how Conn had watched him over the heads of his advisors. He could see how it might be hard even for a royal son to get near him except at the prize giving. Perhaps Cormac longed for a father's approval as much as Demne needed to know

who his father had been. He would have risked anything to win if kindred had been watching him.

But Bodbmall's spirit was watching, and she had
told Demne to play the game. Samhair said she had
been pleased when he won. Did it really matter who
got the ball across the goal? Surely the honor would
go to the winning team. He scratched his tangled locks
and waited for play to resume.

The yellows looked grim as they came back onto the
field. As the ball was once more set moving, Demne
found himself surrounded by a thicket of waving
camans. He didn't see how Dael could have put
them up to it, but at the moment he was not only
being prevented from stealing Cormac's glory, but also
distracting the opposing team's attention pretty effec-
tively just trying to stay alive.

A swinging stick grazed his skull and caught the
point of his shoulder as he ducked. Still head-down,
he butted one of his attackers in the belly. He heard
himself roaring like a bull as his shoulder caught
another boy in the ribs and sent him flying. He
uncoiled in a run.

The yellows had the ball. Three youths passed it
back and forth between them, then Oscar mac Mebh,
grinning like a wolf, scooted in and snatched it away,
sending it rushing towards the green goal. There was a
crack of wood on flesh, and a scream of anguish. Two
of the yellows were trying to beat Oscar to death in
their frustration at losing the ball. One of the judges
called a halt just as Cormac mac Airt sent the leather
orb spinning beneath the green goal.

Oscar lay very still. His handsome young face was
crushed in on one side; the hands that a moment ago
had gripped the *caman* curled open upon the grass.
Demne looked down. The boy's uninjured eye stared
unseeing at the bright blue sky.

Demne fought to breathe. Suddenly he was seeing

Bran mac Conail staring sightless at a sunset sky. But it had not been his doing, this time. Men hurried onto the field and bent over the fallen youth. After some conferring, he was lifted to a litter and carried away. The judges shook their heads and examined the sticks of the three yellows who had attacked Oscar. On one, they found a smear of blood and a wisp of golden hair. The boy whose stick it was stood round-eyed, as if the enormity of what he had done refused to penetrate his mind.

"You young fool," snapped the judge. "Clan mac Mebh will not quickly forgive such a brazen act, and it is forbidden to spill blood on the sacred ground of Tailtiu at the fair."

"It was an accident," the boy whined.

"It was deliberate, and you know it. Get off the field."

Dael mac Conain opened his mouth, closed it, and then said, "We will be a player short. That is not fair."

The judge rounded on Dael and looked at him until the boy shrank back. "The team follows the lead of its chief, and this is as much on your head as on mac Aedh's. Both teams will play with one less boy now."

"Why should we be penalized just because Oscar got himself hurt? He got in the way."

"He is not hurt, you young ass. He is *dead*. And he is dead because you encouraged your team to play foul. If Clan mac Mebh comes after you as well, do not be surprised."

"They would not dare. No one challenges the sons of Morna."

"You are as stupid as you are arrogant, my lad." The judge grabbed the youth with the telltale *caman* by one ear and dragged him away.

Demne rubbed his shoulder, which was beginning

to hurt, and bit his lip. He had liked Oscar, who was cheerful and friendly. A shudder shook his large frame. Would all who befriended him perish? He could not help remembering young Bran, and the last gasps of his foster mother only hours before. Why had he ever left his mountains?

The greens were huddled together as if seeking warmth in the heat of the day. The young faces were grim, some smeared with recent tears. Even Cormac seemed subdued. The youths shifted from foot to foot, scratched their bottoms or heads, and fiddled with their *camans*, restless and at a loss. At last, Cormac cleared his throat.

"Oscar would not wish us to grieve," he announced. Several of his team gave him looks of surprise, then disgust, but no one answered. "We must win the game for him." This seemed to hearten them, and Demne realized that all of them would have a spirit watching them now.

For the first few minutes, the game was sluggish, as if the energy had been drained out of the players when Oscar's blood fed the ground. Both teams captured the ball and then lost it again without scoring. Then action began to restore the excitement. They forgot why they were depressed and grew less cautious. As the play became more heated it grew more dangerous. Then the yellows sent the ball above the goal twice in rapid succession, and the greens drooped like wheat stalks in the sun.

As the ball was returned to yellow territory after the second goal, Demne stole it and punted it a short distance down the trampled field. Then, quite forgetting Cormac's order, he swung his *caman* as hard as he could, channeling into the stroke all his rage and sorrow. He felt a savage release as he felt the wood meet the leather. With a sense of foreknowledge, he straightened and watched the ball arch across the blue bowl of heaven, up, up, and over the green goal.

There was a roar like a storm wind striking the forest as the ball spun across the poles. The folk who clustered around the field seemed to become possessed with some strange madness. As the two teams loped down the length of the hurley ground to face each other once more, the onlookers leaped and cheered. Their excitement swirled out to engulf Demne in its fierce exultation, even though everyone on the field seemed to have become his foe. Cormac's glare and Dael mac Conain's scowl burned Demne's back, but he hardly cared. He had discovered that the rush of joy which came from hitting the leather ball as often and as hard as possible could take away his pain.

In that moment, Demne ceased to play for his own team. Now he was alone, as he had always been. Yellows surrounded him, and he broke through them as if they were no more than saplings in the forest. He heard Cormac mac Airt shout at him to pass the ball, but he refused to hear. Instead, he made goal after goal, dodging swinging *camans*, which might have been accidents, and flashing kicks, which were certainly nothing of the kind, with equal agility. A few connected, despite his fleetness, until his knees were bloody and he had a throbbing lump on his head. His thick, unkempt hair had deflected the head blow a little, and the boy who had hit him got a sharp elbow in the belly, which left him gasping.

Then, without warning, it was over. Demne was still running, but the ball was no longer there. As he came to a halt he realized that the judges were speaking. He heard the announcement that the greens had won the game without understanding the words. Empty of all feeling, Demne stood still, his *caman* dangling from his aching hands.

Cormac mac Airt stomped across the field towards him.

"Can't you understand orders? I told you I wanted to make the goals. Curse you, you have cost me my chance."

Demne nodded stupidly, weary beyond words. "You did. I lost my head." He rubbed the lump on his skull tenderly.

Cormac's expression softened just a little. "Well, at least we were the winning team, and I was the chief. A king must have strong warriors. You did play very well," he added unwillingly. "Where did you learn?"

Still stupid, Demne answered, "I never played before today."

Cormac's face went white, then red. He struck a balled fist into Demne's face, and kicked him viciously on one of his already bloody shins. Then hands seized him and pulled him away.

"Cormac, cease!" It was one of the older men. "Remember who you are." The prince shuddered, and with a visible effort seemed to get himself in hand.

"Next time we meet, you will bow to me!"

THE OTHER GREENS SURROUNDED DEMNE AND DRAGGED him away. They pounded his back and held his arms while they bore him off the field, fending off the press of enthusiastic well-wishers from the crowd. It was as if he were encased and protected by the other boys. He savored the sweetness of this as they led him to the bathhouse. If only poor Oscar had not died, and Bodbmall had been there to enjoy his success, he would have been totally content. As it was, his joy was made bitter by the memory of loss, and he had to struggle to pretend he was pleased. He could not wait to be alone again.

HIS CLOTHING, EVEN THE NEW BREECHES, HAD BEEN utterly ruined in the game. After a luxuriant bath,

Demne put salve on the worst of his cuts, and unpacked the splendid garments with which Donait had gifted him. It was that or go naked, and Bodbmall was not here to forbid his wearing them now. The other boys were dressing around him, and putting on their best as well.

Aonghus came into the House of Youths just as Demne finished tying the thongs of the wonderful leather shoes. He paused and for a long moment studied the clothing Demne wore.

"You played well, lad," he said finally, "though I fear you have made an enemy of Prince Cormac. Here, let's see if we can get that hair of yours in some order." He pulled a comb out of his belt pouch and began to drag it through Demne's wet hair, ignoring the little sounds of protest from the boy.

"I seem to have a talent for making foes, Aonghus," Demne replied. *And if you knew I had slain your brother,* he thought, *you would be one as well.* "Dael mac Conain hated me on sight, and Cormac said we should let him make all the goals. I tried, but I couldn't help myself. The yellows would have won if we had done it the way he told us to."

"Cormac wanted to impress his grandfather. That is perfectly natural," Aonghus answered neutrally.

"Did not all the boys wish to please their fathers and their kin?" Demne asked, thinking once more how wonderful it would have been to have a father to please, even if he had lost.

"Truly said, Demne. But king's sons have a greater need to excel than other men."

"That was what he meant when he said I stole his glory, I suppose. I didn't understand. If only he had been here for the footrace and the spear throw."

Aonghus laughed. "It would have made little difference, I suspect. I do not think there is a youth here this year who can touch you in anything."

"I must explain that I did not understand, and beg his forgiveness, then," Demne insisted.

"You must do nothing of the sort. Cormac will have to learn to deal with disappointment if he is ever to succeed the *Ard Ri*. One can hope that he will emulate his grandfather also in magnanimity. If he is worthy of the high seat, he will learn to value you."

"Do you really think so?" Demne asked dubiously. That had not been his experience so far.

"If it were Dael mac Conain, now, I would not be so hopeful. There are men, lad, who cannot bear to see another succeed, who cannot rejoice in another's accomplishments. They hate those who outreach them, and feel lessened by the feats of others." Aonghus tugged a particularly snarled section of hair free, and Demne winced.

"How do you know that?" He liked the way Aonghus answered his many questions. If only Bodbmall had been so easy to talk to.

"I have two uncles who aspired to the *filidecht*, and failed. They are only a year or two older than I, and when they were not accepted, and I was, they came to hate me. They lacked the gift of memory that is required to master three hundred and fifty tales, and bear me much ill will for succeeding where they failed." As he spoke, he began to work the hair beside Demne's face into two plaits that would hang down on either side.

"Your own kindred hate you?" he asked in amazement.

"Where have you been raised, not to know that the bitterest disagreements are sometimes between kin?"

Demne stood very still while Aonghus bound the end of the braid with a length of leather, and moved to the other side. "I am so ignorant sometimes, I do not even know what questions to ask. My fosterers instructed me as well as they could, but I know much they never told me." He bit his tongue, instantly regretting his boastfulness.

"What might that be, Demne?" The voice of the *fili* was very soft below the cheerful babble of the boys around them.

"Just things," Demne muttered. He liked Aonghus, but did not trust him enough to speak of the song of earth that ran along his bones or to mention the bounteous lady who had gifted him with the fine clothing he wore.

"Hmm. For all your great size, you are still very much a boy, are you not?"

"At Midsummer, I passed twelve."

"Just the age my brother Bran would have been, if he had lived. I hope you live long enough to become a man, for I think you will be remarkable. Now, I've braided two plaits, and I think a band around your brow will keep the rest of these untamed locks in their place. You will want to look your very best when we go." Aonghus removed a narrow strip of embroidered stuff from his belt and bound it across Demne's wide brow.

"Where are we going?"

By now the House of Youths was almost empty, and Demne was glad. He had had enough of people for the day. When Aonghus mentioned Bran, Demne had flinched inwardly, as if he had just cast the stone. He ached for Bodbmall and even for Oscar, smashed upon the field. He needed time to think about what had happened in the game, and about his loss.

"It is time to go before the high king and receive your reward."

"What do you mean?"

"For victory, lad. You have outshone the other youths in all things, and in those clothes, with your hair attended to, the fairness of your face rivals the sun."

Demne felt his face redden. He did feel very fine in the garments of Donait, but no one had ever found his face or body worthy of remark before. He cast an astonished glance at Aonghus and looked away, confused by a flush of pleasure that reminded him of the warmth he had felt with Donait. Without the *bendrui* to advise him, he felt very lost in the strange world of men.

But he could think of no way to evade the summons of the high king. He followed Aonghus out of the House of Youths and across the enclosure. It was almost deserted except for a few dogs and some slaves going about their tasks. But beyond the walls, the field was thronged with folk, all in their finest garb. Many of the warriors wore breeches, some of them with only a half-circle cloak to cover bare torsos that gleamed with jewelry of gold. Others wore the knee-length tunic and mantle, but the most important men wore long gowns like the king's, and cloaks whose golden fringes swept the grass. The late afternoon sun flashed off ruddy tresses, washed and braided and coifed in a hundred fantastic ways. The smell of clean bodies, of hair scented with oils and perfumes, mixed with the smell of beer.

Demne hesitated at the sight of so many. Then he seemed to hear Bodbmall's voice telling him to straighten up and stop being a fool. He squared his shoulders and followed Aonghus through the throng with a confidence he was far from feeling. Big, hearty men buffeted him across the back and breathed beery gusts into his face. Beautiful women smiled at him, and patted his face. Some of the boys he had come to know, or played with, wrung his hand and grinned at him. Did they think something of his skill would rub off on them?

Before the platform where the high king sat in his carved chair, there stood men with spears and others

finely dressed and adorned with jewelry. Behind him
were the druids, dressed in gowns of bleached linen
and fringed mantles of many colors, and the *fili* with
mantles as blue as the sky. Demne hardly noticed
them, for he was fascinated by the sharp-eyed man in
the chair. He had felt the king's clear gaze even across
the field, and close to, the sense of mingled curiosity
and understanding was overwhelming. Conn of the
Hundred Battles might be old and gnarled like a tree
that has faced too many storms, but there was a twinkle in the pale eyes, as if they shared some secret.

Flustered, Demne looked away, and realized that
someone else was staring at him. Straight as a sap-
ling in the shadow of the ancient tree, Cormac mac
Airt was standing behind his grandfather. He too had
been scrubbed and burnished, and encased in new
clothes. For a moment Demne met his eye, and then,
very deliberately, he bowed. The older boy's carven
features did not change, but the betraying flush crept
up his cheeks, then slowly faded again.

He knows, thought Demne, *that I bowed to his name,
not to him.*

Another man strode forward to stand before the
king, rudely jostling Demne aside. The boy recognized
the redheaded man whom he had first seen when he
entered Tailtiu. "*Conain the Swearer . . .*" came the
whisper through the crowd. Demne shrank back in
revulsion. He could smell the beer-heavy breath of
the man, the slight bitter scent of sweat and horse on
his skin and clothing. He swayed, and his red braids
flapped against his broad shoulders as he lurched
closer to the platform.

The *Ard Ri*'s grey eyes grew hooded, as if he were
displeased. Demne stood a pace or two behind the
other man and waited. The redhead's hands were
balled into fists, shoulder muscles bunched beneath
his tunic. If he had been a dog, Demne was certain he

would have snarled, even at the man in the chair.

"I have come to claim what is mine," he muttered, then belched enormously.

"All can see that, Conain mac Morna," the king replied gravely. There were snickers among the spearmen, swallowed quickly when Conain glared at them. "As you have run the best race upon your steed, I grant you one cow of the royal herd as your reward."

"What!" Conain's roar of dismay did not suprise Demne, for even he knew that the reward the king offered was a deliberate slight. "One cow! One! What sort of putrid turd of a gift is that!"

Unmoved, the high king made a small gesture, and the spearmen below the platform shifted to alertness. " 'Tis more than you deserve, considering all the trouble you have made during this fair, and that which your son has caused. The House of Youths has had no peace under his authority, and the Men's House has been little better. Be glad of any gift at all, son of Morna, and keep your tongue well within that foul mouth of yours."

Conain mac Morna swelled like a toad, and Demne could see his skin redden across the back of his thick neck. Three others pushed forward to stand behind him. Again came the whispering: *That's Airt Og of the Hard Strokes, and Garra . . . and big Goll. All the sons of Daire are here.* For a moment they all faced the high king in tense silence. Then the biggest of them grasped one of Conain's thick arms and pulled him away.

"Come along then, ye gibbering fool. You've drunk too much, and you've lost what little wits were in ye before."

As the big man turned Conain around, Demne saw that he only had one eye. That eye fixed on Demne, and for a moment it widened in simple surprise. There were lines of laughter graven into the florid face, but as the moments passed, the expression that filled it was fear. That first look was followed swiftly by fury. He recoiled as if he had been struck.

But if the stranger seemed to have recognized Demne, the boy knew him as well, and he had already hardened himself to reveal nothing. These men were the foes he had seen in the red path of the Goddess, though he could not imagine what ill he had done them.

His hand clenched in the shadow of his sleeve, and he felt the familiar surge of rage kindle his blood. It was not directed at this stranger, but at Bodbmall. The *bendrui* should have told him who his enemies were! That she was gone where he could not even rail at her was even more maddening. If she had been alive, he would have shaken her with his big hands until she revealed to him, not the knowledge of the wise but the secret of his past. Without it, he might not live long enough to use what wisdom she had imparted to him. And there seemed to be none who might tell him what he must know, except the old man Fiacail, if he yet lived.

The high king cleared his throat, and the chatter of the assembly died. In a moment, there was only the sound of breath and the distant low of penned cows. A dog yapped somewhere. The king gestured, and a servant stepped forward with a piece of cloth draped across his extended arms.

"Who are you, boy, to have outdone all the youth of Eriu in fleetness of foot, sureness of hand, and hurley?"

Demne felt his heart sink into his belly. He had no name to give. Still, he could not stand there like a post before this great man who now smiled so kindly.

"Lord, I was called Demne by my fosterers," he answered slowly, his voice cracking in mid-speech.

The *Ard Ri* nodded. "A milk name, but hardly

worthy of such an accomplished youth as you have
become. By the brightness of your skin and hair, you
should be called Fionn, for I have hardly seen such
a fair youth since I was a lad. Tell me, who reared
you?"

Demne was aware of a murmur at this naming, and
wondered why. "The Liath Luachra trained me. She
and the *bendrui* Bodbmall are the only mothers I have
ever known," he answered. He started to add that she
lay dead and he had not even had time to mourn her,
but his throat closed with unshed tears.

"Bodbmall!" said the high king. "I ought to have
guessed that, for she reared me too, long ago, with
her brother and mine, Cumhal mac Trenmor. You
have a look of him about the eyes, and I will not
hesitate to put his name to you. The *bendrui* put her
mark upon us, as she did on you, Fionn mac Cumhal.
For your swiftness and your agility, I gift you with
this cloak, that it may warm you and keep you safe
from all your foes." As he spoke these last words, the
high king looked out across the crowd, as if he were
speaking to someone whom Demne could not see.

When he reached for the armful of russet wool, soft
and too warm in the heat of a summer's day, Demne
was dimly aware that he had finally achieved the goal
that had driven him for as long as he could remember.
He now knew the name of his father, and that he had
his eyes. But it was an empty victory, now that it had
come, and from the sound of some within the crowd,
one which bore a legacy of strife. He bowed slowly,
and pressing the cloak against his breast, he turned
defiantly to face the assembled clans.

Blinking into the blaze of the setting sun, he heard a
shout that shook his bones. Demne started, then realized that they were praising him. No matter who he
was, or who the father whose name he had just learned
had been, he was a hero here. If only Bodbmall had

been here to see it, he thought as someone thrust a carved wooden bowl of beer into his hands and drew him into the celebration. If only she had been able to hear the people of Eriu shouting his new name—

"Fionn! Fionn! Fionn!"

Chapter 11

THE DEERHOUNDS STRAINED AND QUIVERED ON THEIR leads, rough-coated brindled pelts glistening with the mist that had settled there. Demne quieted them with a touch and looked to the hound master for the signal to let them go. Old Liam's weather-browned face creased in an approving smile, then he shook his head. Distant halloos told them that the beaters had started a beast, but it was still far away.

The youth stifled his impatience, rubbed his hand over the brush of his shorn hair, and drew his cloak a little closer about him to ward off the chill of standing still. He brushed a leaf off the russet wool and realized how threadbare it had become. He could still remember how warm and soft it had seemed when he had received it from the hands of the *Ard Ri* after defeating all the other youths in the games at Tailtiu. Where had the two years gone?

A flood of memories overwhelmed the present. Once more Aonghus mac Conail was wakening him from a beery slumber, muttering something about danger. As Demne pulled the cloak the *Ard Ri* had just given him around his shoulders and fumbled with the belongings the poet pressed into his hands, the name of Morna had shocked him back to consciousness.

"You must leave Tailtiu," Aonghus had told him. Despite the prohibition against blood feuds in that sacred ground the sons of Morna were plotting to murder him, the flames in their heads fueled by liberal doses of beer. "Shear your hair so folk will think you an outcast, and get far away from here."

And that was no more than the truth, thought Demne. He seemed to have been running ever since; his entire, brief life had been an endless race against invisible competitors.

His flight had taken him steadily south and westward, away from the lands of the Gael. He served as a cowherd for the Fir Bili, and when he left there, the headwaters of the Boann had sung to him that Aonghus mac Conail had been drowned. Demne had wept for this curious knowledge, never questioning it. All who befriended him seemed to perish. He was alone, always alone.

Demne had wandered south past the skirts of the Sliab Bladhma to toil for a season in the fields at the headwaters of the Siuir, always cropping his hair and darkening his skin, and keeping himself out of sight as much as possible. After that he had made his way to a rath tucked into the hills of the Mumu border where they let him tend horses and gather wood for the kitchens, and remained there almost three seasons more.

But even there he heard news of Clan Morna. So he had made his way deep into Mumu, land of harpers and women of wonder, seeking the mountains of the Sliab Luachra whose beauties the old warrior woman had so often described. In Dun Coba, nearly within sight of the sea, he found employment in the service of the King of Benntraige, working the hounds for old Liam by day, and sleeping among them by night.

The summer was past, and autumn had colored the

woods in gaudy reds and golds. This was the last hunt of the season, for Samhain was but a few days away. Game had already become scarce and the greybeards prophesied a hard winter. The king had sent to the druids for a foretelling, but Demne did not know if he had received any reply.

Demne forced himself back into the present moment, and stroked the lean flank of his favorite bitch, Caer. He had discovered that he liked working with dogs, who responded to his care with such open and unquestioning affection. Perhaps there were no real answers. Certainly discovering the name of his father had solved nothing. Bodbmall had been right, and if he had not insisted on going to Tailtiu she might still be alive, and he would have had her counsel. He grimaced ruefully. He had not valued her wisdom while she lived, only when she was gone. What a fool he was, to be sure.

There was a faint rustling in the underbrush, and an enormous red stag soared over a deadfall between the trees. Liam snapped his long fingers, and Demne loosed the dogs as the tail of the animal vanished. The three great hounds leapt after it, and Demne followed them, jumping a fallen log. All his vain musings were forgotten in the pure pleasure of movement. He barely heard the spearmen following him as the dogs gave tongue, voicing their own delight in the chase.

The breeze which had stirred the leaves quickened into a gusting wind, and rain began to pelt down. In a brief time, Demne was drenched. He hardly noticed. Ahead, the trees thinned for a moment, and he glimpsed the stag. It paused, looking back as if it were mocking its pursuers, then leapt away before the hounds could close. It was a magnificent beast, the very thing for the Samhain feast, but Demne found himself hoping it might elude him and the panting spearmen who followed. It must be a cunning beast

to have survived so many seasons, for he was certain
he had counted seven tines upon its proud rack of
antlers.

Demne pushed himself to keep up with the hounds
as the wind whipped branches against his face and
shoulders. The men grumbled at the wet and the cold,
but they complained about everything, so he paid no
heed. Soaked, he stank of dog, so he could hardly
smell the wet earth beneath his pounding feet. Then
a tremendous clap of thunder rattled the ground and
a flash of lightning dazzled his eyes into momentary
blindness.

In his sightlessness, his toe caught a stone and
Demne sprawled on the sodden earth, his breath
knocked out of him. Blinking, he scrambled back to
his feet and looked for the dogs in the driving rain.
They would lose the scent of the stag, and would
have to depend on their eyes and his. Furry grey hind-
quarters disappeared into a thicket and he dove after
them. The spearmen followed, cursing the weather,
the stag, and anything else that moved. Then he heard
the deep voice of the king ordering them to silence,
and repressed a smile.

The trees opened into a wide meadow, its grasses
flattened by the driving rain. Beyond it was another
line of trees. The stag leaped across the open ground,
the hounds snapping behind him. The youth opened
his stride and rushed ahead, his feet barely touching
the bracken. Someone yelled astonishment as he sped
past the hounds. The stag was nearly out of the meadow. If he reached the dense trees, they would have to
find another guest for the Samhain feast.

The bitch Caer tried to keep pace with him, her pink
tongue lolling as if they were playing a good game.
Then Demne's strong legs left even her behind. The
great seven-tined stag was almost to the safety of the
forest. Demne had no spear to cast, but he had his

hands. His thighs bunched as he launched himself forward.

Demne felt an instant's surprise as he landed across the huge beast's bony spine. Then the antlers swept back to dislodge him, and he realized his peril. He clung to the strong neck, feeling the deer's pulse beat beneath his fingers as he ducked away from the slashing horns. The stag twisted, snorting, its hooves tearing up bunches of rain-soaked fern. Demne could not decide if he would be in more danger where he was or aground where the lashing hooves could strike him.

Then a spear flew past Demne's head, and he decided to take his chances on the ground. He slipped off and rolled agilely into the trampled ferns. He came to his feet just as the king drove his spear into the throat of the stag, just beneath the jaw. Blood spouted around the wound, washing down the heaving breast and paling into pink in the downpour. The beast staggered as another spear thrust home. One of the dogs bit through the sinew of a hind leg, and the stag collapsed, still lashing with hooves and horns.

The great head crashed to earth before Demne's soaking shoes. The dark eyes stared up at him as the life drained away, mute and accusing. Tears blinded Demne's eyes, but the rain washed them away. He groped for words to express his sorrow for that fallen splendor, but could find none. Then he recalled something Bodbmall had taught him. He bent to stroke the stag's brow, opened his awareness, and felt the spirit of the wonderful stag touch his own.

Brother, you ran well! We thank you for the gift of your life—it will not be wasted. We will salute your spirit with those of our fallen brothers when we light the Samhain fires.

His throat ached as if the king's spear had pierced it instead of the stag's.

The other men were crowding forward now. He

sat back, roughly wiping his tears away. To cover his emotion Demne started to check out the hounds. It was then that he saw the body of Caer, caught beneath the weight of the stag as it had fallen, her skull crushed by a lashing hoof. The rain was washing the blood away, and the flesh seemed already cool. Demne pushed the body of the stag aside, and cradled the broken hound against his breast, resting her head against his shoulder. He hardly knew he was crooning his sorrow into her unhearing ear as the huntsmen jerked out their spears and began to gut the slain stag so that it could be carried back to the dun.

The king, a square-shouldered man with a little white showing in his brown hair, looked at the carcass of the dog in Demne's arms. Demne went still, biting his lower lip until he tasted his own blood. It suddenly occurred to him that tackling the stag in that manner had not been the best way to remain obscure. He shivered with cold, and more.

The King of Benntraige stared at him. At last, the rain was slackening. A final clap of thunder rang far away, and a flash of brightness cast sharp shadows across his face. The day was near to ending, and the torches would be soaked through. It looked like a long, dark walk back to the dun.

The huntsmen tied the dead stag's feet to two stout poles, hoisted it onto straining shoulders and set off across the wet meadow at a rapid pace, eager to be out of the weather and into dry garments. Demne started to follow them, but the king laid a hand upon his arm.

"Who are you?"

Demne shifted the burden of the dead bitch in his arms. He was cold and wet and weary to the bone, and he knew from the tone of the question that he was in trouble again. "Demne crop-head—the dog boy. I have been in your service since Midsummer."

"Indeed. I never saw a dog boy so fleet of foot."

Forcing a laugh he did not feel, Demne answered, "To keep pace with the hounds, one must learn fleetness." *And my sister can still outrun me, but even she seems to be leaving me alone.*

"You do not bear yourself like a lad who has known nothing but the hounds."

"The hound master can tell you I work hard," Demne answered defensively.

"Oh, I am certain that you do. He is a stern taskmaster and permits no slacking. But the rain has washed the grime from your face and I can see that it is pale beneath what is left of your bright hair. That fairness, and the set of your eyes, puts me in mind of one I knew long ago. He too was fleet, and headstrong enough to leap upon the back of a stag at bay. My heart went to my throat when I saw you jump," the king said then.

Demne resisted an impulse to cover his revealing hair, and another to drop the body of the dog and run for the woods. Instead, he stared at the king with as much stupidity as his weariness could muster.

"Was he your dog boy too?"

The King of Benntraige gave a snort of bitter laughter. "Cumhal mac Trenmor was no man's dog. That was just the trouble. No one could restrain him. He was cunning as no other I have ever known, but a fool for all of that."

"A fool?" Demne asked, stung. He had only a few scraps of information about the mysterious man who was his father, for he dared not ask about him openly. Folk were reluctant to speak of Cumhal for fear of the wrath of Clan Morna who had defeated Cumhal and his *fian* in some battle. But what he had heard gave him the picture of a very brave man who was anything but a fool.

"He was a madman to have taken away the daughter of the *drui* Tadhg mac Nuadat, and more to have kept her."

Demne shifted the body of the dog in his arms as he digested this. "All men are mad when Aonghus Og afflicts them, are they not?"

"The love god had less to do with it than pure stubbornness. And I can see by the set of your jaw that you are possessed by the same spirit." The king fell silent and turned to follow the huntsmen from the meadow, and Demne followed.

"Tadhg himself will come to my holdings to read the omens at Samhain, *gilla*," the king said then, using the term for a wellborn boy in his years of service, not a slave. "I think 'twere best if you were away before he arrives. I want no blood on my hands, especially a boy's blood."

Demne sighed. "I understand."

He did not, for he could not see why his grandfather would bear him malice for simply existing. But in the two years since Bodbmall died he had learned that asking folk why they acted so incomprehensibly only got him a buffet across the head.

"Tell me one thing, if you will," he said instead. "Was she fair, the daughter of the *drui?*"

The king paused in mid-stride and shook out the folds of his sodden cloak. "Muirne? Fair does not begin to describe her loveliness. The summer roses hung their heads with envy where she passed. Every man in Eriu desired Muirne Fair Neck, boy."

"And Cumhal?" Demne's hunger for some sense of the two people who had died before he began to live made him careless.

"A fine figure of a man, as you will be, if you live to grow a beard. He was my friend, but even for memory of him, I will not risk the wrath of Tadhg. Before the sun rises, be away. Do you hear?"

"I hear. Still, will you answer me this? If Cumhal

was brave and fair to look upon, why did Tadhg refuse his daughter?" It was a question that had plagued him ever since he had first heard that his hawk-eyed grandfather had rejected the suit of Cumhal. "Was he lowborn?"

The king laughed with real amusement this time. "Hardly that, lad. But surely you should know—"

"My foster mother, Bodbmall the *bendrui,* hoped that if she could keep me from finding out anything of my parents, she could keep me safe from harm."

"I see. An odd decision for one of the wise. Cumhal was the son of that fair woman who was the wife of the *Ard Ri* Tuathal until Trenmor ran off with her."

Demne opened his eyes at that. He had not realized that eloping with forbidden women was such a tradition in his family.

"She had already given birth to the great Conn of the Hundred Battles, who rules now in Temair. Good blood runs in your veins, lad, but that will not stop Tadhg from doing you an injury if he can."

"Why is that?"

"You know not of the prophecy?" The king shook his head once more. "It was written before the world began that Tadhg mac Nuadat would lose all that he possessed to his first grandson."

"Why would I want anything of his?" Demne muttered. He was cold and tired. He did not want to have to run again. "Tell me, is there anywhere in Eriu where I will come to no grief?"

"If there is, fair *gilla,* I know not where it might be." They fell silent until they reached the holding, then the king strode into the hall without saying farewell.

Demne did not pause to change into clean, dry clothing. Instead, he found tools to dig a hole in the wet earth big enough to hold a dog. He put the dead Caer into it tenderly, stroking her soft muzzle with one hand. Then he covered her up, blinking away the tears that leaked out of his eyes.

His shoulders ached from the weight of the dead animal, or perhaps he had wrenched them holding onto the stag. His hands were raw from digging. He went and stood beside the kitchen hearth, and let the fire warm him while he ate a bowl of boiled grain and a withered apple. Then he fled to his own familiar bed, ripe with the scent of dog, almost staggering with fatigue.

In the hour before dawn, Demne roused. The brief sleep had hardly refreshed him. He rubbed one shoulder, then pushed the blankets aside, yawned until his square jaw cracked in protest, and stretched. At the foot of his bed was a bundle that did not belong there. He pulled the thing over into his lap and opened it. It was a very thick wool cloak, a little worn, but still good, a tunic of the same stuff, and new trousers. Everything was a dull brown and unadorned, but it was warm and comforting. There was also some food—cheese, a loaf of bread, some strips of dried meat, and three shriveled apples.

The youth smiled over these gifts. The King of Benntraige was a good master, unlike a few he had served. He was touched by the kindness in the gift of the clothing and the food, as he had been touched by the concern of Aonghus mac Conail in hurrying him out of Tailtiu. It was not a thing he was accustomed to, and it touched some unspoken hurt within him and made it less. He hoped there would never be a time when small kindnesses lost the power to move him.

He wished he could get a look at the old man whose fear was forcing him to go away. But the boy could not return the king's kindness by letting himself be killed after all. As Demne gathered his belongings, the unwisdom of remaining nearby was slowly penetrating

his not quite awakened mind. He knew well the powers of the wise, and he did not doubt that Tadhg
would notice him if he were nearby. That fierce old
man had wished him ill even before he was born; now
at least he knew why. He dressed in the new clothing,
and wriggled his feet into still-damp brogues. Then he
slipped away into the rising mists of dawn.

Demne trotted through the empty fields, eating an
apple to break his fast. It was chill, and the sky was
dark with rain to come. The sun rose above the rounded hills shrouded in cloud, and offered no heat he
could feel. But his muscles had loosened with his
exertions, and he did not feel the cold, even when
the wind began to pick up at mid-morning. The first
wet snowflakes surprised Demne, and he left the narrow track he had been following, to get beneath the
shelter of the trees. He snuffled a little, rubbing his
cold nose across his sleeve.

A faint jingle of metal made him start, then freeze
where he stood, listening intently and sniffing the air
through his stuffy nose. Presently he heard the clop
of hooves and voices and caught the warm smell of
horses and men. Curious, he was creeping towards
the road, when a warm gust of wind brushed his
cheek. A small, unseen hand gripped his wrist. The
air sparkled beside him, and Demne could almost see
the shape of a head shaking in negation.

As the horses drew nearer, Demne retreated into
the deep shadow of a large oak tree. He leaned back
against the trunk, feeling the sluggish movement of
the sap within the tree. After Bodbmall's death he had
abandoned the ways of the wise, because to use them
was too painful a reminder of his loss. He still heard
the constant murmur of stone and water, but only
rarely did he give it heed. The waters had sung to
him of the death of Aonghus mac Conail in the depths
of the Boann, and more, the fact that it had not been

chance. But he needed the earth magic now.

He felt the warmth of his invisible sister leave him and longed to follow her where she dwelt. He would not waste her warning. Demne frowned, shutting out the voices that spoke of ages past and others yet to be, and concentrated on the present. He could feel the fury of the oncoming storm hanging just beyond the horizon, and knew he must find some shelter before it arrived. He expanded his awareness to encompass the hills that rose above the forest, and located a tiny cave, a cranny almost, but sufficient to shelter him if he could find it with his open eyes.

As he slipped back into his shivering body, Demne glimpsed riders moving past him along the rutted track. There were warriors, a dozen or more, pressing forward eagerly to reach Dun Coba before the snow fell. In their midst, on a cream-pale steed, there rode a straight-backed ancient with hair like snow and brows like night. His eyes were hooded, as if he dozed while he rode. But as he passed the oak the eyes snapped open with the gaze of a hawk. As he rushed back into his own body, Demne saw the proud head turn. He pressed against the rough trunk and let the oak song flood his mind and fill his limbs.

The slow sap song became his only thought. Demne felt himself dissolve into the tree, and then into all the oaks that had ever been since the world began. A tiny portion of him fluttered in terror, then went still. Unseen eyes raked the woods and found nothing but leaves and branches and stones. The great oak "heard" a voice speak.

I must be getting old, starting at shadows. There is nothing there. My powers are as vigorous as ever. Perhaps it is holding off this storm that has wearied me.

This thought was followed by a confused memory of a rainstorm over a field where men battled. Then, distantly, there was a command, and the horses began to move away more rapidly.

Demne could never determine afterwards how long he hid in the oak, nor what restored him to himself, bone-cold and trembling. He rubbed his hands up and down his arms and legs, then stamped his feet to restore some circulation. The wood was still, except for the slight whisper of snow and the murmur of the wind. He pulled his old prize cloak out of his pack and laid it over his newer one, but the cold seemed to have seeped into his bones. He headed deeper into the wood and toward the little cave that he had spied in his mysterious journeying.

The wind rattled the tree limbs, sending down drifts of wet snow, and Demne began to run. His breath misted before his face and the blood pulsed in his flesh. He slipped and slithered on icy stones, banging into trees and low-hanging branches. The wind rose higher, screaming its fury at having been delayed, and the snow thickened until he could barely see a stride before him.

Demne was soaked now, and so cold his teeth chattered. The full force of the storm nearly knocked him down as he left the cover of the wood. He slipped onto his hands and knees and began to crawl up the incline that he hoped led to his shelter. His hands and knees scraped icy stone, were cut, and bled, but he felt no pain. By the time he finally reached the rocky heights, he was almost too tired to go on.

Pausing to gasp for air, Demne hardened himself to his exhaustion. Before him, the rock narrowed into a ledge. Almost numb, Demne rose slowly and pressed his back against the cold stone, then began to inch his way along. Great gusts of wind pounded his chest and drove spears of ice against his exposed skin. How could the storm be trying to slay him when the *drui* had not known he was there?

Demne's foot slipped and for what felt like an eternity, he flailed between air and an unknown drop to a stony death. Then the wind slammed him back against the cliff, knocking his remaining breath away. Little spots of brightness danced in his blinded eyes. He could feel the bulge of his belongings pressing into his back and promising some comfort if he could ever find the opening of the cave. Weak and dizzy, he reached into the stone and groped with his mind for some guidance. Spread against the wall, numb hands clawing icy rock, he crept upwards.

After a torturous time, the ledge wound out of the direct path of the wind, and Demne could see a little better. He blinked the snow out of his eyes and rubbed his fingers together until he could feel a tingling. Then he gritted his chattering teeth and pressed forward.

An ice-rimmed growth of bracken thrust out from the ledge. Beneath it lay a opening hardly bigger than his wide shoulders. Demne pulled his bundle off and pushed it into the hole first. Then he thrust his head in and wriggled his long body through the passage. It was dark and smelled of cold and old, dead moss.

After a long, slow, puffing time, Demne felt space around him. He groped until he found the walls of a chamber perhaps four paces across and three wide, cramped and cold, but warm compared to the wind. Quickly, he stripped away his soaking cloaks and removed his wet clothing. Then, by feel, he fumbled his pack open. He rubbed his body briskly with his old, worn tunic, smelling of dog and sweat, until he was fairly dry. He pulled an old linen tunic he had been given one Midsummer over his damp head, and coughed. Old leaves crackled beneath him, and he began to gather them into a pile. Even if he choked, he must try to make some fire.

A cold gust brushed the back of his neck, and Demne realized in relief that there must be another opening to the outside. He fumbled in the blackness and found his fire-making flint and steel. His hands were stiff with cold, and it took several tries before a spark flashed, caught the curl of a dried leaf, and blazed into flame. The tiny fire nibbled its way through the little pile of leaves, and Demne held his hands over the faint warmth.

With the little light, he could see more leaves at the very back of the cave. He gathered them and pulled some dried vegetation off the stone walls as well. It was not much. Wood was what he needed, but all he possessed was the shaft of his light hunting spear and his bowl. Still, even a fire of leaves took some of the chill from the tiny space, and he fed it carefully. He hung his old cloak, soaking and now so faded it had almost no color, from a jutting rock and the newer brown one, almost as wet, from another. The new tunic and trousers were damp, but not soaked, and he spread them on the floor at the very end of the tiny chamber. Soon the place began to stink of wet wool.

He removed the outgrown clothing Donait had given him and folded it into a pillow. Then he curled up beneath his dog-reeking blanket, turning his face longingly into the folds of clothing that still retained some of the apple-blossom scent of their maker. From time to time, he added a handful of moss to the fire, though the effort seemed to grow greater as time went on.

Despite the warmth and the sweat on his brow, Demne began to shiver. He coughed with increasing violence. He could feel the fever grip his limbs, and there was nothing he could do but wait. He had some willow bark, which Bodbmall had taught him to brew for fevers, but no water. He swallowed and coughed and wished he had the strength to crawl back to the mouth of the cave where he could lap snow with his bare tongue.

After a time, the fire died, and Demne slipped into an uneasy slumber. He could hear the wind howl, but it seemed to him it was not the wind, but the voices of Bodbmall and the Liath Luachra, screaming at each other in one of their interminable arguments. He tried to call to them, but no one heard. He gasped and tossed beneath the thin folds of his blanket.

Then a cool, smooth hand touched his damp brow. There was a light around him, pale and golden. He could smell spring. Demne struggled to open his eyes, but his body was leaden and all he managed was a moan. An arm clasped his shoulders and he felt his head pillowed against soft breasts. A faint crooning came to his ears, like a song the *bendrui* had made when he was small. But it was not the deep voice of Bodbmall that rang in his ears.

"Donait," he whispered.

"Hush, dear one. I am here with you."

"I have longed to see you again."

"Shh, now. I too have yearned. But you must sleep and gather your strength. You are very ill."

"Do not leave me!" Did he speak the words or only think them?

"Never will I leave thee. Rest now. There's a good boy."

Demne wanted to protest that he was a man, or very nearly. The serving girls in the various places he had labored had often offered him their favors, brushing him with rounded breasts or bumping into him. The feelings which rose in him at those collisions of flesh confused him. When he exchanged a clumsy kiss with a rosy-faced dairy maid beside the Midsummer fires, he felt his loins grow hot, but something held him back from pursuing it further. But Demne found he was too weak to explain anything. The heat in his loins was nothing beside the fever that raced along his veins.

Something pressed against his lips, cool and hard. It was a cup, and he gulped the liquid within it greedily. Bitter as it was, he drained the contents. Sleep seized him then, dragging him down into dreamlessness. Demne roused from time to time, drank more of the brew, and slept again. He felt the ache of his weary young body, and in rare moments of alertness heard the rasp of his laboring lungs. He imagined he was in two places at once: in the cold cave, burning with fever, and also in the fair house of Donait.

When at last Demne became fully awake, the first thing he saw was a small fire burning an arm's length away. He stared at the blazing branches stupidly. Then he looked across it and saw the fairy woman curled like a cat upon the farther side. Her long braids gleamed in the hearth light, and her face was even lovelier than he remembered.

"I thought I dreamed you," he whispered hoarsely.

"You did, and so I came to you. Dreams have the power to make real what the heart desires. That is a mystery even the Sidhe do not fully understand. Now, you must eat something and regain your strength. Samhain draws to a close, and I must return to my home." She held out an enormous apple.

Demne sat up and wrinkled his nose at the sour scent of his body. Then he closed his fingers around the gleaming orb and forgot his filth as he tasted the sweetness of the fruit. He was as ravenous as a wolf, but somehow he managed to eat slowly, savoring each morsel.

He was nearly done when a sharp cracking sound caused him to pause in mid-mouthful. Donait poured a handful of broken hazelnuts onto a plate with a noisy clatter, a real, homey sound. She held it across the fire, and Demne took it. She seemed amused, but not at him. He dug the meats out, one by one, and ate them solemnly until he could consume no more.

"Did you sing to me, Donait?"

"I did." She held out her hand, and he returned the plate to her, covered with hazelnut shells and the bare core of the apple.

"It was beautiful. Everything about you is so beautiful. I wish I could stay with you forever."

Donait shook her head slowly. "Your place is not in my world, not yet. You have much to accomplish first."

"What? All I do is run like a stag with a pack of hounds at my heels."

"That is how it appears to you, but you are learning while you run, and you must complete your education."

Her answers were as obscure as Bodbmall's! "Where shall I go now, Donait?" He expected another riddle or vague reply.

"To the west. Seek service with one who will make you a place beside the hearth, Demne child."

He let a great sigh escape him. It was better than he had dared hope for. "I see. Thank you for caring for me."

"It was not difficult," she answered.

"I wish you would cease thinking of me as a child, though."

Donait gave a soft laugh. "Already you have learned some wisdom from the hazel. Our times are different, yours and mine, and one day they will touch, and you will no longer be a child to me. Restrain your impatience, and learn all you can."

"It seems to me I have done nothing but study since I was a babe. But I will do as you bid me, though I can't understand it." Old habits, he decided, died hard. Obeying a woman seemed a natural thing, and yet, he knew now, it was not the ordinary way.

"I do not doubt you are weary of it. But I am yet

a student myself, and will be until the end of all things."

Astonished, he gaped at her. "I always thought you knew everything."

"Hardly that," she replied, somewhat tartly. Then she stood, shook her skirts free of bits of shell, and cast the contents of the plate into the fire. It blazed hotly as she circled round and came to him. Her soft arms enclosed his shoulders, and her rosy lips pressed against his mouth. The kiss went on until he thought he would happily drown in the sweetness of her. "Until we meet again, dear one," Donait murmured into his ear.

Then she was gone, and the golden light went with her. The fire, however, remained, and the scent of her mingled with the wood smoke. Alone, Demne wept.

Chapter 12

❦

THE SOLES OF HIS BROGUES WERE THIN AND WORN when Demne came to the lands of Gléor Lamraige in the moon of the first budding leaves of the birch. Benntraige lay leagues south, beyond two rivers and dozens of little raths where Demne had rested for a night or two. The winter just past was a blur of rain and snow, cold and hunger, interspersed with brief periods of warmth and companionship. His hair was growing back, and it had been too cold to cut it again.

The westlands were milder and warmer, and the people were shorter of stature and darker of hair than those he had seen before. Demne felt a little awkward among them. Still, they were not hostile. They never denied him a place to sleep or a share of what provender remained after the long winter. Woodswise as he was, he usually managed to snare a bird or some small beast at any place where he sought a night's rest.

Even from a distance, the holding of King Gléor Lamraige was clearly large and wealthy. The stockade surrounding the dwellings seemed almost as big as that at Tailtiu, and the meadows melodious with lowing as the cattle were gathered for the drive to the pastures in the hills. Within, the buildings were in good repair, the folk busy about their daily work. The warm, wet scent of porridge boiling made Demne's mouth water as he passed the cook house, but he silenced his hunger and sought the steward of the household.

He finally found the man discussing pasturage with the chief herdsman, and waited patiently. Demne had learned in other places he had served how much authority was held by the man who ran a household for a king. When the herdsman was gone, there were others, so the day was well advanced before the man turned to him.

"So, what brings you to the lands of Gléor Redhand, lord of Lamraige?" Clearly the house chief was a no-nonsense man with little time for amenities.

"I am called Demne Mael, and I seek service."

The steward eyed his cropped hair and nodded. "Humph. We have sufficient field-workers and herd boys. What would a wanderer like you do here?"

Demne looked down at the ruin of his brogues, then lifted his head and offered his most beguiling smile. "The folk at the rath of Feradalg said you could use someone to tend the fires."

"What do you know of hearth fires? You look like a wild man."

"I can tell an oak from a birch, and I am a hard worker." He held out his long hands, callused and work-worn.

"It takes more than that to keep the hearth fire well nourished. You are too old for such work!"

Demne shook his head. "I am just big for my age. And I am a good student."

The steward narrowed his eyes thoughtfully. "Are you now? So, tell me which woods to gather in what season?"

Demne searched his memory for any scraps of knowledge on the subject he had acquired along the way. Some things he had learned from Bodbmall, the rest from his wanderings. "Oak burns warmly, if it is old and well dried, and pine makes many sparks, though it smells sweet. I know to cut the hawthorn in the fall, not the spring, and that birch burns too fast for the hearth."

The steward nodded. "And alder?"

Demne shook his head. "I have never burned that tree."

With a snort, the older man stood and smoothed the folds of his tunic. "Very well. I will give you a week's trial. Our fire boy died during the winter, and we have found no one to take his place. Just remember to keep out of the way!"

"I thank you for the chance to learn," Demne replied.

"We shall see," the steward answered.

DEMNE ALREADY KNEW THE GENERAL NATURE OF HIS duties—to gather wood and to maintain an even heat in the hearth fire. He had not realized that there was a right way and a wrong one to choose branches and to cut them. The ancient whose task it was to attend to wood gathering was half mad and feeble. He addressed Demne by a muddle of names of other youths who had served him. Still, even in his madness, he possessed a vast store of lore, and Demne listened with care. Some of Bodbmall's stern lessons returned to memory, and he found a deep satisfaction in the simple act of laying a fire and feeding it.

For the first time in many years, he felt content and secure. Demne began to observe the manners of his new household. Crouched beside the hearth, his face sooty and sweating, he watched Gléor's two concubines vie for the attention of the king, and the red-haired, unhappy wife, Muirne, restless in her discontent, snapping like a dog at those around her when they intruded upon the sorrow that kept her gaze turned inward. The king seemed to treat her with affection, despite the concubines, and one of the kitchen maids told Demne that the queen was unhappy because she had no child.

Muirne was a lovely woman, with oddly dark brows above glass grey eyes, and if she had smiled more, he thought she would have been beautiful. She had the same name as his mother, and he wondered sometimes if his own mother would have looked like that, if she had lived. She moved through the hall to take her meals like a whisper of music, and then returned to the sunny Grianan where the women stayed again. Once her skirts had brushed him as she passed, releasing a wave of scent that made his head swim. It was tantalizingly familiar, almost like the smell of the fairy woman Donait, but subtly different. He was certain he had smelled it before, but for the life of him he could not remember where or when. The distant woman never looked at the sooty lad with his raggedly cropped hair, now grown into an unsightly bush.

But if the queen ignored him, her giggling maids were not so shy. He pretended not to hear their speculations about what lay beneath his stained tunic, for he went bare legged like the other servants now. And he tried not to wonder about the softness of the breasts beneath their linen gowns. He did not wonder long, for several of the more forward maids found occasions to press themselves against him, so he could feel the soft flesh of thigh and belly against his own.

His memories of Donait kept him from following his natural inclinations, for somehow it seemed that to lie with one of these giggling girls would be disloyal to the fairy woman. After a time they decided that he was too stupid to understand, but at night, when he listened to the sounds of lovemaking from behind the curtained partitions in the hall, his loins ached, and he could not help longing to hold a girl in his arms.

The days passed, the seasons turned, and autumn began to touch the land. When a wandering bard arrived one evening just before dusk with his harp in a worn sealskin case at his back, he was welcomed eagerly. Demne watched the man, a lanky blond with fine hands, as he lounged on a couch, eating and speaking. He was full of news of the *Ard Ri* at Temair, and gossip about the goings-on there. The name of Clan Morna came up more than once, and the *gilla* was not surprised to hear that his old foe Dael mac Conain had been rude once too often and gotten his head bashed in.

The sons of Morna were famed throughout the land for their hotheaded, contentious ways. At least none of the listeners expressed any surprise at the news. Demne found himself surprised that he was sorry Dael was dead already. Something within him had hoped to do the deed himself. The harper said that Goll mac Morna, chief of the seven *fianna* of Eriu, had successfully repelled an invasion by some folk Demne had never heard of, and then demanded one of Conn's daughters as reward.

"Goll acts as if the blood of Cumhal mac Trenmor had curdled his brain," the bard commented as he ended his tale. At these words, Queen Muirne paled and pressed her hands to her wide brow.

Gléor put a firm hand on her shoulder. "What is it?"

"I . . . have a slight headache," she whispered, looking worse with each passing moment.

"Then this is no place for you. Off you go to the herb woman for a sleeping draught." Gléor Lamraige brushed her chalky cheek with his lips, and sent her away.

Demne watched Queen Muirne pass, and he thought he saw the shimmer of unshed tears in her grey eyes as she hurried from the hall. He wiped his sooty brow, and put another log on the fire. He wished he could ask the harper what he meant by his remark, but he might as well have been invisible. As hearth boy, he saw and heard much, but he kept silent unless some-one spoke to him.

"Will you favor us with a song, then?" Gléor asked, to cover the slight awkwardness of the queen's departure.

"Surely, oh king. I am only a bard, not a *fili,* and so it is not the great tales but my own songs that I sing, yet this talk of the sons of Morna brings to mind a lament that my master left unfinished when he died. I have ventured to complete it, and I hope I do him credit, for I am yet young in my craft."

He retrieved his instrument from where he had set it beside the door. Demne watched him stroke the curved pillar as a man might fondle the long throat of a woman, and listened to the work of tuning the harp with a pleasure that was almost pain. Meanwhile the serving lads passed back and forth, making certain all the horns were brimming. Demne decided to add a bough of well-aged pear wood to the fire to sweeten the air.

The bard struck the strings with an assured hand, and sounded a chord that chilled Demne to his bones, though he could not have said why. When the man began to sing in a clear, sweet tone, a hush fell over the listeners.

> *"The wind blows cold on Cnucha's heath."*
> *Colder still, the sleep of death.*
> *So sleeps the slain son of Trenmor,*
> *But I shall sleep in peace no more."*

As Demne looked around him, he thought there was something odd about their attention. It was the harper's words that were disturbing them, not his skill. Demne's cold deepened as he realized that the bard was singing about Cumhal mac Trenmor.

> "On Almu's hill my father stands,
> His eagle gaze engulfs the lands;
> White are the walls that ward my home,
> But there I can no longer come."

Suddenly Demne could *see* those gleaming walls, and with that sight came a wave of desolation for every loss he had ever known. *I was there,* he thought, *for this is Muirne's song. Before I was even born I lost my home. . . .*

> "By Morna's envious sons is slain
> The Champion; we shall not see again
> Fennid and king, born of one mother—
> Where shall Eriu find such another?"

Demne's eyes stung. As the harper sang, the chance-heard fragments of his father's life fell suddenly into a pattern, vivid as the tapestries in Donait's hall. Whatever the truth of it, for this moment, Cumhal's life had meaning.

> "My love, of men most fierce in fray,
> Cumhal, who carried me away
> From hearth to a home upon the heather;
> Happy was I while we dwelt together."

Blinking away tears, Demne thrust another log into the fire, and as the flame leaped up, saw King Gléor's lips twist as if he too felt some pain. Was it the same anguish Demne felt, or some vision of his own? What was this magic of word and music that could reach past a man's thoughts and pluck the strings of his heart as easily as those of the harp?

> *"Lost is the love and lost the laughter,*
> *Wild in his wrath and tender after,*
> *No more shall Cumhal's like be known,*
> *But Muirne's left to mourn alone."*

Harp music drew out the final tone in plaintive harmony. No one moved as the last notes faded reluctantly into silence. Demne's throat ached, and he did not know if it were his father or the ending of the song that he mourned—or himself, and all that he had lost. He reached for a piece of wood, but until the bard lifted his hands from the harp strings and the stony expression in the eyes of the king at last began to ease he dared not lay it on the fire.

"No doubt you do your master credit," the king said in a voice that seemed even harsher after that sweet sound, "but you are indeed young in your craft."

The warriors shifted uncomfortably on their benches and the women whispered behind their hands.

The harper turned an ugly red. "If I have given offense in some fashion, lord, I humbly beg pardon."

Gléor shook his head. "You have not offended, but you have sung of times better left forgotten."

One of the concubines sighed, as if she had expected some explosion of wrath. Demne wondered what had been wrong with the song. He understood why his own eyes were wet and why his throat was aching. But why should these people care what had happened to Cumhal mac Trenmor?

"Perhaps you have something in a less serious vein?" Gléor asked.

"To be sure, my king." The harper retuned his instrument and struck a bright ripple of notes, like sunlight on a freshet. A comical piece tripped from his tongue, bawdy and rich with a play of words that seemed to amuse the listeners. Half of this lewd frolic was lost on Demne, and he felt stupid and ignorant. It brought back his old longing for the mastery of words. It was a hunger that came from time to time and seized him, for the third path that coiled away from beneath the shining gown of Brigid to the river and the fisherman which he suspected must be the way of Poetry. It was also the portion of the puzzle he had not yet solved, for Demne knew that the red way led to the sons of Morna, and the green way to the fierce old man he had glimpsed on the road a few moons before. If Aonghus mac Conail had lived, Demne would have sought him, for he was certain the young *fili* would have completed his studies by now and been able to advise him. But he was gone.

Demne sighed and turned his attention to the fire as the harper put his instrument away. The night was well advanced, and many were stifling yawns and rubbing bleary, weary eyes. The company began to disperse to the beds in their curtained partitions against the wall, and in a few minutes the youth was alone in the hall. Carefully, he banked the hearth fire and settled down beside it. He closed his eyes, but sleep eluded him.

The soft fall of footsteps on packed earth brought him up, scattering his coverings. Gléor Lamraige stood, staring at him in a way that made Demne uneasy. But after a time his expression softened.

"*Gilla,* do you know *fidchel?*"

"I have played a little," Demne admitted cautiously.

"Good. Let us have a game, for this night sleep has abandoned me. Build up the fire while I get the board."

Demne did as he was bid and soon the embers were ablaze. The chill of early spring was like a mouse gnawing at the walls of the hall. The king laid the playing board on a small serving table and stretched out on a dining couch. Demne sat cross-legged on the earthen floor, facing the king, and examined the board and the pieces. It was a fine set, not as grand as Donait's, nor as simple as the one he had played upon at Tailtiu. The board was inlaid with white bone and dark wood, and the pieces were carved from the same materials. Whatever artisan had created it had formed the pegs with such cunning that each seemed unique and distinct, like a faceless man.

The lord of Lamraige allowed Demne to play the attackers, which had the advantage of making the first move. They pegged their pieces into place and began. Demne concentrated deeply, quite forgetting that it was not good manners to best a king. It was not until the game was almost over that he recalled watching Gléor play with others, and remembered that the man did not like to lose. Clumsily, he pegged the final piece, tensing for a fiery reproach.

When none came, Demne looked up and found Gléor Redhand staring at him once again. "Very good—and very quick. You are a better player than I expected. This time I will let you defend."

They set up their pieces once more. Demne knuckled his eyes, for he had been awake since before dawn, and his young body ached with weariness. Maybe he could get some sleep if he let Gléor win.

Demne's first and second moves were quite deliberately ill chosen, and then the sense that the pieces were real people snared him, and he began to play with cunning once more. He quickly recovered the advantage he had lost, and Gléor found himself quite unable to capture Demne's king. When he realized his mistake, he turned hot with mortification. If only he had not become so involved! To conceal his embarrassment, he turned away to add a fresh brand to the hearth, and the smoke stung his aching eyes.

The king had already reset the board, again giving the defenders to Demne. "Get us some beer, boy, for my throat is parched, and I daresay yours must be the same."

He rose to obey this command, glad to stretch his cramped limbs. Outside, in the cool darkness of the night, Demne felt his head clear. He filled the bowls at the vats beside the stillhouse, and returned to the hall. Gléor was leaning back on the couch, his square, strong fingers laced across his flat belly. The older man sat up as Demne approached, his face thoughtful. He took the bowl without a word and made his first move.

It was an unconventional opening, and Demne pondered a moment before responding. He set his bowl on the floor beside him and forgot to drink as the game seized him once again. This game was more difficult, more challenging, and the victory sweeter for that.

"It is very late, lord," Demne said, rubbing his eyes once more as he watched Gléor arrange the pieces again.

"It is later than you think, *gilla*," Gléor said cryptically. "You have cunning well beyond your years. Now, play."

Demne stared at his opponent, trying to penetrate the mind across from him, then he shrugged. It ought to be easy to lose. If only the pegs did not seem so much like real people, and their loss like real death. The youth was caught between his weariness and his inextinguishable need to excel. It was so fierce a flame within him that he could not bear to sacrifice a single peg if he could avoid it. And so he outplayed Gléor Redhand yet again.

His throat was dry and the beer in his bowl tepid as they began a fifth game. Whether he attacked or defended, the result was the same. The pegs moved almost of their own volition, flashing from hole to hole like night moths. A fine sheen of moisture gleamed on the brow of the king and dampened the line of his hair.

After he won the sixth contest, Demne, exhausted and red-eyed, was sent for more beer. When he returned, the board had been set up again, with black facing him, and white on the king's side. He handed the cool bowl to the older man, and tucked himself back into his place, rubbing his hands across his sooty tunic, and preparing to play once more. He longed only for his place beside the hearth, for rest and untroubled slumber, but Gléor seemed determined to play through the night, or perhaps, from the grim expression upon his face, until the end of the world. Demne drank some beer, but it made his head buzz and the pieces dance before his tired eyes.

The seventh game began like those before, but this time it seemed as if they had both tossed all ordinary strategies aside. This game had a feverish, reckless quality that made the skin of Demne's arms pebble with gooseflesh. He no longer thought of consequences. When he defeated the king once more, the youth looked across the board at his opponent, eyes red-rimmed with exhaustion seeking mercy.

Gléor Lamraige stared at the ruin of his array for a long, silent time. He gave a grunt. "What are you?"

"A boy, lord."

"Then, who are you?"

"Why, Demne, the hearth *gilla,* lord."

The king narrowed his eyes and slowly shook his head. "Not so. I know you now. You can be none other than that Cumhal who was leader of the *fianna* before the Battle of Cnucha. 'Tis many and many a time that I faced him across a *fidchel* board, and until this night,

I never knew another man to play in just that way."

Demne blinked. "Is he not dead, and also his fair wife, Muirne, as I heard in the song of the harper tonight?"

"Some souls return again and again," the king muttered darkly.

Demne had become used to knowing he had a famous father. The thought that he might be his father born again was new. But it was his mother's emotions he had felt as he listened to the song. He shrugged it away with an indifference that only partly hid his confusion.

"Lord, I do not know. But Cumhal is dead. All I know is being Demne, alive in this world." And surely that was hard enough, without adding his father's fate to the load.

"You won't be for long if Goll mac Morna learns that you are here. I would not have you die under my protection. It would upset . . . things. You must go."

Weary as he was, the youth laughed. "It would also upset *me,* for I wish to live and learn all there is to know of the wide world. But unless you tell him, how will Goll mac Morna know I am here?"

Gléor choked on his beer. When he had recovered his breath, he said, "I have no love for the sons of Morna. They are a contentious clan, and grow ever more arrogant. But with or without my will, you are bound to betray yourself, lad. Word would reach him, or he would sniff you out one day. His nose is very keen, since Cumhal mac Trenmor robbed him of an eye."

"Would slaying me restore his sight?" Beer and lack of sleep had made Demne's tongue careless.

"You argue like a *drui,* young Demne. If you are not Cumhal's spirit returned, you must be his son, for in your blood, Cumhal's cunning and Tadhg's wisdom seem marvelously combined. Your death would not give him back his lost eye, but his pride would be comforted."

"To kill a man for pride seems a very stupid thing, lord."

"It is, to a boy. But when you age, there is a stiffness of spirit which seizes you, and makes you commit acts that were unthinkable in earlier years. And you must go now, for the song of the harper, curse him, will set people's minds to thinking of Cumhal."

Demne was not certain if the king cursed the harper or his dead friend. He stared at Gléor for a long moment.

"I will leave, for you have been a good master, and I have no desire to bring you misfortune. But in your eyes I see some secret that troubles you, and I think I will sleep more easily than you."

"That may well be," said the king, "but if so, then the secret is mine to hold. I shall see you decently garbed, and victualed, but I would have you gone tomorrow before the sun has reached the mid-heavens."

Demne chuckled softly, thinking about the last time he had had to depart before sunrise. "I should have tried harder to lose."

Gléor shook his head slowly. "I would have known you even if you had let me win. And that affront is one I would have found it hard to forgive."

"Truly, my foster mother, the Liath Luachra, was most wise."

"How so, child of Cumhal?"

"She always said pride makes fools of men."

A grim smile creased Gléor Lamraige's stern face. He nodded slowly in agreement. "Sad, but very true. It does. Now, get some rest. I want you off my lands by next nightfall." Then, to Demne's great astonishment, Gléor rose and came around the little table. He embraced the youth's broad shoulders with his strong hands, and placed a gentle kiss on his soot-streaked brow. "You do not know how much I wish you were my son, Demne, and could stay," the king whispered into his ear.

Chapter 13

D EMNE LEFT THE LANDS OF LAMRAIGE JUST AFTER
midday, in the brisk chill of a sparkling fall day.
He followed the pale sun, glad of the gift of warm garments given by Redhand. As he left the rath, he turned and looked back, feeling a pang of loss and a great puzzlement at the king's parting words. Then he set his broad shoulders and exulted in the freedom of no longer having to answer to any man. The hills to the west beckoned him, and beyond them, the great sea he had heard in his heart, but never, in all his wanderings across Eriu, yet seen. He could almost smell the salty tang, though the rolling waters lay days away.

As the days grew colder with approaching winter, they fell into a pattern, a sameness that made each one like the last, indistinguishable. He would rise with the first light, break his fast on remnants from the night before, gather up his belongings, and walk westward. The land was nearly empty of men, and he could travel for several days without seeing another human being. Those he did see were small and dark and wary. Here was none of the arrogant hospitality of the great raths. Another might have been frightened by the vast reaches of trees, but Demne was

forest bred. In late afternoons he hunted for a pigeon
or woodcock to fill his belly. He caught fish in rushing streams, when he could, standing stone-still in icy
waters until a trout swam close, and snatching it up
with his bare hands. When game and fish were not to
be found, he gathered late berries, and such nuts as
the squirrels had overlooked, and told his grumbling
belly to be still. In the silent nights, he slept deeply wherever he laid his head. The sons of Morna,
Bodbmall, the *drui* Tadhg mac Nuadat, all faded into
mist in his mind.

The moon had waxed and waned and waxed once
more. Without knowing how he knew, Demne realized it was close to Samhain, and he spent two sleep-
less nights, listening for ghosts and seeking the shade
of Bodbmall. Once he thought he heard the sound of
keening, and ran towards it, banging his knees on logs
until they were bloody. He never found the source
of the noise, and the next morning, he shrugged the
whole matter away. He had no food to share with the
dead, and could hardly feed himself. From the thick
coats on the few animals he saw, it promised to be a
hard winter.

The form of the land shifted before him. The woods
thinned, and the bones of the earth poked through its
thin skin of soil. A brisk, chill breeze that cooled his
cheeks was heavy with moisture, and it smelled of
salt. As he climbed a rise a seabird swooped over his
head, screaming. Then he had reached the top, and
he saw for the first time the great, heaving vastness of
the sun-gilded sea. Blinking, Demne picked his way
down the rocky slope to the shore.

For a long time, he merely stood and stared at the
surge and suck of the waves. Spray glittered in the air
as they crashed upon the rocks, then snaked in a hundred hissing rivulets back to the ocean. Light blazed
back from every water-slick rock, but when he closed

his eyes it was no better, for he was surrounded by the passionate sighing song of the sea. It was like the earth song that he heard always, but far louder.

The gleaming grey waters blurred into a bank of mist that hung offshore. Had he reached the end of the world? At one of the raths Demne had heard of a warrior who launched his ship across the grey plains of the sea and came at last to an island of fair women. The description of it sounded like Donait's hall. He understood now the sea-longing that was celebrated in so many songs.

He sighed, and began to walk along the rocky shore. The stones here were all rubbed shining smooth, and bits of shell the color of sunrise jeweled the tangle of driftwood and dark seaweed. A strange creature with enormous wicked looking claws scuttled down a hole before he got a good look at it.

The wind shifted and brought the smell of smoke to his nostrils. He turned and sought its source. Behind him, the slow rise of land became a mountain as it drew away from the sea. On its immense knees, he could see several small round stone huts, almost invisible but for the telltale curls of white rising from their smoke holes. Further up the mountain, the dirty white dots of grazing sheep stood out against the green grass. The dark shape beside them must be the herder, watching him.

Curious to discover what sort of folk lived here, Demne began to walk towards the buildings. It struck him as odd that there was no stockade around them. Did those who lived here have no enemies? It took him longer than he had expected to reach the foot of the mountain and find the path that led up the slope to the settlement. As he drew closer, a hot smell of fire and something else curled into his nostrils.

The complaints of the sheep reached his ears before the animals and their guardian came into view. It was a girl with hair like night, and rosy cheeks beneath her tanned skin. She stood hardly as high as his chest, but ripe breasts swelled under her woolen shawl, and her wide hips swayed as she walked. Despite the chill of the autumn day, her skirt came barely past her knees, and her little feet winked in and out of the grass as she skipped forward. This was not the perfect beauty of Donait, or the cold loveliness of Queen Muirne, but Demne liked the way her little nose turned up, and her generous mouth curved into a smile when she saw him watching her.

Then a bandy-legged man not much taller than the girl emerged from one of the stone huts. He was clad only in a kilt and a leathern apron. His face and upper body were wet with sweat and streaked with smears of soot, and his eyes were reddened with smoke. Even at a distance he smelled of fire and leather and hot metal. His black hair was streaked with grey, and his skin was a crazed collection of lines and wrinkles. Though the man's back was slightly bowed, Demne had never seen shoulders so broad on any man, nor hands so powerful. What craft could develop the body in that way?

The older man scrutinized Demne grimly. The girl shut the sheep into a stone-walled croft and came back, brown eyes twinkling. As she crossed her arms beneath the knot of her shawl the outlines of her soft breasts were suddenly clear, and Demne's generalized pleasure focused suddenly in his loins. He felt himself reddening, and looked quickly back at the man.

"I bid you good day, master."

"Good? Good for some and not for others. One of the cats pissed on my charcoal, and the stink is all over the forge. What do you want?"

Demne shrugged and tried not to look at the girl. "A place to put my head for a night, and some food, if you have any to spare." The cold wind from the sea began to chill him, and he wondered how the girl could stand with her bare legs exposed. A night in the open here was unappealing.

"No one eats in my house without laboring," the older man grumbled.

"Oh, father!" The girl tossed her head and took a step forward. "Pay him no heed. He is always grumpy over his old charcoal. I am Cruithne, and this is Lochan the smith. He hates to take the time from his metalworking to make the charcoal, you see, and—"

"Stop rattling on, Daughter. This stranger has no interest in our concerns."

"I have served as fire boy at the hearth of the king of Lamraige, master, though charcoal is a mystery to me."

Lochan grinned like an old wolf. "It is a wise man who can admit his own ignorance. Perhaps you aren't one of those cocksure lads who thinks he knows it all."

"The last *gilla* we had was always arguing with Father. He cannot abide anyone disagreeing with him." Cruithne slipped her arm through the smith's and smiled at him fondly.

Demne, suppressing a sharp, sudden stab of envy, nodded. "I do not care much for contention myself," he said slowly, flinching from the memories of Bodbmall and the Liath Luachra in their ceaseless argument. They were both long dead, but the remembrance of their fights was as fresh as if the last one had been yesterday. He glanced across the slopes of the great mountain which loomed above them, scanning the trees with knowledgeable eyes. "What do you use? Not willow charcoal, I should think, for those trees are uncommon here."

Lochan's grim expression softened, and a look of cunning came into his dark eyes. "Come in, boy, come in. You do know a thing or two. I use alder when I can, and poplar when I must. Willow burns too hot and too fast for my work, though it suits some others." The smith's contempt for those "others" was clear.

The girl snorted with impatience. "Wood! Ores! If that is all you can speak of to the first visitor here in moons, I will scream."

"Go ahead," answered the smith. "But do it outside. You know I can't abide a racket."

Cruithne giggled. "After the pounding of your hammer, how would you know what a racket was?"

The smith flicked the girl's cheek affectionately with a work-worn finger. "That's my otter girl! Where's my supper! A man slaves all day over a hot forge, and what does he get?"

"A good mutton stew, if he keeps his tongue behind his teeth," the young woman replied, dimpling in a manner that made Demne's pulses pound. "Boiled oats if he does not."

Demne blinked. He had found the girls of the raths where he had served pretty but resistible. Why did this brown girl make his pulses race?

"Now, you would not make your poor old father eat gruel while he still had all his teeth, would you?"

"I might," she answered saucily. "Go wash your face. And your hands."

"I am a slave to a wooden spoon and a girl's whim. Come, boy. My daughter commands, and we must obey if we want to eat. Her mother was just the same."

Demne began to relax at this easy exchange between the smith and his child. He followed Lochan into a hut which sheltered a small hearth, well banked and glowing. From an opening at one side, water flowed in, passing through a stone channel to the other side. There was a vessel something like a cauldron standing on the floor. For a moment Demne stared at it in perplexity, then he realized it was a pail made from pieces of riveted bronze. He had never seen a pail made out of metal before. The smith began to strip off his leather apron and wool kilt, but Demne's attention was distracted by the pail. It was a beautiful piece, much finer than any he had seen in his travels. With a tender hand, he stroked the cool curve. This was a kind of beauty he had only seen before in the jewelry of kings and queens. To find it lavished on so humble an object as a pail intrigued him.

When he turned, he found the small, broad man watching him intently. Lochan's chest was hidden beneath a mass of dark, curling hair, and his thick arms were scarred. Lochan followed his gaze and shrugged.

"The sparks leap from the forge or the metal, sometimes, and burn." He stroked his grizzled beard with his work-hardened fingers. "Afraid of fire, boy?"

"I was not afraid of the hearth fire of Gléor Lamraige."

"The forge is another matter entirely. It's alive, boy, alive! What's your name?"

"Demne, master."

The smith lifted his bushy brow, but made no comment. "How did you come here? We do not get many visitors until the fishing folk come after Midsummer. 'Tis winter now, and we shall see no one for a handfull of moons."

"I followed the sun and the call of the sea," Demne answered quietly. He had been right. Samhain had come and gone. He wished for the words to express his longing for the sea, and his delight in his first sight of it, but he had none. He shrugged the longing away, and he began to pull off his own travel-stained tunic.

The smith watched him for a moment, then bent, filled the pail from the channel, and poured it into a basin of stone. The smell of smoke mingled with the heavy sweat of the older man. The darkness of

Lochan and the scars on his big arms fascinated the youth, and he forced himself to watch the fire, so as not to stare. Demne, out of sheer habit, slipped another branch into the flames, neatly and without disturbing those below.

Lochan had already picked up a handful of moss and was scrubbing himself. Demne took another from the basket, and began to scour away the stains from his journey. The water felt wonderful, and the coolness brought back good memories of Bodbmall and of the bathhouse at Tailtiu. They rubbed themselves dry with rough cloths hanging on pegs in the wall.

Demne bent to remove his clean tunic from his pack. It had worked its way down to the bottom, and as he slid his hand in, he felt the fine garments Donait had given him years before. He had outgrown them while he labored in the north, but he could not bring himself to discard or give them away.

He tugged the tunic down over his pale hair, and pulled it straight, picking up his belt again to hold it. The smith offered him a bone comb, and Demne pulled it through his tangled locks. His hair had grown out during his journey. He supposed he should shear it again, but it hardly mattered, here. Thrusting the curling locks off his high brow with an unconscious gesture, he handed the comb back to Lochan, then knelt and banked the hearth, ensuring that it would smoulder through the night.

"I can see you do know a thing or two about caring for a fire."

"I do now. When I was young it was just another mouth I had to feed. I did not guess there was an art to keeping it burning rightly. I nearly cooked my master before I learned the trick of maintaining an even flame." He laughed softly, remembering Gléor's curses at his early clumsiness. Lochan's stillness made it easy to go on.

"It seems that all the things of the world must be learned by doing. When I—when those who reared me died, I thought I was done with lessons. To sit and memorize the virtues of herbs, or cast a spear a hundred times at a circle on the earth wearied me. I wanted to be free, but now that I am, I sometimes long for what I hated before. I wonder if I shall ever be content."

"How old are you, Demne?"

"I think I will be sixteen at next Midsummer, but I am not certain."

"You are large for your years then."

Demne shrugged. "I keep growing and growing, which makes keeping a tunic on my back very hard. It was easier when I wore the skins of the beasts I slew. But I like wool or linen better, even if it does not wear as well as hide."

The smith pondered, and Demne waited patiently. Lochan was clearly not a man who hurried over anything. At last he said, "If you will 'prentice to me for a year and a day, until after next Samhain plus a bit, I will have my daughter make you a fine tunic of wool from our own sheep, I will teach you the right way to make charcoal, and perhaps, if you show promise, I will teach you more."

Demne looked at him in surprise. He had always heard that smiths were very jealous of the secrets of their art. The thought of a garment made by Cruithne's little hands excited him in one way, and the idea of learning the ways of the forge intrigued him in another. He could not decide which was the more attractive.

"I would be willing to work, Master Lochan, for my bread and a place to rest. But a new garment would be most welcome." He tugged at the end of his sleeve ruefully. "This covered my wrist two moons ago."

A deep, resonant ring of metal interrupted him. Demne jumped, for he had never heard such a sound before. It was not unlike the noise a cauldron made if one banged it with a stick, but sweeter and more melodious. He glanced around to see where the sound came from, and found nothing close by.

The smith grinned and rubbed his hands together. "There's the girl, calling us to eat. Have you never heard a gong before?"

Demne shook his head. "It is sweet to the ear," he answered as it rang once more.

"As is Cruithne's cooking to the belly. Eat your fill, and do not worry over your growing." He looked Demne up and down. "You already have the size of most men, but soon enough, it will slow down."

They left the bath hut and walked to another. The mouth-watering smell of mutton stew wafted through the doorway. The girl was rosy-cheeked from the heat of the little hearth, and her brown eyes shone like polished hazelnuts. She got wooden bowls from a stack against the wall and ladled them full of steaming food. There was a plate with a stack of fresh oatcakes too, and Demne's mouth watered.

Within the chamber there was only the small table holding the oatcakes. The three of them sat down on the floor around it and began to eat. After weeks of tough, roasted birds, Demne thought it was the best food he had ever tasted. There were chunks of onion mixed with the meat, and bright orange wild carrots, still crisp and crunchy, all swimming in a thick broth that tasted of thyme. His brows lifted as he ate, for he had never before encountered a stew where the vegetables were not boiled into an unresisting mush.

"Is something wrong with the stew?" the girl asked anxiously.

"It is wonderful. I have never tasted its like. But how do you keep the onion and carrots so firm?"

Cruithne beamed at him, and his heart did something strange and not quite comfortable. "I do not add them until the meat is almost cooked. Is that wrong?"

"It seems quite a good idea, and I wonder that no one has thought of it before. I think that no cook in Eriu has your hand with a stew, Cruithne." He felt his cheeks redden as he said her name, and looked down into his bowl to conceal his embarrassment.

The smith grunted and swallowed. "Wait until you taste what she does with fresh fish, lad. I do not think the gods themselves dine better than I."

"Father!" She shook her head and the soft hair bounced across her shoulders. "You must not boast of me," she chided, shaking a little finger at her father. Still, she was delightfully pink with pleasure at these words, and Demne understood that she enjoyed the praise, no matter what she pretended.

Then he wondered if the gods ate at all. He could not, somehow, envision shining Brigid spooning up good mutton stew or dipping an oatcake into the rich broth. Nor could he imagine the beautiful Donait at this simple meal. She seemed to live on fruit and nuts.

The thought of the fairy woman, as always, brought to him the scent of apples. "Tell me, Cruithne, do you ever put apples in your stews?"

She tilted her head to one side in thought, and his heart stumbled once again. "I never have, but that is a good idea. Oh, I can hardly wait now for them! All I have now are small and dried up. I get very bored with making the same thing over and over. Apples would make a good change from carrots." Her gaze met his, then slid swiftly away. "I think you know a great deal more about cooking than you pretend." Her thick lashes shadowed her pink cheeks as she looked down.

"I am very fond of apples," he answered in a stifled voice. Demne sought for something else to look at and found the smith watching him in a thoughtful way. Their eyes met, and Lochan lifted a bushy brow before he looked away.

THE MAKING OF CHARCOAL, DEMNE DISCOVERED, WAS A demanding task, and a tedious one as well. It made his days beside the hearth of Gléor Lamraige seem carefree. Still, always curious, he bent his mind to grasping the properties of woods that could mysteriously be twice burnt. He spent long, cramped hours crouching beside the stone-lined pit oven at one end of the forge house, watching the fire that must be maintained just so. He learned to shape pieces of aged alder to produce neat little blocks of charcoal that would burn evenly in the forge.

Lochan was as much a perfectionist as either Bodbmall or the Liath Luachra, but where Demne had chafed beneath the rule of his fosterers, he felt a quiet contentment with the smith. The backs of his hands were blistered and burnt; his shoulders ached and his legs were cramped from crouching. It did not matter. Cruithne made soothing salves from mutton fat and herbs, and she rubbed them into the burns until the pain was dulled. The touch of her small hands on his skin made his loins burn with desire, and he would bite his lower lip and wish the sensation away. Later he would run along the roaring shore, to ease the knotted muscles of his legs and the hardness of his manhood. Grasping this mystery, which was at once so simple and so difficult, filled him with a sense of accomplishment he had never had from throwing a spear or outrunning a hound.

At the same time, Demne began to know the girl as he had never known anyone of his own age before. In the long winter evenings, while she plied her spindle beside the fire and the smith dozed, they talked. She told the tale of Goibhniu, the smith God, and his two brothers, Credne Cred and Luchtar, and Demne countered with the tale of Tailtiu, as Bodbmall had told it to him on the way to Tailten Fair. From the gods, they went to stories of old heroes, and then to personal stories. Of these, Cruithne had few, for she said her life had been uneventful, and she was avidly interested in the things of Eriu that Demne had experienced. He told the tale of the contests at Tailtiu, but made that boy called Fionn the hero, and never said it had been he.

When spring began, Cruithne went into a frenzy of cleaning, and demanded that he give her all his garments for washing. When she saw the soft clothing that Donait had gifted him, her dark eyes rounded in wonder, and her fingers rubbed the fabric in a way that made him squirm with discomfort. She looked up and smiled. She moved closer to him, until there was not a hand span between their shoulders, and he could smell her sweet flesh.

"Why do you keep these, Demne? They will never fit you again."

"I have my reasons," he growled, misliking her touch on the linen more with each moment.

"You could give them to me—they would fit me very nicely, and I would like to have a robe so fine and soft." Her voice was beguiling, tender, and full of promise. Cruithne turned a little, and one of her rounded breasts slid over his upper arm. At the touch, Demne felt his loins heat, and his face flame. Her face upturned, her little mouth was open, inviting his lips to hers.

Trembling, Demne looked away from her. He could see her hands coiled possessively in the folds of Donait's gift, and his gorge closed until he felt he could not breathe. Gently, he reached out and took them from her. "I must keep them," he muttered without eloquence.

"You are mean! I want them!"

"Want away, Cruithne. We cannot have everything we desire." Demne could not explain that these still-apple-scented garments were precious to him, for he did not wish to reveal anything concerning the fairy woman. Then he made the mistake of glancing at the furious girl. She was, if anything, more desirable angry than she was happy. His skull pounded with blood, and he would have surrendered to her anything but the garments of the Otherworld.

Cruithne sulked. "I want them, and I shall have them—just you wait!"

A FEW DAYS PAST THE MIDSUMMER FEAST AND DEMNE'S sixteenth birthing day, a small fleet of curraghs bobbed up on the shore. They were small round vessels made from skins stretched over a framework of hazel withes, heaped with nets and clothing and other gear, and they looked as if they might sink in the first wave. Demne was amazed that anyone would be mad enough to enter the sea in such unlikely things. He found the sudden enlargement of the community was uncomfortable, for he had come to treasure the simplicity of life with only Cruithne and Lochan.

Then Lochan gave the making of charcoal over to one of the fisher lads, and brought Demne to man the bellows of the forge, and he wondered if he had not done well enough with the charcoal to satisfy his master. Pumping the bellows required nothing more than a strong back, which he certainly had. He pumped until his shoulders ached and his palms were almost raw, and gradually he began to realize that like charcoal making, pumping the bellows looked simpler than it was. Demne began to expend less energy on his pumping and to pay more attention to maintaining an even heat. Lochan, who had complained of his clumsiness, hummed over his work once more. As he worked the bellows, Demne watched the working of the metal, and found himself longing to know its ways.

The fisherfolk were a surly bunch, small and dark and suspicious of his height and fairness, and for the most part, they kept to themselves. They caught their prey each day, then dried and smoked it on the shore. The smell of burning wood and fish mingled with the scent of hot iron and bronze, until Demne was sick of both. Still, if he tried he could ignore them.

What Demne could not ignore was the attention that one of the young men, Eochaidh, lavished upon the smith's daughter. He brought her special fish and handfuls of wildflowers from the meadows where the sheep grazed. Demne had nothing to give her, except the fine garments he had outgrown. He remembered her promise to get the garments from him somehow and the days following their argument, when she had hardly spoken to him. He saw her watching him beneath her thick eyelashes, and he knew she was making mischief. So he forced himself to pretend indifference, for even to best the fisher lad, he would not part with the clothing Donait had given him.

When Eochaidh joined them for the evening meal, the two youths glared at one another. Cruithne pretended to be unaware of this sullen, voiceless rivalry, and smiled upon each of them until Demne was ready to throttle the other boy for merely existing. He could not control the rage he felt, nor the desire that shook him when his fingers touched the girl's as she handed out the food. This frightened him down to some deep core, and he threw himself into his work. He drove himself to near exhaustion and tried not to think of anything but the forge.

On the morning after the feast of Lughnasa that began the harvest, Lochan and Demne came into the forge to begin the day. The *gilla* set about bringing the fire to the proper temperature while the smith inspected his hammers. Then there was a faint rustling sound, like the rush of wings, from above the fire. Demne looked up, blinked several times, and made a little croaking sound.

Shimmering above the forge shone his Lady of the Pathways.

Lochan looked up, grunted sharply, and went down on his knees beside the fire.

"Brigid! You honor me . . ." the little man hissed, trembling.

The Lady smiled, and a sweetness like the breath of all the apple blossoms in Eriu filled the forge. Demne came out of his daze and plopped down on his knees beside Lochan. He had never believed he would see that lambent face again. But he basked in her radiance like a man deprived of light for so long he no longer knows he is in darkness and has been brought out into the day.

The fire blazed higher and the glory expanded to fill the chamber. A finger of fire flared from one lambent hand; before Demne could flinch he felt a touch on his brow. His skin prickled where she touched him. He trembled with fear, but more, with longing for the caress of her hand. His entire body began to tingle with a pleasure that was also pain, and he resisted, then surrendered, his heart pounding with joy. The sensation settled into his hands, and he swallowed a groan that rose from his belly. Demne lifted the burning hands towards the Goddess in supplication, sure the flesh must be seared, and saw around each hand a pale glow. It went on and on, until he thought he could not bear another moment, yet wished it would always be so.

At last the flame began to withdraw, and the Goddess released Demne from her gaze and looked for a long moment at Lochan. The cheerful whistle of the charcoal boy coming up the path sounded impossibly near. Brigid smiled, but already she was fading into the heated air. Demne collapsed onto his hands and knees, shaking. He wanted to call her back, but he could only make small mewling noises in his parched throat.

He heard Lochan rising to his feet beside him. "You have known her before."

Demne knuckled his eyes and nodded. "I saw her once, far away. She showed me where my life might lead. I did not think to find her here."

Lochan snorted as Bodbmall used to do when he had said something particularly naive. "And why not! Is she not the mother of fire?"

"Is she? There is so much I do not understand." Demne stood up and brushed the dirt off his knees. It stuck to his long fingers, wet from his tears. He wanted to go away alone to savor the moment when she had touched him.

"She wishes you to learn my art, Demne. And so you shall. Now there will be someone to carry on the work when I am gone."

Lochan sounded relieved, but Demne shivered with the beginnings of panic. The stone walls of the hut leaned in towards him, and the forge itself gaped to swallow him. Was that what the Goddess had meant? What about the vision she had shown him before? He wanted the secrets of the forge, but he did not want to forsake all those other paths. But perhaps what the Goddess had shown him in the Otherworld did not matter here. Confused, he forced himself to breathe, to make the compressing walls return to their place again.

Still dazed, he nodded. "Teach me, Master Lochan."

The smith chuckled. "Slowly, slowly, lad. It takes a lifetime to learn this craft."

Demne bowed his head, but his inner vision was still filled with the image of the Goddess, and his heart still cried out, *Why?*

THE LONG SUMMER DAY WAS DRAWING TO AN END. Demne raced across a flowering meadow, trying to outrun the nameless terror that made it so hard to breathe. He had gotten out of the forge without releasing the scream that was building inside him, and now that he was alone he found he could not. At last, winded, he dropped onto a rock and stared sightlessly down the mountain at the restless sea. So lost was he in his thoughts that he did not hear the soft footfalls until the girl was right beside him.

Cruithne knelt and frowned up at him. Even seated, he was a head taller than she, and he thought how endearing her smallness was. "I was gathering bilberries, and I saw you running like a wild thing. Is something wrong?"

"I had to get away from the forge," he muttered, acutely aware of her nearness. She looked at him, uncomprehending. "Lochan said he will teach me smithing."

"Demne! That is wonderful!" She pressed her little mouth against his cheek. Soft breasts brushed across his upper arm, and he remembered that in the summer she did not wear anything under the shawl. Without intention, Demne reached for her. For a moment she gazed at him round-eyed, then she smiled a little and very carefully kissed him on the lips. Her mouth tasted of the berries she had eaten on the mountain.

Demne's grip tightened. She was warm and human and very real. He felt her little tongue flick against his lips, his mouth opened, and then he was following her lead, mouth feeding on mouth until his head spun and the image of the Goddess flared away.

Her small hands gripped his broad shoulders, stroked down his chest to his thighs. His loins began to blaze like the forge itself and he groaned.

"You will stay with me now, forever," she whispered. Then they fell over together into the meadow grass. Her basket spilled beside his head, and berries went rolling down the hill in a wave of heady scent.

Demne lost all sense of anything but hands pushing aside garments, hot kisses, and touches of flesh that blotted out the world. He lay in the sun-warmed grass, almost helpless, while the girl lifted her skirts and straddled him. As she wriggled across him and her soft thighs brushed his manhood, he gasped with pleasure. He had been hard already; now his need was plain. He reached for the full breasts that swung just above him, and in the same moment she guided him into her softness. As she slid down upon him his gasp was lost in her deep moan.

Cruithne settled herself more securely, and Demne clutched at the grass. Then she began to rock, softly at first, then more rapidly, until he was aware of nothing but the waves of pleasure each movement sent through him. He tried to touch her face or the bouncing breasts beneath her gown, but consciousness had focused on the pillar of fire between his thighs. He saw her face contort as through a heat haze, and she gave a cry of triumph, long and shuddering, and he arched like a bow and felt himself surrender his fire to her enclosing depths.

Chapter 14

❧

IT TOOK DEMNE EVERY BIT OF BODBMALL'S DISCIPLINE to focus his attention upon the forge in the days that followed. Thoughts of escape were banished by the greater release his flesh had found. His healthy young body ached for Cruithne's, and there were times when all he could do was think about the things they did together and wonder when she would find a time for them to meet again.

The smith's dark-haired daughter proved surprisingly inventive. They lay together in the heather and upon the stored hay behind the croft; she let him take her standing against a wall with her legs wrapped around his waist, supported by the grip of his strong arms. They made love on the beach, mounting waves of passion racing the incoming tide, and in the bathhouse beside the flowing stream. Demne's astonished pleasure began to change to a certain pride as he realized that the stamina and quick responses that had enabled him to excel in other activities were serving him here as well.

It was the greater part of a moon before some disturbing ideas began to bubble through the tide of sensation that had submerged him. The first was that the girl was too skilled in the ways of the flesh for their coupling on the hillside to have been her first adventure. Second, he noticed she often followed their bouts of coupling with fresh entreaties for the fine garments of Donait. The last and most unpleasant was the realization that during the long hours he labored with her father at the forge she was sharing herself with the fisher lad Eochaidh, who glared at him across the evening meal. Demne could smell the distinctive fishy odor in her garments at times.

He pondered this while he pounded heated ingots into shapes Lochan made him file down and forge again. He had observed men and women enough in his wanderings to know that it was not unusual for an unwed girl to share her favors. He could not understand why she should want to, when his passion was fixed solely on her, nor why his heart ached so, but he began to understand why love was called the sickness of Aonghus Og. He did not rage or question, but divided himself into two—the Demne who struggled to master the art of the forge and wondered, and the other who surrendered without thinking to the warm thighs and rounded breasts of the girl.

Demne ignored her demand for the garments and the ugly worm of the idea that she bestrode his body for no other purpose than to get them. The long disciplines of his childhood sustained him now, and he often thought warmly of his two stern fosterers. They had been the forge fire for him, and his only regret was that he could not tell them what great gifts they had given him.

His rival did not manage so well. After several days of sulking, Eochaidh tried to pick a fight with him. Demne sent him sprawling with a single, firm push against the chest, and stepped over the fallen boy as if he were a log. This made Cruithne twinkle with delight, but Lochan scowled and muttered beneath his breath.

Finally, after many restless nights, Demne realized that the way to solve his problem was to marry the girl. Then she would be his and his alone, and he would not have to worry anymore. It was so simple and obvious a solution he wondered why it had taken him so long to think of it. He could remain at the edge of Eriu and pound iron and bronze into wondrous shapes for all his days. What foe would recognize in the famed smith of the seashore the son of Cumhal?

The only question that remained was why this decision did not made him happier, nor why the red-haired sons of Morna, the fierce old *drui* who wished him ill, and the unknown fisher by the river haunted his dreams. Brigid herself had shown him that his path lay here. Demne quenched his doubts as he would have quenched a piece of red-hot metal in water, and sought out Lochan.

The smith was turning over a lump of ore in his thick fingers, fondling it as Demne fondled the full breasts of Cruithne. The *gilla* had seen him do this before, and wondered if the smith heard the voice of the earth in the materials he worked with. They spoke to Demne, telling him which piece of rock would yield iron or copper or tin, and which were barren. But it was an abstract kind of knowledge. He did not handle the metals the way that Lochan did, with love. Still, he had developed a profound respect for bronze and iron and gold, as he had for the trees he made into charcoal to melt the metals down.

"Master."

"What is it?" Lochan did not sound pleased to be interrupted.

"I wish to marry Cruithne," the youth blurted out, forgetting all his carefully constructed arguments.

The smith put down the ore and for a long time looked at Demne in silence from beneath bent brows. "You do, do you? And what sort of bride-price do you offer me?"

Demne had not thought of this, and he was stunned. He had his clothing, the brooch he had received from the Liath Luachra, the outgrown garments from Donait, and little else. He could offer neither cattle nor sheep, nor lengths of fine linen nor ornaments of gold. He was without kin or clan to help him. Property had never before mattered to him. Now he needed it, and he felt as if he had been cheated of an inheritance. If only his father had not been as foolish as he was brave!

"I have nothing to offer but my skills," Demne replied numbly.

"It is a wise man who accepts his limitations. But your talent for the forge, however promising, is not enough to win a wife. You have barely begun to learn—" Lochan broke off in mid-sentence with an expression that Demne could not read, but instinctively mistrusted.

"Yet you do have other talents that may serve. In the upper reaches of the mountain called Sliab Muicce, there is a sow named Béo that has long troubled our winters here. Before you arrived last year, she ravaged the flock and killed the best ewe we had. We were fortunate she was content with that and did not return. Her head will suffice as the bride-price."

Demne gaped at him, remembering quite vividly the sow that had torn his flesh as he ran from the men of the rath years before. He could still smell her hot and fetid breath. To confront such a beast with nothing more than his light hunting spear and his knife was madness, even to win Cruithne. He frowned. He had never heard of a wild sow attacking the houses of men, and he felt a tickle of suspicion darken his thoughts. Lochan was up to something.

Satisfied on this point, Demne focused his attention on the fear that gripped his belly at the thought of facing any member of the pig family. It was not just that he lacked the proper weapons. He knew that his blood had mingled with that of the sow he had slain, that she had become a part of him. To slay a sow or piglet was, in some way he lacked words to express, to kill a part of himself. Then he thought of the berry-sweet girl, and decided he must take the risk. The fear did not disappear, but Demne knew he could accept it, and whatever consequences it brought.

"I have nothing to hunt a pig with, Lochan," he said at last.

"That is true." The look of mischief returned to the old man's eyes. "You yourself must craft the spear that will serve you. I may not aid you, nor can you do it in the time you owe to me. No more tumbles in the meadow with my daughter, or staring off at the sea for hours at a time, dreaming. Does that trouble you? I have taught you enough to forge a good weapon, for indeed, I have never had such a student as you."

Demne felt his face flame, both from the praise and because he had not known that the smith was aware of what he did in the meadow with Cruithne. "What about Eochaidh?" If the old man knew about him, perhaps he knew about the fisher lad as well.

"Eochaidh will depart with his people soon, and return next summer. He has asked me for my daughter too," Lochan said smugly, and Demne wanted to hit him.

"He did?"

"Do not fear. He has no more to offer than you do, and he has no hand for smithing at all. Besides, I do not wish my dear girl to go off to live somewhere else for half the year, and I would not want him hanging around here all winter long. You are a sensible lad, and do not bother me unless you must. My girl is all I have, you know. . . ."

Something in his voice told Demne that Lochan did not wish his daughter to wed at all, but he refused to consider the thought. Instead, he remembered how Cruithne's sweet flesh encompassed his as she sat astride him, and the sweet taste of her kisses.

"Come, we have work to do. You are a good lad, with good instincts, but you are too much of a dreamer, Demne. Brigid herself has marked you for the forge. Put all else from your mind."

Demne scratched his head, and touched the place on his brow where the Goddess had laid a shining finger. He had never told Lochan about his earlier vision. Would he ever understand what the Goddess really wished him to do?

DEMNE BARELY NOTICED THE DEPARTURE OF THE FISHER-folk, nor did he respond to Cruithne's hints regarding the seashore or the meadow, and it never occurred to him to tell her why. Without intending to, he had fallen back into his childhood habit of keeping his own counsel and not telling even those to whom he was closest what he thought or planned. He bent his mind to one thing alone: making a spear capable of slaying the sow. By day he served the smith, and by night he struggled with the forge. The ways of iron were more complex than he had imagined.

The first reasonable-looking spearhead Demne fashioned broke the first time he tested it, and the next one bent. He took to putting pieces of crude iron beneath his lumpy pillow, to listen to their voices during his few hours of sleep. He sought just the right combination of elements, but after half a moon, even his powerful young body began to show the strain. His fingers trembled with fatigue, and his eyes were heavy all the time. He would have given up the whole thing but for the memory of Cruithne's feverish caresses.

When he was weary to near exhaustion, and close to despair, a night came when all went well. Demne sweated over the crude casting he had made the night before, heaving at the bellows to bring the coals to incandescence, watching as the dark shape among them began to glow. After the first quenching, he took up the hammer and began to shape the malleable metal, first with powerful blows, then tenderly, as if he were stroking the feathers of a captive bird. This time the thing he laid among the coals was identifiably the head of a spear. Once more he thrust it into a pail of water. The hissing covered all other sounds, and he nearly jumped out of his skin when Cruithne appeared in the doorway. For a moment he stared at her dumbly. He was vaguely aware that he ought to be glad to see her, but why did she have to interrupt him now? The hissing of the spearhead had ceased. He dared not let it cool further.

Cruithne started towards him, but Demne turned abruptly away from her, lifted the spearhead from the pail, placed it on the anvil, and grasped a smaller hammer in his hand. Muscles developed by months of ceaseless labor swelled and bunched as he began the final shaping of the leaf-shaped blade. He would have been outgrowing his tunics every few weeks here as he used to do when he was a boy, but like Lochan, he now wore only a kilt and a leathern apron when he worked in the forge. In moments he had forgotten that he was not alone. The metal gleamed in the ruddy glow of the fire. The leaf shape had a balance to it that felt right, and satisfaction warmed him. A little more hammering now, while the steel was still warm, and then he could begin the sharpening.

As he laid the spearhead upon the workbench, Cruithne came around the forge and pressed herself against him. She rested her head against his chest, and

Demne looked down at her. Her dark lashes shadowed her cheeks, and he could feel the firm rounds of her breasts pressing against him. He stroked the top of her little head with a grimy hand.

"Cruithne—" He found words at last. His arms tightened around her as he remembered that the reason for all his labor was this girl who nestled in his arms. "The spear—"

"I don't care about the silly spear!" Cruithne laid a finger across his lips. "I want you!"

There was a hunger in her eyes that both drew and repelled him. But the power that had forged the spear still throbbed through him, demanding release. Cruithne's hand slid around his neck. Her mouth opened, dark and wordless, and he let her draw him down.

The hard-packed earthen floor of the forge hut was not as tender a couch as the meadow, nor as sweet smelling, but Demne hardly noticed as his loins took fire. Cruithne was like some wild thing, biting and clawing at him until what clothing they wore was gone. Her hand closed hard around his manhood and he groaned, sure it must be glowing as the spearhead had blazed in the forge, but already her hips were arching, she pulled him into her body, and gasping, he quenched himself in her wetness. Her eyes were glazed and stupid; her teeth were bared in a feral snarl. For a moment, she looked like a stoat, and he tried to pull away. Then fire swept through him once more, and now his flesh was the hammer and hers the anvil. He heaved and grunted, battering himself against her as he had beaten the steel. Her legs vised around his body, and her moans became a scream as all his strength exploded in a last convulsion that left him lying half conscious across her body.

Demne slipped into an exhausted sleep almost before Cruithne had slid from beneath him and sprawled onto the floor. But his sleep was not restful. He dreamed he stood above the anvil, admiring the barb he had just made. The forge was bright, too bright. It hurt his eyes. He looked up and saw the blazing figure of the Goddess. Eager for approval, he lifted up the spearhead. Blue eyes studied it, and the perfect brow was marred by a slight frown. After a time, Brigid gave a little shake of her head and looked back at the forge. Demne felt a protest rise in his throat; he had worked so hard! But the Goddess lifted her hand, and serpents of flame darted upward, twisting and twining in patterns of dizzying complexity. When they faded, the Goddess had disappeared.

When he roused, he was alone. Confused, he looked around him. The forge was glowing, the chamber still warm. He was sweating, and he could smell the odor of his own body and Cruithne's musky perfume. With a groan, he reached for his kilt and staggered to his aching feet. His hair was heavy with dirt from the floor of the hut, and he felt filthy and tired.

Demne picked up the spearhead, now cold, and turned it from side to side. What was wrong with it? Why had the Goddess of the forge frowned? Brigid was just like Bodbmall and all other women, thought Demne: never satisfied. He splashed some water from the bucket across his sweaty face. His eyes stung, but he felt wide awake at last. The metal had cooled completely, but it only needed a few more strokes of the hammer to be done.

It was then that his fingers felt a roughness that should not have been there. A few pulls at the bellows sent the flames leaping. Demne peered at the spearhead, and in that fitful light he saw the faintest of cracks marring its sheen. He stared at it, unbelieving. Surely it had been perfect before.

But he knew that whether he had been too tired to see it, or whether the metal had cooled too quickly because Cruithne had distracted him, the blade was flawed. He shuddered, his vision suddenly filled by images of a monstrous beast charging while he tried to fend it off with half his spearhead gone.

Goddess, forgive me! You yourself marked me for the forge. Show me what I must do.

He waited for the vision to form around him once more, but all he could see was the final image of interlacing serpents of flame. But this time it seemed to him that they were different colors. He could see the patterning within them; and suddenly they were not flames but real serpents, with glittering metallic scales.

Blinking, he looked around him. He had seen something like that before. Most of Lochan's work was cast, but there had been one piece, a dagger whose surface was all shifting patterns like a flowing stream. He had plied the bellows while the smith welded and twisted a bundle of metal rods into a single blade. The unused rods rested on one of the shelves. Pattern welding, Lochan called it, a craft that made blades both flexible and strong. Perhaps, he said, he would teach his apprentice someday. But Demne needed that knowledge now.

He filled the forge with fresh charcoal and pumped the bellows until the fire roared. Once more Cruithne was forgotten. It was Brigid's image that filled his mind, Brigid whom he asked to guide his hands and mind and to show him the meaning of the pattern he had seen. He untied the bundle of metal rods and weighed them in his hands.

They were not all the same. Some of them were dark and dull. When Demne held them he heard a song of stillness at rest in earth's heart, unmoving as stone. It seemed to him that the second kind had a slight spring to them. Their song was of moving water and willow trees bending in the wind. The third kind seemed to leap in his fingers, and he thought they had a brighter sheen.

"Earth you were, ore prisoned in stone, then freed and fashioned but still without form. Do you tire of inaction?" He spoke to the rods. "I will give you blood to drink. Listen to me, bend for me now!"

He bound the ends of several rods of the first and second kinds with thin wire and thrust them into the fire. Then he hauled at the bellows. The firelight glowed along his bare arms, coloring the pale hair on his fair skin. The singing of the coals grew louder.

Tongs snatched the metal from the flame, and the hammer crashed down upon the end until there was only a single point. Then it was back to the coals, and this time the rods were clamped and twisted into a spiral, a few inches at a time, until he had a single thick rod whose surface rippled when he turned it to catch the light of the fire.

This he set once more in the forge. The fire song whispered in his ears; he could hear words tickling in his mind and felt the old frustration because he did not know how to weld them together as he was welding the blade.

"*I am oak, I am strong, Rowan am I, repelling wrong!*" sang the spirits the charcoal released as it burned. "*I am beech, fast I stand, I am willow and I bend!*"

When Demne began to hear a faint moan from the metal itself he swung it up to the anvil and the hammer crashed down, beating the stiff stuff into the shape he had envisioned.

From the fire to the anvil and back again, Demne worked the metal for his spear. His mind was empty of all but the metal that glowed and faded, the feel of the hammer in his hand, the slide of muscle beneath his skin. He found a kind of subtle music in his movements that grew as he labored, until it vibrated along

his very bones. Though he had neither the skill nor
the breath for singing, he was the song.

> *"Steel spiral in,*
> *the blade grows thin,*
> *power grows within,*
> *The spell is laid,*
> *the supple braid*
> *is strongly made,*
> *As powers blend,*
> *though death it send,*
> *life has no end."*

As the harp hears the melody it is playing, Demne
heard the song. With an understanding beyond words
he beat the metal back across itself, over and over,
hearing its tone deepen with each fresh enfolding. He
knew when the sound was right. For the first time, he
felt it the way Lochan must, as if it were alive.

Strength and suppleness were now built into the
steel, but without an edge it would not matter how
strong the spearhead was. In his vision, Demne had
seen the pattern surrounded by an aura of light, but
thinking back, he realized that the radiance came from
a paler band along the edge. That must be what the
third type of rod was for. Whistling between his teeth,
he heated two of the pieces, then bent them around
the rough spearhead, snipped off the extra, and bound
them there.

Once more the bellows wheezed and sighed. The
dull glow of the forge brightened until he could hardly look at it; the whispering from the coals grew louder. Then from the heart of the fire came a thin piping
like the cry of a newborn child. Shielding his eyes
with his hand, Demne fumbled for the tongs and felt
them close on something that quivered like a live
thing in his hand.

The fire died down as soon as the spearhead was out of it. Demne peered at the metal and saw that the new piece had melded into the old with only a ripple of changing color to show the join. He struck it with the hammer, and the air rang. There was a pain of longing and of need in that sound that made Demne's belly clench in sympathy.

"What do you want?" he whispered to the steel. Once more the hammer fell, and the metal cried out again. "Without the beating you will be nothing! I must do it for you to become what you must be!" he said desperately, grabbing one tool after another to finish the final shaping before the metal cooled. As he worked, the tone deepened to the groan of an animal in labor, but the swelling leaf form of the spearhead became more distinct with every blow.

And then, without volition, his arm stilled. He let it drop to his side, and overused muscles began to scream. The hammer slipped from his numbed fingers and hit his foot before it slid to the floor. The forging was finished. A part of him wished to keep working, but some deeper wisdom restrained him. Sunk deep in the struggle, he had never known when something was complete before. Perfection was beyond his grasp, until he learned to be still.

Why had this been so hard to learn? Was it because nothing he had done had ever quite pleased Bodbmall? He had labored as others ordered, but never for love of the work alone. He had worked on the other spearheads to win Cruithne, but this one was different. He tasted the sweetness of achievement like a food he had not even known he longed for, and as lying with Cruithne had fulfilled one part of his nature, now, something within him that had always been empty was finally satisfied.

The spearhead was still warm, pulsing with energy in his hands. He stroked the smooth surface lovingly.

"Sa . . . sa . . . there's no need to tremble. The pain is over and you are whole, and soon—" Demne broke off abruptly, remembering how Bodbmall had scolded him and then bound up his wounds. Once again he thought of his fosterers as the forge fires and himself as the metal. The harshness of their demands no longer seemed as terrible as it had when he was young. They had been shaping him, forming him into something strong. Brigid too had shaped him, like a mother. What, then, was the shape that he was meant to be? Had he begun to achieve it?

The vibration in the spearhead flashed through his own body in a single rush of mingled joy and pain.

What are you? Demne asked the weapon he held. *What am I?*

My name is Birga, and I am thirsty. . . . The answer to the first question reverberated through his brain. But to the second there was no answer at all.

His awareness of the spear's hunger was all the more acute because its making had satisfied his own. Tomorrow he would sharpen it, bend the collar around the strong ash shaft he had made, and punch the rivets through. And then they would go hunting.

"Birga . . ." He spoke the name aloud, caressing its cooling surface once more. "Be easy. Soon you shall drink the blood of Béo and be filled!"

Demne let a long, deep sigh escape his lungs. Through the open door of the forge the autumn stars glowed like the eyes of the Goddess. Gratitude for the gift of the spear's making swelled painfully within him. Words could have released it, but the song which had pulsed through him while he labored had faded with the fire. He had glimpsed the power that a magesmith might put into a piece through poetry, but he knew that whatever magic had gone into this spear's making was Brigid's, not his own.

In the other hut, a soft bed awaited him. But Demne

knew that he would never make it that far. He wrapped the spearhead in a piece of soft doeskin, banked the fire with care, and then curled up beside the familiar warmth of the forge.

THE NEXT MORNING, DEMNE WALKED OUT INTO A WORLD all silvered with frost. Somehow, while he worked, the season had turned towards autumn. Now each day was shorter than the one before, and a chill wind came in off the sea, promising cold to come. Soon the winter storms would begin to blow, and then the sow of Sliab Muicce would come down from the hills.

When Demne showed his work to Lochan, the smith was silent for a long time, fingering the spiraled patterns that glimmered in the steel. In his eyes, Demne read a grudging wonder, and something that was almost fear. For once Demne did not feel the lack of praise, for Brigid had guided his labors, and if she had not found them satisfactory she would have shown him. He could feel Cruithne's eyes upon them, and blushed, remembering how he had battered her when they lay upon the floor of the forge. Would she hate him? He reminded himself what all this labor had been for, and forced himself to turn.

It had been weeks since he had really looked at her in the full light of day. Now he blinked, for her tiny waist had thickened and her round breasts strained against the cloth of her winter gown. He had not noticed that, the night before. But he had heard enough kitchen gossip to know what such changes in a woman's body must mean. She was undoubtedly with child. He wondered whether the baby was his own. He was not ready to be a father, especially to Eochaidh's child. Then her eyes met his in a long, sultry look that set his loins aglow with remembered fire.

It took him two days more to get the spearhead sharpened and the shaft seated to his satisfaction.

Each night he dreamed of the sow, but in his dreams she would change into the sow he had fought when he was fleeing from the men of Mag Life, and it was she whom he was carrying to the lake, she who sank beneath the grey waters and was transformed into something terrible. He realized that if he did not go soon to the mountain, he would not have the courage to go at all.

On the third morning, Demne donned his oldest clothing, packed some food in a small sack, and started up the shoulder of the mountain. When he reached the meadow he heard a light footfall and saw Cruithne, puffing a little as she tried to match his long strides.

"Demne, do not go today." There was a tone in her voice that made him shiver.

"Why? I am as ready as I will ever be, and soon the sow will come down and ravage your flocks."

She looked at him with her big, dark eyes. "But why must you go?"

"I swore to your father that I would kill the beast so I might marry you."

"Is that why you are doing this?" Color flamed into her face, then faded once more. "You could have told me!" she said angrily. "You never talk to me anymore. You are getting just like Father!"

"I thought that he would—" Demne began. Women knew things and gave you orders, like Bodbmall or Donait. But how could you discuss things?

"That he would tell me? Did it never occur to you to find out if I even want to marry you?"

His gaze sank to her middle, and she colored again.

"Do not go. Listen. Perhaps the beast is dead. It has been around since before I was born. It must be very old by now." She sounded sincere, but she would not meet his eyes.

"Before you were born?" Demne halted. He was

not certain how long a pig lived, but more than fifteen years seemed a very long time for a beast. "How long?" He sensed a great wrongness here.

Cruithne was silent for a time, pondering. "Béo has ravaged these lands since before my father even came here. Do you understand now why he set you to kill her?" Demne stared at her blankly.

"I am trying to tell you it isn't a real pig, you dolt," she went on. "They say it comes from the Otherworld, and what weapon will work on a creature from there? I don't want you to die or be maimed. I want you to live and see our child. Come back with me!" She took his arm and lifted her dark eyes fetchingly.

Demne looked down at her, and found that her glance still made his pulses pound. At the same time, there was a hunger in her face that somehow reminded him of Bodbmall. He recalled her expression as she pulled him down onto the floor of the forge, and he shivered with a chill that had nothing to do with the brisk breeze.

"I gave Lochan my word. I will slay the sow as your bride-price. That is why he let me make the spear. How can I dishonor my promise?"

"You will get killed; I know it. Do not leave me alone." Her dark eyes hardened and narrowed, and her little fingers dug into his arm. "At least do not go today."

"What is special about today?"

"It is nearly Samhain."

Demne gaped at her. Lochan had not told him, and he had lost all track of time while he labored on the spear. He remembered two years before, and the great stag he had helped to hunt. He had come near to death then. At Samhain, the black sow's season, the doorways opened between the worlds. Death was very easy then, and if Béo was an uncanny beast, she would face him with extra power. It dawned on

him then that the smith did not really expect him to
survive the hunt, and Cruithne knew it. Perhaps he
should have talked to her before.

Her eyes were still upon him, devouring him. Suddenly he wondered why the old man had allowed her
to escape his watchfulness at just the moment when
he might expect Demne to be completing his work at
the forge. Cruithne did not want him dead. She had
not even known why he was making the spear. Unless
she was lying too, and had changed her mind after she
lay with him . . .

Demne shook his head to clear it and took a deep
breath, and the crisp breeze made the blood sing in
his veins. Lochan had not expected him to go after
the sow with a Goddess-blessed weapon in his hand.
The thought of a lifetime with Cruithne was frighten-
ing him almost as much as the prospect of fighting the
sow, but he felt a perverse determination to outfox the
old man.

He wanted to shove the beast's snout into the old
man's face, and neither love nor fear could stop
him from seeking it now. He shook off Cruithne's
clutching hand and bounded towards the first line
of trees.

DEMNE PAUSED BENEATH A NUT-LADEN HAZEL AND
breathed to calm himself. How many moons had
passed since he had done any serious hunting? The
stink of the forge had faded from his nose, and he
savored the familiar scents of trees and growing
things, released as the sun reached its noontide
strength. It was as if he had crossed some invisible boundary, as he had when he had jumped the
chasm to Donait's realm. He gazed at his spear,
saw its excellence, and knew that despite Brigid's
blessing he did not belong in the forge. He had
believed for so many years that discovering the

secret of his parentage would give him place and
peace, and all it had brought him was trouble.
Even here, in the apparent security of Lochan's
domain, he was in peril. He scratched his head in
exasperation.

Then the stillness of the mountain began to seep
into his bones, drawing Demne back to the simpler
time when he went skin clad and hunted for the
two old women. He could not return to that soli-
tude even if he wished to, but he could appreciate
it now. He heard the sigh of the trees and the murmur
of a brook nearby, and he felt their songs stir in his
blood. Enchanted by the ringing of the forge and the
rosy-cheeked Cruithne, he had not listened to those
fair melodies in a long time. Now she swelled with a
child, and he felt snared by the very softness that had
drawn him to her. He still desired her, but his breath
caught as he realized that her love constricted him as
much as the *bendrui*'s care.

But he had given his word, and in a way, Lochan
had challenged him. He could not run away even if
he no longer wanted to marry the girl. And the Liath
Luachra had taught him better than to go into danger with his thoughts in such turmoil. He shook his
head to clear away the distractions, and set himself to
climb. He crossed a brook, and paused to listen for the
sounds of bird or beast beside it.

Long bars of light and shadow slanted through the
forest as the sun sank towards the sea Demne could
hear hurling itself against the jagged rocks far below.
But among the trees it was quiet, too quiet. He tilted
his head back and looked up. A large crow sat silent
in the branches of a tall yew tree, watching him dis-
passionately. He made a little caw in his throat, but
the bird did not answer.

It was unnatural, this silence. The hair at the nape
of his neck bristled. Carefully, he began to move

through the underbrush, straining his ears for any sound but the distant rush of the sea. He wished he could hear the rapid footfalls that would tell him that the invisible sister whose laughter had so often irritated him as a youngster was near. For the first time in his life, Demne was afraid of the quiet of the wilderness.

The urge to run back to the stone huts disgusted him. He had never been afraid in the wild before. This fear must come from living too long within walls of stone. Had he ever really believed he could be content in such a hole?

A soft grunt some distance ahead sent the nagging questions out of his mind. There was a crashing, crunching noise of something heavy moving through the bracken. He froze in the shadow of a yew tree. The breeze was flowing from behind him. A snorting, grunting snuffle caught his ear, followed by a roar of piggy fury.

The beast had found his scent. Demne listened as wood tore beneath the assault of curved tusks and sharp hoofs. He gripped his spear and discovered his palms were damp with sweat. The beast burst out of the underbrush, and the youth gasped as he swung himself astraddle a branch. He had not imagined any pig could be so big!

The beast was not black as he had expected, but an odd, unhealthy silver grey. It stood, swinging its huge head back and forth, as large as Gléor's best bull, and much more intelligent. Only the pig's feeble vision kept it from discovering him in the shadows. The hide looked like leather, and white tusks gleamed in the huge jaws. Tusks! That was wrong, but before he could think why, a stronger gust of wind gave him away, and the animal charged the trunk of the tree, squealing.

The impact of the pig's broad shoulder upset

Demne's precarious balance, and he rolled off the branch, the spear encumbering him. Demne hit the earth running as it tore after him, screaming with furious anticipation. He could smell the hot and fetid breath as he dashed around the trunk of an enormous oak and charged back again.

Demne jabbed at a flank and heard a shrill squeal of astonishment. He had only time to tear the weapon free and lope away ahead of slashing tusks. The pig's hot blood dripped down the yew shaft of the spear and stung his skin. His vision wavered, and he nearly ran headlong into a tree. For just a moment his legs felt short, stubby, and powerful, and he was seized with terror as he felt himself begin to change into the beast that pursued him, as he had been transformed by the sow he had slain so long ago. He scrambled over a tumble of rock and wrenched himself out of the memory.

Demne swung around and struggled for a firm footing on lichen-covered stone. The pig scrambled over the rocks, snorting and squealing, blood spurting from the wounded flank. The monster was too close already for the spear. The youth hurled his knife into its mounded chest as it charged and saw it sink deep into the flesh. The snick of deadly hooves scrabbled against stone, and blood colored the pale lichen in the fading light.

He sprang to a larger rock, a slashing tusk just missing his calf as he climbed. Demne wiped a bloody hand on his tunic and gripped his spear. The pig struggled and grunted, rested its front legs against the boulder, and thrust its great head up, jaw gaping. The smell of blood and pig made Demne feel weak and dizzy with a strange sense of kinship, not with fear.

I am empty. . . . Come to me and I will be filled. . . . I am hungry . . . let me feed on you. . . . There is no struggle in the darkness; you have only to give yourself to me. . . .

Those eyes were not red, but a deep and luminous brown, and he began to sway forward.

Then Demne smelled the scent of decay; his gorge rose and he jerked away. The spear slipped, he grabbed for it, and smeared the steel with the blood that still stained his palm. He almost dropped the spear again as it leaped in his hand.

Thirsty! sang the spear. *Give me blood to drink!*

Blood, yes. Demne gripped the ash shaft in both hands.

"Don't look at me that way!" he yelled at that luminous eye. It was not brown, could not be— He thrust at it with the shining point of his spear.

The pig's scream rattled the branches as the steel entered its brain. Demne leapt back as the liquid of the eye spouted out, afraid to let it touch him. The tusks gouged two grooves in the rock. Then the pig shuddered, fell backwards, and collapsed belly-up on the ground below. Demne peered over the edge of the rock. The beast lay still, its stubby legs thrust upwards, with the spear shaft angling towards the darkening sky. Demne felt his own male members shrink in reaction as he saw that what he had slain was unmistakably a boar.

At last, when he was certain it was truly dead, he clambered downward and removed the spear from the animal's eye. It must have caught the last of the sunset, because for a moment the spearhead seemed to glow. Demne shook his head, jerked his knife from the pig's chest and began to haggle the head free of the body. He did not know if the thing had somehow changed its sex to unman him, or whether local legend had been wrong. It had certainly fought like something from the Otherworld.

The mountain was an uncanny place even with the

boar gone and Demne had no desire to spend the night there. Cutting through the tough flesh was a long, hard task, but there was surprisingly little blood. He lifted the ruined head up by the stiff hair between the stubby ears and made a sound of disgust. The smell of rot was overpowering, as if the boar had been decaying before he even killed it.

Demne began his long descent from the mountain, pausing only to wash his hands, his spear, and the noisome trophy in a gurgling stream. A small sliver of moon rose to light his way, but even so, he stumbled with weariness and more than once bumped into trees. But he was not tempted to stop in any of the hollows where the pine needles lay thick and soft. The wind had died with the sun, but the treetops were full of whispering, and the darkness beneath them glimmered with lights that owed nothing to the moon.

When he finally reached the edge of the meadow where he had first coupled with Cruithne, Demne rested and looked down at the huts below, then back towards the forested sides of the great mountain, torn between the two domains. He still could not decide where he should be. But he was too weary for such ruminations now.

Lochan emerged from the main hut as Demne stumbled in. His features were almost hidden by the darkness, but the youth was certain the smith was not pleased to see him return. Wordlessly, he held up the huge head. His arms screamed with agony, and he wanted to throw the terrible thing into the sea.

The smith stared at the stinking, hideous head for a long moment. "That is not Béo," said Lochan.

Demne stared at him. Given his suspicions, he had not expected praise, but he did not even feel the old rage at being deprived of his due. If this was not Béo, than what had he killed?

"I did not think to ask its name when it attacked

me." Just now, with the Samhain wind chilling his sweaty skin, he was not sure he wanted to know.

The older man's shoulders slumped. "I suppose it will have to do."

Chapter 15

❦

THE SECOND WINTER BESIDE THE HOWLING SEA WAS cold and dreary. Demne chafed as the winds blasted the stone huts on the shoulder of the mountain, and the rain beat in through chinks in the walls. As the moons passed, Cruithne's body swelled, and she lost the bloom in her cheeks and the twinkle in her dark eyes. She was irritable and snappish, and disinclined to sport beneath the covers during the night hours. No longer did she smell of meadow grass and taste of berries. Now she stank of wet sheep like the rest of them, and her rare kisses were flavored with bile. They told no tales beside the fire now, but sat in sullen silences.

Lochan had been sunk into a bleak mood since Demne's return, and nothing pleased him. The youth found the older man staring at him sometimes, and it made his skin roughen and the nape of his neck bristle. Worse, his sense of being trapped increased with each passing day.

One evening a moon past Midwinter, the three were huddled in the hut while a storm tore at the stones. Demne lifted his eyes from the flickering fire and stared at the skull of the pig which now hung from the wall of the hut. All the flesh had been removed, and the bones had been dried. Lochan had bound the jaw with a chased band of iron which gleamed dully in the firelight. One eye socket had been ruined by the thrust of Demne's spear, and the smith had pinned a bronze roundel across it. It made the youth think of that one-eyed son of Morna, Goll, who was the high king's *rigfennid*, and his sworn enemy.

Demne had not thought of his foes in some time. They would never find him in this wilderness, but sometimes he wondered if he would not rather face Goll mac Morna's sword than stay prisoned here. He found himself revisioning the paths of his future as they had swirled from the hem of the Brigid's gown. So vivid was his memory that he could almost smell the scent of the light-filled house of Donait over the stink of tallow and smoke in the little room. Nowhere in those colored paths was there the slightest hint of this desolate place, or of the smith and his daughter. Still, he had seen the vision when he was in the Otherworld, where the fairy woman and his invisible sister dwelt, and he was not certain how to interpret its meaning in the world of men.

Not for the first time during this endless winter, he wondered why the Goddess had appeared to him in the forge. He was bored with making charcoal, pumping the bellows, forming ingots and then deforming them. He was heartily sick of the smell of hot metal and smoke, and weary of Lochan's sullen silences and sudden rages, and Cruithne's whining. The smith's claim that he had slain the wrong beast was clearly untrue, for nothing had disturbed the flocks since he had returned from the reaches of the mountain. It must have been said from spite, to enrage him.

A ripple of movement beneath the folds of Cruithne's gown caught his attention for a moment, and he looked away in disgust. The presence of that life growing within the girl made him at once angry and uneasy. He was not ready to be father to what was probably the fisher boy's child, to be shackled to a face that had swollen to grossness. She had begged him to talk to her, but what was there to discuss, except her progress upon the loom and his at the forge? It was not enough, and he knew it. The sense of being smothered which he had felt when he had started up the mountain returned, all the more oppressive because now it was familiar. He wanted to run, shouting, out into the storm. Instead, he glared at the skull upon the wall of the hut, and wished he could slay the beast again.

Later, Demne lay awake, listening to the snores of Lochan and the labored breathing of the girl beside him. The storm was dying outside, and the hearth fire barely glowed within. He slid out from the warmth of the covers and tugged his clothing on, shivering. He must get out and stretch his legs. He would walk down to the shore, he decided, and see what the sea had cast up.

Sometime later, Demne was astonished to discover he had gathered all his belongings, including his spear, and was striding towards the meadow where he had first tasted the berry sweetness of Cruithne's lips. He hesitated in mid-step. Was he crazed? The last sputterings of sleet damped his hair in the darkness. He had taken no food, just his clothes and old blanket, his tattered brogues, and his cloak of worn wool. But without a backward glance, he crossed the puddled meadow and began to climb the mountain. His eyes adjusted to the darkness, and he moved slowly into the trees above.

A gusty sigh escaped him, and he felt as if he had laid down a burden he had not even known he bore. When dawn began to streak the sky he was high upon the mountain, free and happy for the first time since he had taken Cruithne to wife. He reached the summit as the sun began to gleam, shimmering like the gown of Brigid against the fair blue sky. He eased down on a damp boulder and allowed himself to listen to the murmurs of earth, the morning chirp of birds, and the soft rustle of leaves. For a time he gazed back at the distant blur of the sea, knowing he would not see it again. Then he rose, shouldered his bundle, and began to travel eastward, towards the mountains whose ragged crown snagged the clouds.

The descent of the far slope took most of the brief day. Demne's sling brought down a hare near the foot of it, and he roasted the flesh over a tiny fire. It was delicious, after months of mutton and dried fish. He found himself savoring the plainness of the meal, and he sharpened a twig with his knife to pick his teeth clean. Then, content, he curled up in his smelly blanket and slept until the cry of birds aroused him once more.

Some distance away, he could hear the chatter of crows discussing something of interest. Demne scratched his tangled locks and yawned. Then he washed his face in an icy spring and set off to investigate. The clean, green smell of the forest was refreshing, though his clothing still stank of the forge. The spear in his hand gave him confidence.

When he drew near the glade where the crows were gathered, Demne pushed aside a branch and peered through the leaves. All he could see was a cloaked figure, bent over and making a terrible sound. Whoever it was seemed to be quite alone. Still cautious, he left his hiding place and moved closer.

A twig snapped beneath his foot despite all his care, and the figure turned abruptly. It was a woman about the age of the wife of Gléor, tall and sun tressed. She would have been beautiful, but her face and breast were streaked with gore. Her eyes widened when she saw him, and drops of blood coursed down the pale cheeks and dribbled onto the heaving bosom of her gown. Demne gasped as the woman retched and vomited up a red clot that lay on the earth like a jewel. No wonder the crows were excited—the smell of blood could draw them for miles.

"What ails you, woman?" Demne asked. He was not certain she was real. He had never heard of anyone crying blood before.

"My son is slain," she answered, and fresh red tears spilled down her cheeks. She keened eerily until she spewed blood once more. The sound made him shiver, and he was glad she had paused.

"You are red-mouthed, woman. I have never seen such a wonder."

She cast him an odd chilling look that made him shiver. "That is fitting, for a terrible, great warrior has slain my child, and I shall spew up blood until he is avenged."

"But surely you yourself will perish if you go on," he said practically.

She shook her head, and her long braids dragged through the red wetness on her breast. "I shall live to see my son's murderer die."

Demne scratched his head and shifted his weight from foot to foot. "Tell me of this warrior," he said feeling both distressed and revolted. Would his mother weep blood for him, he wondered, if she were still alive?

She lowered her eyes to the ground, but not before Demne had seen the look of mischief there. "He is a monster, four times the size of any man, and each day he eats the head of some hapless warrior. He enchants them with a song he keeps in a treasure bag, and draws them to their deaths. He has skin like leather and eyes like coals and his hands are made of iron."

Demne raised an eyebrow. Where in this wilderness would the monster find enough warriors to keep him supplied? Bodbmall had taught him that the things people said were not always to be taken literally, but this seemed an odd moment to be exaggerating.

"Have you seen this, then?" he said carefully.

"I have not, for his song keeps women away, just as it draws his victims. Can you hear it?"

Demne listened, but heard only the rough caw of crows and the whisper of the breeze. The woman began her keening once more, drowning out even the voices of the birds. The hair bristled along the nape of his neck at the sound. Something was wrong here, something that went beyond the woman's bloody tears and heavings. He frowned, searching for a clue to the puzzle, and found nothing.

The breeze shifted around and brought the woman's scent to Demne, and for all her fairness, it was the odor of something that has lain long rotting in the ground. He gripped his spear and took a step backwards. He had smelled this taint before, on this very mountain. His stomach clenched with the beginnings of an awful certainty.

"Who was your son, red-mouthed woman?"

Her lips stretched across very sharp teeth. "Mac Béo the Brave was my son, and his death must be avenged. Never was there a better son in all of Eriu."

Demne blinked, for as she spoke, her long, pale hair appeared to coarsen until it looked like strands of hempen rope. She stretched out bony hands; her nails were like talons of iron. "Soon you will hear the song the monster makes. Will you not avenge my son's death?"

Demne took another step backwards, and slipped on a gout of her blood. "What is the name of this great warrior," he squeaked.

The eyes of the woman narrowed, and another bloody tear slipped down her cheek. "The warrior is called Luachra," she hissed.

The sound of that name stopped Demne in his tracks. He touched the cloak clasp at his throat. She had to be lying—he had left the creature that had once been his foster mother in Loch Lurgan far away. But even if the Liath Luachra had somehow come here, he could never slay her. What mischief was this red-mouthed woman up to? Where had she gotten that name? His limbs felt like the water of the loch where the warrior woman now swam.

Demne gasped for breath, and the stench of the red-mouthed woman sent a wave of dizziness through him. Gritting his teeth, he shifted away from her, retreating towards the edge of the glade as quickly as his trembling legs could carry him. With each step, his vigor increased and his strength returned.

The woman howled, and around her contorted face her golden hair stood out in a stiff brush, and her shapely body began to expand. Already she loomed above him. Demne did not wait to see her complete her transformation. He loped as fast as his feet would carry him away from her screams of rage. As he whipped between the trees more wood crashed close behind him, and he put on another burst of speed.

Something whizzed over his head, and a whole birch tree sailed into the tops of some wide-shouldered oaks, showering him with earth from its dangling roots as it passed. Behind him a golden head reared above the forest, a crimson mouth opened, and teeth like the barbs of spears gleamed in the sun. An enormous hand plunged towards him, and he dove through a tangle of hazels, cursing the undergrowth.

It seemed to him he could already feel the hot blast of Béo's breath on his back when at last the wood thinned before him. He took a deep breath and launched himself across the open ground at his best speed. He heard the groan as more trees were uprooted, and the ground trembled with great footfalls. What use was his spear against a giantess? He flogged his mind for some idea as he flogged his body across a small meadow, through a thin stand of alders, and into a wider stretch of grass just as the huge bulk of the red-mouthed woman burst through the last of the trees.

She was four times the height of any man he had ever seen, and her hair was bristled and twisted. Her once fair skin had thickened and sprouted short, stiff hair. The mouth which had spewed up blood was now a crimson cave, bristling with fangs. Biting off the heads of her victims would be no trouble at all. The eyes of the face glared like those of the boar, and tears of blood continued to fall. Where they struck, the earth sizzled, leaves wilted as her body pushed through the trees, and the grasses her great feet crushed grew brown and sere. He shook his head. A hundred spears could not have pierced the leathery hide that now covered her bones.

Demne raced up the meadow and onto some scree that slowed his pace. Swiftly, he shifted his spear to his left hand, and scooped up a rock, twisted, and hurled it into the gaping maw.

The giantess grunted and staggered for an instant. He scrambled over the slippery shale and grabbed another likely stone. The howling had ceased, and she was spewing up gouts of stinking blood. The sweet meadow was a smoking ruin around the torn hem of her gown. Demne took advantage of the pause to cast his rock. It crashed into the top of her skull and bounced away with no apparent effect.

There was an infuriated snarl, and Béo straightened, blood dripping from the cavern of her mouth. Demne raced higher. He could hear the huge body slipping on the scree as she began to climb after him. At last he had an advantage—the only one he was likely to find! He pivoted and dashed back towards her, light feet dancing across the scree. Stone slithered where he trod, but he was always a step ahead, circling out of the monster's reach while she struggled to stay upright on the treacherous footing. Béo lunged, and he dashed back down into the stinking meadow.

The reek of burnt grass made him reel, but Demne forced himself to gulp a lung-searing breath and raced directly at the gibbering monster. Taloned fingers scored the air before him, and he danced to one side. She swiped at him once more and slid down the slope, bringing half of it crashing down with her. As Béo flailed, he cast a sharp, flat piece of shale at the wide brow beneath the bristling hair. It tore through the flesh, and blood began to spill into the gleaming red eyes.

The giantess wiped her eyes on her huge arm and made a little grunt of what he guessed was pain. Her great legs bunched as he moved backward. But already she was leaping; her shadow engulfed him, and he was crushed to the earth beneath one stinking shoulder as she fell.

Demne could hardly breathe for the weight upon his chest and the stench; already the vigor was leaving his limbs. Then the monster lifted and turned above him, her great mouth gaping. Demne pulled his left arm free, focusing his remaining strength in his arm, and thrust the spear upward as the stinking maw opened to encompass his head. To pit his human spear against this monster was a futile gesture, but he felt joy pound along his veins as he aimed the barb. At least he would die fighting! There was a shock as the Goddess-forged barb bit through flesh and bone, but it was the monster's own weight that forced the spear through her eye into the brain beyond.

Béo reared backward as pain's message mastered greed. There was a scream that seemed to come from the depths of the earth, and then the earth was quaking—No, it was the giantess whose tremors shook the soil. The great body rolled away. Dazed, he realized that it was shrinking, shriveling before his eyes. Demne tore at his tunic where a drop of blood had burned through to his flesh, and crawled a few feet, gulping for air.

"The blood of my son," howled the red-mouthed woman. "I taste the blood of Mac Béo on this spear." The taloned hands clawed at the ground as the flesh began to fall from the contracting bones. "Murderer!"

Demne scrambled further, retching as the stench of the giantess's final decomposition exploded through the air. His vision began to blur. His limbs could not hold him, and he sank to the earth as the screams began to fade. He rested his head on a stone and the pain of her blood upon his skin became the world. He felt the darkness rising around him, and then there was nothing.

AN ETERNITY LATER, DEMNE WAS AWAKENED BY THE caress of soft spring rain upon his skin. He felt as drained, but he finally managed to get upright. Immediately he regretted it. His skull throbbed, and there was an open wound on his right shoulder that hurt worse then anything he could recall. But as the cool rain trickled into the wound the pain eased until he could almost think again.

He gritted his teeth, then breathed slowly, as Bodbmall had taught him. The breeze brushed his hot cheeks, bringing the stench of decay, but also the clean smell of leaves and young grasses. With his knees bent and his good arm resting across them, he sat gathering his wits. As his weakness lessened, he realized that the rain felt so welcome because his skin was burning. The fever in his blood could almost dry his soaked garments, and his throat was parched. Ignoring the jolt of pain and the spots that danced before his eyes, he tipped back his head and began to lick the raindrops that fell upon his lips.

The smell of the rotting carcass made him sicker every time the wind changed. Cautiously he got to his hands and knees and began to creep away. It was slow going, and at times the pain threatened to overwhelm him. His palms and knees were scraped and bloody before the dreadful smell faded, and by then he could hear the gurgle of a spring nearby.

Demne plunged his throbbing head into the clear waters which bubbled from the earth, dragged it up again, and pushed his long, tangled hair out of his eyes. Then he opened his mouth and sucked in the icy water like some beast. It tasted cleaner and sweeter than honey wine, and the fire in his blood began to ease. He plunged his torn hands into the churning waters, then splashed it on the wound on his shoulder. He did not know if there was some virtue in the spring or if the simple act of cleansing was what was needed, but the wound became numb, and he realized he was weary beyond words. He curled himself into a ball beside the spring and let his eyes close in sleep.

Hunger roused him, sharp and demanding. Demne drank some water to still his growling stomach and twisted to peer at his shoulder. There was a small star-shaped white scar where the blood of Béo had touched his flesh, but at least there was no longer any pain. Perhaps the water of the spring had washed it away. He wobbled to his feet and started off to reclaim his scattered belongings.

His cloak had been torn in two by taloned fingers, with the brooch of the Liath Luachra still holding the rent pieces together. He sighed and picked it up. His pack had fallen from his shoulder at some point in the fight, and it took him a long while to find it among the boulders. He pulled off the ruin of his tunic and found an old one in his pack. The sleeves were too short, and it pulled across his broad chest, but it was warm and dry and smelled of sweet herbs. He wondered once more when he would cease to grow, or if he would end up, though more slowly, like the fearsome creature he had slain.

Cautiously, Demne approached the place on the shale where the red-mouthed giantess had died. He wanted his spear back, and he thought he could risk the poisonous fumes of the corpse one more time to get it. Brigid had helped him to make that spear, and he valued it for that reason, even if it had not been his only weapon. But the body was not there, and neither was his spear. He cast around him, thinking he must have mistaken the place. But all that he could see to mark their battlefield was a dark hole in the scree. It was a cave mouth, really, and he was sure that it had not been there before.

Demne hunkered down and peered into the hole, sniffing suspiciously. The only odor that reached his quivering nostrils was the clean smell of fresh, damp earth and crushed fern. He scratched his head for a moment, then crawled inside. A kind of tunnel led into the side of the hill, dark after the soft light of the day, but he could feel his way forward. He listened intently for any sound of danger, and used his keen nose continuously. After a time, he smelled water, though he could hear no gurgle, and his exploring fingers found the edge of what seemed to be a deep, still pool. He crawled closer and peered down.

In the darkness of the chamber, he should not have been able to see anything, but his face was mirrored in the surface of the water. His pale hair gleamed faintly, and a soft fuzz of beard disguised his square jaw. His light blue eyes seemed huge in his lean face, and he looked wild and unkempt. Then, like a double image below his reflection, he saw a bag of some soft, supple leather, and beside it, his spear. He plunged his arm into the water, reaching for it, and it vanished. Astonishingly, the water was not icy, but warm.

Demne chewed his lower lip in thought. As the water stilled, the objects reappeared. They seemed to lie but an arm's reach below the surface, but that must be an illusion. Was this the sack of treasures that the giantess had mentioned? He touched a finger to the water and the objects vanished. It was almost as if the bag and the spear were not in the pool, but only appeared to be. He looked up from the water, but this was the end of the tunnel.

Shivering, the youth removed his clothing, folding it tidily beside the edge of the pool. Demne lowered himself into the shimmering liquid then gasped. It was hot—more than hot. It was almost boiling, though no bubbles rose around him. He treaded water for a moment, took a great breath, and dove.

The heat of the water seemed to increase as Demne swam towards the bottom of the pool. He was going to be boiled like a duck. He expelled a little air through his nostrils as the Liath Luachra had taught him, gritted his teeth, and kicked his powerful legs while his hands groped ahead.

At first they closed on nothing but scalding water. Demne's ears began to ring and his lungs screamed for air. He released a little more breath and swallowed, which lessened the discomfort somewhat, but made him all the more aware of his need. Deeper and deeper he moved, until he lost all sense of purpose in the simple struggle not to open his mouth and gasp. Did the pool go to the heart of the world? How was he going to reach the surface once more?

At last, his flesh would be denied no longer. Demne fought a instant longer, then inhaled the searing liquid that surrounded him. The water flowed down his mouth and into his lungs. He waved his hands like waterweeds, and waited for his end. Now, he thought with quiet regret, he would never discover what waited on the paths the Goddess had showed him.

After a few moments he noticed that he was not dying. In fact, he was breathing water as if it were air, and it seemed marginally cooler as well. Fear and sorrow were replaced by curiosity. Tiny bubbles spun from his lips as he breathed, but the water seemed as comforting as the bath of Donait, and as invigorating.

Something gleamed ahead. For a moment he thought it was his spear, then a boneless wriggle brought it towards him. He saw the flicker of a fin, then the long, smooth curve of a silver-speckled side. It was a salmon, larger than any he had ever seen. *You should be cooked,* he thought, giggling. Then his gaze was caught by its glowing golden eyes. It was still nearing; its shining back arching gracefully beneath his floating hand. Demne stroked the smooth scales, and felt a thrill of delight. Now the salmon hovered close before him. Demne gazed into those luminous eyes and was filled with a longing for which he had no words. He only knew that it had been within him since he was born.

Then the great fish darted away and vanished into shadow, and Demne realized that he had reached the bottom of the pool. The skin bag and spear lay before him on the silvery sand. He closed one hand around the yew shaft, and grasped the cords of the bag with the other. As he pulled the long cords over his head, he felt the wood of the spear quiver in his hand. The bag settled against his bare chest and seemed

to snuggle close to him. That was curious too, but
this was no time to wonder. Demne launched himself towards the surface of the pool. The water was
cool against his skin now.

Without warning, he began to cough and choke on
the liquid he had been able to breathe but a moment
before. He flutter-kicked in panic and clawed at water
that was suddenly cold. The chill ate into his flesh,
and he could feel the strength slipping from him. His
mind started the spiral into endless darkness just as
his head thrust through the surface.

Demne sucked in air and choked as water spewed
from his throat. He thrashed weakly to keep afloat. In
spite of his efforts, he went under twice and came up
sputtering before his flailing hand touched the edge of
the pool. He clutched at it, poked his spear above the
water and thrust it out onto the ground, then dragged
himself up onto the earth.

Runnels of water dripped from his long hair and his
skin as he lay catching his breath. The skin bag he had
taken lay warm against his breast. When at last he sat
up, he found it dry to the touch. He rubbed himself as
dry as he could with a piece of his torn cloak. Then
he put on his garments once more, hiding the bag
beneath the tunic, and started back up the passage.

As he moved, Demne became aware once more of
the spear shaft in his hand. It tingled under his touch,
and as the opening of the tunnel drew nearer, he
looked at it carefully. The head shone with a reddish
light, and though the spiral patterning still gleamed,
it no longer looked quite like steel. The leather thongs
that strengthened the joining of spear and shaft seemed
quite ordinary, but the ash wood glowed yellow.
Uneasily he remembered the glimmer he had seen after
the death of the boar. He shuddered to think what the
blood of the red-mouthed woman might do. But as the
spear poked into daylight, its shimmering vanished,

and it seemed to be his familiar weapon once more.

When Demne emerged into the dim light of a cloudy afternoon he blinked, and sat down hard on a nearby rock. The trees, which had only been beginning to leaf when he had entered the cave, were now bronzed with autumn, and the meadow where the giantess had left a smoking ruin was golden with drying grass. His stomach growled, and he rose shakily to gather a handful of late berries, in his hunger, careless of the snagging thorns. The breeze was chill and smelled of ripe wild apples. He stumbled across the meadow and found a tree heavy with the fruit. Somehow, two seasons had passed since he had entered the cave. He wondered if more than seasons had gone.

He turned his hands back and forth, and noticed that all the cuts and scrapes of his battle with the red-mouthed woman were healed, and realized that the pain in his chest was gone as well. He pulled aside the throat of his tunic and peered at his shoulder. The starlike scar where the blood of the giantess had touched him remained the same, and he scratched his head, wishing that Bodbmall were there to explain it to him.

But whatever had happened could not be changed now. Demne gathered some dry branches and set about making a little fire. He was cold and tired, and there was nothing in his belly but some berries and an apple or two. In the flickering light, he noticed that his wrists stuck out of his sleeves even further than they had what seemed to him only a few hours before.

To distract himself from his hunger, Demne drew the skin bag from beneath his tunic and pulled the cords off over his head. The bag was not of any great size, and when he ran his fingers across it, it seemed to be empty. He turned the bag over and found it unadorned. He could not imagine what value it might have. Then he began to draw apart the cords that closed it. Suddenly there was a faint sound, and he lifted the supple leather closer to his ear.

From within the bag came the most haunting voice he had ever heard. It was the song of a crane, but it filled his awareness like the roar of the sea. He lowered the bag and frowned. The sea was on the other side of the mountains. He stared uneasily at the mouth of the bag, dark and apparently empty. There were knots at either side, and he prudently memorized the pattern in which they had been tied. Then he pulled the mouth open until it touched the knots, which promptly undid themselves without his aid. The cords slid eagerly between his fingers, and Demne jerked away.

When nothing happened, Demne peered into the mouth of the bag. It was dark, but he smelled salt and seawrack. Then he turned the bag towards the flickering light of the fire. Instead of bare leather he saw a glittering tumble of weapons and fine gold jewelry. There were spears far too long to fit into the bag and swords too sharp not to pierce its soft leather. There were torcs of chased and carven gold, earrings and wristlets, as well as enough weapons for a hundred men.

His bewilderment was broken by a sighing song like the moaning of the breeze through evergreens.

> *"I was Aife, Manannan's wife—*
> *By strife and spite, my rival, my bane,*
> *A crane me made, but kept from flying*
> *Though trying at season's turning;*
> *My yearning now you hear—"*

Demne dropped the bag, but the singer continued.

> *"Fear not, fair Cumhal's son,*
> *Known by hand's touch. Aife was I,*

By magic made, treasure bag of the brave.
That knave, Béo's son, bore me for the fian,
Still a man, struck Cumhal, whose blow—
Slow death—he fled. Hurt sore,
As boar survived, and I in his captivity."

Demne blinked, at last understanding. The boar
he killed who had been the red-mouthed woman's
son, transformed by her into beast-form to stave off
his mortality. The crane skin bag, the *corrbolg*, had
also once had human form and been transformed.
Although Bodbmall had occasionally mentioned that
such changes were possible, Demne had never really
believed her.

"Beyond the mountain's gates
Waits old Crimall son of Trenmor.
For all thy years, his brother's son,
Fair one, he's sought. Thy birthright's there
Where Cumhal's fian *look for their lord—"*

An uncle? Demne had thought all of his kindred
gone! Heart pounding, he whispered, "Oh, *corrbolg*,
where shall I find Crimall?"

"My word will lead thee well;
Dwells Crimall in Connachta lands. . . ."

The bag sighed and was still.

Demne sighed too, for Connachta was far to the
north of anywhere he had been during his wanderings, and to get there, he must pass through the lands
of the sons of Morna. Still, his wounds were healed,
and he saw now that in addition to the treasures, there
were rounds of cheese, dried meat, and hard bread in
the bag. And best of all, he was no longer a clanless
man. He ate the food, and after offering his thanks to

the *corrbolg,* knotted up the cords at the crane bag's mouth as they had been tied before.

Then, much heartened, he slung his gear about him and started northward across the hills.

Chapter 16

❦

A S THE SEASON TURNED TOWARDS WINTER, DEMNE hurried north to the mouth of the Sinnan estuary, and then along the banks of the river. When he reached Loch Dergdeire, the stronghold of Red Daire whose other name was Morna, he traveled by night for fear of his enemies. In the dawning he glimpsed the slopes of Sliab Bladhma, dim with distance as a dream. But though he longed to return to them, the voice in the crane bag instructed him to cross the river above Bri Élé, and make his way north and westward again. He never remained more than one night in any place, and Aife advised him where to stop and where to go past. The crane bag also told him to trade a pair of golden earrings from the treasure sack for a good wool cloak and a pair of new shoes.

To thrust his hand into the depths of the sack was disturbing, even with the soft voice of Aife to reassure him. He knew that when he opened it he reached into the Otherworld and listened to a sea that was not the same as the one which flung itself upon the shores of Eriu. Twice he had been into that world—when he had leapt the chasm to Donait and when he had swum in the charmed pool to recover his spear—but

to reach into it while remaining in the land he knew
made the flesh of his arm go cold.

Whenever possible, Demne ran, streaking past small
settlements where round-eyed children stared in wonder and men reached for their spears as he flashed by.
Each day was colder than the last, and shorter, and
only hunger slowed his feet. He crossed ranges of
mountains and valleys filled with the lowing of cattle
or the bleating of sheep, sped as quickly as he could
through murmuring forests and forded icy streams and
rushing rivers, and his hair flew out behind him like
a golden banner as he ran.

At last, after the moon had twice reached her
fullness and faded to sickly thinness again, Demne
reached the range of hills on whose crags the *fian* of
Crimall mac Trenmor were said to dwell. The folk
nearby said they were like eagles, swooping down
to snatch a cow or a sheep, clearing a field of corn
like ravenous crows, and looked askance when Demne
asked directions. It seemed that the men of the *fian*
were little better than the thieves whom they sometimes fought, for they neither herded nor tilled, but
took what they desired. And there was no reason for
it—the people would have given food gladly, though
they grew angry when it was a young woman that the
warriors stole. Only fear prevented folk from climbing
the mountain and chasing them away. Demne found it
hard to understand too. He had always worked at one
thing or another to earn his keep. Surely the bread that
came with curses would choke the thief as he gulped
it down.

It was the end of a brief day, and Demne was climbing the lower reaches of the mountain when he heard
a birdcall that came from no beak or bill. He paused
and fiddled with the thong of his shoe, letting his
awareness extend around him without appearing to be
alarmed. He was being watched from the hazel thicket

ahead of him, though he was unable to spot the spies. He gripped his spear more firmly and moved off at an angle, ignoring the tense pebbling of the skin upon his forearms as he passed. Instead, he began to hum under his breath as if to keep up his courage. It was a little melody he had heard the sad Muirne, the Queen of Lamraige, sing over her distaff beside the hearth.

A mist curled between the trees, and birdcalls rang around him. His invisible observers were signaling. Demne tried to identify the pattern so that he could guess at its meaning, and his lip curled. Who but a fool would twitter spring mating calls when the leaves were autumn brown?

Then seven men materialized out of the mist, surrounding him. Demne grinned, impressed at last, for not even the rustle of a dried leaf had warned his quick ears. He stilled like a beast before the hunter, only too aware that the two men behind him had poised their spears.

"You're no lad of the village! What do you want here?" The speaker was a big man in his middle years, with a grizzled bushy beard and a pate nearly bald, wearing a vest of wolf skin above grey breeches, with a shaggy cloak over all.

"I seek Crimall mac Trenmor," Demne replied as calmly as he could, feeling sweat break out on his brow despite the chill of the evening.

"And what would you be wanting with Crimall?" another asked. His hair was bound into a topknot from which bobbed a dozen braids whose ends were bound with leather from which dangled bits of bone.

"That is for him to hear and me to say," Demne answered, beginning to feel angry. These men were ruder than the rath folk, and more suspicious. His mouth was dry, and he swallowed with difficulty. "I bring him something he has long wished for."

"Many have come to offer Crimall a hero's death,

and none have returned," the greybeard announced.

"Death?" Demne blinked in surprise.

"What else does a warrior desire but a good death?" the man asked him, straightening and puffing out his chest.

Demne grinned. "Pretty women, if the rath folk are to be believed, plus the odd sheep and a cask of honey wine not three days past."

"Those are our fair wage for defending those hen hearts from their foes."

The youth suppressed a desire to laugh. He sucked his cheeks against his teeth and tightened his grip on his spear.

"I mean no harm to anyone here."

What a contemptible lot they were, preying on the hardworking villagers, and puffing themselves up with pretense. The voice of the *corrbolg* had insisted that he must speak of the crane bag to no one but his uncle. Crimall might be any of the men around him, or he might be in the fort the rath folk said stood at the top of the mountain. So close to a kinsman, Demne was hard-pressed to control his impatience or his temper.

"It's harm to yerself you should be fearing," said someone nastily. This man's hair had been bleached with lime so that part was an odd orange color, part the natural brown, and part as pale as Demne's own.

"I say we just kill the boy," one of the men behind Demne began.

The old rage boiled up in his blood without warning, and without turning, Demne jammed his spear butt backwards. It struck a leather jerkin and the flesh beneath it with a most satisfying thunk, knocking the wind out of the speaker before he could finish. He heard the other man moving, and leapt in the air so high he nearly brained himself on an overhanging limb to dodge his swing.

All his frustration was unleashed in a few moments

of furious action. As he fell back to earth, Demne
whipped the blade of his spear around like a scythe,
cutting three hurled weapons in twain as they flew.
The other had already landed harmlessly where he
had stood but a moment before, and he stood upon
the pieces as the men gaped at him. He could hear
the spearhead humming and a singing in his head that
whispered, *Thirsty . . . feed me!* With an effort he shut
out the sound.

"Who *are* you?" hissed the big man.

Demne considered this question as he watched one
of the men lean forward to retrieve his spear. The
youth put a foot on the shaft, and their eyes locked.
After a moment, the other man looked away and drew
back.

"I am called Demne," he said then.

"Whatever you are called, be off with you," snarled
one of the men whose spear had been severed, his
braids trembling with outrage at having been disarmed
by the youth. "Crimall doesn't see anyone but the men
of his *fian*."

The boy looked from face to face. Half the men
before him were twice his age. They might have
fought beside his father, and survived the Battle of
Cnucha where Cumhal had been slain. The faces were
hard, scarred and aged with years, weather, and combat. Some had a familiar look, and for the first time
in years, Demne thought of old Fiacail. He could hear
the sound of the old man's voice speaking to Bodbmall
and the Liath Luachra on his last visit. Demne remembered straining to hear when he was supposed to be
asleep. Surely it was of these very men, some of them,
that Fiacail had spoken.

"Does Fiacail still dwell with you?" he asked, ignoring the rudeness.

Clearly this question had startled them. They traded
quick glances, and shrugged uncertainly.

"That name is not uncommon. What man do you mean?" It was the big greybeard who spoke, and Demne guessed he was the leader of this band.

Demne strained for the rest of the old warrior's name, and for an instant found nothing. He had not cared about such things when he was nine years old, and it was the sort of knowledge that Bodbmall had tried to deny him. It was the boys of Mag Life and Tailtiu who had taught him that to the men of Eriu a man was more than himself, he was a heritage. Then, in a flash, it came to him.

"It is of Fiacail mac Conchinn that I speak, a wise and courteous warrior." Demne looked pointedly at the man who had told him that Crimall only saw his *fian.*

The greybeard appeared to take this mild rebuke personally. He bristled and eyed his severed spear shaft, and chewed on a tuft of his beard. "He might be," he said finally. "What is that to you?"

"I knew him when I was a child. He used to visit my fosterers, the *bendrui* Bodbmall and the warrior known as the Liath Luachra."

The big man choked and the white showed around his bulging eyes.

"By the gods!" He coughed, and another man pounded him on the back until he could speak again. "Bodbmall's fosterling! Then you are Cumhal's son, boy! Why did you not say so?"

"I have learned that it is not wise to speak my father's name too freely."

"They said you won all the competitions at Tailtiu, and then for years there was no word—"

"We believed you must be dead," one of the younger men muttered, sounding as though he wished it were true. "Cumhal brought us nothing but trouble, and I doubt you will do better."

"You hold your bitter tongue, Aghmar. I am Reidhe

mac Dael, shield bearer to Crimall mac Trenmor, though it has been many a season since we took the field." Suddenly the greybeard was garrulous. "We regret our inhospitality, son of Cumhal, but these are hard times. Truly, you have the look of your father about you, and we might have guessed, had we been less quick with our spears and more quick with our minds. Come along."

"Are you mad, Reidhe? If Clan Morna hears of this, we—"

"And how should the sons of Morna hear anything, unless you run off and tell them? The lad has already shown us he's not made free with his name. There is no need to borrow strife, man. It comes unbidden. Let us go now. The day is almost over, and the mist rises."

This was true. The twilight was silver with a fog that hid the trees further than a spear length ahead, and the chill of approaching winter hung in the air. Grumbling, the men gathered their weapons and trooped rather noisily behind Demne and Reidhe. As they ascended the mountain, more out-of-season birdcalls twittered and were answered. Men materialized like spirits from the mist to join them, conversing in hushed voices, until Demne counted more than thirty in all, as varied and fantastic in their hairstyles and gear as the men who ambushed him had been. He could feel their eyes upon his back, some curious, but most wary and uneasy. It was hardly the welcome he had imagined.

His belly growled with hunger, but his heart felt leaden. Demne tried to understand the bleak mood which was overcoming him, and slowly realized it was their suspicion and wariness that were weighing on him. He had thought the *fian* would greet him with delight, but why should they? He had never brought happiness to anyone, and from the sound of it, nei-

ther had his father. When the *corrbolg* had told him
to find Crimall, he had thought he was going to the
family he had always yearned for. Instead he found
fear—of himself and of the red-haired sons of Morna.
Would there never be any place where he belonged?

A well-maintained stockade, its logs well chinked
and braced, loomed through the mist ahead. They passed through the open gate, whose posts were crowned
with the skulls of stags, and Demne looked around
him. The palisade enclosed a central round hall and a
number of smaller buildings. In the twilight he could
see the flicker of the hearth around the edges of the
hide that hung before the door to the great hall. The
smell of boiling meat wafted across the compound,
and his mouth watered. A hound, white-muzzled
but still strong, rose stiff-legged and growled at him.
Demne growled back at the beast and the snarl died
in its throat. A baby howled its hunger somewhere in
one of the buildings, then stilled as a woman crooned
a soft song.

Reidhe led Demne toward the hall, and pushed
aside the hide. Shadows leaped within as the central fire flared, momentarily highlighting the jut of a
man's nose or the curve of a brow. Then it sank and
Demne saw only the shapes of the men seated there.
But he had marked one of them already, reclining on a
bench beside the hearth. He was somewhat bent with
years, his reddish beard lightened with grey, but his
belly was flat and the muscles upon his arms corded
and hard. A golden arm ring glinted as he sat up to
see who had come in.

Demne followed Reidhe forward, and once more
the fire brightened. The man with the arm ring came
halfway to his feet, blue eyes widening, and his hand
lifted in the beginning of a warding sign. Then Demne
moved fully into the firelight.

"It is not yet Samhain, and this is no spirit come

again," said Reidhe with the hint of a tremor in his tone. "Yet he is very like Cumhal."

The other man straightened fully and let out his breath in a long sigh.

"It was my brother's very walk, and the shape of him—but I see now that this one is young." He looked Demne up and down, and the first hint of a smile began to glimmer in his blue eyes.

"Ah, lad—it has taken ye long enough to come to us, an' we all thinking you had no use for the old men of your father's *fian!*" His voice cracked, and he caught Demne in a sudden bear hug that left him breathless.

"I-I didn't know," he stammered when he could speak again. "Bodbmall never told me!" Clumsily, he returned the hug.

"But at last, you are here," Crimall said finally, letting him go. "Come, sit by me near the fire. Long have I waited for the day when I could lay my burdens down." He looked at Demne again, smiling delightedly.

Demne stiffened. What did this man want of him? It seemed that all his brief years had been spent in learning other people's lives, in picking up what they had let fall. Bodbmall had chosen the way of the wise for him, and the Liath Luachra that of the warrior. The smith Lochan had surely believed he would follow the smith's craft. He had never yet chosen what *he* wanted to do.

Reidhe grunted dubiously, and it seemed to Demne that Crimall's words did not please the warrior either.

Slowly, he tugged loose the pin of the Liath Luachra's brooch and laid his worn and shabby cloak aside. The hall was warm after the damp chill of the wood, and it smelled of smoke, wet wool, and dog. The youth eyed the hearth critically. The wood had been poorly laid, and his long fingers itched to do it over again. Across the flames, a surly-faced lad of perhaps ten summers scowled as if he could read Demne's thoughts and resented them.

One after another, the men of the *fian* gathered around the hearth, pulling off damp cloaks and stretching out chilled hands. Outside there had been shouting, but here, except for the crackle of the fire, all was still. The silence seemed to grow until it was almost an invisible presence, oppressive and hostile. They were all looking at him, but except for his uncle, not a one of them seemed to find any pleasure in the sight, and no one would meet his eyes.

Reidhe cleared his throat. "The lad is surely his father's true son, for he stood against seven of us and did not even work up a sweat. He cut through three spear shafts in a single sweep, though it seems more than any mortal blade could do. His spear is a wonder, for it sings for blood, yet none of us were slain. Coll mac Diarmaita will have an aching chest for some days, for he got a spear butt rammed into it, but there was no other harm." He stared at Demne. "Where did you get that spear, lad, eh? The Otherworld?"

"Hush," muttered one of the men, shifting uncomfortably. "Do not speak of that so near to Samhain!"

Demne looked down at the spearhead that gleamed so innocently in the light of the fire.

"It was forged in the south, in a smithy near the sea," he muttered. This did not seem to be the moment to mention Brigid and the boar.

"It is what I would expect from Cumhal's son!" said Crimall. "Welcome to your father's *fian!*"

"Are we now to be making a *fennid* for the dodging of a few spears?" someone exclaimed. "What of the training and the testing? The rules should be the same for all!"

There was a mutter of agreement from the men.

Crimall nodded, his four braids of hair swinging forward. "It is true, Dithrambach, but the lad is wearied from his journeying. Before the initiation we must give him a chance to rest and learn our ways."

"How much chance did ye give *me* to prepare?" came the rough demand.

"Or me?" said another. "It was into the woods with me before I had been here an hour!"

"There is no need for you to change your rules," Demne said quickly. "I have only come to bring something that belongs to your *fian,* Crimall mac Trenmor."

He spoke as he would have addressed any of the chieftains he had served, having discovered through hard experience that it was safer than familiarity, no matter how kind they might seem. He had learned a great many things since he had accompanied Bodbmall to Tailtiu, and he could nearly taste the fear and hostility in the hall. But somewhere within him a voice cried out, wailing the loss of his dreamed-for kinship.

Crimall frowned. "Surely you have come to take your rightful place among us. Tomorrow we will test you"—he looked swiftly round the circle—"though I have no doubt of your fitness to run with your father's *fian*—"

"Son of Trenmor, if he does, we will have Clan Morna down upon us like wolves who hear the bleat of a trapped lamb," one of the men interrupted.

"And do you fear them?" Crimall responded, his contempt making the veins stand out along his thick neck.

"Only a fool would not fear Goll mac Morna and the royal *fennid* of Eriu. Even here in our fastness we have heard how they search for this boy."

Crimall took a deep breath and seemed to increase in size. "The royal *fennid!* Time was when *we* were the royal *fian!* And it is thanks to the sons of Morna that we scratch out a living here instead of living on the fat of the land. My brother's blood is still unavenged. It is we who should be going after those scum who strut in Temair!"

"Then you are as much a fool as Cumhal!"

The two men glared at each other while Demne squirmed with discomfort. Everywhere he went, contention arose. He had already set his father's *fian* at odds, and at the moment they were a greater danger to him than the red-haired sons of Morna. The weariness of his wanderings settled around his shoulders like a ragged cloak. When would he find a place he could call home? His throat constricted, and he squared his jaw to conceal his despair.

"Your spines are all made of water," snarled Crimall. "You dishonor me and yourselves by these words."

"We lost everything *except* our honor because of Cumhal. Why should we look kindly on his child, who will surely bring us woe if we let him remain?" Coll mac Diarmaita said. "We bear the lad no malice, and there is no question he is strong and cunning. But is this enough?"

Crimall almost growled. "It has always sufficed for the *fian*. You say he comes with a spear that sings for blood. Can you doubt it is the blood of Morna it cries for? How came you by your spear, son of Cumhal?"

Demne shrugged uncomfortably. "I made it. For a time I was apprentice to the smith Lochan, who taught me the craft of the forge." He paused, for the vision that Brigid had shown him was too sacred a thing to speak of, and the killings of the silver boar and his red-mouthed dame too uncanny. Still, he knew that the spear Birga was no longer simply the weapon he had fashioned. In his two battles it had undergone some incomprehensible change.

The soft rustle of the door hanging being pushed aside and a damp draft along the back of his knees made Demne turn. Forgetting the contention around him, he leapt to his feet at the sight of the man who was coming towards them, then blushed as eyes that were still sharp examined him with the wry humor he remembered.

"Demne! My boy, how you have grown!" Fiacail mac Conchinn embraced him with joy, and Demne felt truly welcomed at last.

Fiacail had seemed an ancient when Demne was a child, and he did not appear to have changed at all, as if he had reached a certain age and halted there. But the youth could feel the brittleness of the bones, and he knew his eyes did not see everything. There was a smell of age about the man that reminded him of Bodbmall. Still, to see the man of his childhood yet hale and in possession of his senses was comforting.

"Caught any salmon lately?" Fiacail asked, chortling until he began to cough, and Demne had to thump him lightly between the thin shoulders until he was breathing again.

"What's all that about a fish?" asked Reidhe.

Fiacail grinned, showing gaps between the few remaining teeth. Demne frowned, recalling his fosterers and the old man chuckling over something about a salmon once long ago. All he could think of was the great silver fish that had swum in the pool where he had gotten the *corrbolg*. He could almost feel the touch of its skin on his fingers, sweeter than the caresses of Cruithne. He had a feeling that the story was going to embarrass him, but already the tension in the room was easing.

Fiacail paused until he had everyone's attention, and nodded, smiling. "It was Midsummer Day, and this boy was hardly dry from his mother's womb. I was leading my old woman Bodbmall and the Liath

Luachra through the wood as fast as we could go. Old Tadhg mac Nuadat was hot on our trail, do you see, and he would have killed the child."

"His own daughter's son?" asked someone. "For shame!"

"At last, we came to a swift river and began to cross," Fiacail went on relentlessly, clearly enjoying every word he spoke. "Bodbmall was midway when her foot betrayed her, and this squirming rascal spilled into the stream. Thrice dove the Liath Luachra into the foaming waters. I was already seeking words to tell my stubborn old woman it was useless when the Liath Luachra broke the waters, cursing, with the babe wriggling in her arms. But the remarkable thing—" Once more he paused, letting anticipation build. Demne willed him to go on. This was more than he had ever heard from Bodbmall!

"The remarkable thing was that he was clutching a salmon almost as big as he, and the warrior woman swore he had been playing among the fishes at the bottom of the stream." Fiacail nodded slowly. "It was a most succulent salmon, the sweetest I ever ate."

Someone laughed, and it was clear they were trying to decide how much of the old man's story to believe.

At last Reidhe spoke. "Demne said that his reason for seeking us, Crimall mac Trenmor, was to deliver something to you."

"Is this true? You did not come to join the *fian?*" For a moment hurt showed in Crimall's eyes.

Demne nodded slowly, refusing, in the face of so many who a moment ago had been hostile, to speak of his yearning to belong to the band. "I did not know I could—I would not bring trouble upon you. But I found—"

The words died in his mouth. The *corrbolg* had

been most clear that he must to reveal her existence to none but Crimall.

"It is a thing for my uncle alone," he finally managed. The men stirred uneasily, but Crimall gave a little grunt and motioned the youth to follow him to the far end of the chamber.

Away from the hearth it was chilly, and the light was dim. The walls smelled of damp mud, and the pile of woolen blankets onto which Crimall settled, of mildew. Voices rose from around the fire as Demne squatted on the packed earth floor. He searched the face of his uncle, seeing the blurred reflection of his own features, knowing how he would appear in age. The older man folded his big hands and waited calmly.

Demne bent his head foward and lifted the cords of the crane-skin bag over it. Then he drew the supple *corrbolg* from where it had lain against his breast for so many days. He had thought he wanted to be rid of it, but without realizing it, he had become quite fond of Aife's soft voice, as if she were still a woman and his friend. For a moment more he held it, then thrust it into his uncle's hands, not trusting his voice for words.

The catch of breath made him look up sharply.

"How did you get this, Demne?" Crimall's voice was very low and gentle, as if he knew what it had cost the boy to give the crane-skin bag away.

"I cannot tell you as Fiacail told about the salmon." The young man fought for words. "I have only the bare bones of it, and it deserves to be said with blood and beauty, as the *fili* sing in the royal hall. I can hear the song of it, as I can hear the murmur of the world, but I cannot sing it."

When Demne had finished his tale, Crimall sat, turning the bag over and over in his hands.

"So, it was the Grey Man of Luachar who took it

after all! He was the son of a woman of the Sidhe by a mortal man, and always uncanny, but for many years he served Cumhal faithfully. Your father made him the keeper of the *corrbolg*, thinking an Otherworldly man a good custodian for such a thing. But the lust for it must have eaten at him. I saw the Grey Man wound Cumhal and run away, but was too hardpressed myself to go after him. After the battle, the crane bag was gone. Now it only remains to discover what happened to your father's sword. . . ."

For a few moments there was silence, then came a burst of laughter from the hall. Crimall roused and looked at Demne curiously.

"Do you know what this is?" He pointed at the bag.

Demne nodded. "She told me her tale, and much else as I journeyed here."

"She?" Crimall lifted his bushy brows.

"Aife, the crane woman whose skin is now the treasure bag in your hands."

"I see. She does not speak to any but those who rightfully possess her. Any man can open the cords, and some may even see the riches within, but only the chosen can hear the voice of the *corrbolg* and none before you have known its name. This has long been one of the wonders of our *fian*, and the loss of it was grievous. Cumhal could hear the voice, but he never heeded its counsel. I could never hear the voice, though when the tide is right, I can reach within and take what I need. I shall hold this in trust, until you can claim it and the leadership of the *fian* as well."

"You think I can lead the *fian?*" Demne scratched his head. "But the men do not want me."

He was glad to know that he had not lost the *corrbolg* forever, but the price might be more than he was willing to pay. How could he command men like Reidhe mac Dael who were twice his age and perhaps more?

Bodbmall had taught him that the way of the wise was one of service, not rule. Indeed, she had only contempt for *drui* like his fearsome grandfather Tadhg, who used their skills to amass wealth and power.

"They will, lad, they will—" Crimall chuckled. "By the time we return to the hearth, old Fiacail will have them so enchanted with his tales of your youth that they will be fighting to stand beside you."

Demne doubted this, but held his tongue. He had learned the futility of arguing with his elders when he still wore skins and went unshod. He seemed to be plagued with a gift for finding people who were convinced they knew what was best for him. And all of them were wrong. It was a pity that he lacked even a hint of what his actual destiny might be. His uncle's warm welcome cheered him, but already he knew that he would not be content for long.

Crimall pulled the strings of the *corrbolg* around his thick neck and tucked it beneath his shabby tunic. Then he led the youth back towards the hearth. Two gangling boys were starting to hand out bowls of steaming stew, and it smelled delicious. Demne forgot his doubts and concerns as his mouth watered.

"Tomorrow Demne will undergo the first part of his testing," Crimall told the men sternly. They looked at one another. There were a few shrugs and shakes of braided heads, but their mouths were filled with hot food and no one objected. Clearly Fiacail's joking had helped, but Demne felt the cold finger of peril tickle his straight spine.

"Think you it is wise to have this son of Cumhal in the *fian?*" Coll mac Diarmaita finally asked, and several of the men looked relieved.

Crimall shrugged, scowling. "Am I a *drui,* to see into tomorrow? But no man may escape his destiny. Demne has come here to fulfill his. That much is clear to me."

"And if his destiny costs us all our heads, what then, Crimall mac Trenmor?" asked Reidhe.

"Then that is our fate," said Crimall, and this time, only silence answered the old warrior's words.

Chapter 17

THE MIST WAS STEAMING OFF THE TREES IN WHITE trails like smoke from a cook fire in the first light of day. A child howled in the compound, and a tangle of dogs scattered across the yard after a leather ball thrown by a shouting boy. The smell of boiling oats rose from the cauldron in the cook shed, and a toothless woman churned it with a wooden spoon almost as tall as she was.

Demne yawned, stretched, and sniffed appreciatively. Food and sleep had refreshed him, and the forebodings of the night before were vanishing like mist at the coming of day. What would this one bring to him? Above the reek of dung and the nutty odor of the cooking porridge there was a crispness to the air that promised snow. Another winter would soon be upon them, and he was glad of a roof above his head, no matter how hostile those who shared it with him might be. He might sleep alone, but at least he would not be bored.

Then he saw Fiacail mac Conchinn heading purposefully towards him, a fine comb in one hand, and a coarser one in the other. "Come along, Demne. Let's see if we can get those untamed locks of yours into some order. The ends are all ragged! What have you done to them?"

Demne followed Fiacail over to a bench beside the great hall. "A *fili* I knew in Tailtiu counseled me to shear my hair and go in the guise of an outcast to hide from the sons of Morna. Was my father pale haired, Fiacail? Crimall's hair is ruddy, though I can see by the set of his eyes and the line of his jaw that we are kin."

"Hmm. Well, Cumhal's hair shone like the sun in springtide. It was good enough advice," Fiacail went on, "but you have your father's features stamped upon your face, and any who knew Cumhal in his manhood would know who you must be."

"Shall I wear a sack over my head to hide my face from my foes?" Demne's tone sharpened as he remembered his friend Aonghus, the death of Bodbmall, and how the sons of Morna had plotted his destruction even in that sacred place. "I am weary of running away."

The old man chuckled as they sat down on the bench by the water trough. "I hope you are not *too* weary, for today you must run as perhaps you have never run before. You must break no twig, nor rustle any leaf in your passage, for the men of the *fian* will pursue you like a hind. Neither may a hair of your braids be displaced during your race—that is, if I can get this cursed tangle into any order at all!" He dragged the coarse comb through Demne's hair.

Demne snorted to conceal a yelp of pain. "Does the *fian* always demand three impossible things before the porridge, or just on certain occasions?" He gritted his teeth as Fiacail worried the worst snarls out of his silky hair.

"I did it, when I was young, and so did every man here."

"Perhaps," Demne muttered darkly, hardly believing the old man's claim. "But when you ran, there were none who wished you ill."

Fiacail's hand jerked. "What do you mean?"

"There are several here who fear the sons of Morna. They would be relieved if I did not survive this race. I can see it in their faces, and hear it in their voices as well."

"These are men of honor!" The old man's voice was thin and reedy now.

Demne twisted around and glared at the warrior. "There is no room for honor in the heart that is filled by fear—the Liath Luachra taught me that. Crimall wishes me to take his place only because I am the son of Cumhal, for what does he know of me? As for the others, I could be the son of Lugh, and it would not allay their fears." He turned his back and allowed Fiacail to continue his efforts.

"At Tailtiu, I won every contest against the youth of Eriu. But even as the *Ard Ri* named me Fionn, the fair one, the men of Morna were watching with the red eyes of rage, and scheming to slay me by night. If my friend, the *fili* Aonghus, had not warned me, I would have died as I lay in the House of Youths. Do you see now why I am so mistrustful, even of my uncle, who is, after all, only a man?"

"The sons of Morna must have been mad to think to slay you on Tailtiu's sacred ground." Fiacail's voice shook and the hand holding the comb yanked out a snarl. "This is how Eriu has fallen. Such a thing would never have been countenanced by a man like your father—nor, I would have thought, by Goll mac Morna. Has time so changed him that he stoops to murder children?"

Demne shook his head. "I have thought much on that, and it is my belief that Goll did not know what his relatives had in mind. He saw me when I was before the high king, and he knew me for Cumhal's son. He could not but wish vengeance upon me for the loss of his eye, but he seemed a man who would rather wait for a fair fight when I came to manhood than sneak through the night to murder a sleeping boy. Goll is not Clan Morna, Fiacail. He may be its head, but he is not its limbs."

"You speak with a wisdom far beyond your years, Demne. Truly, you do your fosterers proud." He smoothed the youth's hair with a gentle hand and began to use the finer comb to separate the soft, wavy locks into sections.

"I would be wiser still if I understood why the men of Morna hate me so," Demne muttered. "Bodbmall once told me to beware them and of the Luagni tribe in Midhe as well, but never why. I know that Cumhal was outlawed because he carried off my mother and would not give her back again, but what had that to do with the sons of Morna?"

"It is a long story, and an old one." Fiacail sighed and paused with the comb poised in his hand. "And many strands have gone into the weaving. The high king rules now in Temair, but long ago the south was ruled by its own kings, sons of the men who came to Eriu from Gaul. When the sons of Mil rose in might to restore the rule of the Gaels they made the Gallic kings their subjects, but the Gallic warriors were at the service of the high kings. It is from these warrior bands that the *fiana* come. Cumhal's *fian* were originally all men of the Ui Failghi tribe of Laigin, though now we are a ragtag band. But the *fian* of Clan Morna come from Loch Dergdaire, the red lake where Goll washed the blood from his lost eye."

"That I know," said Demne, shivering. "I passed through that country on my way to you."

"Indeed, before ever Tuathal reconquered the land

they were our foes, and when Conn made his half
brother Cumhal *rigfennid* of the royal *fian* it only
increased their enmity."

"And Clan Morna were envious of their power?"
asked Demne as Fiacail began to comb the strands out
smooth. "That I can understand, but why did the high
king allow them to attack his own kin?"

"I think it was because Cumhal grew too powerful, and began to dream of wresting Laigin from the
high king's rule. It might even have come to pass,
had he not run afoul of the great druid who served
the Luaigni king. Your father was a great man, but he
had a genius for making enemies."

"You mean my grandfather Tadhg?" Demne shivered once more, remembering how the old man's spirit
sight had nearly found him. "He did not wish Cumhal
to marry my mother, I know."

"Muirne Fair Neck was the flower of the south."
Fiacail smiled, reminiscing. "All the princes of Eriu
were courting her, but it was Cumhal she chose. Never doubt that she went with him willingly, though
her father cried rape when he complained to the high
king."

"And so Cumhal's king, his own half-brother,
betrayed him," Demne said bitterly. "But when he
gave me the prize at Tailtiu he seemed glad to see
me. He is old now, and sad. But he seemed kind."

"We are all old now, except you!" Fiacail's laughter
turned to a fit of coughing. "In his day Conn Hundred-
Fighter was a great warrior, but when he turned against
your father I think his strength was already beginning
to fail him, and his son Airt had been killed raiding in
Britain across the sea. He had to keep the land peaceful
until his grandson Cormac is grown. Perhaps he meant
only to weaken Cumhal, not kill him, but the end was
the same. He loosed Clan Morna and the Luaigni and

the sons of Uirgriu, and Tadhg worked battle magic against us, and they brought us to battle at Cnucha and Cumhal was slain."

The old man fell silent and Demne felt the sharp tug and twist as he began to braid his hair.

"But my father is long dead, and I a wanderer," the boy said finally. "Why do they still hate me?"

"Because you are the son of Cumhal in whom his blood runs true, the one born to avenge him. All unknowing, you began the work of retribution with the killing of that traitor, the Grey Man of Luachar! Crimall told me your tale after the others were abed last night. And if you survive this morning's testing, you are the one who can restore this *fian* to its former power."

"Do you think so?" Demne asked bitterly. "Wherever I have gone, my father was there before me, and the chieftains sent me away, lest I bring strife to their raths. I thought to find something different here, in my father's own *fian,* but it is more of the same—I can see it in their eyes. My name should be Trouble, not Demne, for I seem to cause disruption wherever I rest. Even Lochan thought to send me to my death on the tusks of the boar." Demne sighed again.

Fiacail nodded and continued braiding, his old fingers surprisingly agile on the boy's hair.

"Fiacail, if I had known what the world was like, I do not know if I would have asked Bodbmall to take me into it. She did not wish to leave the mountain, and it cost her her life to please me."

Fiacail's hand gave a braid a vicious yank, and Demne choked back a yelp. "Bodbmall dead? Are you quite certain, lad?" There was a tremor in the old voice, as if it held unshed tears.

"As certain as I am of anything. We came down from the mountains during the summer rains, journeying to

Tailten for Lughnasa. She got wet and chilled, and began to cough. When we reached Tailtiu she worsened, and just before the hurley game, she breathed her last." He ached with the loss, as if it were only yesterday.

"When was this, Demne?" Fiacail seemed calmer.

"That is hard to say, for I do not know any longer the number of my summers." Demne did not wish to admit the seasons that had passed while he swam in the pool of the Otherworld.

"In the years of the world, you passed ten and seven last Midsummer, though you are unusually large for one so young." The old man gave a feeble chuckle, followed by a fit of coughing. "I was there," he gasped, "when you first proclaimed yourself, and a lusty cry it was."

Demne did some rapid reckoning. "It was five years ago then, for I was past my twelfth birthing day. But I went from eleven to twelve in what seemed to me a single sleep. So much has happened I do not understand."

Fiacail scratched his beard and frowned as if something were puzzling him. "Five years, hmm?" Demne saw his wrinkled lips open as if to speak. Then he closed them again with a sigh. "If you have more questions, you must ask them now, for I am almost done, and you must be ready for your test."

Demne wondered what the old man was concealing from him, and the hair on the nape of his neck stirred slightly. Then he put it from his mind and concentrated on making some sense of his tale.

"There is still one thing—the red-mouthed woman that I met on my way told me that her son had been slain by a fearsome warrior who enchanted with song, and she named this warrior the Liath Luachra. I thought she was trying to confuse me.

"But I know she lied, for I myself cast the old woman into Loch Lurgan and watched her become a great beast, all covered in hard skin. There I am sure she remains."

"I do not doubt you. The Liath Luachra was born from the waters, of no ordinary mortal kind. Of course she would return to them in the end." Demne started to insist she was not dead at all, not like the *bendrui,* but he stopped himself.

"But I do not wonder that the red-mouthed woman confused you," Fiacail went on. "It was not the Liath Luachra, but the Grey Man of Luachar whom she meant—the names are almost the same. Béo is one of the oldest race who dwell beneath the hills, and sometimes takes the form of a great sow who roams the mountainsides."

"When I speared the red-mouthed woman she screamed that she tasted the blood of her son," Demne said slowly, "and I realized that the terrible warrior who had slain him was me! Then she died, and when I reclaimed my weapon, it was no longer the same. The steel is still steel, and the ash still ash, but when it scents blood, the spear awakens."

Fiacail tied a thong onto a braid and twisted the ends neatly out of sight. "The blood of the Otherworld is strange stuff, Demne. And such creatures as this giantess and her son are not of our world, even when they tread its soil. Everything there is the same and different—the food, the air, even time itself." He cleared his throat. "I have not been there, but this is what I have heard. In your few years I suspect that you have seen more of that land than I, but I shall not press you. Now you are ready for the chase. Run well, as the swift-footed Liath Luachra taught you."

"And if I fail?"

"You must not. You will not."

Demne took a long, slow breath. If he did not run this race well, he knew he would never see his eighteenth summer. There were too many of the *fian* who would be eager to save themselves some trouble by speeding him to the Otherworld. With a fatalism born of long acquaintance, the youth shrugged, and then, slowly, he grinned.

"Well, perhaps I shall not be doing so badly. Have the men of the *fian* ever run with the wind?"

"The wind?" Fiacail mac Conchinn echoed, staring.

"My twin sister is like the wind," was all the answer the youth gave as he stood and strode away. The old warrior stared after him in wonder.

THE MEN OF THE *FIAN*, ARMED WITH LIGHT HUNTING spears, were ranged in three groups outside the walls of the stockade. A few joked with one another as Demne approached, but for the most part they were silent and grim. He recognized Reidhe mac Dael, and old Coll, and the hot-eyed young man called Dithramhach, but though their eyes darted towards him, no one would meet his glance. Pretending nonchalance, they gazed at the mist-shrouded forest below. The morning chill, with its smell of coming snow, was sharper now. The only sound was the rattle of spear shafts and the stamping of feet against the growing cold.

Crimall mac Trenmor came up beside Demne, pulling his cloak around him. The boy could see gooseflesh along the older man's bare arms. His uncle grunted, hawked, and spat onto the ground.

"You're ready? Well then, listen to the first part of the Law of the *Fianna,* for it is by this Law that you will live or die." He straightened and seemed to draw dignity around him with the words.

"No man shall enter the *fian* unless his kindred and

his tribe give security not to seek compensation for him should he be slain, for it is to the *fian* alone that the *fennid* shall look for vengeance."

Demne nodded. They needed no security for him, for all the kindred he had in the world were here. But who would avenge a *fennid* if it were by the *fian* that he were slain?

"Not a man shall be taken into the *fian* till his hair be interwoven into braids upon him and he start at a run through Eriu's woods while the others, seeking to wound him, follow in his wake. Should he be wounded, he shall not be taken; should his weapons quiver in his hand he shall not be taken, nor if a branch of the wood should disturb his hair's braiding, nor if he cracks a dry stick beneath his foot as he runs. Unless at full speed he shall jump a stick level with his brow and stoop beneath one even with his knee, and without slackening, extract from his foot a thorn, he shall not be taken, but who shall survive this testing shall be one of Cumhal's people. That is our Law."

Demne lifted a hand to touch Fiacail's careful braiding. It was worse than he had thought, for if they were supposed to come after him with weapons, who could say if a blow were meant to wound or kill? He could see Fiacail frowning as if this had just occurred to him too.

"In the spring, we will undertake the second part of your testing, but now you must run to the foot of the mountain, and return unscathed," said Crimall.

"How will you know if I have broken a twig, with this great herd of men trampling after me?"

"My men do not disturb the forest!"

Demne shrugged. "When they approached me yesterday, I heard a twig snap. And before I ever saw them their birdcalls told me someone was there. The spring song of the robin sounds odd at this time of year."

Crimall glared at him, then at his men, his naturally ruddy complexion growing redder still. "Surely I am growing too old to be leader of this *fian*. We have become lazy and careless. Win the race for me, lad, so that I may surrender the rule to you." He spoke very softly, so only the youth heard his words.

Demne stared at him. "You may be too old, but I am too young. Do you really believe you can force them to accept me?"

"I think you can win their approval, Demne. I think you must. If you do not, then the leadership will fall to your brother Dithramhach, who may be ten years older than you, but lacks even such wisdom as you have gained already."

"My brother?" Demne's voice cracked and involuntarily his eyes sought the young man. This was the most startling thing he had learned today. In daylight, he thought he could trace a resemblance to Crimall in the curve of the brow and the blue eyes. But he read no sense of kinship there.

"He is the son of a bondwoman who said that Cumhal lay with her on one of his journeys. He was twelve summers old when she brought him to us. We had no choice but to believe her and hope he might make an heir for Cumhal if the son your father had by his first wife, Torba, never returned from Alba, and if you did not survive. Dithramhach has always expected my mantle to fall to him one day. That he is quite without the qualities he needs does not occur to him." Crimall stepped away, leaving Demne's head so awhirl that he scarcely realized that his question about how the race would be judged had never been answered.

"Now, we begin," the old warrior cried out. He lifted an arm. With an effort, Demne forced his seething emotions under control.

"Catch me if you can!" he yelled. Suddenly all the

turmoil within him was released as energy. Before Crimall even lowered his arm he was leaping away. There was a roar of astonishment and outrage as he darted among the mist-cloaked trees. The footfalls behind him thundered like a heavy rain.

Demne ran swiftly, but with care, using protruding rocks whenever possible, and jumping over patches of slippery leaves. His feet hardly seemed to touch the earth. A spear parted the mist and thunked into a tree trunk not far from his fair head. Barely pausing, Demne tugged it free, then ran onward. He barely noticed when the first wet flakes of snow touched his brow and cooled his skin.

He ducked a low-hanging branch by a hair's breadth, and delight thrilled through his loins. He was no longer afraid, even when another spear struck the ground a hand span away. The *fian* was intent on doing him harm, but he could outwit as well as out-run them. In that moment it ceased to be a race for him, and became a game. He grabbed it, and grinned fiercely as he heard them behind him. They were fast, and quiet, but he could still hear the pant of breath and the scrape of shoe leather over stone.

Demne changed course, running crosswise instead of straight down, through a natural alley between some trees. He laughed silently when he heard one group blunder past him not ten lengths away, their attention focused downward when their quarry was elsewhere. If he had wished, he could have sent his two captured spears into the men. Instead he began to descend into the swirling brightness of the falling snow. The wetness of it damped his braided hair and began to soak the wool of his worn tunic.

He paused for a moment and drew a long breath, closed his eyes and tried to listen to the song of the trees and the rocks around him. His belly growled a little, hollow with hunger, but he silenced it sternly, and when he opened his eyes, he had an image in his mind of the lay of the land. Confidently he ran on. In a minute he had passed the group of pursuers who were taking a route parallel to his path.

As he crossed an open glade, one of the *fennid* spotted him despite the thickening fall of snow. A spear hurtled towards his side, and without thinking, Demne reached out and grasped the shaft as it flew. He added it to the other two he had reaped and ducked beneath the low-hanging branches of some yew trees, careful not to disturb them. Behind him, he heard two groups merge into one, and the sound of spring birdcalls allowed him to locate the third. Fools! They might be strong and courageous, but they lacked the sort of cunning he had learned from his warrior foster mother.

Demne knew he had reached the bottom of the mountain when he saw a length of rag tied around the trunk of a slender birch. With a swift movement, he plunged the butt ends of the spears he had gathered down against the hard earth, breaking the thin crust of snow that had formed around the tree. Two stood, and one wavered and fell over. He tugged the rag free from the birch and looped it over his neck, tucking the ends into his belt that they might not catch on anything. Then he turned and darted back into the forest at a sharp angle from his descent. He had no intention of returning the way he had come.

Below, he heard the noise as some of the *fennid* reached the birch tree, and was so amused by their snarls of fury that he nearly ran headlong into the third part of the *fian*. Only the shimmer of falling snow cloaked him as he scooted around the base of a large oak and froze. The men rushed downward on the other side of the tree, so close Demne could smell the sweat on their skins and the scent of stale beer on their rasping breaths.

Silently he slipped away from the shelter of the tree, and darted across rocks now slick with snow. Demne listened to the noise of the *fian* rushing after him, the rattle of spears almost merry in the cold air. Moving more slowly now—for the ground was treacherous—he turned to one side and crossed the trampled path of his pursuers, wary of leaving a trail. He could hear that they had regrouped and split up once more, and mockingly he whistled one of their signals. As he began to run again, he could hear their confusion. It was all he could do not to laugh aloud.

The wet snow slackened as suddenly as it had begun, and Demne wiped his eyes. A spear whizzed past, almost touching his braids, and he scooped it up as he rushed away to hide in the shadow of some yews. He was hot with anger, and enjoying himself immensely at the same time. A perverse mischief swelled in his breast, and he turned and ran a short distance back down the mountainside.

Demne found the trampled track of one group and lengthened his stride until he could see the broad backs of the men. They were running in two ragged lines, with the space of a spear length between them, all their attention focused before them. He braced himself, gathered his strong young limbs, and spurted into their midst.

"Boo!" he shouted, and watched them jump and whirl. He had a quick glimpse of their astonished faces as they raised their spears, but they dared not cast them for fear of hitting one another. It was not until he had passed through their ranks that they tried to bring him down.

It was at that moment, when Demne was buoyed by confidence, that his foot slipped on a bit of rock, and he went down. The youth curled into a tight ball, landed on his shoulder, and rolled back to his feet, braids untouched, as a spear struck the ground where he had been. He did not pause to retrieve this one, but sped away so fast the trees were a blur to his eyes. He could feel his energy beginning to flag, and bent his mind to conserving what remained.

So intent was he upon escaping the shouting men behind him that he nearly ran into Reidhe mac Dael, who was crouched in a thicket ahead of him. For a moment they gaped at one another. Then Reidhe threw his spear, and Demne leapt straight up. The spear flew harmlessly beneath him, and he grabbed the weapon as he came back to earth.

"Here. You need this more than I do." He tossed the spear back to the old warrior shaft-first, then darted back among the trees. At last his second wind had come upon him and he praised the Liath Luachra and her harsh lessons with all his strong young heart as he rapidly slipped between the trees. When at last he saw the walls of the fortress, his breath was a little ragged and his chest burned, but he could have run an hour more.

Crimall and Fiacail and several other elders were standing beside the gate, stamping their feet and rubbing their hands against the cold. Demne put on a last burst of speed to reach them as the men of *fian* boiled out from the forest like an overflowing cauldron. His tunic was soaked with sweat and snow, and he could feel the cold of the air. He pulled the sopping rag from around his neck and held it up triumphantly.

Before he began to really shiver with the cold, Fiacail draped his thick cloak around Demne's shoulders and patted him on the back. Crimall inspected the braids intently, and finally gave a little nod. Then he looked at his men.

"So," the *rigfennid* asked, "how went the race?"

There was a tense silence, and the caw of a crow came clearly from the forest. At last one of the men said, "It was difficult to judge, because of the snow."

Another gave a snort which might have been humorous or derisive. "Difficult to judge! The lad ran us in circles, as if we were the prey and he the hound. We are fair men here. Admit that we were bested."

"Bested! I would not call it that," growled the man Demne had winded with his spear butt the previous day. "A bunch of tricks, boy's tricks, is what I say."

"You only say that because he caught your spear and left it for you by the birch tree, Coll mac Diarmaita."

Grudgingly Reidhe mac Dael stepped forward, his face stern. "Demne ran a good race, swift and cunning. If he were other than the son of Cumhal, none here would even hint at any fault in his skills."

"We have never run this test in this season before. It is not a fair—" Dithramhach began, then gave a tremendous sneeze.

Before the young man could recover his breath, Reidhe went on. "It is too cold a day to stand around talking. If anyone saw Demne touch leaf or twig, let him speak. I think we may assume the skills in bending and leaping were covered in the run down the mountainside. If not, let us retire to the hearth. I, for one, am chilled to my bones, and Dithramhach there looks to have caught a chill."

Crimall nodded. "Come within. Some dry clothing and hot soup will do us all good."

Fiacail smiled at Demne as they walked through the gate. "Well done, lad, well done. I never saw a fleeter start, even when the Liath Luachra was in her prime. How I longed to follow you!"

Demne savored this praise for a long, slow moment

as they entered the compound. Then his sense of mischief pricked him. "If you think I am fast, you ought to run with my sister, old man."

Fiacail made a long, hissing sound, and looked into the boy's wet face. "This is the second time you have mentioned her! Your sister died the day you were born, Demne."

"Do you really think so?" the boy asked.

The old man frowned, but made no reply.

BY THE FOLLOWING MORNING, THE FOREST WAS GLEAMing white with a heavy fall of snow, and Dithramhach was burning with fever. He lay beside the fire, gasping for breath and coughing up thick yellow gobbets. Watching the young man toss in his blankets, Demne remembered Bodbmall doing the same in Tailtiu. It made him shiver, as if this illness were something he had caused. He did not want another death on his heart, not like this.

And they said this man was his half brother. He could not bear to lose any kinfolk, even if Dithramhach hated him.

Demne opened his pack and sorted through the contents. There were many untidy little packs of herbs Bodbmall had taught him how to use. Some were ancient, from five summers before, and some were newer, Cruithne's gatherings or his own. Sniffing them, he wondered how long their virtue remained. In his mind he could hear the voice of the *bendrui,* teaching him the ways of plants, and for a moment thought he could see her ancient hands pointing to various packets. Taking the small trail pot of his own crafting, the youth set water to boil on the hearth. When it was bubbling, he added willow bark and feverfew, and set the potion to cool. The sharp smell of willow soon floated into the air.

When it was ready, Demne poured a bowl of the stuff and carried it to the warrior. Gently he cradled Dithramhach's shoulders, and trickled a mouthful of the potion between the fever-cracked lips. The man's flesh burned beneath his fingers as he watched Dithramhach's grimace at the taste of the brew. His half brother made a feeble attempt to push the bowl away "Drink it!" Dithramhach groaned, but obeyed.

The coughing eased after a time, and Demne could feel Dithramhach's skin begin to cool, so he lowered his half brother and watched him go into a restless sleep. Demne added more water and set his pot on the fire again. As he turned to look at his patient, he found Dithramhach glaring balefully, but a clear gaze.

"That stuff tastes awful. Are you trying to poison me?" the sick warrior whispered.

Demne smiled and shook his head. "It is a remedy I learned from my foster mother, the *bendrui* Bodbmall."

"Ah, her. I saw her once, when she was with Fiacail. She had the tongue that would curdle milk." He made a slight gagging noise. "No wonder her recipe tastes foul. Still, I feel a little cooler. Must the potion be so dreadful to have healing virtue?"

Demne would have given a great deal to hear that sharp voice once more. He shook his head. "If I had a little honey, it would doubtless be better. I had not thought of that."

Dithramhach sighed. "The kitchen women can give you honey. I am relieved to find you do not think of everything. I was starting to believe you were perfect."

Demne blinked, and found Dithramhach's blue eyes twinkling with amusement. And suddenly he saw in them a mirror of his own. He let the beginning of a smile touch his mouth, and saw his half brother grin

like a wolf. Perhaps they could be friends and not
foes. The hope swelled in his breast, the yearning for
companionship. . . . With regret, he let it go. It was too
much to dare to hope for.

Chapter 18

◈

AFTER SAMHAIN, THE WHITE FIST OF WINTER CLOSED over the mountains. The first snowfall choked the valleys, but icy winds scoured the tops of the hills. The continuing cold leached the last color from the reeds, and day by day the skin of ice crept further across the pools and stilled the voices of the streams. The dark days drove men indoors to huddle around the hearth fires, gambling and grumbling and sometimes quarreling when they had been cooped up together too long.

"D'ye remember the ale vats of Temair?" said Coll mac Diarmaita, gazing mournfully into his beaker of thin beer.

"And the skins of mead," said an even older man called Mongan Mael, who had gone completely bald with age. "When we wintered in Temair, all the raths of Eriu were bound to supply us with their best brewing, so that though we drank ourselves into a stupor each night from Samhain until Beltane we should never run dry!"

"And the beef that was kept boiling in the great cauldrons, and the pigs hanging in the smokehouses through the winter," said another of the greybeards.

"Indeed, we were the high king's own darlings. There was never any lack of food or drink in Cumhal's day. . . ."

Demne continued gnawing at a rib of the two-prong buck that he himself had brought in and sighed. It was true that he had eaten better winter fare at some of the raths where he had served, but he could remember sharing the boiled bones of a hedgehog stewed up with a few rotten roots with the Liath Luachra and Bodbmall when their stock of grain ran out before the end of the winter storms.

"Well, it is the sons of Morna, plague take them, who lie now at their ease before the *Ard Ri*'s fire," said Coll, "while we must skulk in the hills beneath the royal ban!"

A chill draught set them all to shivering as two more of the men came in, stamping the snow from their feet and cursing the cold.

"A curse upon Cumhal, who could not be content with what he had!" came a mutter from behind them. "Were it not for him, we might be feasting in Temair now!"

"Were it not for Cumhal we would not have been in the *Ard Ri*'s service at all," Reidhe mac Dael reproved them. "In those days we were all heroes, and would you have followed a prudent man?"

Coll shrugged and drained his beaker. "There is no place for prudence on the battlefield, to be sure. And in action he was a joy to see. I mind how that sword of his one time took off six men's heads at one blow."

"What became of his sword?" Dithramhach asked then.

"The sons of Morna have it, I suppose," Reidhe replied. "We could not find it after Cnucha, when we took his body up from the field."

Demne worried the last bit of flesh from his bone and tossed it to one of the dogs, then bent to slide a new log into the fire. Leaping flame revealed in momentary high relief the gaunt features of old men who had outlived their valor, and young ones soured by lack of opportunity. Demne looked around the circle and grimaced. In the past weeks he had come to know them, their scents and their voices, and the track each one left upon the muddy ground. He realized with a start that beneath his mistrust and exasperation were growing the beginnings of a rueful affection.

"Cumhal did not lose that battle on the field of Cnucha, though he met his death there, but in the council hall!" Crimall said heavily. "I think that it was after Airt the Lone One was killed that his father, Conn, turned against Cumhal. With the other prince, Connla, gone off into faerie there's none but the grandson, Cormac, left of the *Ard Ri*'s blood. I think Conn feared what Cumhal might do if he himself died before his grandson was old enough to rule."

Demne frowned. Fiacail had said it was Cumhal's ambitions for Laigin that had turned the high king against him. He wondered which story were true. Perhaps both of them. The gossip of old men was often boring, but little by little he was beginning to understand some of the undercurrents that had mystified him when he was a boy at Tailtiu.

And often enough the topic during those long evenings was the deeds of Cumhal mac Trenmor. Gradually Demne developed a sense of what kind of man his father had been. The knowledge was not altogether comforting, for the character which emerged from their stories was arrogant, willful, and headstrong, as well as cunning and brave. Demne recognized in himself the same tendency to be headstrong, but not the perilous pride that had caused his father to abduct the druid's daughter. Bodbmall and the Liath Luachra had schooled most of that out of him before he was old enough to understand.

Demne sat back. The fire was sinking once more, but he had no heart to build it up again. He was as restless and irritable as any of the others; but unlike them he was lonely, for though he had survived his testing, he remained outside the *fian*. After his physicking of Dithramhach, several of the men had asked him for remedies for coughs or chilblains. But their appreciation stopped short of friendship, for they were unable to forget that he was the trueborn son of Cumhal, who seemed bound to upset their precarious existence whether he willed it or no. In his dreams Demne sometimes thought he was still with Cruithne, and woke, grinding his body against the blankets with need. Sometimes he wondered if he had been right to run away.

Anxious to escape the endless bickering over anything and nothing, in the days that followed Demne began to explore the rest of the fort's other buildings. He was chased out of the kitchen by a toothless old woman who put him in mind of Bodbmall, and the only horse in the stable was an old beast scarcely fit for the plough, no use if he had wanted to learn to ride. At last he entered a small building set against the back of the stockade, and found it to be a modest forge, half buried by years of old leaves.

With a sense of fresh purpose, Demne began to clear the debris from the floor and repair the crumbling walls. When he had removed most of the litter, he examined the forge itself, and found it still sound. He scraped rust off several hammers, shaking his head at such mistreatment of good tools, and carved a new handle to replace one that snapped at the first blow. He begged some fat from the kitchen mistress, which she gave him with much scolding and chafing, and he rubbed the hammerheads with it until they gleamed dully in the light of the short winter days.

In one corner of the hut he found the charcoal oven hidden beneath a discarded blanket that fell to tatters when he touched it. There was a pile of willow limbs, well dried after years, and he began to hum to himself as he cut them into the right lengths to be used. He would have preferred alder, but there was none, green or dried, to be found within the compound. The call for the evening meal made him realize how late it was and how dark it had become. With great reluctance, he left the forge and went to the great hall to eat.

At first light, he was back within the forge hut, his belly growling for porridge, but too eager to stop for food. Demne laid the pieces of willow he had prepared in the charcoal oven with great care and precision, as Lochan had taught him, and started the fire beneath them, nearly burning his hand before he snatched it away from the hungry flames. He laid the stone cover over the oven and turned back to the chamber.

Then Demne began to search in the corners which had been too dark to see before and found a rotting hide sack almost invisible in the shadows. Within were ingots of copper, tin, a little silver, and rusted but usable slabs of iron. He wiped the slabs clean without caring that the rust powdered his clothes and left ruddy streaks when he ran his fingers through his pale hair.

Next he cleaned out the forge itself, a messy task that crossed his red streaks with smears of grey ash. The sharp smoke of burning willow made his eyes water, but it was a familiar sensation, and he simply dragged his filthy sleeve across his face and kept on. So deep was he in his labors that when he heard the sound of a footfall, he looked up, half expecting to see Lochan's frown or Cruithne's mischievous smile.

Instead, Crimall stood in the doorway, his bushy brows lifting as he saw what was going on.

"I noticed the smoke," the older man began, "and came to see. I might have guessed it was you, lad. We have not had a smith since Aitherne mac Connla died five winters past."

"Had he no student?" Demne asked, surprised.

"He did try to teach the craft to several of the younger men, but they had no feel for the working of metals, he said. It is not a common gift, the forgecraft. Besides, Aitherne was jealous of his knowledge and impatient if he had to repeat himself, when he was willing to speak at all. You're as closemouthed as he was, lad. I wondered where you had gotten to yesterday."

"The hearth fire bickering gives me a sour belly, Uncle," Demne answered. He dropped a scoop of ash into a leather bucket and resumed his work. "At first I liked the tales, but so much contention becomes wearisome. It makes me think of Bodbmall and the Liath Luachra, except the voices are less shrill. I never cared for it when I was a child, and I do not now."

"My men chafe for lack of work, and mourn for their lost honors."

Demne looked up from the forge and fixed Crimall with a hard stare. *"Idleness is the maker of illness,"* he said, quoting the *bendrui.*

"True, but my men are warriors and hunters, not craftsmen. More, they miss the comforts of wintering in Temair or some other king's hall, with enough women to warm their beds and enough drink to keep away the cold."

Demne pursed his mouth. "I know. I heard about the raid they made last winter from the folk of the rath in the valley as well as from those boasters in the hall."

"Boasters?" Crimall was frowning like a thundercloud now.

Demne gave a little shrug and continued his work in silence. He was unaccustomed to offering criticism to those older than himself, but he thought the remnants of his father's followers lazy and undisciplined. The last thing he wanted was to challenge the leadership of Crimall mac Trenmor, but his service as a *gilla* had left him with a great respect for the people who herded the cattle and tilled the soil. The men of the *fian* called them dull and stupid, but Demne could remember pulling tares from among the sprouting corn until his long fingers bled. Now when he ate bread, he thought of his labors. He had milked swollen udders into birch wood pails, and carried the warm sweet milk to the dairy to be transformed into white cheese or thick butter. It was beyond his understanding how these men could believe that strength of arms alone was worthwhile.

"Come the springtime they will spend their energy in raiding the woods for game or the raths for beer," said Demne. "Is that more honorable than telling tales of past glories by the fire?"

Crimall coughed. "Men are not like those dogs you tended for the chieftain of Benntraige. They need more than a pat and a bone!"

Suddenly Demne understood one reason why he was not happy here. He had been Bodbmall's pupil too long to be content when fighting and hunting were all there was to do. But he knew he would have been just as frustrated if he had done nothing but stay indoors brewing up salves and simples. The conflict was a very old one: within him, the Liath Luachra still praised the way of the warrior, and Bodbmall extolled the way of the wise. But even Bodbmall had known nothing of the third path that Brigid had shown him, that led to the fisherman by the river. Nor had the Liath Luachra, with all her love of weapons, known the way of the forge. What more might lie in this lovely turning world that neither of his fosterers had known?

As long as he stayed here with the remnants of his father's band he would remain firmly on the warrior's way. Across that road stood the sons of Morna and their allies, and at its ending, more men lying dead in their blood. The red path had betrayed him into killing friends already, but then he had killed from rage and need. It had given Demne no joy to kill the red-mouthed woman and her son. If he set his feet upon the path of vengeance in cold hatred he feared the red tide would sweep him away.

"Men need honor, boy, if they are to survive!"

"What is honor?" asked Demne. "Can you eat it? Will slaying my father's killers bring him back alive?"

"You talk like a druid!" Crimall spat out the door. "Bodbmall had the teaching of you for too long!"

Demne hauled another bucket of ashes out of the forge, wondering. Bodbmall had thought that he would be safe on her path, but Brigid had shown him that the green way led towards his powerful and arrogant grandfather, and a battle of wills and magic.

"Do you think so?" Demne asked quietly. "My grandfather is a druid, and more dangerous than any warrior. Cumhal was a hero, but he ran to his own destruction when he challenged the lord of Almu. I nearly died when Tadhg's mind but brushed my own. If I am bound to vengeance, then I must tackle him as well. I fear no fair combat, but in such a battle he would best me as easily as I outran your men, and what good would that do?"

"Justice . . ." Crimall shook his head. "Ah, lad, I have not the words. But Cumhal had a dream that was more than his own glory. Are we to allow our dreams to be destroyed by the envy of small-minded men?"

Aonghus had known the words, thought Demne sadly, and there had been knowledge in the lament

of Muirne that the young bard had sung so touching-
ly in the hall of King Gléor Lamraige. The only path
that remained untrodden was the blue path which led
to the fisher by the river. If he could find Fionnéices
and learn it, then would he understand? The *filidecht*
was the forge of the mind, wherein a man might work
words as Lochan had taught him to work iron. He
sighed, for even in this season of silence the earth
song pulsed from the ground beneath him, demanding release into the world. But only a *fili* could find
words for that song. Demne knew he could not be
content until he had walked that path as well.

"You must not despise the men of your father's
fian," said Crimall. "They have not the words either,
and the dream was taken from us before we could
understand."

Demne scowled at his uncle. "Then why are they
forever talking about it? From the beginning I have
told you my doubts that I can be the leader you wish
for, but surely I shall not let my men sit idle, telling
tales of past prowess and boasting of their successes
with women, if ever I come to rule any *fian*!"

Crimall snorted. "It has not always been so. When
Cumhal was *rigfennid* in Eriu, we defended the land
against foes, and we were respected. It is only because
we have lost our proper place that we idle and boast
now."

Demne regarded his uncle quietly, carefully, and
saw only a frustrated old man bound to past glories.
He could not decide if Crimall was a good leader or a
poor one. True, he had kept the remnant of Cumhal's
fian together for some seventeen years. The boy realized what a remarkable feat this was. He also understood that his uncle was weary of commanding his
contentious band, and longed to pass the unpleasant
task into the youth's ash-grimed hands. He held back
a shudder as he wondered if, when he was old, he too

would press his cares onto his sons or grandsons.

"Well, I am a poor hand at idleness," he replied. "And at boasting. I have no deeds to tell."

"Do you not? Tell the tale of how you slew the great boar and his giant mother and returned the *corrbolg* to the *fian*—and tell it as you told it to me and to Fiacail—and you could kindle men's hearts like that fire. But you scarcely speak to the men except when you are physicking them, and the rest of the time you sulk in the corners of the hall. Young as you are, I think there is more than one tale in your past!"

Demne shook his rust- and ash-streaked head. Would they praise him for killing the boys of Mag Life or getting Cruithne with child? He had longed for praise from Bodbmall and the Liath Luachra, and that yearning had brought him only sorrow.

"I don't believe the men when they boast of their deeds, so why should they believe me? I would rather heal their illnesses and forge new heads for their spears!"

"You are so big." Crimall sighed. "I keep forgetting that you are also young. But one day you will understand the reasons for our ways." He heaved himself to his feet, but his shoulders still sagged. Demne wondered if the words were intended as a command or a suggestion.

As Crimall stalked off through the new-fallen snow Demne looked unhappily after him. During his wanderings he had wanted nothing so much as a home and kin, but now that he had them, he found himself longing for freedom once more.

"Everyone seems to be so sure they know who I am and what I should do," he told the empty forge. "Everyone but me. . . ."

AT THE FIRST RIPENING OF BIRCH BUDS, THE REST-less men of the *fian* began to leave the warmth of the hearth to roam the mountainside. New iron spearheads of Demne's making gleamed in the pale sunlight as the warriors passed between the greening trees. Spears made by Demne sped true and kept their edges longer than other weapons. There came to be a certain competition for those spears, and with them, the warriors began to accept the man who had made them.

To his great surprise, Demne found himself developing a real friendship with two or three men. The lad who kept the hearth was called Glanna, and once he was sure that the newcomer did not mean to take his place he was glad to learn all the fire lore that Demne would share. Grimthann the dog boy took to him also when he found that Demne had a way with the hounds. But the best of it was the trust which was developing between Demne and his half brother, Dithramhach, as slow and steady as the seeds hidden beneath the warming soil. They did not speak of it, but often as not it would be Dithramhach who made sure that food was saved and waiting when Demne labored late at the forge; and when they went hunting, Dithramhach who ran at his heels.

After the turning of spring, the earth softened in the drenching rains, and one fairly clear morning, several of the men began to dig a deep pit just outside the wall of the stockade. As Demne came out of the home wood with a load of branches to burn for charcoal, one of them saw him and nudged his fellow, laughing. Demne raised an eyebrow, but he was preoccupied with thoughts of a new cauldron for the kitchens, and the laughter had seemed friendly. Without thinking any more of it he went on.

He was cleaning out the charcoal pit when Fiacail mac Conchinn came to find him. The winter had been cruel to the older man, and he had lost the last teeth remaining to him and much of his wispy hair. His back was bowed, and the sound of the blackthorn staff he now used had told Demne who was coming even before his shadow filled the door.

"Leave that be, lad," wheezed the old man. Carefully he eased his old bones down on a bench by the forge. "You have more important things to do."

"Without a clean oven I can burn no charcoal, and without charcoal, I can forge no more spearheads for the men." With brisk strokes of his bundle of willow twigs Demne swept the last of the old ash away.

"Spears!" Fiacail made an odd choked sound, and Demne turned in alarm. It took him a moment to realize that the old man was laughing. "They've spears and enough for what they need to do!"

Demne sat back on his heels, eyes narrowing, and waited until Fiacail could speak again.

"The spear test, boy. Don't you remember, the race was only the first part of your initiation into the *fian,* but the rest of it had to wait until we could dig the ground?"

"The pit outside the walls . . ." said Demne. Thinking back, he remembered references to another test when spring came. He had paid little attention, probably because he had not expected to stay here so long.

"They are digging it for you to stand in," said Fiacail.

Are you sure it is not to bury me? thought Demne, but he did not say the words aloud. The old man's flesh had the sweet smell of approaching dissolution. Whether or not he himself survived this next testing, he did not think that Fiacail would last long. *It is because I came here,* he thought then. *Now he will die like the Liath Luachra and Bodbmall and leave me alone.*

He stood up and brushed his hands together to remove the ash, trying to manage a laugh.

"I should be honored. I have not seen the men of the *fian* work so earnestly since I arrived."

Fiacail gave a long sigh. "Crimall has said you do not approve of our ways. But when you are one of us you will see the glory of the warrior's path, and how we defend Eriu from its foes."

Demne held his tongue with difficulty. His uncle had regaled him with tales of old glories until he was sick of the word. There was a time, after he fled the sons of Morna at Tailtiu, when he had dreamed of punishing the foes of Cumhal mac Trenmor. But since his encounter with the red-mouthed giantess, the shedding of blood had lost its savor. The place on his shoulder where a droplet of her blood had touched him was nearly invisible now, a fair, star-shaped white scar, but sometimes, when he remembered her, it still burned.

"What is so glorious about a hole in the ground?" he asked the old man.

"It is a test. You will stand in the pit with a hazel wand in your hand, and fend off the spears of nine men, nine times."

"Without mussing a hair of my head, of course," he said with a forced laugh. The men of the *fian* spent an inordinate amount of time and energy grooming their locks. Demne preferred to drag a comb through his hair a few times, then bind it back with a thong.

"Exactly," Fiacail answered seriously.

"Tell me, old one, were my father's braids all tidy at the Battle of Cnucha when he died?"

Fiacail's rheumy eyes filled with tears. "They were red with his blood, boy, when Goll mac Morna struck off his head. But that is an old sorrow." He brushed his sleeve across his face and straightened. "It is your survival that we are concerned with now. Listen to me, Demne. You must keep both your feet on the earth at all times, and you may not duck, though you may bend your body from side to side to escape the spears. Your only defense will be the wand, with which you must deflect the weapons. If you move, you will be disqualified. If you show fear, you will fail."

Demne nodded, understanding at last that the old man had come not to try to sway but to save him.

"Did you endure such a test?"

"I did, and lived to tell of it."

"Very well." Demne turned away to conceal his expression. Suddenly his mouth was dry. He knew that despite the friendships he had made during the winter, there were still many in the *fian* who were uneasy in his presence or who feared the wrath of the sons of Morna more than they cared for him. But he knew that he was no coward. He touched the Liath Luachra's brooch and felt the old woman's spirit tingle along his fingers. *These men are mad,* he thought, *with the madness that brought my father to an early grave.*

ONCE MORE DEMNE ALLOWED FIACAIL TO DRESS HIS HAIR, and out of a kind of bravado he put on the embroidered tunic that Cruithne had made for him a year ago. This day was even brighter than the one before; the kind of shining spring day when light sparks from each new-washed leaf and gleams from every stone. In the woods the blackbirds had already begun a joyous song.

Demne felt tension edge his nerves as he saw the men awaiting him and breathed deeply of the sweet air. In the shadowless sunlight of noontide, everything around him seemed to have an inner glow.

Is it because I am in danger, he wondered, *that I can see the light in all things?* It occurred to him suddenly that perhaps some men sought battle because only when they were facing death did they feel truly alive.

Fiacail handed him a stout hazel wand as long as his arm and led him towards the pit. Beyond it were waiting the nine men of the *fian* who had been chosen to test him. Beside each of them nine spears were driven butt-first into the soft earth. Some of those spears he himself had crafted. At the thought that his work was going to be literally thrown back into his face Demne began laughing. The grim frowns on the faces of the men who faced him faltered; he read the play of expression and knew that some thought it bravado and admired him, and the others thought him mad. Only Demne knew that his laughter was a reaction to fear.

But at least Crimall had chosen the spearmen with an attempt at fairness. Neither the men who had become his friends nor those who were most against him stood before him, although he could feel hostile stares from elsewhere in the waiting crowd. Still laughing, he surveyed them, and winked as he met Dithramhach's uncertain smile. Then he walked the last few paces to the pit and leaped lightly in.

Upon his head the sun shone warmly, and the air smelled of leaf and bud. The pit was waist-deep and large enough so that his arm could move freely. Demne scuffled his feet around until he felt secure and lifted his wand.

Crimall mac Trenmor and the older men of the *fian* stood behind the spearmen, waiting to judge the contest. Demne wondered how well they could see over the shoulders of the warriors, and his heart began to pound. And what good would the hazel wand be against spears of iron and bronze? He breathed long and slow, waiting for the signal to begin. Unlike the race down the mountain, this was not something he could manipulate. The earth walls seemed to rise around him. Suddenly he felt like a cornered beast in its hole and fought for control.

He did not realize the word had been given until he saw the first spear hurtling towards him. Demne resisted the natural impulse to duck, though it would have ended this mad contest before it was even begun, and struck the spear stave aside with his wand. He thought he had no more than touched it, and at the sound of snapping wood he nearly leaped from the hole. Until this moment, he had never known how much he depended on his fleet feet to keep him out of trouble. He hated the pit and the men who had put him into it as a trapped beast hates the snare.

He settled himself firmly as two more spears spun towards him. Fiacail had warned him that each cast would include more spears than the previous one, so he knew what to expect. He knocked one aside and turned his body to let the other go by. Sweat beaded his brow and cascaded down his sides as four spears sped towards his breast.

Demne whipped the wand against the foremost weapon, knocking it into the one behind it. The barb of the spearhead caught the next and shattered it, and Demne had a moment to bless the skill of his smithing. The wand quivered in his hand as if the life of the tree still filled it. Eight more spears flew towards him before he had time to wonder why, but he let that energy enhance his own as he batted to one side, then the other, dashing the spears away or breaking them in twain. One only flicked past his slim waist and buried itself in the side of the pit. As if from some far distance he heard the sound of cheers.

He shifted his footing, awaiting the cast of sixteen. Now he understood how one might survive this test. The very number of spears being thrown became an advantage. A slow grin touched his mouth as the shadow of many shafts darkened the air. But the moment he took to choose a strategy was nearly fatal. Demne sucked in his belly to the backbone, striving to get the wand up in time to deflect the one missile that would knock the largest number of others away. A spear flew past his skull so close he could feel the rush of air over his braids, and another sank into the wall of the pit, so close the shaft almost hit him in the stomach. His vision was blurred by sweat dripping from his wide brow.

He drew his sleeve across his face, gasping, furious with mingled anger and fear.

The next throw of spears was like a cloud across the milky sun. Demne saw it, and suddenly his flesh grew incandescent with the familiar heat of his own rage. The hazel wand quivered like an extension of his arms, a flash of lightning to either side that smashed the spears. He drew in breath in great tearing gasps.

The final cast came from all directions at once, and Demne twisted in a long, sweeping strike. He heard a pop from his back, and felt a sharp pain. It vanished before he could tell if he had been hit, and he spun around to smash the spears coming from the other side. He swung and met nothing, and beat the air for several seconds more before he realized there was nothing there. There was a dense silence around him.

Bit by bit, the fury ebbed away. When he could see again, he realized that he was up to his knees in broken spears.

"Now, that was a proper waste of good spear shafts," he announced, and wondered why they laughed. "All my hard work, turned to firewood! Well, they will fuel my forge." Many hands were reaching to help him out of the pit. Instinctively he grasped them.

"But not yet," murmured someone, Dithramhach perhaps, at his shoulder. "First we'll sweat the aches out, and then we will feast your victory."

Hands clapped him on the shoulders, and he heard the mingled thunder of many deep voices, all shouting his praise. It was the same as when they had cheered him at Tailtiu; he felt as if he had emptied himself of all emotion with his battle rage. As his heartbeat gradually slowed and he began to relax he could sense the pride of the men who surrounded him, but he could not accept it. He wanted to turn to them, and at the same time he wanted to flee. He shook his head in confusion as they bore him away in to the stockade.

Chapter 19

THE MEN OF THE *FIAN* LAY STEWING TOGETHER IN THE sweat house like the fish that Bodbmall used to bake, encased in clay in the ashes of the hearth. It was the first time Demne had used the sweat house with the others. If he had felt smothered when the warriors gathered around him, he felt now as if he were drowning. Surely this was another test for him, though the rest of them seemed to consider it a reward. Demne lay gasping with his eyes closed and wondered how long he could endure.

The sweat house was a low round building of whitewashed stone with stepped benches surrounding the sunken pit where they piled the glowing stones. Demne and the men who an hour ago had been doing their best to spear him had been given the benches closest to the hot rocks, and the others crowded in on the higher benches. Now and again someone would cough, or a board creak as a man turned. But mostly what Demne heard was the rasp of breathing hoarse as his own. Light from the oil lamp that hung from the ceiling caught the gleam of sweaty bodies. The smell of men's sweat, and onions and the sweet herbs they had scattered across the stones lay heavy on the air.

Demne remembered the seals that beached themselves on the sands below Lochan's mountain to breed. They had seemed to enjoy being crowded together. How could they bear it, after the freedom of the open sea? And every spring the migrating waterfowl settled together onto the lakes in a single mass of squawking feathers. Why were creatures who could fly to lands he had never heard of compelled to seek one another's company? In his first testing Demne had raced like the wind, but it had not occurred to him to run away. And he had stood still to face the spears. But now all he could think of was fighting his way to the door.

His muscles tensed. In another moment he would heave himself upright and dive for the doorway. In another moment he would scream. But all the strength seemed to be running out of him with the sweat that poured off his skin. He tried to raise himself upon his elbows, but he could not move.

If the way out was closed to him then Demne would have to escape inward. He tried to control his breathing as Bodbmall had taught him, and seek the core of stillness within.

But instead of shrinking, his awareness expanded suddenly to fill the building, and his individual identity merged with the composite consciousness of the *fian,* a many-bodied beast whose life flowed back into the earth in a single salty stream.

He was Reidhe mac Dael, who had cast the first spear and whose wrenched shoulder the heat was at last beginning to ease. He was Aghmar mac Domnaill, content as a good hound by the fire. He was Mongan Mael, turning so the heat would bake the hip that always pained him when it came on to rain. He was Crimall, letting his cares flow out of him with tho wetness that dripped from his sides, and Dithramhach, smiling gently at the shadows that danced across the thatch above. He was all of them. A wave of emotion like nothing Demne had ever known swept through him. It was the song of each man's soul that he was hearing, as he had heard the earth and the trees, and in that moment he loved them all.

And then it passed, and he was only himself once more.

Demne ground his face against the damp wood of the bench, grateful that no one could tell that the moisture upon his cheeks was tears. Then someone pushed open the door and cool air flowed over their backs like a blessing. With a chorus of curses and ribald commentary, the warriors clambered out into the yard, bodies steaming, to douse each other with buckets of chill water from the well.

THE SUN WAS SINKING BEHIND THE POINTS OF THE palisade when the men of the *fian* escorted Demne to the feasting hall. Combed and cleansed, their faces still aglow, the warriors had decked themselves out as if they were going to a festival. And for once in his life, Demne was not behind in finery. When he had returned to dress, he had found a new tunic and pair of breeches laid out for him. There was a new belt there as well. As he was buckling it, one of the warriors came in with a light cloak of heathery wool for him to pin with the Liath Luachra's brooch. As they moved towards the hall others came up to offer their own gifts with a mumbled word of congratulation or a clap on the back and laughter as Demne felt the betraying flush redden his cheeks once more.

He did not know how to respond to them. No one had ever given him so many presents before. Gradually it dawned on him that they must have been preparing these things all winter. He had not noticed, just as he had not known that they planned to test him. And he would never have suspected that they wanted him to win.

When he took his place next to Crimall, Demne realized that the glow of the sweat house was not all that remained. He was still sensing the emotions of the men around him. It made him uneasy, as if he had turned into someone he did not know. When Duibhne came around with the great horn of mead, he held out the carved beech wood cup that someone had given him. Perhaps he could drown this overwhelming awareness if he drank enough. At least they had plenty of it. The wrought-iron tools and cauldrons he had sent down the mountain had fetched a good price in trade.

Demne leaned against the pillar, feeling the warm glow as the liquid gold of the mead went down. There was a shout as two of the warriors appeared in the doorway, carrying a plank upon which a haunch of beef fresh from the great cauldron steamed. Grinning, they set it down in front of Demne and Crimall.

"Cut it, lad," said the *rigfennid,* and laughed as Demne felt his face go blank with surprise. "Today you are our hero, and the Champion's Portion is your due. In times to come, when you have grown accustomed to the honor, remember this day!"

Demne swallowed. The rich scent of the beef was making his mouth water. *A hero,* he thought. *Is that what I am?* The Liath Luachra had once told him a tale of a battle caused by a quarrel over who should have first cut of a hog. Demne wondered if accepting this honor doomed him to lead these men to their deaths someday.

But tonight the warriors were waiting, eager as a pack of hound pups when the kitchen drudge brings his basket of scraps into their run. Belatedly, Demne shook his head in a vain attempt to clear it. Then he knelt before the plank and drew the long bronze dagger that he had crafted that winter, its edge keener than any but the spear Birga's steel. He looked around him, seeking for words.

"I slice this meat for you all. It is you who are the heroes, and I will even forgive you for making me spoil all those spears." He forced a grin to meet their laughter as the pink, juicy slabs peeled away beneath the sharp blade.

"Fionn!" came a shout from the hall. "We drink to Fionn son of Cumhal!" And the rafters echoed with his name. Demne blinked, remembering how the people had shouted for him at Tailtiu, and a shimmer of warning flickered down his nerves. The last time men had hailed him by that name he had been forced to flee.

I am Demne, he thought. *Fionn mac Cumhal is a hero they are inventing—someone I do not know.* He did not want the name. "Fionn" was heir to more than a *fian*. With that name came a fate that would force him to kill.

The boys who served in the hall were bringing in the rest of the beef, baskets of bannocks, hard cheese and soft curds with honey, boiled puddings, and sausages fragrant with garlic and onion and thyme. Demne stared at the food and wondered if he were really expected to eat it all. He had lived on short rations for too long to be easy with excess.

At the other end of the hall someone raised his voice in song. The mead horn went round again, followed by many beakers of ale, and the noise level rose. Even listening to the Liath Luachra bicker with Bodbmall would have been easier, thought Demne, wishing he could cover his ears. Then it occurred to him that he had heard men shout at their drinking before and never minded. It was that uncomfortable awareness again. And these men liked him. He would have been a gibbering wreck if he had been so open to emotions in the House of Youths or some of the other places he had been. And all he had to fight it with was the mead. Demne had never been able to get really drunk, but it occurred to him that this might be a good time to try.

By mid-evening, he realized that his plan must be working, for he was feeling no pain. When the man they had left as gate guard came in and whispered to Crimall he did not even try to listen. But he was not as befuddled as he thought, for the word "Morna" penetrated his haze.

"What is it?" He shook his uncle's shoulder when the man had gone. "What is wrong?"

Crimall drained his cup. "Warriors of a sept of Clan Morna were seen down the valley. A lad from the village came to tell us so."

From the slurring of his words, Demne knew that his uncle had been trying to get drunk too. But even garbled, he understood the older man's words.

"Will they come here?" he asked.

Crimall belched loudly and then began to laugh. "We'll be ready for 'em if they do!"

Somehow the word had spread through the hall. The singing became more aggressive and louder.

"*Aedh was the name of Daire's strong son.*" Old Coll had staggered to his feet, waving his cup. A mutter of recognition ran through the hall.

> "*Till radiant Luchet's deed was done—*
> *A spear in the eye left Aedh but one,*
> *And now we call him Goll!*"

"One-eye! One-eye!" cried the men. "Let him come here and we'll darken the other for him too!"

> "*But Goll slew Luchet bye and bye,*
> *At Cnucha's field—it is no lie*

That bright brave Luchet there did die,
To Morna's son he fell."

"Ah, the fine fair lad!" On the other side of the
hearth, Fiacail lifted his horn. "Like the first light
of dawn was he when he rose in his splendor. But
his light was put out at Cnucha's field!"

Demne felt the old man's sorrow as if it had been
his own. Why did men seek battle so eagerly when
there was always such grief at its end?

> *"Morna's sons fought in that fray*
> *And Luaigni of Temair, all day,*
> *For every warlike king to pay,*
> *The* fianna *of Fal!"*

There was a roar of rage from the men that shook
the rafters of the hall.

"Death to the sons of Morna!" they cried. "Death
to Goll! Death to Art Og of the Hard Strokes, and to
Conain the Swearer and Garra their brother, and disaster to the Luaigni and to the men of Uirgriu!"

But Coll was still singing.

> *"By Goll at last Cumhal was slain,*
> *Where bled the hosts on Cnucha's plain,*
> *The* fian's *leadership to gain,*
> *For this cause did they kill!"*

The rage had become a passion of mourning that
wrenched Demne's bones. The men cursed Goll as
their chieftain's murderer. Demne wondered why they
were not cursing the Grey Man of Luachar as well.
Even as he trembled with the backlash of their grief
it occurred to him that Goll could not have killed his
father single-handed, especially when he had just lost
one of his eyes. It must have taken many wounds to

bring down a man like Cumhal mac Trenmor.

Demne's senses were coming back to him, and he dared not drink any more. The warriors of the *fian* thought otherwise. They lifted their cups and their horns again and again, calling out the names of warriors who had been cold in their graves when Cumhal's son was born. It was in that moment that Demne felt on his cheek the touch of chill air, and heard above the shouting a shimmer of laughter.

Sister? He sat up, looking around him, but saw only the hearth fire blazing as if a wind had passed through the hall. He turned back to Crimall.

"Uncle, where were the Mornas when they were sighted?" he asked urgently. "Are they looking for me?"

"You're one of us, now, lad!" The boy recoiled from a blast of beery breath as Crimall's arm fell heavily across his back. "We'll defend you! Down at Rath Sinsar, they were. Wish they *would* come here— we'd show 'em . . . Cumhal's men . . . not all under the sod!"

That was just what Demne was afraid of. Suddenly he remembered how Bran mac Conail's empty eyes had accused the sky. But the Morna men had been sighted at the other end of the valley. At least Crimall and his warriors would not have to rush out in a drunken frenzy to fight their ancient foe.

It had been a mistake, he thought absently, to let all the men of the *fian* attend the feast at the same time. If he ever led them—He realized what he was thinking and swallowed sickly. He didn't *want* to lead these men. The Mornas would not come tonight, but if they arrived tomorrow, what would the *fian* do? At least if they died drunk they wouldn't feel the pain!

Demne gazed around the hall, trying, for the first time, to see these men with the eye of a commander. The younger men were extra sons or wanderers who were good enough on a woodland path, but who had never seen a battlefield. The trained warriors were all greybeards. With a pang he remembered how the Liath Luachra had chafed when her body would no longer obey her will. But he doubted that throwing any of these into a lake would do more than drown them.

My foes may not attack this time, the thought came to him with painful clarity, *but after tonight there will be no hiding my name. Crimall means me to be leader here. The sons of Morna won't know how little that idea appeals to me. And they'll want to stop me before I get too strong.* He shivered, and for a moment the red firelight turned spilled ale to blood and it was a hall full of dead men feasting there.

And at that moment he felt his own hand grasped by small, cool fingers and tugged gently in the direction of the door.

"Uncle, thank you," he said softly, but Crimall was already snoring. Gently Demne slipped out from beneath the older man's arm. He picked up his cloak and began to drift towards the door, staggering artistically and trying to assume the expression of a man who is not sure he will reach the privies in time. One of the younger men began to spew beside the fireplace, and while the others were cursing him, Demne slipped through the door, wondering if a phantom hand had tickled the fellow's throat to distract them.

Demne circled behind the latrines and moved stealthily towards the forge, where he slept and kept his things. When he had moved there he had told the others it was because he needed to keep an eye on the fires, but in truth he had found it hard to sleep through the snoring and grunting of the crowd in the hall. He gathered his belongings soundlessly, replacing the new clothing with which the men had gifted him with the comfortable, stained garments he wore every day. Better that they think he was rejecting their gifts than believe he had abused their trust and run away.

The noise from the hall was still enormous, but the yard was empty. Demne slipped from shadow to shadow, nearly stumbled over a sleeping dog, and silenced the beast with a word. A warm tongue lapped his hand and for a moment he fondled the soft ears. He would be sorry to leave the hounds. Then he heard someone talking ahead of him and remembered that however inadequate it might be, Crimall had set a guard. He would have to escape by the back way, then, where the last snowfall had loosened some of the logs of the palisade.

He turned, and was beginning to make his way around the end of the cook shed when he heard the scuff of a shoe on stone.

"Are you too drunk to find your way back to the hall," said a shadow behind him, "or are you running away?"

Demne could not see features, but he recognized the movement and straightened with a sigh.

"I thought you might be sick and need help," Dithramhach went on. "But I suppose that our gifts are light enough—"

"I left everything in the forge!" Indignation unlocked Demne's tongue. "If treasure were what I wanted, I could have kept the *corrbolg!* And if I were a coward I would not have faced your spears!"

"*Why*, then?"

With a wrench Demne realized that what he was hearing in his half brother's voice was pain.

"Don't you know that Crimall would have given you the *fian?* What kind of a madman are you, to endure all our mistreatment without complaining, and then, when you have made us love you, to run away!"

Demne's breath caught as if he had taken a belly blow.

"You and Crimall are the madmen if you think I know enough to lead you all!" he said desperately. "Or if you think this band can face the force that will come against it once the sons of Morna know for certain that I am here! I am not afraid to fight, but I've let you come too close to me. What's left of our father's *fian* will die, and it will be my doing as surely as if they fell by my hand!" He bowed his head, clinging to the shaft of his spear.

"And that's what you're afraid of?" Dithramhach's tone held only wonder. "That's why you're running away?" There was a long silence, and then, "I never had a chance to give my gift to you—" Suddenly the other man moved and Demne felt something hard and warm pressed into his hand.

"It's a piece of amber, pierced for a thong. Cumhal gave it to my mother when I was born."

"But it's all you have of him—"

"I saw him, Demne. At least I know what he looked like. And I know now that though I am his son, you are his heir. Wear the amber, and remember him, and me. Wear it, and when you have finished your learning, let it guide you back to us once more."

Demne stared at the shadow shape of his brother in utter confusion. Dithramhach reached out and caught his hand in a warm clasp, then wind swirled in his hair and Demne felt the pressure of his sister's fingers, drawing him away.

"I will remember you!" Choking back a sob, Demne fled towards the gap in the palisade.

IN SIX MONTHS DEMNE'S FEET HAD LEARNED THE LAY of the land around the dun. He moved through the forest without sound, almost without thought, knowing only that he must get away. But the earth song

soothed his spirit, and gradually he became aware of
the gurgle of a stream ahead of him and the whisper of
young leaves in the night breeze. An owl called overhead, telling his mate that he had fed and now was
moving on.

Demne did not know whether anguish or relief were
clamoring loudest. Each time Dithramhach's amber
bounced against his chest he felt new pain, but there
was relief as well, as if he had dropped a burden too
great for even his broad shoulders to bear. When he
came to the stream, he knelt beside it and scooped up
the chill water in his hands.

The clean taste of it washed away the last fumes
of the mead, and more of it cooled his burning brow.
When at last his thirst was eased, Demne sat back on
his heels. He had gotten away, but where was he trying to go? Here, the stream broadened into a small
pool, flickering with light and shadow where the trees
cast their nets for the reflection of the sickle moon.
As Demne stared into it, he caught a flash of brighter
silver. For a moment he thought it was a trick of the
light, then realized it was only a fish that he had seen.

Do fish ever sleep? he wondered. Bodbmall would
have known. No doubt his terrible grandfather, Tadhg
mac Nuadat, knew as well. When Demne peered
beneath the shimmering surface, the pool seemed
to have no bottom at all. Suddenly he remembered
how he had touched the salmon in the pool where the
corrbolg had lain hidden. And that memory brought
him another—his vision of the man who fished beside
an unknown river—and suddenly he knew what he
would do. If he followed this stream to the river he would find the fisherman. It was the only
path that held no peril for himself or other men.

Suddenly a great weariness was on him. Demne had
only the strength to curl himself between the project-

ing roots of an ash tree before sleep swept down and
carried him away.

THE HALL OF DONAIT ROSE AROUND HIM, ITS EN-
twined branches shedding a golden light upon the
spiraled floor. He could smell Donait's sweet scent
upon the air and looked for her, but it was Brigid
whom he saw, shimmering above the flickering hearth
fire, lighting the world with her smile. Demne felt his
heart leap at the sight of her bright face, and peered
eagerly at the paths that spun out from her swirling
skirts once more. But they were no longer separate.
Now the three ways crossed back and forth until they
were a plait of red and green and blue that dazzled the
eye.

The Goddess lifted a graceful hand and pointed
towards the rising sun. For a moment three faces
floated in the air. He saw the one-eyed, red-haired
son of Morna roaring with sardonic laughter. The
druid's white hair glimmered like moon silver as his
dark eyes searched the land. The third face was one
that Demne had never seen before. He thought it was
noble, but marred by some inner turmoil still unre-
solved. Then the faces faded. Again Brigid pointed
to the rising sun. She too disappeared and there
was only the fluttering hearth fire and the spiraled
floor, from which the colors faded until the differ-
ences between the three paths could no longer be
seen.

DEMNE'S EYES OPENED SLOWLY AND HE STARED UP AT
the trees. They were only ordinary beech and hazel,
and it was with the honest sunlight that they shone.
On the other hand, they were green and living, and
if the forest was a less pleasant place to awaken than
Donait's hall, it was better than the smoke-grimed

pillars of Crimall's dun. By the time he had washed the sleep out of his eyes and broken his fast on the tender leaves of some spring greens, he felt ready to tackle the world. And at least he now knew in what direction he must go.

Whistling under his breath, Demne strode eastward, towards the rising sun.

FOR A MOON OF DAYS DEMNE TRAVELED EASTWARD through the little hills and valleys. He crossed the Sinnan near the Grey Lake, made his way among the many lakes and forests of the center of Eriu, and came down at last into Midhe, moving carefully, for these were the lands of the Luaigni, his enemies. He came to a dark-flowing stream that men said flowed into the Boann, and followed its windings through the settled lands. At times the forest grew down to the edge of the river, but the stream here was nowhere as wide as the river of his vision, and so he went on.

It was hard sometimes to live on fish and spring greens when he could smell meat cooking in the settlements he passed, especially when he reflected that it was his own fault he was a fugitive. He moved like a ghost through the margins of field and forest, walking by night when he must, and lying up where the deer hid during the day. The occasional hunting party was easy enough to avoid, but even a pig boy guiding his herd to root for mast in the woods sent Demne fading back among the trees.

And as the season turned towards Beltane it was no hardship to walk the woodlands. Demne's heart lightened as he saw the rich color of the primroses poured out beneath the trees, and the first flowers of the hawthorn began to blaze white on the bough. Cowslips and anemones jeweled the meadows; the new grass was springing thick and green through last year's straw. Even to breathe the air of that season made one drunk with a delight sweeter than the mead he had drunk in Crimall's hall.

When he passed the plain of Tailtiu he could not help slipping to the edge of the forest to stare. But the ranks of tents and bothies that had filled it at festival time were gone, and only the royal dwellings, with their thatch still ragged and walls not yet re-whitewashed after the winter storms, remained to remind him. There was not even a scent of cattle upon the clean wind. For a moment he longed to be twelve years old once more, tromping up the dusty road with Bodbmall. Then he remembered that he had run from her, too.

As he went onward, Demne began to realize that there were worse perils in the world than the sons of Uirgriu, the allies of the Clan Morna. The warriors of the Luaigni could be avoided; it was the more subtle pitfalls of affection that had driven him this way. Bodbmall had wanted to keep him a child. Cruithne had tried to prison him between her soft thighs. Crimall had tried to bind him with honors and the love of the *fian*. They were all fetters, and he had to be free. He watched the flowing river and swore that never again would any other human choose his destiny.

And he was determined that his destiny should not be the bloody road that Crimall had mapped out for him. He would abandon the way of the warrior and become a *fili* like his friend Aonghus, whom no man was allowed to strike or slay. Surely enough blood had been spilled in Cumhal's name already without contributing his own.

But how was he to find his teacher? Already the river was widening, and when the main branch of the Boann joined it at An Uaimh, he began to fear that he would follow the river all the way to the sea and be no closer to his goal.

That night he settled himself to sleep against the

sturdy trunk of a great oak tree, willing his limbs to relax, his breathing to ease. The murmur of the earth song welled up around him; he sighed and let it pass through him, embracing him until his body was as much a part of the earth as the grass or the tree. His spirit tugged at its moorings, striving to be free. Sleep took him finally, and a little before the dawning, he found himself flying, as he often did in dream.

This time he was riding the wind like an owl above the forest, scanning the land below. Bright to the southward burned a flame. The face of Brigid shimmered within it, and red-robed women watched and sang. He tried to draw closer, but the Goddess held up her hand to warn him away. This was not his goal, though he longed for it.

Be patient, came her voice in his soul. *You will come here one day.*

Accepting that, he veered away, and saw nearby a gleaming white wall that crowned a hill. It was a fortress finer than Crimall's, finer than anything he had seen, but a dark magic burned around it, and there was a stink like the breath of the red-mouthed woman upon the breeze. Something within him screamed to cleanse it, but how that might be done was beyond his understanding, and he knew that this must wait as well. He wheeled away northward once more, seeking the shining ribbon of river and his goal.

To the eastward, the sky was growing brighter. Below him, something began to shimmer upon a hill that sloped down to the Boann. At first it seemed one of the mounds of the old ones, though he had never seen one faced with white stones. Then that light which was neither that of night nor of day shone full upon it, and Demne saw fully revealed the noble walls and spiraling passageways of the Brugh na Boinn—the palace of Aonghus Og to which the mound on the hill was only the entryway.

For a moment it glimmered before his sight, and Demne recognized the radiance of the Otherworld. Then the sun rose upon mortal lands, and he saw only the white walls once more. As he drew away in disappointment, he heard someone singing. In the sky above the wood a lark was warbling; but there were words in this song.

With double awareness, Demne realized that he was wakening. He clung to the dream, forcing himself to follow the voice down to a pool cut into the bank of the river where fish leaped at the first flies of the day. A man in a white robe was sitting there, holding a fishing pole.

A cuckoo called from the branch above him, and Demne found himself whirling back to awareness of his body again. He was looking upon all the splendor of a spring morning, but to his inner vision the pool below the white mound was still clear—

The pool where Fionnéices was waiting for him.

Chapter 20

❧

DEMNE RAN INTO THE NEW DAY LEAPING LIKE a stag through the young leaves. He need save his strength no longer, for his goal was near. Mortal sight recognized landmarks from dreamscape, and his pace quickened. The sun rose up before him, hovered for a space as if amazed by his speed, and then began her slanting descent westward, caressing his back with her warmth as he ran on.

As dream sight had seen the white walls of the Brugh na Boann glimmering through the dawning, Demne's mortal vision showed him their glow in the last rays of the setting sun. Then, at last, he paused. Through the trees below the mound water gleamed. A faintly marked trail led down towards the river, and he followed it. A stillness had fallen on the land, and he found himself moving more and more slowly, as if after all his running something within him were suddenly reluctant to reach his goal.

This was the place of his vision. Demne knew he was not mistaken. But what if Fionnéices refused to take him on? He licked lips gone suddenly dry with apprehension. Why, after all, should the *fili* want him? In the past few years Demne had realized that nature and the Liath Luachra's training had given him a body that mastered physical skills more quickly than most, but Bodbmall had made his deficiencies in the skills of the mind very clear. What possessed him to think that he could follow in the footsteps of the golden-tongued Aonghus?

I am no better than a beast of burden. He stopped short on the trail. *One might as well try to teach a lowing cow poetry!* And yet even Bodbmall had found uses for his strength from time to time. *Then let me be a cow!* he thought. *I will say nothing of apprentices—let me offer myself to him as a servant, to get him food and tend his fire.* Demne started forward again.

The moist earth of the path told its own tale to his woodwise eyes. Only one man had used this trail since the last rain, a man whose gait was clumsy, who wore tattered sandals and walked with a staff. Demne's lips tightened as he saw where the old man had fallen. Fionnéices had not looked so feeble in his dream. The way led through a clearing where a clumsily patched brush hut surrounded by scattered debris made the boy frown. Perhaps his skills at making and mending would win him a welcome here.

Another path led towards the riverside. Even in the dusk Demne could see that the prints upon it were fresh. He unshouldered his pack and leaned his spear against an oak tree, then followed them.

> "Seven silver ripples on the stream,
> Agleam at evening, even so
> The silver salmon scribes with fin,
> within, the wisdom I would know. . . ."

The voice was thin and a little breathless, but in the gathering darkness there was an eerie sweetness to it that made Demne shiver. Those words held a power beyond their meaning. He had found himself a poet indeed.

Demne heard something sing through the air and then a muffled splash, recognized the sound of a fishing line hitting the water, and smiled. He pushed through the bushes. Before him the river gleamed like a polished shield, reflecting the last light of the sky. Widening rings were spiraling across the still pool. His gaze moved inward to their source, saw where the line disappeared into the water, and then the pole and the man who held it.

A cloak that had once been blue was wrapped around his shoulders, and his beard flowed down over it, mingled gold and grey. There was nobility in the man's high forehead, but his eyes were sunk deeply into their sockets, and around his brow and mouth were graven lines of pain.

"Art there, old one?" whispered the fisherman, leaning forward. "Art hiding in the darkness, mocking me?" He shook his head, swaying. "I am a willow by the shore . . . I am the wind that ruffles the water . . . I am thy fate, old one, and thou art mine!"

The old man stiffened as another splash broke the stillness. Demne glimpsed a flicker of silver from the corner of his eye, but his fascination with the old man had blurred the boy's customary alertness. A new set of ripples was rolling shoreward, but of their source he could see only a glimmer beneath the smooth center of the pool.

"The fish!" cried the poet as the first ripples broke against the bank. The pole dropped and he lurched forward. "Wise one, wise one, come to my hand!"

Fionnéices's next step entangled him in the draggled folds of his robe. Without even trying to save himself he pitched forward into the water, grasping at some invisible prey. His robes billowed around him as he flailed helplessly. Demne unhooked the belt from around his waist, kicked off his sandals, and launched himself forward in a long, flat dive that brought him to the old man's side just as the water soaking into the heavy cloth began to drag him down.

Demne's fingers closed on wet wool. He got his feet under him and heaved, spouting like a whale. The cloak came away in his hands and he grabbed again; his fingers closed on a thin arm with a certain whipcord strength still in it. With a catch at the heart he remembered how light the Liath Luachra had been in his arms. But this one he could save.

As he lifted, the old man began to fight him, but he shifted his grip and staggered shoreward. Coarse grass grew down to the river here; gently he laid the old man belly down and pressed on his back until Fionnéices coughed convulsively and spewed river water in a long stream.

"I felt him! He was there!" the poet muttered when he could speak again. "The salmon of my prophecy!"

"Maybe he was," answered Demne, "but you are not dressed for swimming. Even I could not catch a fish bare-handed if I were swaddled in a *fili*'s robes!"

He sat back on his haunches, as the older man's gasping breaths began to ease. Presently he coughed and rolled onto his side, brows bent as if he were listening. He reached up, fumbling for Demne's arm.

"Strong . . ." he muttered, "and young. Did you see him, lad? Did you see the Salmon of Wisdom in the stream?"

Demne thought of the glimmer of silver that had troubled the water, and wondered what he *had* seen. But he dared not encourage the old man in his fantasies.

"A trout jumped," he said calmly. "What salmon do you mean?"

"When I find him, nothing shall be hidden from

me," came the whisper. "It was promised me in the prophecy, and for six years I have fished this pool. Even now I can feel when the veils between the worlds grow thin. The air was tingling with change just now. He was close to me, I know!"

"Did you see him?" Demne asked as he helped the poet to sit up.

"See him?" Fionnéices's cough turned to a bark of bitter laughter. "But that is why I want to catch him. When I eat the Salmon of Wisdom I will see again!"

He turned to Demne, eyes opening, and even in the dimming light the boy could see that there was no focus to the blurred grey stare. Fionnéices was blind.

BY THE TIME DEMNE HAD HIS CATCH WARMING before a crackling fire, the question of whether the *fili* needed a servant seemed to have been settled without ever having been raised. *Or perhaps I am to be his keeper,* thought Demne wryly as he set the last good grains from a sack of barley he had found in the hut to boiling in the cauldron that hung over the fire. A few strips of dried meat from his own pack would give it a little more substance; clearly it had been too long since the blind man had been properly fed. Why was a man who even blind could have claimed the hospitality of any chieftain's hall moldering out here alone?

"My thanks to you," said Fionnéices as Demne ladled the gruel into his bowl. "My apprentice used to do such things for me. The folk from the rath bring me food, but I cannot bear such clumsy fools about me. You are soft-footed and deft of hand, lad. I will allow you to stay."

Demne grinned. This man certainly had all a poet's pride, despite his poverty. But that arrogance had sparked something within the boy that burned away

his self-doubt. Or perhaps it was the wisp of water-
weed that still clung to the *fili*'s beard.

"Teach me," he said.

Fionnéices's bushy brows lifted.

"I have come here to learn the *filidecht,* not to fish
the *fili* out of the river like that salmon you are so
eager to find. But I am willing to do both if that is
what is required."

The blind poet laughed suddenly, and Demne saw
like a reflection in his face the features of a much
younger, merrier man.

"You are old to be starting this, from the size of
you. Are you as intelligent as you are strong?" The
fili raised one bushy eyebrow, and Demne felt like
an overgrown lout once more. But he held his peace.
"Stay then, if you are so determined, and I will try
you. For a year and a day stay with me, and if you
are teachable we will see. . . ."

THE SUMMER THAT FOLLOWED THAT EXUBERANT SPRING
came in strong and golden. Asters appeared in the
meadows like a sprinkling of multicolored stars, and
the grain grew high in the fields. Demne threw himself
into the task of making the poet's hermitage habitable
as he had tackled rebuilding the *fian*'s forge.

By Midsummer, there was a new hut for the *fili* in
the clearing, a structure of tightly woven willow twigs
thickly plastered with mud and thatched neatly with
river reeds. Then Demne repaired the old hut to use
for a storage shed, and made a smaller dwelling for
himself nearby. The paths that the blind man regu-
larly used he smoothed and edged with round stones.
Demne hunted deer and snared conies, ranged the forest for useful herbs and traded the surplus to the folk
of the rath for a new robe of heavy linen for the *fili*
to wear.

While Demne worked, the poet talked. The things

Demne's clever hands had made were a visible achievement, but when he looked at them he saw the stories that Fionnéices had told while he was building them—heroes and sages and fair women, hideous monsters and the unearthly beauty of the Sidhe.

"SO, DEMNE, LIST FOR ME ONCE MORE THE CATEGORIES of Prime Tales that a *fili* must know—" Fionnéices fixed Demne with his sightless gaze.

Demne jumped, then realized that the old man must have heard him scraping out the cauldron. During his first months with the *fili,* he had considered unlearning some of his quietness so that his master would know where he was. But Fionnéices's ability to locate things by sound alone bordered on the uncanny. Bodbmall had taught him how to *see,* but from Fionnéices he had learned how to *hear.* Sometimes when he was with the old man he found himself closing his eyes, trying to perceive the world as the poet perceived it, interpreting the messages of sound and scent and air pressure and other senses for which he had no names.

There was a gentle rustle as a leaf settled to the ground, for the harvest was ending and the leaves beginning to turn. Then silence as if the whole wood were waiting for him to reply.

"Destructions and cattle raids and courtships and battles," Demne said quickly. "And feasts, adventures, elopements, slaughters, eruptions or invasions, visions, loves, expeditions." He paused for breath, trying to remember the rest of them.

"Is that the whole of it?"

The voice of Fionnéices was always low and melodious. He knew now where Aonghus had learned his teaching style. Perhaps that was why the *fili*'s questions did not make Demne as angry as Bodbmall's. Or perhaps it was because now he was older, and had chosen this teacher of his own free will. Still, it was probably the *bendrui*'s endless training in memorization that enabled him to gobble up all the learning that the *fili* would give him.

Demne laughed. "There are tales of voyages and caves. And sieges . . . and of conceptions and births and boyhood deeds. That is all I can remember just now."

"It is enough," answered Fionnéices. "You might also have added violent deaths and frenzies. And how many of these tales must a man learn before he can be called an *ollamh?*"

"Seven times fifty," came the quick answer.

"And how many of them," asked the *fili*, "do you know?"

Demne stared. Could the cauldron say what had been put into it to make the stew? All the stories that the poet had been teaching him bubbled together within him in glorious confusion. But at that moment he could not have identified a one. Fionnéices sighed.

"Name a tale of invasion in which a salmon appears."

When Demne was fishing, his hands moved into position to grip with no need for thinking at the first flicker of silvery scales. As the poet spoke, the same thing happened within his mind, and from his lips the words began to come.

"Tuan the grand-nephew of Partholon, who was the sole survivor of the first folk to live in Eriu, was in the shape of a stag during the time of Nemed, and a boar when the Galeóin came into the land, and a hawk in the heavens when the Tuatha de Danann conquered them. But high king of the salmon he became when the Sons of Mil invaded, and he ranged all the rivers of the four fifths of Eriu and all the seas of the world, until he was caught and eaten and reborn to the wife of Cairell mac Muirtach as a man once more."

Demne drew breath, blinking. How much more, he wondered, was locked now in his memory, awaiting only the right question to flow free?

"So," said Fionnéices, "the knowledge is there. When you have mastered sixty tales you will enter the fourth rank of *filidecht,* and I can begin to teach you the stories of the second category which are told only among the wise."

With a shock Demne realized that this was nearly as far along as Aonghus had been before he died. His heart leaped, and only then did he realize that he had begun to fear that he would never make any progress, and be rejected at the end of the year after all. At that moment Demne's only regret was that the older youth was not here to share his learning. Fionnéices never spoke of Aonghus at all.

In the storage shed joints of smoked meat, onions and garlic and bunches of herbs hung from the rafters, and baskets of nuts were stacked on the floor. When he had come here, the old man had looked as if a good wind might blow him away. Now Demne observed his master's ruddy cheeks with satisfaction. Nothing could be done about the man's sight, but Fionnéices was certainly healthier now. Looking at the old man helped him to bear the memory of how he had failed the Liath Luachra and Bodbmall.

"Very good, but it is not enough to know them. You must know how to use them." Fionnéices smiled. "Say, then, what tales you would tell in the house of king to whom a son had just been born, to that same king as he prepared for battle, and after the fighting, when the bodies of the warriors were brought home to the hall?"

Demne grinned back at him. He was beginning to understand the way of it now, and how the choice of tale must always be triggered by need.

"If the king were a Gael, it is the story of the birth of Cuchulain that I would be telling, and the battle of Cuchulain and Ferdiad at the ford that I would sing as the men sent 'round the drinking horn in the hall. And it is the ending of Cuchulain himself that I would proclaim when the women raised the keen for those who fell!"

"It is well," said the *fili*. "But you must know more than the one cycle of stories so as to pick the right one for each occasion. This is the function and purpose of the *filidecht*, lad, that by telling the fates of the men of old, you may give to the men who hear you a meaning for their present lives."

"That is true," said Demne, "but what stories can one tell in the halls of the Galeóin? Is there a poem on the death of Cumhal mac Trenmor?" The bard who sang for King Gléor Lamraige had tried to make one, but Demne knew there was more to the story than he had been told.

"Cumhal!" Fionnéices's voice sharpened. "Why do you say that name? Cumhal . . . the most splendid . . . the most brave . . . the most foolish of men . . ." His voice sank, and Demne stared, trying to understand.

"Did I never tell you that I was his *fili* for a time?" Fionnéices said finally. "I stood on the hill above the battlefield with the poet who had been sent by the sons of Morna, that we might make a true account of it for the world. But it was all a muddle in the end. I have tried to tell that tale, boy, but even now it will not come clear for me. Oh, it is a terrible world, and terrible men living in it, and not a one of us but has done some deed that would sound better as a story than it was to live through."

Fionnéices's face took on the bleak look that meant he was remembering the past. Demne had never asked what evils the *fili* was regretting. Young he might be, but he already had too many unhappy memories

of his own. Demne suppressed an impulse to ask
Fionnéices about Cumhal. He had rejected the right
to that knowledge when he had run away from the
fian.

SAMHAIN BROUGHT THE TURNING OF THE YEAR, AND
in the woods beside the river a chill wind harvested
the leaves. Demne traded deer meat for a woolen cloak
for his master, and cobbled together a winter wrap for
himself out of badger and beaver skins. As the season
deepened, he woke to late dawnings when a glitter
of frost glazed the fallen leaves, and at day's ending watched the sun's cold fire trapped by the bare
branches of the trees. He and Fionnéices spent most
of their time huddled near the fire, but Demne hardly
noticed the cold, for it seemed to him that the fish he
himself was seeking was rising to the lure at last.

"So," said Fionnéices patiently as Demne thrust
another stick into the fire. "What is the difference
between a chance gathering of words and poetry?"

Demne blinked. Had they not been talking about
that very thing every day for a week or more? He
wondered which of the traditional answers the poet
desired.

"A poem is the true learning of sages—" he began.

"But is every expression of wisdom poetry?"
Fionnéices snapped.

"A poem is the true harmony of sounds in conjunc-
tion," Demne offered then.

"And how then does it differ from the singing of
birds?"

"Because it has meaning—" Demne stopped himself, remembering how the earth song sounded for him
sometimes with an intensity beyond human words.
But all that was part of the life he had left behind
him. Even to his master, Demne would not speak of
that now.

"Because when a true thought is expressed by an elegant linking of sound and sense the form of the words *is* the meaning, and a thing said in just that way means more than the separate significance of the words."

He gestured helplessly. A perfect line of poetry was like the moment when the stag leaped to meet the perfect arc of his spear, an eternal moment in which the deer's death and Demne's life were one. But if he had known how to put that understanding into words he would not have been sitting in a snowy wood beside this totally inadequate fire.

Viciously he jabbed wood into the blaze, while Fionnéices laughed.

"Well, you have the longings of a poet, surely. In time, we shall see if you have the manhood to fulfill them."

"Why not now?" Demne asked.

Fionnéices grimaced. "My dear, who is preventing you? Surely not I!" Suddenly he groped for the staff propped against the side of the hut, levered himself to his feet, and strode out along the path that led to the river, jabbing at the frosty ground as if his staff were a spear.

Now what set him *off?* Demne wondered. *If he does not pay more attention to where he is going he will he will surely slip on a patch of ice where the puddles froze after the last rain.* He hugged his knees, head half turned to listen to the scrape of wood on the hard ground. The daylight was dimming—not that darkness would make any difference to the blind man—but when night came it would get colder, and then Fionnéices was bound to return.

The forms of poetry were not the problem. Demne had memorized enough verse to understand how the music of the word sounds must mesh with the rhythm of the lines. He knew the rules. It was how to find the right words that eluded him, and even more essential, where to find something to say.

That is what I want the fili *to teach me*, thought Demne. *Why will he not understand?*

Very well, he would show him! He would compose a poem. Now. And his subject would be—this fire!

"Fire that freely flickers here . . ." he murmured, then shook his head. The form was well enough, but what did it mean? Could he find something more interesting in the contrast between the red fire and the white woods around him? It must be Midwinter Eve, or nearly. Perhaps he could work in something about the rebirth of the sun.

> *"Red fire burns the wood's hot heart,*
> *Frost fire freezes now the forest . . ."*

There was a certain satisfaction in the parallel structure that began the two lines. But the thing was not going anywhere. Demne banged his forehead against his knees. Was this why the *fili* had taunted him? He felt like those clumsy boys at Tailtiu. He had thought then that his knack for running a race and casting the spear was the result of the Liath Luachra's training. It had seemed to him that anyone could have done as well, given such a teacher, and time.

He could see them now, stepping, turning, swaying to the weight of the spear shaft as they threw. They knew all the moves. They had been following the rules. But the harmony of movement that made the spear fly to its target like a homing bird had not been there. It had been painful to watch, sometimes, as they tried to force the weapons to take wing.

Was it training or some inborn gift, something inherited, perhaps, from that great warrior who was his father, that made a spear leap from Demne's hands like a live thing?

But there had been no poetry in Cumhal mac Trenmor.

Anguish burned in the boy's heart. If poetry was not a thing that could be learned, then he was no poet, could never be a poet, and was doomed to the purposeless conflicts of the *fian*.

Demne leaped to his feet as Fionnéices had done, but it was his spear, not a staff, that came without conscious intention into his hand. And there was no clumsiness when the pressures of youth and strength and all the harmony of body that was his inheritance were released into action and he began to run.

Ice crunched loudly as Demne's feet found the path. Instinctively he slipped aside between two young oak trees and continued onward through the woods that edged the river, moving as silently as if the men of the *fian* were hunting him once more. Trees blurred past: rough-barked oaks whose lack of leaves revealed their strength, ash and alder arrayed in sturdy grace, willows with a few leaves of pale gold still clinging to the twigs that trailed above the congealing surface of the stream. Once he startled a hare from its form and leaped aside as the white scut blurred through the fading light and disappeared.

Imperceptibly Demne's pace slowed. He moved now through a forest of shadows, weaving among tree shapes that were sensed rather than seen. An icy wind had risen at nightfall, sweeping the sky clean of cloud. Then, suddenly, there was space before him, and beneath his feet, the combed clods of a ploughed field. Demne came to a faltering halt, drawing in deep breaths of frosty air.

Dim shapes of hill and treetop defined the land around him, lying quiet beneath the restless glitter of the stars. A shift in the wind brought him the scent of wood smoke and cooking meat. He turned, and realized that he had run all the way to the nearby rath. Firelight set the air above the round houses aglow; the wind strengthened, and he heard a snatch of song. It must be Midwinter Eve indeed, then, and the people of the rath would feast and drink the night through to drive the darkness away. Demne had only to knock at their gate and they would give him hot food and a place by the fire, for on this night, as on Samhain, no one would refuse hospitality to a wanderer. But he did not move.

Who would give Fionnéices his dinner? Who would keep up the fire? It was already near to freezing. Would the old man have the sense to cover the coals to keep them smouldering and wrap himself in all his furs?

Why had he been so angry? Demne wondered then. It was not the *fili*'s fault if his apprentice failed.

He started up the slope towards the cart road that led towards the Brugh, stumbled as his foot sank between two furrows, and almost fell. The energy that had sped him here had vanished. Like his dreams, he thought dully, leaning on his spear. It was as much as he could do to put one foot before the other, and though the going got easier when he reached the road, surely even the *fili* could have outdistanced him at the rate he was going now.

Demne felt the world wheel towards midnight, and the winter darkness gripped the land in an icy fist until it was an effort even to force air into his lungs. Demne could not understand it. He had ranged the woods in a blizzard, scorned to stay inside even in the worst of winter storms. The men of the *fian* would have laughed to see him surrendering to a little cold.

He came to a halt on a rise, feeling the air sear his lungs as he breathed. He pulled his furs over his nose in an attempt to warm it and shivered as cold crept up his thighs. Somewhere nearby he heard the sharp crack of a freezing stone.

Demne had been abroad in all kinds of weather, but

never on this night, when the world stilled, balanced between the forces of light and darkness. At Samhain the spirits of the dead wailed upon the wind, and the fairy roads glimmered with light at the passing of the Sidhe. But at Midwinter, more ancient forces walked the world, and even the Tribe of Danu clung to the shelter of their mounds. On Midwinter Eve Bodbmall had sent him to his bed at nightfall, but he remembered how the air had tingled as she chanted her spells.

His skin prickled now as senses that were not of the body awakened within.

Before the Galeóin and the sons of Mil, we were here; we ruled this land before the Tuatha de Danann. . . . sang the wind. *Like a spark in the darkness is the life of a man, and then it is gone. Only the powers of Night are eternal and shall endure. . . .*

The stars pulsed cold in the heavens, but as Demne looked, one fell in a long streak of light and was gone.

The Hounds of Darkness were abroad, hunting the stars. Perhaps this was the year that they would pull down the sun. What did it matter whether or not Demne learned how to make poetry if life and light were lost to the world?

He forced himself to keep going, as if returning to his master would somehow strike a blow against the dark, but his steps grew ever more feeble as he went on. The stars fled slowly across the heavens. If there were to be another dawn, it would come soon. The road curved towards the river and Demne knew that he was almost to his goal, but as the pale glimmer of the Brugh na Boinne rose up before him, he fell, and had not the strength to get up again.

He could still crawl, though. Dragging his spear, Demne pulled himself towards the white stones that studded the wall of the Brugh. Its entrance was a maw of darkness, but in the lee of the mound it seemed a little warmer, or perhaps some of the power that the place collected was still stored in the quartz stones. He sagged against them, and the darkness took him as a drowning sailor is swallowed by the sea.

But for Demne, there were dreams in that darkness. It seemed to him that he heard singing, and saw fair faces glimmering out of the gloom. He saw Donait's golden hair, and then for a moment, the glowing countenance of the Lady of the braided paths. He saw light and darkness intertwined in endless spirals that drew him deeper and deeper within.

For a moment, then, he thought he understood the meaning of their combat. He saw Light shaped by Shadow, a seed of radiance blooming in the womb of Night, and the heat stored by summer leaves released by burning logs.

> Sunfire sets alight the life
> That's hid in winter wood. . . .

And then he was drawn upward like a salmon being pulled from the depths of a pool.

"Sunfire—" Demne said aloud.

"The sun has risen. I can feel the change on my skin," said a hoarse voice close by.

"Alight!" Demne opened his eyes, but the rest of the phrase was fading as the growing light of dawn was making the shadows flee. He grabbed as if he could hold the words and his fingers closed on coarse wool.

"It's gone!" With a groan, Demne sank back again. "I had the words, Fionnéices! I had them, and they were poetry! Why could you not teach me how to make them stay?" He turned his face to the cold ground, weeping for every dream he had ever lost.

"Lad, lad," murmured the poet, "I will give you

everything I have! But if I could compel inspiration do you think I would still be waiting beside that stream? The tools of the craft are all I can give you. The life in it must come from within!"

The pain in the old man's voice brought Demne upright, but as he turned to his master the rising sun cleared the treetops on the other side of the valley. Radiance flared from the stones around him and poured down the dark passageway into the heart of the Brugh na Boinne, and gazing, Demne forgot all except the light.

Chapter 21

"I HEAR THE CROWS SUMMONING THEIR KINDRED AS they fly home from the fields, and the soft calling of the doves." The *fili* sighed and lifted his face to the sky. "Tell me, Demne, does the sky grow red in the west?"

"The larks wing homeward across a sky that is turning the color of Brigid's flame," Demne said, smiling. "Surely the fish will be biting in the pool of Féic. Do you go down and catch one for our supper now, but take care that you do not fall in!"

He realized suddenly that a year had passed since he had pulled the poet out of the pool. Once more the new leaves blazed upon the branches like spurts of green flame, and the warmth of the approaching summer was like the touch of a lover, drawing abundance from the land. For the forest, the day of his arrival could have been yesterday. But the neatly kept huts around the clearing, repaired now from the ravages of the winter's storms, were different from the dilapidated structures that had been here when he came.

And though it seemed sometimes that all he had found out in the past year was how much there was left to learn about poetry, Demne knew also that he, too, had been changed by this year.

"Perhaps it will be tonight that the Salmon of Wisdom comes to me," said Fionnéices wistfully. "On Beltane Eve the doors to the Otherworld stand open. 'Tis there that he dwells with his brothers, where the nine sacred hazels drop their nuts into the white-walled well. But sometimes he ventures to mortal lands. Do not you think that this time he might swim through?"

"Surely, he will come one day, for was he not promised to you by the prophecy?" Demne was already bringing the fishing pole and bucket from their place by the wall.

"My sight shall be restored and nothing shall be hidden from me. . . ." muttered the old man. "For seven years I have waited. Surely he will come. . . ."

Demne shook his head indulgently as the *fili* made his way down the path to the river, using the fishing pole as a staff. The prophecy that when Fionn the Poet caught the Salmon of Wisdom that swam in the pool of Linn Féic, he would see clearly at last had become as familiar as any of the traditional tales. During the stormy days of winter Fionnéices had seemed to forget it, but as soon as the days began to lengthen towards summer his longing had returned, like the refrain to a song. Demne knew better than to be scornful, for he still dreamed of the salmon he had seen in the pool of the *corrbolg*.

When darkness fell, the old poet would return. But his absence gave Demne time to start the evening gruel, and to prepare for the questioning that would follow the meal. When the oats were beginning to bubble in the cauldron, spiced with garlic and leek and onion and some bits of leftover smoked pork, Demne unwound the linen that wrapped his hazel wand.

This, at least, was one of the skills of a poet that
Demne could master. Three months had been spent
in learning the incantations that would lead him to
the right tree, waiting for the moment when moon and
sun were propitious, and gaining the assent of the tree
to take a branch the length of his forearm for his wand.
Three months more he had spent in drying and shaping the wood, and in carving into it the four fives of
up and down slashes that represented the sounds of
human speech.

The Liath Luachra had used the ogham for brief
messages, and Bodbmall employed it in her spells,
so Demne had not come to the learning completely
ignorant. But he had not realized that the signs could
be used to guide one through the mazes of knowledge
as surely as he tracked a deer through the wood.

"This is the science that was invented by Ogma
son of Elatha, the god most skilled in speech and
poetry: the ogham of trees, the ogham of birds, the
ogham of colors, the ogham of fortresses . . ." he murmured as Fionnéices had taught him, sensitive fingertips slipping across the smooth wood to trace the
shapes carved there.

Each day he gave himself more easily to the discipline of this learning. The torrent of feeling still surged
within him, but he was learning the rules by which
it might be controlled. Half-remembered memories of
Midwinter morning sometimes troubled his dreams.
But it seemed to him that he must have misunder-
stood Fionnéices's meaning, and he had never dared
to ask.

When he was ready, surely the *fili* would demon-
strate the trance of poetic inspiration which he had so
often described. Then all the teaching would fall into
place in one glorious pattern of sound and meaning,
and Demne would find peace at last.

"The first sign is *bcith*, which means the birch tree,

and signifies also the pheasant, the color white, and the fortress of Bruden. . . ." The only white fortress that he had ever seen was the dun of Almu, thought Demne, and that was in vision. He shut away memories of the terrible old man who lived there and forced his mind back to his task.

It was growing darker. Crickets were beginning their night song in the undergrowth, and a warm breeze rustled the leaves. Faint on that wind came the scent of the Beltane fires. The hearth fire burned steadily and all was calm around him, but there was a tension in the air, as if somewhere beyond the hills the gods were brewing thunder.

"*Huathe*—hawthorn, is the next ogham sign, which is the raven, a color of terror, the fortress of h-Ocha. . . ." Somehow he had gotten to the second set of five. Demne did not remember reciting the intervening sounds. He scratched his head in puzzlement for a moment.

Demne looked up then, for the wind had grown colder. The fire leaped, and he poked at it until the flame burned evenly once more. Surely Fionnéices would be returning soon. With a sigh he sank back into the trance of learning.

"*Ruis* is the elder, a rook, red, roigne—"

Demne jerked upright, staring, as thunder drummed in the distance like an echo of the Beltane dancing in the rath up the hill. But that was not what had disturbed him. Awareness flicked backward—there had been a splash! He got to his feet, staring down the path.

"Demne . . . Demne, come!"

The boy dashed forward. Had the old man fallen in after all?

They met halfway up the path, and even in the twilight Demne could see the silver sheen of the great fish in Fionnéices's arms.

"What a beauty!" exclaimed the boy as he reached for the salmon. But Fionnéices still clutched at the slippery armful as if trying to convince himself of its reality. In the end, Demne put his arms around the old man and half carried him and the fish up the path together.

"He *is* Beauty!" said Fionnéices when he had got his breath again. "Does not the magic in him shimmer from each scale? I felt the shock of it like lightning when he took the hook, and the line sang like a harp string as I hauled him in!"

Demne eyed the dead fish with interest. From the tip of its fluted tail to the fiercely jutting hook of the lower jaw, the salmon was certainly splendid. The body above the midline shone a speckled greenish silver in the firelight, and the belly blushed like sunrise. In truth it was early in the year for him to be coming upriver to breed. But magical? Was the sensation Demne felt as he stroked the curved body a tingle or only the catch of scales against his fingertips?

"Seven years!" babbled the poet. "I never lost hope of him, and the gods have been good to me at last! It is the Salmon, boy, the Salmon of Wisdom himself that has come to me, and now I will see all the truth of the world! Build up the fire with all your skill—this fish must be cooked as carefully as ever you did anything in all your days!" His long fingers fluttered once more across the sleek body, then he pressed it into Demne's arms.

"I will roast it to perfection," said the boy. "I will describe for you each sizzle of its flesh and every flicker of flame!"

But Fionnéices was already hurrying towards his hut. "I must wash myself," he muttered. "I must be purified! Watch the Salmon for me, boy, and do not taste even a morsel of it until I return!"

"This fish will be as safe with me as the virgin

daughter of a king," said Demne, smiling.

The poet would want the fish cooked quickly, so he could not bake it among the coals. After a moment's thought Demne selected some well-aged middle-sized oak logs from the woodshed, and built them into a cone. While the logs were burning down, he slit open the salmon's belly and gutted it. Whistling under his breath, he threaded two long pieces of hazel through each side of the fish, set their butt ends into the earth and rested their tops against the crossed bars of the tripod so that the carcass was held parallel to the pyramid of flame.

Full dark had fallen, and the night seemed unnaturally still. Even the crickets had fallen silent. Perhaps there was a storm coming, thought Demne, and the shock that Fionnéices had felt when he touched the fish an effect of the energy in the air. He jumped at the pop and crackle as the fire bit into the oak logs.

Brigid, Lady of inspiration, breathed Demne, *let it indeed be the Salmon of Wisdom for him. Let Fionnéices find what he has been seeking for so long!*

As the fire blazed, Demne felt a warm flush of gratitude. His relationship with the poet had been characterized by a kindly courtesy unique in the boy's experience. The source of the rules and requirements that his master laid upon him was the poet's craft, not anyone's notions about Demne's destiny, and Fionnéices accepted the service that the boy offered without complaint or commentary.

Demne jumped and blinked as a drop of juice from the fish sizzled upon the fire. For a moment the flame had seemed to blaze blue where it fell. He took an appreciative breath of the rich scent of the cooking fish and rubbed his eyes, for surely this was the same shimmer he had seen on the hearth of Donait's hall.

"Blessed Brigid!" he breathed, staring around him. "Has the old man caught the right salmon after all?" He could feel the presence of the Goddess all around him though he could not see her, but with every drop of juice that fell from the salmon there came another rainbow ripple of flame.

The savor of the salmon was overwhelming. Demne licked his lips and wished that Fionnéices would return. *I shall compose a poem upon the cooking of this salmon,* he thought vaguely, *when I have mastered the* fili's *craft.* The colors of the fire were becoming quite wonderful, crimson and blue, vibrant green and shimmering silver and gold. *The flames are as gold as the first sun of Beltane glowing upon the flowers of the broom,* he thought dreamily. *The red is like the blood of a slain deer upon new-fallen snow . . .*

The images flickered through his awareness. Fionnéices had been right. The fish was magic. A golden glow shimmered around it, a little sparkle of light seemed to edge each scale. Taking a deep breath only intensified the strangeness. Demne dug his fingers into the cool earth, trying to keep control.

I promised I would cook it perfectly. . . . He poked at the glowing logs so that the flesh of the salmon was not so near the flame, and multicolored sparks swirled around his hands. Fionnéices had better get here soon, he thought then, for the salmon was almost done. Already a blister was beginning to form as the rich juices bubbled beneath the smooth skin. It seemed a pity that anything should mar that perfection. Without thinking, Demne leaned forward, and pressed the bubble flat with the ball of his thumb.

Agony exploded through his body. It was far worse than the time he had touched a coal in the forge. With a moan, Demne jammed his thumb into his mouth, trying to suck out the pain.

—And his world was unmade.

He tasted salt and sweetness, a rich savor beyond all the food of men or faerie. The fire in his thumb burned his tongue, flared outward to sear all his senses. Sensation rioted through his awareness in an explosion of beauty that fell back into consciousness in a shower of shining words.

Beltane! The earth song that he had been hearing since childhood clamored within him. His ears rang with memories of the music of rain and waterfalls, with the songs of corncrakes and larks, blackbirds bursting into music at the break of the day. It was Beltane! But it was not enough to see and hear it. Demne's tongue tingled painfully. He understood now in its fullness all that he had almost grasped when he lay beside the Brugh na Boann.

"Beltane, oh Beltane, blossoming beauty!" he cried aloud. "At new day the blackbirds burst into song! The strong sturdy cuckoo sings welcome to summer, calmed are the harsh winds that brought branches down."

That was better, but the riot of sensation was still almost beyond bearing. He searched for the deeper pattern that bound all this scattered splendor into one magnificent order, and suddenly the words became a song that satisfied in the same way that forging the spearhead had fulfilled him, a marriage of form and function, all the more a marvel because now he had words for what he knew.

> *"Summer shrinks streamlets, swift horses*
> *   seek water,*
> *Wild hair of the heather and white bog down*
> *   lengthens,*
> *Strengthens the sea swell, soothing sleep*
> *   bearing,*
> *Deer browse the whitethorn, and flowers fold*
> *   the world."*

In memory he saw a fawn that he had tracked in the woods of Sliab Bladhma and petted when it was only a few hours old. More images fountained into music. This was what all of the rules and the practice had been for!

"Golden the burden of blossom that bees
    bring,
A king's feast the ant finds, kine to the hills
    fare.
Where peace fills the woodland, soft the
    wind's harp plays,
A haze on the cool lake, colors blaze on each
    hill.
Swallows soar circling the hillside with sweet
    sound,
Abounding with fruit the tree; quagmire's mud
    chatters,
Water like ravens' wings shines, such a
    wonder,
Yonder the speckled fish leaps from the
    stream."

INTO HIS SONG WENT ALL THE BEAUTY THAT HAD haunted his childhood, and in singing, Demne reclaimed it. Beneath all the grief of his growing had lain this joy. He understood now that the Liath Luachra and Bodbmall were not his only fosterers. The mother who had loved him best was this wild and lovely world.

"Warriors wax in their boldness, maidens in
    majesty,
Trees in their fullness; wheat stalks strive
    sunward.
Done is wild winter when white was each
    oak bough,

> *Now find we fair seasons, and peace and*
> *   good cheer."*

Once more he was seeing Tailtiu, and the splendor
of the men and the horses on the green plain. There
had been beauty there too, all things rejoicing in the
summer sun. Laughing, he claimed the memory.

> *"Graceful birds settle, the white streams rush*
> *   wildly,*
> *Through green fields the hosts march, bold*
> *   riders are racing;*
> *Tracing the bright shaft shot into the land-*
> *   scape,*
> *And the waterflags, sunstruck, explode into*
> *   gold."*

As the song surged to its climax Demne felt another
presence, an alien passion that threaded itself through
his music like a minor harmony. It had been there for
some time, but he could not have stopped singing if
he had tried. All of his life, it seemed, this knowledge
had been waiting for him to set it free.

> *"Though fearful, the wren is persistent,*
> *   proclaiming*
> *The name that the high flying lark can cry*
> *   clear.*
> *Hear how the stutterer sings the glad*
> *   tidings,*
> *Abiding in beauty, blest Beltane is here."*

Growing ever softer as it moved to its ending, the
song flowed through him and out into the world as
the wind passed through the trees. And then there
was silence. At rest in that stillness, Demne became
aware at last that someone was weeping.

Slowly he turned. Fionnéices stood leaning on his staff at the edge of the firelight, resplendent in the white robe of his calling and the deep blue mantle of an *ollamh* with its fringe of gold. But his cheeks were wet with tears.

"Demne . . ." After the music, the old voice seemed to hold all the world's pain. "What have you done?"

"I cooked the salmon!" the boy exclaimed. "Cannot you smell the wonder of it, whole and perfect over the fire!"

"You have tasted it . . ." Fionnéices said heavily.

"I did not!" Demne frowned, trying to remember. "Only . . . on the skin a blister was forming. I pressed it down to keep the skin from being spoiled and it burned my thumb." His thumb still ached and he put it to his mouth, felt the rush of awareness returning and jerked it away again, staring.

"Your thumb—" Fionnéices moved carefully towards him and felt for his hand. "All the power of wisdom was in that blister, boy." Demne could feel the tremor in the fingers that gripped his own. "Who are you?" the poet whispered then.

"What do you mean? I am called Demne."

"Not so!" The old man straightened. "*You are Fionn!*" It was a voice that Demne had never heard from him before, and it rolled through the wood like thunder, the voice that a *fili* uses when he is in the trance of inspiration and cannot lie. "Your name is Fionn, and it is for you that the Salmon was intended."

"How did you know?" the boy stammered. "Fionn is the name that the high king gave me, and the name they shouted in the *fian!*" Three times that name had been given him, and he would never be free from it now. "It was the truth saying of the *filidecht,* was it not? You have known my name since the beginning, and known that I was the son of Cumhal!"

The staff slipped from Fionnéices's hand, and

Demne leaped to keep it from falling into the fire, a little surprised to find that he could move.

"Eat the fish!" said the poet harshly.

The boy looked at him sharply, hearing in his voice undertones of rage and despair. Perhaps if he ate a little he could persuade Fionnéices to join him. It was a large salmon. Surely all of its magic could not have been in that one taste he had. Carefully he lifted the fish away from the fire and laid it upon a grass mat by the hearth to cool. The scent that rose from it was still mouth watering, and he found himself furiously hungry.

With some trepidation, Demne cut a slice and put it into his mouth. The flesh was cooked to perfection, a deep orange pink, so tender that the fragments flaked apart in his hand. The rich taste of it alone would have been enough to send him into an ecstasy. He had downed several mouthfuls before he realized that his mouth was tingling, and that there was more than satisfaction in the golden glow that filled his belly.

"Please eat some." He held out a piece to Fionnéices who still stood on the other side of the fire. "There is too much here for one."

"Are you afraid, Cumhal's son?"

Demne frowned. That tone had certainly been hostile, but he supposed it was only to be expected.

"Shouldn't I be, considering what one taste of it did to me? I think there is enough meat in this salmon to inspire half the poets in Eriu!"

"You are generous," said Fionnéices more easily, though he did not move. "Your father was a great one also for sharing, whether it was the game that he killed or the gold that he won. All his prizes he shared freely with his followers . . . all of them but one. But in the end it was death that Cumhal mac Trenmor shared with his *fian*."

Once more Demne heard truth in the poet's words.

"I have your father's sword," whispered Fionnéices, turning. "I saved it after the battle. Now I know it was for you. . . ." He shuffled away into the darkness, and Demne took another bite of salmon.

He could hear the coals of the oak logs singing softly of the sweetness of sun fire feeding their leaves and their joy in giving that heat back again. That was the meaning he had been striving for when he glimpsed the first light of the Midwinter sun.

He trembled with pleasure when the wind stroked the treetops with a gentle hand. The earth beneath him was warm and welcoming as the body of a lover, and deep within it flowed the waters from which the salmon had come. If he listened carefully, he could hear them singing of rainfall and waterfall, of the dark depths of rivers and the deep, slow surges of the sea.

Overhead an owl called, and he knew that it had killed a squirrel and was soaring across the river to hunt mice in the fields of men. The reply of its mate came faint from the west where the people of the rath had built a great fire. *Is the secret of all language locked in the flesh of this salmon?* he wondered. When he had first heard the earth song, he was like a man who recovers the hearing of one ear while those around him are still silent. But now it was as if he had never really listened to anything before.

Then Fionnéices came back with the sword.

The sheath was bloodstained, but when the poet drew the blade Demne saw that it had a smooth steel sheen. The boy examined it with a professional eye. It seemed a good piece of forge work. He itched to try its balance, but the poet was clinging to it as he had held the salmon before.

"Cumhal's sword," said Fionnéices. Again the mix of tones; Demne wondered why. Could he hear the hidden meanings in men's words, too, if he tried?

"It was a gift to him from the high king, that last wintertide that we guested at Temair. That was the winter when he met Muirne."

Demne opened his eyes. He had encountered far too many men who knew his father, but he had never met one who would speak of his mother before. And he could hear in the old man's voice that for Fionnéices, her image was as vivid as if it were the day before that he had seen her last.

"My mother . . ." he said softly. "What was she like, Fionnéices?"

"Muirne of the White Neck was the flower of the world." In the *fili*'s voice Demne heard only wonder, and he began to relax again. "She was slender as a white birch tree. Her hair was the deep, smoky red of smouldering coals, and when the sun was on it, all the little curling wisps would burst into flame. But her eyes were the cold, clear grey of the winter waves. A man could drown in that clarity, but Muirne was as innocent and without mercy as the sea. . . ."

This man had loved his mother, thought Demne, listening. He could almost see the woman as he spoke of her. . . . A flicker of memory teased at his awareness, of a scent like apple blossom and firelight striking red sparks from dark hair. There was something more recent, too, but the poet was continuing.

"She was the druid's daughter," Fionnéices continued, "but she performed no magic. She *was* magic, and every man who looked upon her desired her, that winter at Temair. Only Cumhal appeared to ignore her, among them all."

"But you knew otherwise," said Demne. The more he ate of the salmon, the more acute his senses became, his ears almost tingling at each word. "He loved her, and so did you. . . ."

"I did, and I did not believe she could give her love to a man who argued his points with his spear!" Fionnéices's head came up, his eyes widening as if he were trying to see. "The red slash of a sword blade was the only ogham that man knew, though indeed, he wrote it very well. But of those who came to the *filidecht* in my generation, I was the brightest and quickest," the poet went on. "Cumhal was king of the *fennid*, and I thought to become king of poets by singing his exploits. As a hound scavenges in the hall I fawned on him," Fionnéices said bitterly, "gathering the scraps of his deeds to make my songs."

"And my mother loved him—" Demne spoke into the silence.

"She confided in me!" Fionnéices exclaimed. "They both confided in me! And I listened to both of them, and the agony grew within me as tree trunks tangle in a river until the flood breaks them free."

"You must not tell me this," said Demne. Suddenly the salmon he had eaten lay like lead in his belly. He shivered as the poet went on, because he realized that from now on he would hear the truth in every word the old man said to him.

"And I listened to Aedh mac Morna, whom men now call Goll. And it was I who put into his head to tell the druid that Cumhal, whose indifference he had trusted, had stolen the heart of his girl. And that was the first betrayal, for Cumhal had won loyalty even from his clan's ancient enemies when he led the *fian*, and Goll had been the most faithful of Cumhal's warriors before."

"And that is how the sons of Morna became my father's foes?" asked Demne. Crimall had said that Cumhal was a victim of ancient enmities. Fiacail had said it was because the high king feared the *fian's* growing power. But for Fionnéices, the cause was jealousy.

"When Cumhal carried off Muirne, Aedh left him,"

said Fionnéices. "But I remained. I watched their happiness, and hated it. I watched her belly swell with his child. And in the end I watched the *fian* of Cumhal march out to die on Cnucha's field."

There was more, but Demne did not want to know it. Already he seemed to see the grey dawn and feel the damp wind off the ocean, to hear the creak of leather and the clink of metal, the low-voiced mutter of speculation and the edged joking of brave men who see before them an overwhelming foe. Was it still Beltane Eve, or had the years rolled eighteen seasons backward? As Fionnéices spoke a thing, Demne saw it, both the things that the poet said, and the truths behind his words.

The damp air rang with the battering of spears against hide-covered shields, and men's deep voices, raised in song. The mist swirled in from the seacoast, borne by no wind of the world. It was a sorcerous mist that Tadhg had sent upon the armies, and only the gift of poetic sight enabled Fionnéices to distinguish between friend and foe. He saw how Cumhal battled and the warriors fell before him. The Grey Man was the first to wound him, and only because Cumhal never thought to guard himself against a friend. He slashed at his leader's sword arm, and the answering blow sent him reeling from the field. Then Aedh mac Morna came against him, and they fought as the gods fought in the first days of the world.

Somehow the day had sped and darkness was falling. Most of the warriors who marched out that morning had fallen, and instead of their battle cries the harsh calling of ravens filled the air. Cumhal's arm was still bleeding. More than once he staggered, and was saved only by the magic of his shield. Then it looked as if Aedh had him, for Cumhal was falling, but in that moment bright Luchet sped between them, and his swift stroke took out Aedh's eye. The next blow of the son of Morna killed Luchet, but now the shock of the head wound felled Aedh and he collapsed to the trampled earth by Cumhal's side.

"And then I crept down the hill to see who had lived and who had died," Fionnéices spoke into Demne's vision.

Slowly Demne pulled his awareness back into his own body. The *fili* was a dim shape picked out in light where the gold fringe of his cloak and the steel of the sword reflected the dying fire. Behind him the dark tangle of branches blurred into a featureless darkness, but Demne could hear the uneasy rustling of new leaves as the moist wind grew stronger. Light blinked to the northward, closely followed by the thunder. The warriors of heaven were beating on their shields.

Storm coming, thought Demne, feeling the fine hairs prickle along his arms. *Not long to wait now.*

"I tried to make a song of it afterward, but the words would not come," said Fionnéices. "The mist swirled around us, blotting out the world, but it never lifted for me. . . ."

"It was not your sight but your vision that you wanted the Salmon to restore," said Demne, understanding suddenly why the *fili* had been able to give him only the forms of poetry.

"You stole it!" whispered Fionnéices. "Your father stole Muirne and you stole my Vision, and you did not even need it, for the poetry was in you already. Aonghus was the same, until I killed him. . . . Thief! Traitor! I will have my vengeance! The Salmon gave himself to *me*!"

A sword of light clove the world asunder; the sword in Fionnéices's fist flared towards Demne; then the dark wings of the thunder clapped above them, obliterating sight and sound. The white streak of the sword's path was etched still across Demne's vision. He uncoiled upward, reaching, felt the cold blade slide by him and the hard, knobbed grip of the hilt and the unexpected strength of Fionnéices's thin hands.

Night chill and darkness, the screeching of ravens. . . . A man's face, white with blood loss, the slow stirring of his chest as he groans . . .

A sword hilt, cold from the mud it's lain in; surprise at how hard it is to poke the tip through the tough skin of the breast, to lean on the sword. . . .

Blue eyes open, fury changing to shock as Cumhal sees who is driving in the blade. The lips open, but all that comes from them is a bubble of crimson. Then all meaning fades from the face, the dark mist of magic rolls over them; all meaning fades from the world. . . .

Rain drove down and the coals exploded with a serpent hiss of steam. Demne and Fionnéices rolled over and over, struggling for possession of the sword. The old man fought as if possessed by the lightning. Sight was no advantage here, it was all heavings and grapplings as Demne strove to immobilize limbs grown slippery with mud and rain.

And blood. Demne realized that the strength that opposed him was ebbing, and he stilled, feeling the fragility of the body between his hands. The wetness that covered them was warmer than the rain. Lightning blinked once more and he saw the sword embedded in Fionnéices's side. Then the *fili*'s blank gaze focused and he met Demne's eyes.

"Cumhal!" In the dark that followed the lightning the *fili*'s hand moved unerringly to the boy's face. "I *see* you! I will sing . . . your song!"

Demne reached up to grip the hand, sobbing. There was a rattle of breath, then the poet's arm grew heavy, and the boy knew that Fionnéices had left him. He blinked, and thought for a moment that he had taken on the poet's blindness, but it was only tears.

* * *

THE SUN OF BELTANE MORNING DRIED THE WOODS. THE
earth was soft from the storm and digging a grave
for the old man was easy. As Demne worked, he
waited for the familiar ache of guilt, but it was as
if he and Fionnéices had been picked up and shak-
en by some convulsion of nature, a passion that had
passed through them like the storm. The earth song
was stronger than ever this morning, and the birds
sang lustily, little caring that a man lay dead below.

It seemed to Demne that the vision that had come
to him when he ate the Salmon was worth a man's
life. Perhaps Fionnéices had thought so too, for that
was the price the poet had paid for the Sight that had
come to him at the end.

Demne wrapped the fragile body in the deep blue
cloak of a master poet and laid it in the earth with the
fili's staff and the remains of the Salmon. And then
there was no more to do.

It was a little after noon when he found enough
strength to gather his things together and leave the
forest. The rath whose bale fires he had scented the
night before stood on a rise above the river. Now
smoke twined lazily from its cook fires. Demne's belly grumbled and he realized that he had eaten nothing
since the fish the night before.

Dogs came out in a snarling tangle to greet him, but
by the time he reached the gate the tenor of their barking had changed, for he spoke to them in the voice of
one who understands what they are saying, and in his
sweat they smelled no fear. A woman came out after
them, scowling as she wiped her hands on the cloth
tied over her gown. She would be harder to convince
than the dogs.

"What d'ye want then? We're a poor place, with no
food to spare for those who cannot earn their keep,
and I must warn ye that we have warriors already."
She frowned at his sword and spear.

"My blessing on the house and the woman of it," he said, smiling in spite of himself, for she looked so much like a grey goose defending her patch of reeds.

"And glad I am to hear that you are so well defended. Indeed I am a warrior"—*and a murderer,* he thought, but he did not say those words aloud—"and a smith and a forger of words as well. I can poultice a sick horse or a dog or a man, and put up a good fight at *fidchel.* If you have any use for a man who can do all of these things, then I will beg your hospitality."

He grinned at her expression, and suddenly the woman herself was laughing.

"Oh, indeed! And is it Lugh Samildanach himself that we're to be welcoming?"

He took a deep breath, hearing his words echoing across all the years of the world and all the leagues of Eriu.

"My name is Fionn mac Cumhal."